LINDEN WOODS

LINDEN WOODS

Michael Taylor

This first world edition published in Great Britain 2007 by
SEVERN HOUSE PUBLISHERS LTD of
9–15 High Street, Sutton, Surrey SM1 1DF.
This first world edition published in the USA 2007 by
SEVERN HOUSE PUBLISHERS INC of
595 Madison Avenue, New York, N.Y. 10022.

British Library Cataloguing in Publication Data

Taylor, Michael, 1942 May 1-
 Linden Woods
 1. Black Country (England) – Fiction
 2. Love stories
 I. Title
 823.9'14[F]

ISBN-13: 978-0-7278-6517-5   (cased)
ISBN-13: 978-1-84751-018-1   (trade paper)

Typeset by Palimpsest Book Production Ltd.,
Grangemouth, Stirlingshire, Scotland.
Printed and bound in Great Britain by
MPG Books Ltd., Bodmin, Cornwall.

One

'How do I look, Dad?'

Dad hesitated, but merely for effect. He had just returned indoors after an enforced spell in the back garden, out of respect for his only daughter's occupation of the tin bath. Now the tin bath was emptied, removed from the hearth, she was ready, spruce and raring to go to the dance.

'Passable,' he said after a moment, with a wink to Gladys, his wife.

'Only passable?' Disappointment was manifest on the girl's lovely face. 'What's amiss then?'

Joseph Woods smiled affectionately at Linden, the light of his life, and looked at her with fatherly admiration. 'There's nothing amiss, my flower.' He put his hand on her arm reassuringly. 'You look lovely . . . just lovely . . .'

Linden beamed back at him, her hazel eyes spectacularly alive. 'Honest? You're not just saying that? He's not just saying that, is he, Mum?'

Joe laughed, turning to Gladys. 'Hark at her. She knows very well how nice she looks.'

'I feel nice, Dad, but a girl likes to hear it confirmed. Even if it is a biased opinion.'

'Biased?' said Gladys. 'I should say he's biased. Anyway, what time's young Ron calling for you?'

'Any minute.'

Joe looked at the clock, steadily measuring their lives from the mantelpiece as it had done for the past twenty years, gaining about five minutes in the process each day and having to be put right every two days. Beyond two days Joe lost track of when it had last been adjusted, so could never be sure of the correct time. 'That clock'll be fast, by about four minutes,' he hazarded.

'Oh, it'll be near enough for Ron. It's not often he's late.'

'Well just mind your time getting back,' Gladys cautioned.

'Well, for goodness' sake don't wait up for me,' Linden replied beseechingly. 'The dance doesn't finish till eleven. We'll be chatting outside for ages after, then we've got to walk back.'

'Just keep your eye on your glass slippers,' Joe said. 'It'd be nice if you was back here by half past eleven.'

'Cinderella had till twelve,' Linden countered with a girlish pout. 'Her fairy godmother said she could. Why can't I have till twelve?' Linden looked at Gladys with an irresistible plea in her eyes.

'Because I'm not your fairy godmother. I'm your mother.'

'Oh, Mum . . .' Linden implored. 'Don't expect me to rush back. Not tonight. The dance is specially for us school-leavers. I might not see some of the girls ever again – nor the teachers come to that. And we've all been such good friends.'

Gladys looked at Joe for his assent, and got it. 'Very well, young madam. Twelve, but no later. And mind what you'm up to. Not that I shall sleep a wink till you get back.'

'I shan't get up to anything I shouldn't,' Linden assured them. 'So you can sleep in peace.' They heard footsteps in the entry. 'Hark. That'll be Ron. I'll be off. See you in the morning.'

Linden swished around in a flounce of summer cotton dress. She gave them each a kiss and breezed out to a delicious whiff of Chanel and a string of glass beads chinking around her neck. As she opened the door, Ron called his greeting to Joe and Gladys.

''Bye!' they responded in unison.

'You look nice,' Ron said as she linked her arm through his. 'You smell nice as well.'

Linden beamed up at him as they began walking through Kates Hill's narrow, terraced streets towards the town. 'Thank you, Ron. You look nice, too.'

'And do *I* smell nice?'

She pretended to sniff him as they walked. 'Nothing special,' she teased.

'Thanks. I should have expected nothing more from you. So how did it go, your last day at school?'

'A bit strange, really,' she answered. 'Happy to be leaving after all those years studying hard, but sad as well to be leaving all my old school mates behind. I shall miss them.'

'Life moves on,' he remarked, affecting to sound worldly. 'Life does that.'

'Yes, and all I've got to do now is get a job.'

'You'll have no bother there, chick. You're eighteen and you're smart. Some girls would go to university with the education you've had.'

Linden sighed. 'I know, and I'd love to go to university, but Mum and Dad could never afford to send me.'

'It makes no odds,' Ron asserted with a reassuring smile. 'Girls going to university is a bit of a waste of time and money, if you ask me. They end up getting married and having kids, so never make use of the qualifications they get. Anyway, you've done all that shorthand and typing malarkey. Firms are always after good shorthand typists.'

'Dad's got me an interview at the Blower's Green Steelworks where he works – did I tell you?'

'So you'll be in with a chance.'

'Hope so. He had a word with the personnel manager. They want somebody, he told him.'

'Well, it's always good if somebody like your dad can put a word in.'

'He is a bit biased, though, my dad. And he's worked there so long, maybe they only agreed to interview me to humour him. Have you thought of that?'

'What, and waste everybody's time by going through the motions?' Ron said scornfully. 'Big firms don't do that. Time's money. If they've said they want to employ a new shorthand typist, then you can bet your bottom dollar that's just what they intend to do.'

Linden squeezed his arm. 'D'you really think so?'

'I do, so let me give you a tip. Wear your least showy skirt and blouse, in case it's a woman who interviews you. If it's a chap smile nicely – as if you might be interested in him – but don't be too brassy of course, and the job's yours.'

'Lord! I'm getting nervous already at the thought of it.'

'We'll soon settle your nerves when we get to the Saracen's Head. It'll be a nice gin and lime for you.'

The dance had been organised for the leavers of the Dudley Girls' High School and the boys of the grammar school, both excellent educational establishments that existed symbiotically.

Their extensive grounds shared a long boundary fence that materially divided them – for fraternization could never be encouraged, leastwise during school time. Many pupils struck up romantic liaisons outside school, whether or no, since the girls could hardly be prevented from meeting the boys around the marketplace after lessons.

The Saracen's Head was a town pub about five hundred yards from the grammar school, and word had got round that many of those attending the dance would be meeting there beforehand. Soon it was buzzing with young folk, most only just old enough to be drinking legally. The stale odour of beer and tobacco smoke, indelibly fused into the very fabric of the building, was familiar to Linden; not that she was a hardened drinker – she was not – but as a child and even as an adolescent, she had accompanied her mother and father to a pub called the Shoulder of Mutton, Joe's favourite, and had been allowed to play with other kids in the 'children's room'. Hence the familiarity, and it reminded her poignantly of long-gone summer evenings.

Linden got her gin and lime, sipped it and pursed her lips at its sourness.

Ron had a pint of best bitter and extravagantly lit a cigarette. 'Can you see anybody you know?' he asked, for he was a stranger in both camps, having never been fortunate enough to attend the grammar school, although Linden always reckoned he was bright enough, if a bit lacking sometimes in the gumption department.

'Look, there's Irene . . . and Doreen, from my class.' They spotted each other simultaneously, and Linden beckoned them over. 'I'll introduce you.'

After the introductions Ron gallantly squeezed his way to the bar to buy them drinks too. He brought another gin and lime for Linden and she thanked him with a dazzling flash of her clear eyes, the colour of the sherry he'd brought for her friends. They laughed and joked about leaving school, and discussed which teachers they were happy to leave behind and which they wouldn't mind seeing again. Inevitably, talk veered towards the future and hence their prospects.

'Did you listen to the wireless before you came out?' Irene asked the others ominously when they'd each revealed their hopes and dreams.

'No, why?' Linden at once sensed Irene's concern.

'Looks like there's more trouble brewing. This time between China and Japan.'

Ron shrugged. 'Well I heard it, but I can't see as how that's going to affect us.' He took a nonchalant swig of his beer.

'I think it's a sign of the times,' Linden remarked, her expression delightfully intense as she tried to make herself heard over the hubbub of young, enthusiastic voices and the chinking of glasses. 'What with civil war in Spain, Italy overrunning Abyssinia last year and using mustard gas to do it—'

'And Germany overrunning the Rhineland,' Irene added with a grave nod.

'Not to mention the king abdicating and marrying his beloved Wallis Simpson,' Doreen interjected.

'And don't forget, either, that they're mass-producing gas masks in this country, one apiece for each of us,' Irene reminded them. 'Why would they do that unless they think we're going to need 'em?'

Ron shrugged again and took another slurp of beer. None of this was his concern.

'War is looming,' Linden said. 'Has been for ages. My dad swears there's going to be a war. He says you can smell it a mile off. He reckons Hitler's got his heart set on making Germany bigger, reclaiming land they reckon used to be theirs, like parts of Poland and the Rhineland. He reckons you could never trust Hitler.'

'I don't reckon there'll be a war,' Ron commented. 'We've all got too much to lose, especially after the last war. And anyway, the Rhineland used to be part of Germany before, so Hitler's only reclaimed what was rightfully theirs anyway.'

'Yes, Ron, but it puts him a hundred miles closer to France and us,' Irene argued.

'But he's predicting twenty-five years' peace.'

Linden sipped her fresh glass of gin and lime. It was going to her head and she did not want to be made morose with uninformed speculation about war. She wanted to be happy, for tonight was supposed to be a time for letting your hair down, forgetting the unpredictable future for now, and celebrating the past few tremendous years at school.

'Oh, enough of this,' she exclaimed. 'Anybody else who talks of depressing things like war will be sent to Coventry. All agreed?'

They all agreed.

The dance was a great success. As the evening wore on Linden watched an ever-increasing number of her unescorted friends pairing off with the available grammar-school lads or their invited friends. Outside, in the warm July night everybody said their goodbyes with fervent best wishes for the future, all promising to keep in touch no matter what.

'We should hold reunions regularly,' one girl suggested.

'At least every four years,' another recommended with fitting exuberance.

'Like the Olympic Games,' said another.

'So we'll be due to meet again in 1941,' Linden remarked. 'I suppose it had better be in Dudley.'

'Well, Dudley would be most appropriate.'

'And central for everybody. We'll arrange it nearer the time.'

Linden and Ron said their goodbyes to the rest and walked arm in arm in silence. She realized this night had been a turning point in her life. From now on, her daily routine would change inexorably. She had become comfortable in her school life, confident with her friends. Now she had no idea what the future might hold, but she did not fear it; rather she considered it a challenge, a time of new opportunities which she would embrace with enthusiasm . . . barring war.

'You're quiet,' Ron remarked at last.

Linden turned to him. 'I was just thinking about the friends I've just left.' She sighed profoundly. 'Sad, isn't it? You spend years with these people, practically every day of the week, except for holidays and weekends – in my case at any rate. You become so close to them, get to know everything about them, even about their parents . . . Then suddenly, they've gone, like bubbles suddenly burst – to universities, to jobs, working in different towns where they'll make new friends from other parts of the country. They'll marry, I expect, go to live God knows where, have children . . . I know I'll never see some of them again, yet they've been so close to me all these years. I think it's sad.'

He put his arm around her and gave her a hug as they walked through Dudley's dark, quiet streets.

'There's something I've been meaning to say, Linden.'

'What?' She looked up at him and the feeble street lamp reflected in her eyes, which seemed inordinately wide in the half-light, and so beautifully clear.

'I think we should get engaged.'

Linden stopped in her tracks and looked up at him again, but this time there seemed to be disillusionment in those same pools. Here was one opportunity she had no wish to embrace. 'Did you say what I thought you said?'

He uttered a nervous little laugh. 'I said, I think we should get engaged. What's wrong with that? I mean, I'd ask your mum and dad first if it was OK.'

'What if I don't want to get engaged?' she said, on the move again.

'Do I take it then that you don't?'

'I've only just left school, Ron. I want to see a bit of life, not tie myself to the first person who asks me to get engaged. Engagement means marriage. I don't want to have to even think about it – not for years and years.'

'I thought you'd be pleased,' he said, sounding hurt.

'I'm flattered that you think so much of me . . . but . . .'

'But what?'

'But I don't see the point.'

'Why do I always get the feeling, Linden, that I think a lot more of you than you think of me.'

'I think the world of you, Ron, but not enough to get engaged. Anyway, I'm too young. My dad would have a fit.'

'You mean you don't love me. Is that it? I'm well aware you've never said you do.'

Linden did not want to say outright that she did not love him, even though it was the truth, because she had no wish to hurt him or belittle him. She liked Ron enormously: he was her chum, his attentions gave her confidence, but she did not fancy him like that. She did not feel ready to commit herself, especially to *him*. Somehow, she felt she was on a different mental plane, smarter, more able to think things through. Like the depressing discussion earlier about the likelihood of war; he'd never really thought about it. He never considered important things – he'd never thought them through and it was evident in his attitude and his answers. All he seemed interested in was having a full belly, football, what films were showing that week, and how much money he'd pick up on payday. She expected more than that from a man. Significantly more. She would only ever get engaged to somebody who offered her some mental and not just physical stimulation.

'I'm just not ready to get engaged and start courting seriously,' she stated simply.

'D'you want to go on seeing me?'

Two

The Blower's Green Steelworks was situated in the most dismal part of Dudley, grey with the spoil of coal-mining, and smutty with industrial smoke propelled in thick coils by hundreds of red-brick chimney stacks, and dispersed into the atmosphere by the whimsical wind. Such was this area's desolation that if even a dandelion had the audacity to pierce the dark-grey crust with its bright yellow head it stood out like a beacon, and was worthy of remark. The landscape here was criss-crossed by railways, some belonging to the Blower's Green Steelworks, some to other, even vaster enterprises that melted and rolled and re-rolled steel. And it was noisy; the ear-splitting roar of furnaces, diluted only by distance, the incessant clanging of metal, the unremitting thud of huge forging hammers that made the ground beneath your feet tremble as they formed steel bars into pre-conceived shapes. The hissing and huffing of mineral-hauling locomotives and the shouts of men at work all added to the cacophony.

As Linden walked along Peartree Lane, over and under canal and railway bridges, she feared for the whiteness of her blouse and the shine on her shoes, for the dust swirled around her in the breeze, whipped up by the chugging lorries that passed her by. If she was successful in her interview for this job, she would be walking this route daily, to and from work. She tried to imagine it in winter in the cold and rain, and shuddered at the thought. It was nowhere near as pleasant as the walk to the high school set in the lea of the old castle, among trees and meadows on the more rural side of town. But, as Ron had told her, life moves on.

She pondered Ron and his eager proposal a few days ago. Engagement was the first step along that critical path, a path that was the downfall of some yet the saviour of many. But it *was* a promise to marry. Even if she agreed to go along with it, he must surely understand that they were too young yet. So what would be the point? She was just about to step into the bigger, wider world beyond the restricting limits of school discipline, and she had every intention of seeing what it had to offer before she committed herself to Ron, decent as he was. Of course, she had no wish to stop seeing him; there would be no point to that either. He worked for a living, so could afford to take her out once in a while. She enjoyed his company, she liked his friends, who seemed to like her too. Ron was fun. But commitment? No.

A musty, dusty smell greeted her in the grand entrance hall of Blower's Green Steelworks. In a tiny room behind a hatch two telephone operators sat. One of them, white-headed, evidently a spinster and older than Linden's mother, asked if she could help, and Linden explained that she had come for a job interview. White-headed spinster suggested she take a seat and she would tell Personnel that she was here. Linden thanked her with a polite smile.

She looked around her, at the walls panelled in oak and the lino on the floor that incongruously showed the marks of where it had been recently wiped with a less-than-clean mop. Gazing down at her from a gilt photo frame was a middle-aged man formally posed, clean-shaven, with greying hair and kind eyes behind his wire-rimmed spectacles. This, she presumed, was Charles Burgayne the owner she had heard so much about of this huge and successful enterprise.

Five minutes passed and another spinsterly lady appeared, prim and straight-backed. This was Miss Hardy, who looked Linden up and down and shook her hand. She said how happy she was to meet her, and ushered Linden into a wood-panelled, but spartan interview room.

Miss Hardy switched on the light, closed the door behind her, pointed out which of the chairs Linden should sit in, and took the chair behind the solitary desk.

'Of course, I know your father.' She smiled, as if the revelation might put her in good standing with her young visitor.

Linden, now sitting demurely, her knees together, her hands clasped together on her lap, rolled her eyes as if to apologize for her father's very existence.

'He's a fine man and a good worker, and has been employed here many years.'

'Since just after I was born, I think, Miss Hardy,' Linden replied, relieved that her father was decently revered after all.

'All right. Down to business. This appointment. We are seeking a smart and reliable girl to work in our typing pool. She must be proficient at shorthand and typing, and be an excellent timekeeper. Are you straight from school?'

'Dudley Girls' High, Miss Hardy,' Linden answered, inordinately proud of the fact.

'I presume you attained your Pitman's Diploma there?'

'Yes, Miss Hardy. Ninety words a minute.' She opened her handbag and withdrew the certificate, which she handed over.

Miss Hardy scanned it and handed it back. 'That seems very satisfactory. And your typing speed?'

'Sixty words a minute.'

Miss Hardy handed Linden a shorthand notebook and a pencil which she took from a desk drawer, along with a typed sheet of foolscap paper. 'I would like you to take down in shorthand what I am about to read.'

She read out a letter containing typical words and phrases used in steelmaking, some of which were strange to Linden. Then Miss Hardy asked her to read back what she'd said.

Linden took a deep breath and read. Some technical words had given her a little trouble, and she glanced up at Miss Hardy apprehensively.

'Don't worry, I'm not concerned at this stage over your unfamiliarity with some of the more technical words. Regular use would make them familiar, of course. Apart from that, you are very accurate. How old are you, Miss Woods?'

'Eighteen, miss.'

'And do you have any plans to get married in the foreseeable future?'

'No, Miss Hardy.' Linden smiled, recalling again Ron's proposal. 'Definitely not.'

'Very good. The appointment will carry a salary of twenty-two shillings and sixpence a week, and the successful applicant would qualify for two weeks' annual holiday after ten months' service. Do you have any questions you'd like to ask me, Miss Woods?'

'Yes, Miss Hardy. When can I start?'

* * *

Ron called round that evening, wearing grey flannels and open-necked shirt.

'How did you get on today, chick?' he asked as he sat down in the tiny scullery.

She grinned contentedly. 'I start on Monday.'

'Great!'

'And with my first week's wages I'll treat you to a night at the pictures.'

'I should hold her to that,' Joe Woods exclaimed from the depths of his armchair in front of the black-leaded fire grate. ''Tain't often you get an offer like that from a woman. Leastwise, not in my day.'

'No girl could afford to pay for her chap to go out in your day, Joe,' Gladys chimed in, in defence of her sex. 'Times was hard.'

'Times am still hard,' he responded. 'But we've done all right. At least we put our Linden through high school, even though it cost twelve guineas a term.'

'It's as well you had a good job, Joe. Otherwise, we wouldn't have been able to do it.'

'I'll pay you back,' Linden exclaimed sincerely. 'It's always been my intention to pay you back when I can afford it. I realize how much you've sacrificed over the years for my sake.'

'Aye, well I shouldn't worry about it too much, my flower,' Joe said. 'It was money well spent. It's given you a bloody good education and a flying start in this world. That was the intention, and I wouldn't have had it any other way. To see you like you are now, with the world at your feet, is repayment enough. I desire nothing more.'

'Oh, Dad . . .' Linden leaned over, kissed her father and ruffled his thinning hair affectionately. 'Don't think I don't appreciate it. I do.'

'So make the most of it. Now go out and enjoy yourself.'

'I thought we could go to the pictures tonight, chick,' Ron said. 'To celebrate you getting this job. That film *Top Hat* is on again at the Criterion.'

'The one with Fred Astaire and Ginger Rogers?'

'Yes. You enjoyed it when we saw it last year. Fancy seeing it again?'

Linden beamed. 'Ooh, yes, I do,' she replied dreamily. 'I'll go up and get changed.'

'Well, be quick. It starts in half an hour.'

On her first day at work, Linden decided to walk to the Blower's Green Steelworks. The blue sky was daubed with billowing white clouds but rain looked unlikely, so it would be a pleasant walk that would take her the best part of half an hour. No doubt she could get there by bus and tram, but decided not to rely on those on her first day. Her father never did. He always walked, and had left earlier to begin his shift at six.

When she arrived, she reported first to the Personnel Department. Miss Hardy took her to the typing pool, and introduced her first to Miss Mayhew, the pool's supervisor, then to a Mr Webb, who was in charge of the Wages Office.

'You will be working mostly for Mr Webb, Miss Woods.'

Mr Webb was in his fifties, staid, wearing a stiff collar that looked a mite too uncomfortable, and unfashionable spats. It did not seem in his nature to smile, and Linden wondered if she was going to be happy working with such a person. Before giving her a chance to settle in the typing pool Mr Webb called her for dictation. She duly skipped along to his office with notebook, pencil and eraser, avoiding the eyes of other nameless, unfamiliar employees, male and female, who milled about the corridors, but whose eyes she felt weighing her up as another newly arrived office girl.

Most of what Mr Webb gave her was internal memos to other departments or people, but before she could type it up she found it necessary to rummage through the drawers of the desk she'd been assigned in the typing pool for the correct headed paper.

'What are you looking for?' the girl at the desk to her right enquired.

Linden smiled back amiably. 'I've got some internal memos to do for Mr Webb, and I don't seem to be able to find any blank ones.'

'I got some you can have,' the girl said helpfully. She opened a drawer and pulled out a sheaf of paper. 'Here, this lot should keep you going a while. I'll take you to Marjorie in the stationery stores after, and you can get everything you need. I'm Vera Bytheway, by the way.'

Linden wondered at first if that was a double-barrelled name, but the girl's easy smile told her she had made herself the butt of a little joke. 'How do you do, Vera?' she replied, relieved the ice had been broken with at least one girl. 'I'm Linden Woods.'

'It makes you feel a bit awkward when you start a new job somewhere and you don't know anybody, I always think,' Vera remarked. 'Awful, it is. I remember my first day here. Didn't know a soul, didn't know where anything was, or who was what. Same as you, eh? You'll soon get used to it though.'

'What did you say your name is?' the girl on her left asked, butting in.

'Linden Woods. Hello.'

'Hello, Linden,' the girl said pleasantly. 'I'm Hilda Homer.'

'Nice to meet you Hilda. How long have you two been here?' Linden asked them collectively.

'Two years, me,' Vera answered. 'Hilda's been here about a year, eh, Hilda?'

Hilda confirmed the fact with a nod.

'D'you think I'll like it?' Linden asked. 'Mr Webb seems a bit of a stick-in-the-mud.'

'Oh, he's all right. Nora, the girl who used to do his work before, got on all right with him, didn't she, Hilda?'

'He's harmless enough.'

'So why did she leave?'

'She got married. I reckon she had to get married, to tell you the truth, but she never admitted as much to anybody, did she, Hilda?'

'No, but she was starting to get a bit of a podge on her. She didn't need to tell anybody, it was obvious.'

'Anyway,' Vera continued, 'they don't operate a married-workers policy here for women. So she had to leave.'

'You're not married then, I take it?' Linden commented as she separated three sheets of quarto with two sheets of carbon paper.

Vera laughed out loud. 'Do I look daft? Sort of courting, but I ain't about to get married. Not for a long time yet. I'm only twenty. There's plenty time for all that softness.'

Linden offered the sheets of paper to the rollers of her un-familiar typewriter and began to turn the knob on the side of the machine to feed them through. 'So who do you work for, Vera?'

'Mostly for Mr Vickers in Sales, but we all have to swap about a bit from time to time, to even the work out.'

'Do you see much of Mr Burgayne?'

'Which one?'

'Oh, is there more than one?' Linden queried, with some surprise.

'There's the old man, Mr Charles Burgayne, then there's Mr Hugh Burgayne, his eldest son, who's also a director. He's in his mid-twenties, I reckon, and he's got an eye for the women, I can tell you. So you want to watch out for him – a nice-looking girl like you.'

'Thanks for the warning, Vera.'

'There's another son besides, but we rarely see him.'

'So Mr Burgayne has two sons?'

'And a daughter. Penny, her name is. She's nice. She comes in and helps out sometimes when the staff get busy. Keeps her away from her horses, though. They say she's mad about horses.'

'And men,' Hilda added. 'Or so I heard.'

'So how old is this Penny?'

'Our age. Nineteen or twenty. Have you brought sandwiches with you, or d'you intend to go to the canteen at dinner time?'

'I thought I might go to the canteen.'

'Great. You can come with us. We'll show you the ropes, eh? It's always good to have somebody who can show you the ropes when you're new, I always reckon.'

'I'm really grateful,' Linden said with a smile as she began typing. 'You're really kind, both of you.'

'Think nothing of it. It'll give you the chance to get to know some of the other girls as well.'

The other girls seemed a friendly lot, and Linden soon felt at ease with them. Mr Webb showed no sign of proving himself the ogre he first appeared to be; rather she found him mild-mannered, perhaps a little self-conscious with a young and very pretty girl whom he seemed unwilling to even look at. Their relationship seemed to get off to a reasonable start, especially when her first batch of letters and memos came back to her all duly signed and ready for the post room.

It had not been a bad first day at work.

Three

Before Linden knew it, the works' annual shutdown had arrived. Office work was slack since many, barring staff and those involved in maintenance, were on holiday. Linden enjoyed the easy relaxed atmosphere, but found the days passed more slowly and was glad one day during the second week when her supervisor asked her to go to the boardroom with her notebook and pencil to take dictation. Apprehensive as to whom she would be working for, fearing it might be Mr Charles Burgayne or, worse, his son Hugh, she tapped on the door nervously and was surprised when a woman's voice asked her to enter.

'I was told to come here for dictation,' Linden explained hesitantly to a girl who was slim and very attractive, with sun-bleached blonde hair, bright-blue eyes, and about the same age as herself.

'I asked for somebody,' the girl said with an affable grin. 'Do come in and sit down . . . We've not met before. Are you new here?'

'This is only my second week,' Linden replied. 'My name is Linden Woods.'

'Then, how do you do, Linden Woods? I'm Penny Burgayne.' She offered her hand and they shook.

'Oh . . . So you're Mr Charles Burgayne's daughter.'

'The one and only.'

Linden's surprise was matched only by her smile. 'I'm really pleased to meet you. The other girls said you dropped by from time to time.'

'I could drop by more often, I'm sure, but Daddy insists I only get in the way. Anyway, I do hope you don't mind, Linden, but I have some rather pressing correspondence to get done, and it would be such a help if you could do a bit of typing for me. I'm hopeless at typing.'

'I'd be glad to,' said Linden, at once at ease with this girl. 'There's not much to do at the moment with the works' holidays and everything. I'm itching for something to do.'

'Well, just to explain, we're hosting a garden party at Kinlet Hall – that's the family pile, you know – on the twenty-first of August, and I do desperately need to write to some of the suppliers to confirm the orders for food, etcetera, etcetera. Otherwise our poor guests will have sweet Fanny Adams to eat and will be bloody-well totally unimpressed. And I shall get the blame, of course. I can type a bit myself, you understand, but by the time I've got letters done without a page full of typos I could have driven here and got somebody else on the case who really knows what they're doing. Hence the reason you're here.'

Linden chuckled aloud. 'I don't mind a bit.' She really liked this Penny. There was a warmth about her and, despite her cultured tones, she was unaffected, a quality which surprised her, for she would not have expected it in a girl from her elevated background.

When Penny had finished dictating half a dozen letters, all in a similar vein, Linden left her to type them up on the Burgayne family's personal headed notepaper. Within half an hour she was knocking on the boardroom door again carrying the finished articles, complete with typed envelopes, all in a neat pile. Penny was ending a telephone call, and put the receiver down as Linden approached.

'That was impressively quick,' she commented pleasantly.

'I do hope they're all right,' Linden said. 'Shall I wait while you glance over them, in case I need to type any again?'

'If you like, Linden. Have a seat a mo.'

She sat down opposite Penny and studied the girl while she read the letters through and signed them in turn. This girl seemed as though she hadn't a care in the world. Her skin was fashionably tanned as if she had spent a great deal of time in the open air, living the country life. Linden tried to imagine her as a solemn creature, sedate and demure, sitting at her father's right hand with pearls at her throat in the doubtless vast dining room of this Kinlet Hall; but the image seemed wrong. Penny was not that type. She was unlike the preconceived notion that Linden had harboured all her life of how the daughters of the wealthy would be. Penny would be fun, rebellious even.

'They all look good to me,' Penny confirmed at length, and flashed a glimpse of her beautifully even teeth as she beamed.

Linden graciously returned the smile. 'Good. I'll seal them up and take them to the post room for you.'

'Thank you, Linden, that's jolly kind of you. But wait. There's no rush. Do sit down again and let's have a chat. It's rather a novelty for me, you know, to talk to a girl my own age, especially here. Normally, I'm expected to use Miss Evans, my father's secretary, who is actually several decades older than a conker tree, but she's on holiday too . . . thank goodness. Anyway, you say you haven't got much to do.'

'No, but what about my supervisor?'

'Oh, don't worry about old Betsy Mayhew. You're working with me. You say you're fairly new here?'

'Yes. I left high school in July, and here I am thrust into the big, wide world at last.'

'Bit of a sooty world, too, in this neck of the woods, don't you think?'

'Oh, isn't it just? So where is Kinlet Hall, if you don't mind me asking? Out in the country?'

'Yes, out in the sticks. Sort of between Kinver and Alveley if you know where that is. Near the Shropshire–Staffordshire border at any rate. Rather lovely it is, actually, especially at this time of year.'

'The girls here say you're keen on horses. I expect you get the chance to ride loads out in the country?'

Penny gurgled with laughter. 'Keen on horses, cars, bikes, chaps . . . anything that moves.'

Hilda had intimated that the girl liked chaps. 'D'you have a boyfriend then?'

'I get through about one a month on average. Nobody at present though.' Penny shrugged self-effacingly. 'Rather exhausted the supply, you could say. Not too many tasty chaps who are readily available in the sticks, you know . . . And you?'

'Mmm,' she answered wistfully. 'There's this chap called Ron. I've known him a couple of years . . . and I like him. But he's asked me to get engaged, and I'm not sure it's what I want. So I keep him at arm's length.'

Penny gurgled again. 'Best place for 'em, arm's length. Do you have any brothers? Oh, I'm not on the lookout for new conquests, mind, so please don't jump to that conclusion.'

Linden laughed, dismissing the notion. 'I'm an only child. You have brothers though, don't you?'

'Two . . . Chalk and cheese.'

'I've seen Mr Hugh. He always seems to be here.'

'Hugh? Oh, Hugh . . .' There was some disdain in Penny's voice. 'Actually, he's engaged to a jolly decent girl called Laura Birch – you know, the daughter of James Birch who owns a carpet factory in Kidderminster. I'm sure Hugh doesn't deserve her at all, though. I wouldn't trust him as far as I could throw him, but keep that to yourself for goodness sake. *She* thinks the sun shines out of his backside, poor fool. Somebody really ought to tell her.'

'But not you,' Linden suggested.

'Oh, definitely not me.' She turned down the corners of her mouth. 'It's nothing to do with me.'

'And your other brother, Penny. What about him?'

'Edward. It's quite fun having Edward home from university for a while. At least I have somebody to play tennis with.' All at once there appeared a brighter gleam in Penny's eyes. 'I say, do you play tennis?'

'I played quite a lot at school,' Linden replied.

'So you must be pretty good, huh?'

'Not bad.'

'Then you really must come over. I'm desperate for a lady tennis partner – somebody to make up a four.' Penny looked at her watch. 'I say, it's nearly one o' clock. D'you fancy going out and having a spot of lunch? There's this super pub I know.'

'I'd love to,' Linden agreed, delighted, flattered and surprised at being thus invited by no less an entity than the boss's only daughter, whom she rather liked. 'Is it far?'

'Quite a way, but we'll go in my car.'

'You have a car?' Linden queried, incredulous.

'Yea, verily. Come on, leave those letters here. They can go to the post room this afternoon.'

Penny drove the Riley fast and never stopped talking, while Linden felt compelled to cling on tightly but discreetly to the squab of her seat, her eyes never leaving the road ahead. Riding in a car was not something she did regularly. In fact, she could only ever recall having ridden in one other – an undertaker's car on the day of her grandfather's funeral. But this was hardly funereal; this was exhilarating.

The sight of a cattle market, closed today, signified their arrival after about fifteen minutes at the village of Hagley, green with grass, and with quaint houses painted white and black. It seemed a million miles from the industrial conglomeration they had left behind. They quit the main road and ascended a narrow lane before coming to a standstill outside an old redbrick building.

'Here we are,' Penny announced, and clambered out of the vehicle. 'It'll be quiet here today with the cattle market shut.'

They ambled to the front door and entered. Again, the familiar yet unfamiliar aroma every public house seemed to possess enveloped her.

'What's your poison?' Penny enquired.

'Oh . . . I don't know. What are you having?'

'I'll have a pint of bitter. It's excellent here.'

'A pint of bitter?' *Men drink pints of bitter. Girls don't.* 'I don't think I could manage a pint of bitter,' Linden declared.

'A half then?'

'A half of shandy, maybe . . . please.'

'A pint of bitter and a half of bitter shandy,' Penny told the barman, who was waiting for the order. 'And two cheese and ham sandwiches.'

'Coming up, miss.' He grabbed a pint glass and proceeded to fill it from the beer pump.

She placed half a crown on the counter and the barman handed her change. The two girls moved to a table in the window with their drinks.

'Fancy you drinking pints of bitter,' Linden remarked matily, and not without some admiration. 'I wouldn't have the nerve.'

'Why shouldn't women drink pints if they have the capacity for it?'

'But who'd have thought it? I mean, there's nothing to you. I mean, it's not as if you're big.'

'Eight stone, wringing wet. But that's got nothing to do with it.'

'So where d'you put it?'

Laughing, she said, 'Well, I'll have to visit the WC more often than you.' She took a good swig of the beer and sighed.

'Damn good stuff, you know, this.' Then, after a pause: 'I say, do you really fancy making up a four at tennis?'

'Oh, yes. Who plays?'

'Edward, my brother, and his pal, Adrian Farrance. Adrian's sweetheart used to play, but since she gave him up we've been short of a girl. Actually, I'm rather glad she gave him up. He's as pretty as paint.'

'You fancy him?'

'Rather.' Penny grinned impishly, her blue eyes sparkling, and Linden thought she looked very attractive.

'Does he fancy you?'

'Oh, I'll have a jolly good go at making him.'

Linden broke into a chuckle. 'So when is the next match?'

'We could fix something up for Saturday, if that suits.'

'OK by me.'

'Then let's hope the weather holds. I can easily pick you up Saturday morning if you let me have your address before I leave today. You will be able to stay the night, won't you?'

'Oh . . . yes . . . if you'd like me to.'

Even greater surprise. At once Linden's mind was awhirl. She would have to put Ron off. He wouldn't be happy about it, but he didn't own her. Surely her mother and father couldn't object. Anyway, how could she possibly refuse an invitation to the home of Charles Burgayne? If only her friends from school could see her now . . .

Gladys Woods flitted around the cramped living room in Hill Street with a duster in one hand, a tin of Mansion polish in the other, as nervous as a kitten about the impending visit of Charles Burgayne's only daughter. She polished the sideboard, the chairs, the coal scuttle and the fender, then buffed up the black-leaded grate with a damp cloth, and stood back to assess the effect of her efforts. She adjusted the position of the ornaments that sat alongside the confusingly erratic clock on top of the mantelpiece, and even tidied up the pincushion that hung from its chenille pelmet. Then across the table she spread the best chenille cloth, which normally only saw the light of day on a Sunday.

Linden stepped down the crooked stairs and opened the creaking door on to the room to see her mother cleaning the imperfect window panes that looked out on to the veranda.

'I just thought I'd spruce the place up a bit afore that young woman gets here.'

'I wouldn't have bothered, Mum,' Linden replied, glancing around appraisingly. She had no intention of inviting the girl in – not wishing to put her off before she really got to know her. 'Better if I just run down the entry as soon as I hear her car.'

She noticed Gladys's hurt expression that she was not going to be allowed near Penny Burgayne, and she felt for her; her mother was doing her best to make what little they'd got presentable. But the fussing made Linden acutely aware of the smallness, the humbleness of their terraced home, compared to what Penny was used to.

'She probably won't have time to come in and say hello,' Linden suggested placatingly. 'Maybe when she brings me back tomorrow . . .'

'Well, I would like to meet this Penny Burgayne . . . I would like to think you're not ashamed of us, our Linden.'

'Oh, Mum.' She flung her arms around Gladys's neck and gave her a hug. 'Course I'm not. What a daft thing to say.'

They heard the throb of a motor-car engine, the toot of a horn.

'She's here,' Linden said, and collected her things together. 'See you tomorrow, Mum. I'll be back for Sunday dinner.'

'Well, don't show yourself up, and just mind your Ps and Qs, our Linden. But have a lovely time.'

Gladys watched her daughter proudly as she hurried on to the yard and down the entry to the street and the waiting motor car.

Linden jumped into the vehicle as quickly as she could, thinking that if Penny hurried and drove fast through the awful streets she wouldn't have time to notice the grubbiness. She did not know Penny Burgayne well enough yet to appreciate that the girl was sufficiently well educated to understand that modest means did not necessarily mean modest intellect, nor a lack of fascination. Nor did Linden know that from the moment she had first set foot in the boardroom to take dictation Penny had liked the look and demeanour of her, recognizing her not so much as a kindred spirit but more of a complementary personality. They were different, and the difference was what attracted Penny. Despite her lowly background, Linden seemed actually more refined; she was certainly more reserved, and Penny was intrigued by the incongruity of it all.

'You must think it's pretty awful around here,' Linden remarked self-consciously as the uninspiring scenery flashed by.

'Actually, I don't think that at all.' Penny smiled her reassurance.

'But it can't be anything like where you live.'

'It's not. But that makes it all the more interesting. Look at the view from here. It's terrific.'

They drove on and reached the centre of the town crowded with Saturday shoppers. At one point they were stuck behind a tram and Penny honked her horn impatiently, until she could overtake it. Beyond Stourbridge there were fields, ripening gold under the summer sun. The houses they passed were big and beautiful with immaculately manicured lawns; flower beds and borders offered splashes of sometimes brilliant, sometimes subtle colours, but always eliciting a smile of pleasure and admiration from Linden.

Over an undulating, winding road they travelled. Penny swung the wheel left into a narrow lane. On the skyline, a clump of trees stood hazy in the distance, an island in a heaving sea of golden barley. Below them in the middle distance the ground dipped away from the road, cradling a hazel copse that looked dark and soft as velvet. Soon, they were passing between two tall, wrought-iron gates, and on along a sweeping tarmacadam driveway with tall elms and oaks lining its curve, and vast stretches of lawn flanking each side. It seemed to go on for ages, but as it twisted sharply a house stood before them, big and grey, built of limestone and Tudor in style.

It was her first glimpse of Kinlet Hall.

Before Linden knew it, she was ascending the front steps carrying her tennis racquet and her overnight case, with Penny's hand encouragingly in the small of her back. She caught her breath as her meandering gaze took in the entrance hall with its ancient panelling, its arched and timbered ceiling. The antlers of long-dead stags extended from wooden shields and in a vast stone fireplace fir cones lay unlit in a wrought-iron basket. The place had its own distinctive smell, too: a blend of pot-pourri, stone and ancient wood.

At once a maid appeared.

'This is Jenkins, Linden. She'll take your things to your room.'

Linden smiled equally at the girl, who was in her early twenties and not at all unattractive, and offered her the overnight case, which she now realized was rather tatty. She was not used to servants and felt a little uncomfortable; servants normally came from people of her own class.

'Thank you very much,' she said self-consciously as the maid took the case and bobbed a curtsey.

'I'll show you your room later,' Penny said. 'First, let me introduce you to my mother.'

They found Mrs Burgayne in the morning room sitting at a table, writing. She was a pleasant-looking woman in her fifties, neither fat nor thin – a woman who had held on to her figure well.

'Mother, this is Linden Woods, my new friend I told you about.'

Dorothy Burgayne stood up and offered her hand. 'I'm delighted to meet you, Miss Woods. May I call you Linden?'

'Oh, yes, of course.'

'Penny tells me you are a secretary at the works?' It was a question rather than an outright statement of fact.

'I am, but I'm fairly new there, Mrs Burgayne.'

'And here for the tennis, I hear. Do you play much?'

'When I was at school I played a lot. It was very much encouraged.'

'An active body aids an active mind is the theory behind that ethic, I suspect.'

Linden nodded and smiled. 'Yes, I expect so.'

'Edward has gone out,' Mrs Burgayne told Penny. 'He's meeting Adrian. I expect he'll be back soon.'

'He'd better be,' Penny said. 'He knew very well that Linden was coming here to make up a four.'

'Well, why don't you show Linden her room, and then you can have lunch. They might be here by the time you've eaten.'

'Yes, come on Linden.'

Linden smiled. 'See you later, Mrs Burgayne.'

In the hallway again, she followed Penny across the stone flags to a wide flight of stone stairs. In the gallery above, the polished wooden floor was uneven and it creaked as they made their way to the kind of room Linden never dreamed existed any more. In it was a four-poster bed hung with a cream-coloured tapestry in a pink rose design, and thick, colourful rugs on the oak floor. The mullioned windows were curtained with a material that matched the bed hangings, and Linden went across to catch the view outside.

'This is a lovely room, Penny.'

'So glad you like it. There's a bathroom here . . .' She went to the door and into the gallery again, and Linden followed. 'There, look.' She pointed to a door. 'You should have everything you need. If not, just ring for Jenkins.'

Ring for Jenkins! She wouldn't have the nerve to ring for Jenkins; she would rather die than ring for Jenkins.

'Anyway, do let's have lunch now, shall we? I could eat a horse.'

The two of them went outside to eat at a table and chairs set out on a lawn that stretched like a carpet of velvet before them, and shaded by elms. The flower beds were a riot of scarlet, purple, pink and white.

'So what d'you think of Kinlet Hall?' Penny asked, shaking salt over her chicken salad.

'I think it's magnificent. I have to confess, though, to being a bit overawed by it all, especially servants. I'm not used to servants.'

'It seems to me that the trick with servants is to be respectful to them. Then they don't get all hoity-toity. I mean to say, if you really upset them there's no knowing what unspeakable things they might do, especially to your food when your back's turned. I once heard of a chap who was always very hard on his servants and rude too, so they regularly used to wipe their master's favourite mutton chops round the bull-mastiff's backside before serving it.'

Linden giggled infectiously. 'That's disgusting! I take it this chicken hasn't had the same treatment?'

'Not bloody likely. Daddy runs a happy ship.'

'So tell me about your family. Have you always lived here? How far back do your ancestors go in this house?'

'Oh, not as far as you might imagine. We're hardly aristocracy. Not old money at any rate. This house was bought for a song, apparently, by my great-grandfather in the first flush of his prosperity. It was him who began steel-making – rather it was iron-making in those days; there was no steel. As an ironmaster he did rather well and the business has been handed down, and with careful management it's grown. Not everybody has wanted to be part of it, though. I'm not sure what Edward will do yet – all he's interested in at present is aeroplanes.'

'I'm looking forward to meeting Edward,' Linden remarked. 'What's he like?'

'Amiable . . . Yes, that describes him perfectly. He's amiable.'

Linden wanted to ask if he was also good-looking, but such a question might give Penny the wrong idea, so she desisted. Instead, Linden switched the subject to Penny's string of past male conquests, and howled at her host's irreverence where boys were concerned.

'D'you think you'll ever get married?' Linden asked.

'If I have to,' Penny replied, then shrieked, 'Oh, Lord! I didn't mean it like it came out. God, you must think me awful. What I mean is, it'll be sort of expected of me . . . So, if the right chap comes along I might have to . . .'

Four

After lunch the girls played a couple of sets, which Linden won, before two uncommonly appealing young men appeared in whites, bearing tennis racquets and all the coolness and jauntiness of youth.

'You're late,' Penny reprimanded collectively, irked at their casualness.

One of them smiled, an icon of bonhomie. 'Sorry, old fruit. Had to get my racquet restrung.'

So this was Edward. He was wearing a sleeveless pullover over a white shirt and his hair was a riot of unruly curls with some evidence remaining of a conventional parting on the left. Linden did not consider him strikingly handsome – at least not immediately – but there was something about him that appealed. He was the manifestation of what she considered masculine and elegant. His smile was broad and frank, and she perceived an innate warmth in his blue eyes that creased so attractively when he smiled. Yes, he did seem amiable, just as Penny had described.

'This is Linden Woods,' Penny announced to them both. 'Linden, my brother Edward . . . and Adrian Farrance . . .'

Edward greeted Linden with youthful interest. 'Pleased to meet you Miss Woods.'

'Oh, do call her Linden, Edward. You *are* going to bounce about the tennis court with her.'

'Pleased to meet you, Linden,' he said again, less formally as he offered his hand. They shook. 'Such a pretty name, too.'

'Thank you.' Linden smiled demurely, and blushed as she'd never blushed before.

Adrian offered his hand too, and she understood exactly why Penny was interested in him. He was tall, youthful, evidently a rebel like she was, with a mop of dark curls akin to Edward's, and head-turningly handsome with it.

'How do you do, Linden,' he said.

'I'm well, thank you,' Linden replied.

'You don't look quite your usual pristine self this morning, Adrian,' Penny remarked familiarly.

'Oh, I got invited to some stuck-up sort of do last night in Kinver. There were rather too many snooty types for my liking, except for one rather tasty piece who I did my best to woo. She was of the same mind as me, so we left together and I dragged her round one or two hostelries. Last thing I can remember is gazing at a bottle of brandy.'

'You *are* the limit, Adrian. So what happened to the girl?'

'I really don't recall. Pity. She was rather nice, actually. Somebody, though, must have taken me home . . . And now I don't feel any worse than if I'd been shoved through one of your father's rolling mills.'

'It's time you got over Juliet and settled down with a nice girl who'd put a stop to your nonsense.'

'Well, I always seem to be drawn back to you, Penny.'

Linden saw that Penny flushed slightly.

'Should I be excited about that?'

'Are we interrupting a serious game of tennis?' Edward asked, diverting them from their banter.

'Serious for me,' Penny said. 'I've just lost two sets. This Linden Woods is a demon player.'

'Well done, Linden. Are you ready for a four now?'

'I think so.'

'Girls against the boys, eh?' Edward suggested.

'That's hardly fair,' Penny complained. 'You'll skin us.'

'You're joking. The state Adrian is in?'

'He'll soon rally round. I'll partner Adrian, and you can partner Linden.'

'Is that OK by you, Linden?' Edward asked.

She nodded. 'Fine by me.'

'You serve first, Adrian.'

'God. Must I?'

They all laughed, and the two couples parted to take their places at opposite sides of the net. Disregarding his aching limbs and throbbing head, Adrian began the onslaught, which Linden parried effectively, taking the point.

'Love fifteen,' exclaimed Edward. 'Well done.'

'Liven up, Adrian,' Penny called, 'else we're going to be a walkover.'

It was an earnestly fought match, which Linden and Edward won after three sets. This was quite some feat on their part, despite Adrian's self-inflicted incapacity, since Edward was inordinately distracted by Linden's long and shapely limbs as she moved across the court with all the suppleness of a young gazelle. The sun, frequently behind her, shone through the flimsy material of her tennis frock, enticingly defining her form beneath it. Edward lingered to appreciate the treat on more than a few occasions at the expense of several back-hands and many points. Who was this unassuming, pleasant and attractive girl Penny had latched on to? She glowed like a lily in the sunshine. Her dark hair, which was pinned up, allowed errant stray strands to sensuously caress her elegant neck, moist with perspiration. Awaiting Adrian's cyclonic serves and usually returning them successfully, she danced around the court on tiptoes, her very kissable lips pursed with concentration. Yet she seemed so innocent, so virginal, entirely unaware of her sexuality; and that made her all the more appealing.

None of them saw Hugh Burgayne watching, hidden behind the trees that encompassed the tennis court. He had heard from his mother that a new girl-friend of Penny's from the typing pool was playing tennis, and he wanted to catch a glimpse of her. Penny wouldn't normally associate with employees, but their mother had said she seemed a very nice girl, and very pretty too, which aroused his curiosity. He had already spotted an extremely attractive girl in the corridors at the office, a new employee whom he very much fancied. He'd wondered if this was the same girl . . . It was.

At the end of the tennis all four were perspiring madly as they stood facing each other on the grass in the shade of an ancient oak, thankful that Jenkins had come along and planted a collapsible table, complete with two jugs of lemonade and four glasses beneath a tree.

'You played jolly well,' Edward said to Linden as he mopped sweat from his face with a handkerchief. 'Anytime you need a partner at this game do let me know.'

'Well, this doesn't have to be a one-off event,' Penny inter-jected, breathless and radiant with exertion. She poured lemonade for each of them. 'Linden is welcome to play with us regularly, if that's OK with her.'

'Oh, I'd love to,' Linden replied. She accepted a glass and drank.

'Except, Edward, that you'll be leaving for Cambridge soon.'

'I know.' Edward continued to study Linden discreetly. She was to him the essence of femininity. Slim and perfectly proportioned, with all the grace of a ballerina, her skin looked invitingly smooth, her hazel eyes were crystal clear and long-lashed, and her lovely mouth was so obviously made to give and receive delicious kisses.

'Are you staying the night, Linden?'

Linden said she was.

'She's having dinner with us, Edward,' Penny said, and sat down on the grass.

The others followed suit, sitting in a circle.

'D'you fancy joining Adrian and me for a day out tomorrow?' he asked. 'We're playing cricket at Enville Hall.'

'Sorry, I shall have to get back home,' Linden answered with sincere regret, looking from one to the other. 'My folks will be expecting me before one. Sunday dinner's a bit of a ritual at our house.'

As she took another drink, Linden realized she must sound ineffably plebeian. 'They tell me you're keen on aeroplanes, Edward,' she said, diverting the focus from herself.

'And flying them,' Edward replied enthusiastically, always happy to talk about his favourite subject.

'You fly them?' Linden couldn't help sounding impressed as well as surprised.

'He has his own plane,' Penny explained.

'It's a Gypsy Moth,' Edward said. 'Would you like to see it?'

'Yes, I would,' Linden replied with enthusiasm. 'I've never seen a plane close to.'

'Come on, I'll show you.'

All four scrambled to their feet, put their glasses on the table, and made their way in a group across the grass and through a line of trees to a clearing.

'This is the strip where I take off and land,' Edward explained. 'The Moth only needs about a hundred and fifty yards for either.'

Linden turned her head from left to right scanning the swathe of short-cropped turf. 'So where is the aeroplane?'

'Over here.'

She walked alongside him, while Penny and Adrian fell further behind engaged in their own conversation.

'How long have you had it?'

'Oh, nearly a year. My father got it me for my birthday. I'm hoping to fly to Cambridge next week, providing I can get permission to keep it at Duxford. That's the airfield we use. I belong to the University Air Squadron, you see.'

'I didn't know universities had air squadrons.'

He turned and smiled. 'Cambridge was the first, set up in 1925, actually. It's seen as a way of getting chaps with degrees to go on to a career in the RAF.'

'Is that what you want to do, then? Join the Royal Air Force?'

'Absolutely.'

'Doesn't the prospect of war with Germany scare you?'

'Not at all. We would all have to play our parts.' He smiled again deliciously.

'What got you interested in aeroplanes?'

'Oh, ever since I was a small boy and somebody gave me a book on the aircraft of the Great War . . . Look, there it is . . .'

The aircraft lay under a canvas awning, akin to a large, open tent. It was painted silver and blue and had large letters marked on the side. Linden ran her fingers lightly along the leading edge of the lower wing as she perused it. The covering was a material that looked like some sort of tough canvas, and the wings were secured by what she perceived as wire rigging, like sails on a yacht. Controlling rods and wires were attached to the outside of the fuselage.

'It's beautiful,' she said, almost breathlessly. 'Smaller than I imagined.'

'It carries two, you know. Would you like to go up in it?'

'Now, you mean?'

'Why not? It doesn't take long to get it ready. It's already fuelled up.'

'But it all looks a bit flimsy to me,' she said, uncertain now as to what she might be letting herself in for.

He was enchanted by her hesitancy. 'Actually, it's as safe as houses. Even if the engine packed up we would glide safely back to the ground.'

Linden turned to obtain Penny's advice; she must have already flown in the contraption. Penny was giving Adrian her full attention as they approached, and laughing at something he had just said.

'Penny, Edward has asked me to go up in the aeroplane with him,' she said, almost as if he'd made an improper suggestion.

'Then you'll need to wear something warm,' Penny replied. 'It's freezing up there, even on a day like today, and it'll blow you to bits. Forget it in your tennis frock.'

'Have you ever flown in it?'

'Yes. Once. It's quite a whiz, actually.'

Linden looked at Edward with uncertainty in her eyes.

'You'll love it, Linden,' he reassured her. 'Penny has a warm jacket you could borrow, and I have a spare helmet.'

'You'll need some goggles too,' Penny added.

'I have a spare pair,' Edward said. 'Look, why don't you go to the house, get togged up first, then come back here when you're ready.'

'It all seems a lot of bother,' Linden said, full of reticence, but not wishing to appear afraid.

'No bother at all, Linden. Come on, we'll soon have you ready.'

When Linden was walking back from the house with Penny, suitably attired for her first flight, she could hear the thrum and cackle of its engine, already warming up.

'OK,' Edward called, trying to make himself heard over the din. 'Step up here, hold the wing struts for support, then lower yourself into the front seat.'

'The front seat?' Linden screeched into the teeth of the air stream that was created by the turning propeller.

Edward nodded.

She did as he bid, not without some difficulty, for there was very little room. Edward then reached inside and pulled out the safety straps, which he pulled around her in a sort of webbing. It came together at a metal buckle into which all the strands clipped.

'Don't touch the clasp until we're back on the ground,' he instructed in a shout. 'Are your goggles secure?'

She tightened them and nodded. He smiled reassuringly, and clambered into the cockpit behind her. When he had fastened himself in, he tapped her on the shoulder and, as she turned to glance behind her, he gave her the thumbs-up.

The first thing she noticed was an increase in the speed and sound of the engine as Edward nosed the Gypsy Moth into the wind and taxied forward. He opened the throttle fully and waited for the surge of power that would haul them into the blue, and a constant blast of wind from the propeller ruffling the top of the leather helmet Linden was wearing.

The little biplane did not disappoint; it rumbled along the clearing, gathering speed, the whole assembly vibrating alarmingly. Then the vibration ceased, and she was surprised at how quickly the ground beneath her slipped away. She peered over the side as the aircraft banked. Penny and Adrian, getting smaller and smaller, waved enthusiastically. She waved back, scanning the landscape sliding away underneath her for landmarks she might recognize. A canal came into view, glinting like a length of shiny bent wire as it disappeared into the hazy distance.

It was strange and exhilarating to be up here, remote, flying with the birds, although birds seemed to scatter in all directions at the raucous sound of the engine. She had no idea how high they were flying, and even if she'd called to ask the question it was obvious that Edward would not be able to hear her above the phenomenal wind noise and the throb of the engine.

Up here you could watch the world and all its troubles go by and somehow be untouched by it. They flew over countryside patched with gold and yellow and green, lush with trees. To their right, below them was a stately home in magnificent grounds, with two shimmering lakes; it was amazing how many lakes and ponds there were down there. Through the summer haze, the spire of Top Church in Dudley was visible, then Linden recognized the grey hulk that was the keep of Dudley's Norman castle and the new modern buildings in its grounds that were part of the new zoo. She recognized other landmarks too, including her old school playing fields and St John's church on Kates Hill. She looked for the street in which she lived, but before she could locate it she felt the flimsy machine roll to the left. The wings dipped alarmingly, the horizon became seriously skew-whiffed and Linden believed that but for the securing hold of the webbing that was attached to her, she would surely tumble out.

They were obviously turning back. Pity. It was intoxicating.
Shame it must be so short-lived a trip. Linden lost all sense
of direction and orientation. Too soon she sensed that they
were descending, the ground was getting closer . . . closer, ever
closer. They skimmed a copse of trees, then she recognized
the grey Tudor building that was Kinlet Hall. Ahead of her
and below she could just make out the clearing which served
as the landing strip. She braced herself for the inevitable
bump as the wheels hit the ground. But it was so smooth. The
only clue that they were on the ground was when they rumbled
across it and she felt the unevenness of the grassy surface that
made the wings and bracing shudder again, until they came
to a rapid halt and the engine died.

Silence. Silence like she had never known before.

She felt a bump behind her that suggested Edward was
clambering out. She turned her head and caught sight of him
jumping to the ground.

He grinned laddishly as he took off his goggles and muffler.
'How was that?'

'Brilliant!' She beamed back at him. 'Oh, absolutely brilliant. I can't believe I've actually flown.'

'We'd better unharness you.' He reached into the open
cockpit to unfasten the webbings. 'OK. Careful as you climb
out.'

Back on solid ground, she removed the goggles to fully
reveal her flushed cheeks and astonishingly bright eyes that
told perfectly how much she had enjoyed herself.

'How long have we been up there?' she enquired, taking
off the fur-lined gloves Penny had lent her.

'About half an hour, I imagine.'

'It's very cold up there, isn't it?'

'Told you so,' he answered with a grin.

'I can't see Penny and Adrian.' She looked about her, peering
through the trees.

'Shall we go and find them, and let them know you're back
in one piece?'

She smiled at him in unconcealed admiration. 'OK.'

There were six for dinner, which was a very informal occasion. Penny had invited Adrian to stay and he was still wearing
his tennis whites. Linden had brought with her a printed cotton

dress all fresh and summery, which turned out to be an ideal choice, while Penny changed into black slacks and a blouse with a bold floral pattern.

Linden met Charles Burgayne for the first time just before they sat down to dinner, when Penny introduced them.

'I'm very pleased to meet you, Miss Woods,' he said pleasantly as he shook her hand.

'You *can* call her Linden, you know, Daddy,' Penny declared, rolling her eyes. Then, in an aside to Linden that was deliberately audible to everybody, added, 'Daddy is so old-fashioned sometimes.'

'It's an old-fashioned courtesy that I extend to anybody I've not had the pleasure of meeting before,' Charles responded, but with good-humour. 'One just cannot take for granted that people are happy with such familiarities as being called by they Christian name.'

'But Linden is my generation, Daddy, not yours. We don't stand on ceremony. It's just too boring.'

'So, Linden,' he went on, choosing to ignore his daughter's denunciation but taking her advice anyway, 'I understand you've been up in the Moth?'

'Oh, yes, and it was a sensation,' she enthused. 'I loved every minute. It was very good of Edward to go to all the trouble.'

Charles smiled. 'And I expect you're more than welcome to go up again next time you're here.'

'Goes without saying,' Edward asserted.

Charles made no comment about her being an employee of his company, and Linden was relieved that his attitude towards her was kind and considerate, a million miles from his business face. Now, he was in his own home, with members of his own family and their chosen friends.

They sat at the table in the large dining-room, where Jenkins, spruce in a black frock and pristine white pinafore served beef consommé.

'Are you going to the seaside for a holiday while the works are shut, Linden?' Dorothy Burgayne asked when the consommé was served.

'I'm afraid not, Mrs Burgayne. Not this year at any rate. Shall you be going away?'

'Bournemouth. I'm taking Penny. We leave on Monday. We're both very fond of Bournemouth, aren't we, dear?'

'Yes, Mother. I have an aunt and cousins there, you see,' she explained to Linden. 'Damn, I'd forgotten about Bournemouth. It means I shan't see you again, Linden, till I get back.'

'But perhaps Linden would still like to come and play tennis,' Edward suggested hopefully. 'She is rather good. I could always pick you up, Linden.'

'Her mother and father would strongly disapprove if they thought there'd be nobody here to chaperone her, Edward,' Dorothy reminded him.

'Nor do I think her boyfriend would take very kindly to it,' Penny added.

'Boyfriend? Oh . . . Sorry, Linden. I didn't realize you have a boyfriend . . .' He looked embarrassed and disappointed, and Linden felt herself redden as she met his eyes apologetically.

'He's asked you to marry him, hasn't he, Linden?'

'Well, he's actually only asked me to get engaged.'

'Which is a promise to marry after all,' Dorothy affirmed.

'I know, but I want to see something of life before ever I start to think about marriage.'

'Very sensible too,' Dorothy said.

'Yes, good for you,' said Edward. He sighed to himself; her wanting to see something of life would doubtless exclude him as a romantic interest anyway.

'Anyway,' Dorothy went on, 'remember we have to be back from Bournemouth in good time for the garden party.'

'Of course, the garden party,' Penny chimed. 'I say, Linden, would you like to come to the garden party? I think you've earned an invitation after all those letters you typed.'

'I'd love to, but—'

'It is all right if Linden comes, isn't it, Mother?'

'Of course. If she wants to she's more than welcome.'

Penny turned to Linden. 'That's settled then. But that boyfriend of yours will curse me for dragging you away from him another Saturday night. Perhaps you'd better bring him too.'

'Oh, I'd rather not, if you don't mind,' she answered emphatically, which made the others laugh, including Edward.

Five

'My mother is dying to meet you,' Linden said as Penny's black Riley pulled up outside the little terraced house in Hill Street. She had been giving the matter some thought as they drove back, and it seemed the proper thing to do in view of the fact that she'd enjoyed the easy friendship and hospitality of the Burgaynes. The fact that it was so humble and undeniably working-class Linden would have to live with.

'I'd be delighted,' Penny replied eagerly. 'Who knows? – I might have seen your father around since he works for my father.'

'Don't mind the house, though,' Linden said apologetically. 'It's hardly what you'd call grand.'

'It's home, isn't it?'

Linden gave a little self-conscious laugh. 'Oh, it's home all right.'

'And you're comfortable in it?'

'I suppose so.'

'So why should I mind it?'

'Well . . . the comparison between it and your house, I suppose,' Linden explained.

'If you're apologizing for it, because you think it's small compared to the ancient mausoleum I live in, then don't bother. I'd prefer something much cosier. I bet your house is cosy. I bet your mother and father are cosy.'

Linden smiled, grateful for her friend's reassurances. 'It's just that I'm aware of the difference in our backgrounds, Penny,' she said candidly. 'Some people in your position would look down on us.'

'Some would, I daresay, Linden, but I never would. To do so would be to assume that you are less intelligent or less worthy than me, and I flatly refuse to accept such nonsense. I take people as I find them, and what I find in you I like enormously. From the moment we met it seemed to me that we could become good friends. Not because we are similar – we're absolutely not – but because we are different. So please, don't be so dismissive of yourself.'

'Well, I'm not normally,' Linden said. 'I believe I'm as good as the next person—'

'And so you are . . . infinitely better than most. Edward thought so too.' Penny looked at Linden for her reaction. 'I can tell.'

Linden smiled radiantly. 'Oh, do you really think so?'

'Yes, I do.'

'And yet you told him I'd got a boyfriend.'

'Well, so what? If he allows that to stop him making a move on you, then he's not half the chap I thought he was. Anyway, even if you were interested in him, you wouldn't want him to think you were too readily available. At his beck and call. Correct?'

'Correct,' Linden agreed, smiling.

'It will maintain his interest if he thinks there's only a slight chance. So toss him a crumb of hope from time to time.'

Linden laughed. 'You!' she said. 'You're a right one for playing games with men. How are you getting on with Adrian? Have you stirred his interest yet?'

Penny's chuckle was almost musical. 'It's important to play hard to get, you know. Show them a glimpse of the promised land, then pull back to reassure them that you're not a girl like that. It works wonders.'

Linden sighed and reached for the door handle. 'Thank you for everything, Penny,' she said sincerely. 'I've had a smashing time. I wouldn't have missed it for the world.'

'You're welcome any time, you know. We'll get together again when I come back from Bournemouth.'

'I'll look forward to it.' She smiled happily. 'Now, come and meet Darby and Joan.'

Gladys Woods was in the brew house peeling potatoes at the stone sink below the window beside a cast-iron mangle with bleached and cracked wooden rollers. In one corner was the wash boiler, a brick-built affair with a fire hole beneath for heating water on washing day. On the wall hung two maiding dollies for pounding the laundry in the tub, and alongside them hung the tin bath. Against another wall next to the door stood the gas stove, from which was emanating the most wonderful, mouth-watering aroma of lamb roasting.

'My, that smells good,' Penny at once remarked.

'Mum, this is Penny Burgayne.'

'Oh, I am pleased to meet you, Miss Burgayne,' Gladys said deferentially. 'And if you like the smell of me lamb cooking in the stove there you'm welcome to stop and have a bit of dinner with us.'

'That's really very kind of you, Mrs Woods, and do call me Penny. Any other day I would love to, but today I must get back home *tout de suite*. My mother and I are going away tomorrow, you see, and we have to supervise the packing.'

'Well, have a cup o' tea then, eh? Our Linden, why don't you put the kettle on?'

'Course I will.' Linden grabbed the kettle from the hob and filled it with fresh water. 'Where's Dad?'

'Need you ask?' Gladys replied, cutting the eye out of a potato. 'He's up the yard.'

'I didn't see anybody in the yard when we came through the entry,' Penny offered.

'No, Mum means he's in the privy.' Linden was mortified.

'Oh . . . I see . . .'

'He'll be down in a minute. He's been up there twenty minutes already.'

'We don't need to know that, Mum,' Linden admonished, privately squirming. 'Is that cosy enough?' she remarked quietly to Penny and rolled her eyes with embarrassment.

Penny saw the funny side and laughed. She turned then to Gladys. 'Mrs Woods, I've returned your daughter safe and sound, and I really do believe she's enjoyed herself immensely.'

'I have,' Linden confirmed.

'I hope she ain't been no trouble, young Penny.'

'Not a minute's trouble, Mrs Woods. She's behaved impec-cably – a credit to you.' Penny winked at Linden. 'We've enjoyed having her. So much so she's invited back again when I get back from Bournemouth.'

'Well, that's very nice of you. Just so long as she's no trouble.' Gladys rinsed her peeled potatoes in a colander and dried her hands on a threadbare towel. 'Come into the scullery and sit down a bit while the kettle boils.'

The veranda, which linked the scullery to the brew house,

had been erected by Joe five years earlier so that Gladys wouldn't have to endure the vagaries of the winter weather when darting from one to the other. Potted plants adorned the rough shelves and the window ledge, and an aspidistra sat majestically in a brass pot on an ancient but very solid round table that occupied far too much space on the stone-flagged floor.

Linden led Penny into the scullery where a fire was burning bright in the black-leaded grate. A home-made podged rug, made from scraps of Joe's and Gladys's old clothes lay on the hearth.

In that small room a table, adorned with a tasselled chenille cloth, and three chairs stood under the window that looked on to the veranda. On a small cabinet next to the table stood a wireless. In the middle of the room, facing the fireplace, was Joe's old armchair, and behind that with just enough room for a person to slide past, a sideboard bearing crocheted mats and another vase of cut glass, at the bottom of which lay a hotchpotch of buttons and hairgrips. But everywhere was spotless.

'This *is* cosy,' Penny remarked.

'And small,' Linden added morosely.

'But I do like it.'

Joe entered, carrying a folded newspaper. 'You'm back then, our Linden.'

'Hello, Dad. Yes, I'm back, and this is Penny Burgayne.'

'Well, well. Miss Burgayne, this is an honour.' He held out his hand.

'Do call me Penny,' she said.

'If you'll call me Joe,' he bargained, with a broad, affable grin.

'It's a deal – Joe.' They shook hands amiably.

'Dad always takes the paper with him to the privy,' Linden remarked with embarrassment.

'Oh, my father does too,' Penny replied. 'He says it's the only time he gets the chance to read the paper in peace and quiet.'

'I like the News o' the World meself, you know, Penny. The football page is what I like. And the cricket in the summer o' course. How's your father, by the way? I hope he's keeping well. I seldom see him these days.'

'He's reasonably well, thank you, except that he works too hard and too long. He suffers with his chest, you know.'

'Yes, he always did. Is he thinking of retiring?'

'My father? Oh, I doubt it. He'll work as long as he can.'

'Give him my regards, young Penny. If he don't remember who I am − 'cause there's hundreds work there and he can't be expected to remember everybody − tell him I'm the one who pulled him out o' that great big gearbox on the number one rolling mill what he fell into when they was refilling it with soft grease one shutdown.'

Penny laughed. 'I heard about that. He was covered in the stuff, wasn't he?'

'From head to toe. I thought we'd never get him clean.'

'We laugh about that still, you know.'

'We laughed an' all at the time, but I don't think he saw the funny side of it. Not then at any rate.'

Gladys entered carrying a teapot cocooned in a bright woollen tea cosy. 'Tea up,' she declared, and put the tray on the table. 'Linden, will you get the cups and saucers and sugar from the cupboard, while I get the milk?'

That afternoon Ron called round. He was disgruntled because Gladys and Joe were full of this Penny Burgayne who'd called in to pay her respects, and she was the cause of his being thrown over the evening before. Thus, he felt it was not in his best interests to condone either what Linden had done, approve of where she'd been, or who with. So he tried his best to remain aloof as she recounted her visit to Kinlet Hall.

'I flew in an aeroplane, you know,' she wilfully goaded him.

'You what?' He sounded highly sceptical.

'Their younger son Edward has his own aeroplane. A Gypsy Moth . . .' That certainly gained Ron's interest.

'A Gypsy Moth? And you went up in it?'

'We flew over Dudley. I saw the castle, the new zoo − everything.'

'How old is this Edward?'

'Twenty-one . . . And *very* good-looking,' she said coquettishly.

'I suppose he was trying to get round you, eh? You want to watch out for these posh folk with money who live in big mansions and have aeroplanes. They take what they want and then scarper.'

'He didn't seem that sort at all.'

'They never do. So are you interested in this Edward?'

She shrugged, teasing him. 'Wouldn't you be if you were a girl? Wouldn't you be interested in somebody with wealth, health, fine manners, who was handsome with it?' She paused a moment, looking thoughtful. 'And an aeroplane? . . . But then again . . .' She sighed theatrically. 'I suppose a lot depends on whether he's interested in me . . .'

The annual works' holiday was over, and Linden joined the throngs of people walking to their jobs once again on the first Monday morning after the break. Both Vera and Hilda, her workmates, had been on holiday. As they assembled in the typing pool, they were bubbling over with eagerness to tell Linden about their respective exploits, and compare experiences, and she listened to both with amused interest.

'Didn't you go away, Linden?' Hilda enquired, as it slowly dawned on her that Linden had offered nothing to the conversation, only listening to them and laughing with them.

'Don't you remember?' she responded. 'I was here. I'm not entitled to any holiday yet.'

'Lord, d'you know, I completely forgot? You poor thing. So was it quiet?'

'Very. But I did meet Penny Burgayne. I had to do some letters for her. I thought she was very nice.' Linden did not feel inclined to tell them that Penny had since become a good friend and that she'd been a guest at Kinlet Hall. Such information was best kept to herself.

'And how's that Ron?' Hilda queried. 'Is he still as keen?'

Linden shrugged. 'Sometimes I wish he wasn't.'

'Why don't you just give him up?'

'To tell you the truth, Vera, I don't think I could. I think it would upset him, and I wouldn't do that. And anyway, I don't actually dislike him. I just don't want to marry him.'

Their chat was interrupted by the appearance of Betsy Mayhew, the supervisor.

'Miss Woods, if you're not too busy Mr Hugh Burgayne would appreciate you taking some dictation.'

'Mr Hugh?'

'Yes. Miss Roberts, his usual secretary is away this week. He's asked for you.'

Linden glanced at her two friends and the corners of their mouths turned down and their eyebrows arched simultaneously.

'Does he want me right away?'

'I believe so.'

Linden picked up her notepad and pencil and, smoothing the creases out of her cotton skirt, made her way to the office of Hugh Burgayne. He was standing beside a huge oak desk and seemed tall in his dark pin-striped suit – taller than Edward. His hair was starting to thin already and he had a slight stoop, a thin face with large eyes and a pointed nose – not half as appealing as Edward. His desk was a model of neatness; nothing was out of place, and such papers as there were, were stacked in neat, separate piles.

'Good morning, Miss Woods.' He greeted her with a magnanimous smile and gestured for her to sit down opposite him. 'I've a few letters I'd like rattled off, if you could manage that for me.'

'Yes, gladly,' Linden replied.

'Excellent. We've not met before.'

'I'm Linden Woods, Mr Burgayne.'

'Yes, I know who you are,' he said. 'You were at Kinlet Hall over the weekend. I never had the chance to say hello.'

She smiled self-consciously.

'I'm sorry I missed you,' he went on. 'I understand you and Penny have become friends.'

'Yes.'

'So you had a good time?'

'Oh, I had a smashing time, thank you. Your brother Edward took me up in his aeroplane. I think that was the highlight of my stay.'

'Oh, Edward and his aeroplane,' Hugh said, and his tone conveyed disdain. 'He'll get himself killed in that contraption one of these days. When he does, let's hope you're not with him. Be jolly careful, young lady. You're a very pretty girl, you know, and it would be a sin to mar those delightful good looks in an accident with Edward . . . or even worse, get yourself maimed . . .'

'I'm grateful for your concern, Mr Burgayne, really, but I

think it's unlikely I shall ever fly with him again. He's going back to Cambridge soon, isn't he, soon after the garden party?'

'You know about the garden party?'

'I've been invited as Penny's guest.'

'Excellent. Of course, I shall be there, but under sufferance. Mother believes she's doing something to help the church and the community by holding it every year. All we get from it is a whole barrow-load of litter, and lawns that take months to recover afterwards. Anyway, it will be a pleasure to see *you* there, Miss Woods.'

'Thank you.'

'So . . . to the letters . . .'

'Oh, yes.' Linden opened her notepad, and her pencil was at once poised. 'Ready when you are, Mr Burgayne.'

He dictated the letters, disposing of them in a capable and business-like manner, then resumed their conversation.

'Have you ever had photographs taken, Miss Woods? I mean a set of formal, serious portraits?'

'Oh, only some snaps,' she answered dismissively, closing her notepad. 'Nothing that you might call formal.'

'I'm amazed.'

'Really? Why?'

'I'm astonished, actually, that a girl as beautiful as you hasn't. Has nobody asked you to sit before?'

'No.' She smiled, wide-eyed, flattered that he should say as much.

'Such a waste. I happen to be a very keen photographer, you know, and I have a studio and darkroom at Kinlet Hall. I'd be delighted if you'd sit for me.'

'Yes . . . I suppose I—'

'If you could come this Saturday or Sunday?'

Besides the warning from Vera and Hilda that Hugh was a womaniser, Linden remembered what Dorothy Burgayne had said about being unchaperoned while she and Penny were away, and how her folks would have disapproved had she accepted Edward's invitation.

'Sorry, but I can't this weekend.'

'Perhaps when you come for the garden party then? I daresay we could steal an hour to take some serious photos.'

'Yes, I daresay we could . . .' It was hardly possible to refuse. Hugh Burgayne was a director of the company, and she would be enjoying his family's hospitality once again. She confirmed her assent with a smile, and said, 'I'll go and type these letters for you now, Mr Burgayne. It shouldn't take long.'

With the holiday season continuing, Linden found herself standing in for other secretaries from time to time, including Edith Evans, Charles Burgayne's ageing but utterly reliable helpmeet. She'd felt comfortable in the presence of Charles Burgayne as she'd dined with him at Kinlet Hall, but was nervous about whether her work would be up to the standard of Miss Evans's.

'Have you heard from Penny and Mrs Burgayne?' Linden asked him conversationally when he'd finished dictating a batch of correspondence to her.

'Why, yes, Linden,' he replied cheerfully. 'They telephoned last evening, actually. It seems they are enjoying the sunshine and the beach. And I know my wife always sleeps remarkably well when she's in Bournemouth. So do I for that matter. Something to do with the sea air and the trees, I think.' He coughed noisily, putting his hand in front of his mouth. 'Sorry about that . . . Maybe I should seek some of the same sea air to see if it will cure this persistent cough of mine.'

'Yes, you ought,' Linden agreed. 'That's quite a chesty cough, Mr Burgayne. Can I get you something? A glass of water and a couple of aspirin perhaps?'

'No, please don't fuss.' He smiled to let her know it was not a reprimand. 'I'll survive, my dear. I've always been prone to bronchitis, you know. Maybe I'm due an attack.'

'Perhaps you ought to seriously think about joining Penny and Mrs Burgayne in Bournemouth.'

He chuckled. 'I imagine you'd be quite the mother hen, given the chance.'

'But it makes sense, Mr Burgayne. I'm sure you could allow yourself time away from here.'

He shook his head from side to side, weighing up her sage words. Then he burst out laughing, which made him cough once more. 'I say, this is a bit of a turn round . . . Who's the boss here, I wonder? You're giving *me* time off!'

'I – I didn't intend it to sound like that,' she responded, full of apology.

He laughed again, amused at her solemn consternation.

'Don't give it a second thought, Linden. Actually, I think you are quite right. It would do me a power of good to get away from here and have a few days enjoying Bournemouth's clean, unadulterated air. Perhaps you'd be good enough to check the times of the trains for me. If there's one tomorrow morning from Wolverhampton or Kidderminster book me a first-class return, would you?'

'Of course I will, Mr Burgayne. What day would you like to return.'

'The Thursday before the garden party, I suppose. Hang it all, Hugh is quite capable of making any decisions here while I'm away.'

'Wouldn't it be possible for Edward to fly you there in his Moth?'

He roared again. 'My dear, the purpose of this trip is that I survive it, not get blown to Kingdom Come.'

'You're going up in the world,' Vera remarked as Linden put down her notebook and sat at her desk. 'First it's Mr Hugh's work, then it's the gaffer's. They've took a fancy to you, the Burgaynes.'

'Not especially, Vera,' Linden replied diffidently, placing a sheet of carbon paper between two sheets of foolscap. 'It's just the way things happen. There's not much work from the Wages Office at the moment, and Mr Burgayne's secretary is on holiday. Somebody has to step in. I hadn't got much to do anyway.'

'But I just saw you come out of Miss Evans's office. You been given permission to work in there?'

'Oh, it was just to use the telephone to book rail tickets to Bournemouth tomorrow for Mr Charles. His wife's there, and he wants to join her. To tell you the truth, he's got a nasty cough, and I should say the break will do him good.'

'He's always had a cough. But why should you be so concerned?' There seemed to be some resentment and even sarcasm in Vera's tone, which irked Linden.

Linden looked her squarely in the eye. It was time to be forthright. 'I am concerned, Vera. Mr Charles seems a very decent man. At least he's been very nice and very polite to me, so why shouldn't I be concerned? Besides that, he owns the firm that pays my wages, not to mention my father's. It doesn't hurt to give him some respect. Don't you think so?'

'I suppose you're right,' Vera admitted, humbled.

They remained unspeaking for a few minutes while Linden consulted her notepad and Vera resumed typing. Each was pondering what the other had said, and both realized that harbouring resentment might endanger their comradeship. They had to work together and it was common sense to maintain good relations.

'Are you going to the canteen at dinnertime, Vera?'

'I expect so.' Vera smiled affably, relieved at the change of tack. 'Ooh, it's cottage pie today. I'd almost forgot.'

Linden returned the smile, pleased that her matiness had worked. But perhaps it was time to clear the air a little more and reveal some snippets about her relationship with the Burgaynes . . . in strict confidence, of course.

Linden leaned towards Vera and Vera, in turn, cocked her ear towards Linden.

'Can you keep a secret, Vera?'

'Yes, I can keep a secret.'

'Well, if what I'm going to tell you gets out, I'll know it's you that's spread it, because you are the only person I'm telling . . .'

'Go on then. You can tell me.'

'Well . . . When I did that work I told you about in the holidays for Penny Burgayne,' she whispered, 'we got talking about things, and I told her I used to play tennis regularly. Well, she invited me to play with her and her brother Edward at Kinlet Hall where they live. It was only so that she could get a four going with Edward and his friend. She fancies his friend, see. Well, while I was there, I met Mr Charles Burgayne and Mrs Burgayne.'

'So get *you*! No wonder you're going up in the world. See, I was right. So what's the younger son like?'

'Edward?' Her eyes lit up involuntarily. 'He's really nice. They all seem nice, Vera. They made me so welcome . . .'

For the time being it was enough information for Vera to handle.

Six

O n the Saturday of the garden party Penny collected Linden
once more from Hill Street and took her to Kinlet Hall.
It was late morning and the weather was perfect.

'I expect you've all been busy getting things ready.'

'One mad rush,' Penny disdained. 'The gardener has been
up since the crack of dawn, mowing the lawns and, just after
eight o' clock this morning a troupe of men arrived to erect
the marquee. Oh, but they were so bloody comical. If it had
been a circus tent going up there couldn't have been funnier
clowns.'

'What about the food?'

'Oh, that's all under control, thank God. Mother was flapping like a headless chicken because the salmon hadn't arrived,
but it showed up just before I left to collect you.'

'I hope I can be of help,' Linden said. 'There must still be
plenty to do.'

'You're a guest, Linden.'

'Whether I am or not, I'd like to make myself useful. I'm
a dab hand at making sandwiches, you know.'

Penny turned her head and smiled. 'You know, that's just
like you. But you're not expected to do anything. Just enjoy
yourself.'

'Anyway, how's Edward?'

'Oh, he's all right. He said he'd come and collect you, but
as it happened his car broke down. In any case I didn't think
it was such a good idea. We wouldn't want your mother and
father getting the wrong idea, would we? Not to mention that
boyfriend of yours.'

'Poor Ron. He's not happy that I shan't be seeing him
tonight . . . But I don't care.'

'Attagirl!' Penny exclaimed with a mischievous grin.

'Have you seen anything of Adrian, Penny?'

'Nothing. But he'll be there this afternoon, or so his best friend Edward informs me.'

'And he's still unattached?'

Penny grimaced. 'He'd better be.'

'Oh, I forgot to tell you when we spoke on the phone yesterday . . . Hugh wants me to sit for him today. He wants to take some photos of me.'

'Does he, indeed?'

'I did some work for him, and we got talking. I quite liked the sound of the idea, actually. At least I might get a decent portrait out of it that I could give my mother and father.'

They arrived at Kinlet Hall hot after the stuffiness of the car. The temperature had soared to eighty-five, the air was still, the sky cloudless and the views across Shropshire were suffused in haze. Linden noticed that the flower beds seemed more densely populated with bigger and brighter flowers, the edges were well manicured, the lawns greener and cut shorter. Penny and Linden had lunch with Mrs Burgayne then went upstairs to change. Throughout the summer Linden's smooth skin had taken on the creamy glow of a healthy-looking tan.

As they parted at the door to her room, she said, 'Penny, d'you think it would be all right not to wear stockings? I mean, it's so hot and sticky.'

'Brilliant idea!' Penny lifted her skirt and assessed the colour of her shins and calves, thrusting each leg forward in turn. 'You know, I think with this bit of a tan I might just get away with it. How are yours?'

Linden raised her hem and peered down at her legs. 'Not quite as brown as yours, but I think I might get away with it.'

They both laughed, enjoying the youthful excuse to cock a snoot at modesty and convention.

'Then let's forget the stockings.'

People began arriving in waves, shaking hands, kissing cheeks, laughing and joking. Women and young girls were vivid in their summer attire, the men sweltering under their jackets and straw hats in the heat of the afternoon sun. Members of the Burgayne family greeted all their guests in turn, with grace, attentiveness and welcoming smiles. Linden stood alongside Penny who introduced her to so many people, whose names she inevitably struggled to remember. Eventually, a jazz band struck up from inside the sweltering depths of the marquee, its wailing brass and plinking banjo drifting across the lawns.

Edward sidled up to her when the incidence of new arrivals had slowed somewhat.

'Linden, how lovely to see you.'

She turned, recognizing the voice at once, and her broad smile told how delighted she was to see him again at last. 'Hello, Edward.'

'Sorry I wasn't here for lunch.'

'Your racquet needed restringing again?'

He laughed. 'Actually, no. But my blasted car needed some attention. I had to rush over to a little garage in Kinver that does odd mechanical jobs for us. Otherwise I might have called to collect you instead of Penny.'

'That would've been nice, Edward. I like to think I'm your friend as well as Penny's.' She smiled, her eyes wide, her head tilted captivatingly.

'I'm very glad to hear it, Linden.' His eyes creased with such appeal as he returned the smile. 'I like to think so too.'

'If you don't mind, I'll leave you two to it,' Penny butted in, detecting that her company was superfluous right then. 'Seen Mother, Edward?'

'Wherever there's a tea urn . . .'

'See you later, Penny,' Linden said, then turned back to Edward. 'So when do you go back to Cambridge?'

'Oh, probably Thursday.'

'And are you going to fly there, as you'd hoped?'

'Yes, actually,' he answered. 'Fancy you remembering that. Yes, I got permission to keep the Moth at Duxford after all. The only problem is that I'll have to send all my stuff by rail. Can't stow much in the Moth, you see.'

'I do hope you'll be careful when you fly. It beats me how you know where you're going when you are up there.'

He laughed. 'By following special maps that indicate landmarks. It's all fairly basic stuff really.'

'I'm sure I'd get completely lost. I'd be useless.'

'Of course you wouldn't,' he said kindly. 'While you fly you have time to pick out these landmarks and adjust your course accordingly.'

'So when shall you come home again?' she enquired, trying to sound casual, as if it mattered not one jot to her.

'Oh, I expect I'll be home for Christmas. Christmas is rather jolly here. It would be nice if you could come.'

'That's a long way off yet,' she replied. 'Lord knows what I'll be doing. Spending it at home with my mum and dad, I suppose.'

'And that boyfriend of yours, eh?'

She wished at that moment that she had the power either never to blush, or to hide her blushes convincingly, for she coloured up like a peony. 'If he's still around,' she answered.

'Might he not be?'

She shrugged, her colour subsiding a little. 'It's up to him.'

'And not up to you?' he asked.

She did not reply, but looked down, inspecting her big toe as it peeped out of the sandal on one foot.

'I'm sure he thinks a lot of you, Linden.'

'I think he does . . .'

'But?'

She sighed, deciding to be candid. 'But it's not because I encourage him unduly.'

'Your looks and demeanour are the only encouragement he needs, I suspect.'

She laughed at that, throwing her head back, enjoying the compliment, but feeling inordinately self-conscious. 'I wish I could believe that.'

'You'd do well to believe it.'

'It's very nice of you to say so, Edward.' She felt herself blushing again and was thankful for an unexpected light breeze cooling her face. 'Is Adrian here yet?' she asked, changing the subject.

'Yes, he's here. Why? Don't tell me you're interested in Adrian.' He sounded disappointed.

'No, not me. But I know somebody who might be.'

'And I bet I know who . . . I say, Linden, you haven't got a drink. Let's get you something.'

'Thank you. Cold orange juice would be nice. Or even a glass of fizzy pop.'

They moved towards the marquee and the sound of the jazz band playing 'Honeysuckle Rose'. Everywhere, people were strolling in twos and threes, holding drinking glasses, pointing out and naming the flowers, admiring the giant redwood trees that were almost as old as the house.

Although it was shaded inside the marquee it seemed hotter, stuffier than outside, and full of people chattering, vying to be heard over each other and the music. Standing next to the makeshift bar were Penny and Adrian who seemed only to have eyes for each other and were laughing at some shared joke.

'Hello, you two,' Edward greeted them; then to the hired help who was tending to drinks, 'Two glasses of orange juice, please. As cold as you can make them.'

Adrian took out a cigarette case and offered them round. Edward took one, tapped the end against his thumbnail and put it to his lips. Adrian lit it, then his own.

'I say, do you have any plans for tonight, you two?' he enquired casually, exhaling smoke.

'Nothing that can't be changed,' Penny said, looking into Linden's eyes as if daring her to defy her.

'Edward, why don't we take these two delightful creatures out tonight?'

'I'm game,' Edward replied.

'How about it, girls?'

The two girls looked at each other for consensus, smiled and nodded simultaneously.

Edward passed a glass to Linden. 'Orange juice,' he said.

She thanked him and sipped it, feeling it cool on her lips, soothing to her throat. 'Perhaps we ought to stand outside in the shade,' she suggested. 'It's cooler there.'

'Does the heat bother you?' Edward asked.

'Not particularly. It's just a bit cooler outside.'

'But the cakes and sandwiches will be unveiled soon,' Adrian suggested.

'And you've had no lunch, I suppose?' Penny remarked. 'Well, we can always come back for sandwiches. Linden is right. It's cooler outside.'

As they stepped outside again Linden looked around for sight of Hugh Burgayne. She had not seen him at all yet, and while she was enjoying the present company she was still eager to fulfil her promise of sitting for photographs.

'I've never met Laura Birch,' she remarked, turning the conversation.

'Hugh's fiancée?'

'Yes. Is she here? I wouldn't have a clue what she looks like.'

'She's on holiday in the south of France, I believe,' Edward informed her. 'Her family have a place over there. Provence, I think.'

'Doesn't Hugh go with them?'

'Sometimes, but not this time. Too much going on at the works.'

'Here's Hugh now, look,' Edward said. 'He's heading towards us. Minus Laura Birch, of course.'

Linden felt herself colour up once more at the prospect of meeting Hugh, for he was likely to remind her of their photo session, which she had not mentioned to Edward.

Hugh greeted them all in a collective 'hello', and commented how well attended the garden party was.

'Linden,' he said, singling her out. 'I do hope you haven't forgotten that we were to work on some photographs this afternoon.'

She glanced at Edward uncomfortably, before replying. 'Of course I haven't forgotten. When would you like to take the photos?'

'Is it convenient now?'

'Actually, Hugh, we were just contemplating grabbing some food,' Edward said, irked at his brother's intervention.

'Food won't be ready for half an hour yet.'

'In that case, why don't I go now with Hugh?' Linden suggested, it seeming a diplomatic solution. 'And perhaps you three can save me a sandwich or something.'

Hugh looked at the others for their assent.

'Yes, that's fine, Hugh,' Penny agreed. 'Come to the marquee when you're through, Linden, and we'll have a plate of curly sandwiches and fairy cakes saved for you.'

Linden smiled her thanks. 'See you later then.'

'Try to be back in time for the raffle,' Edward said. 'They'll be glad of a pretty face to draw the tickets.'

As Linden walked back towards the house with Hugh in the blazing sunshine, Edward said to Penny, 'I didn't know Hugh was intending to take pictures of Linden.'

Penny thought she detected resentment in his tone. 'He asked her a while ago, apparently. She's been doing some work for him while his own secretary has been on holiday. Why? Do you mind?'

'How can I mind?' Edward responded dolefully. 'I have no claim on her.'

'Even though you sound as if you wish you had . . . Anyway, she rather liked the idea of being able to give her mother and father a decent photograph of herself – something she's never had. I think that's rather sweet.'

Hugh's studio was the conservatory on the north side of the house. Because it was in shade it was cooler than she might have expected under glass. He explained that it was ideally situated for portrait photography, because the diffused light was good and cast no hard shadows.

'I thought we might do a few close-up portraits first, then try some full-length,' he said. 'Do make yourself comfortable while I set up.'

There were a couple of armchairs and a chaise longue from which to choose to sit on, so she opted for one of the armchairs.

'Have you been keen on photography long?' she asked conversationally.

'About ten years, I suppose.'

'It always seems to me that photography is very complicated.'

'Well, there is a lot to learn,' he admitted, screwing the camera to the tripod. 'Knowing what f-stop to use with what shutter speed, calculating the depth of field and all that.'

'Sounds terrifying.'

He laughed. 'Experience does point you in the right direction. It's like everything else, though – if you spend lots of time doing it, it comes easy . . . Right, we're ready. The camera's loaded. If you'd like to perch on that stool, Linden . . .'

She got up from the armchair and went over to the stool, smoothing the creases out of her dress. She wore a sleeveless cotton dress with a full skirt and scalloped neck, ideal for summer, pale yellow with a discreet floral print. It complemented her dark hair beautifully.

'How do you want me?'

'Yes . . . Well . . .' If only it were that easy. He coughed self-consciously. 'Head and shoulders, three-quarter face I think.

It will show us a little of the shape of your nose.' He adjusted the settings on the front of the camera. 'You have a delightful nose, if you don't mind my saying so.'

'Thank you.'

'You're not too hot in here, are you?'

'No, I'm fine.'

'Jolly good.' He adjusted the focusing ring. 'Just a hint of a smile now, Linden . . . Oh, yes, hold that . . .' She heard a click from the shutter, he looked up and smiled. 'Promises to be good. One more at a slightly different exposure . . .' That done, he moved closer with the camera and tripod. 'I'd like to try one in real close-up. You have lovely skin, you know . . . Tilt your head down just slightly so you have to look up at me from under your brows . . . Yes, that's it . . . Gives you such a cheeky look.'

'I hear your fiancée is on holiday at the moment,' Linden said, trying to divert attention from herself.

'Yes, she's in France for a month. Doubt whether I'll have time to miss her, though.'

'When are you getting married?'

'Nothing's fixed as yet. And you, Linden? Are you stepping out with somebody?'

'There's this chap I see . . . Nothing serious though.'

'What's his name?'

'Ron Downing.'

'Does he work at the steelworks?'

'Oh, no, he works for the GPO.' She felt so ordinary, so mundane, so plebeian, having to admit as much.

'But it's nothing serious, you say?'

'No. I don't want to settle down with anybody yet.'

'Especially somebody who works for the GPO, eh?'

She flushed with embarrassment. He must think her so commonplace. 'I want to have some fun first.'

'Good for you.' He wound the film on. 'Two more portraits,' he said. 'One full face, and then one in semi-profile.'

'To show up my nose.'

'Well, to show *off* your nose. And to capture the clarity of your eyes too. You have beautiful eyes.'

He took the next two photos, as he'd intended. 'Right . . . Some full length pictures now . . . Can you jump on that table and sit facing me?'

She slid off the stool and sat on the table, her shapely legs swinging above the floor. He loaded a new roll of film, repositioned the camera and lowered the tripod a little, then refocused the lens.

'A nice wide smile now . . . That's lovely. Hold that . . .'

He walked towards her. 'For the next one I'd like to see your skirt up a little higher, showing a bit of thigh.'

Before she knew it, his hands were on her knees and he'd lifted the hem of her skirt six inches. In so doing he managed to skim his fingers over her bare lower thighs, slicked with moisture wrought by the summer heat. Then he smoothed out the creases of her skirt, stroking her thighs over the material, privately relishing the impression of their firm, young lissomness.

It was over in a second.

It was over even before Linden realized what had happened. He'd stroked her thighs, but what could she do about it? She could hardly complain. There was probably nothing behind it, no malice aforethought, no lewd intention, no over-familiarity. He was a photographer doing a photographer's work. Photographers surely rearranged subjects' clothing for the benefit of the photograph. Besides, he was a director of the company that employed her – employed her father too. And once again she was enjoying the hospitality of his family.

'If you lean back a little . . . Yes, rest on your arms behind you . . . Now another of your cheeky smiles . . .'

Click!

'Capital. Now, would you like to lie on the *chaise longue*, Linden? I want you to look all languid and sensual, as if you're enjoying some scandalously erotic thoughts.'

Erotic thoughts? That would be a turn-up for the books. And how am I supposed to appear all languid and sensual?

She ambled over to the chaise longue, wondering if he was likely to touch her legs again, and reclined on it.

'Would you like to take off your sandals? I think bare feet would look much more effective.'

She raised her knees and unfastened the shoes, letting them drop to the floor.

'Do you want me to raise the hem of my skirt this time?' she enquired, thinking it would relieve him of the responsibility.

'Yes, rather . . .'

'How far?' She pulled the hem over her thighs and looked at him questioningly.

'Oh, a bit further, if that's all right with you.'

She generously complied.

'But would you raise your left knee now? . . .'

She knew very well that the way she was posing he could see directly up her skirt. She smiled to herself. She understood his game and was content to go along with it to some extent. Little by little he was trying to gain her confidence and ease her into exposing more of herself. Soon he would be asking her to shed her clothes and pose in her knickers and brassiere, or even naked, but never would she agree to that.

'How do I look?' she asked perkily.

'Utterly vivacious . . . An icon of feminine abandon.'

Click!

She smiled affably. 'Can we call it a day now, Hugh? I'm getting quite hot and I'm starving hungry. Would you mind?'

'No, that's fine.' He wound on the film. 'I'll have these developed and printed in a day or two.'

'I look forward to seeing them.'

'Er . . . I, er, wondered, Linden . . .'

'Yes?' She looked at him curiously.

'You said earlier you want to have some fun . . . It occurred to me . . . If you're leaving here after the garden party, would you like to join me for dinner this evening? There's this lovely little restaurant I know.'

'Actually, Hugh, I'm . . . I'm staying here the night,' she replied as diplomatically as she could. 'Edward and Adrian are taking Penny and me out tonight. It's already fixed.'

'Oh, you're partnering Edward . . .?'

Perhaps he should have gone to Provence with Laura after all.

Seven

Edward and Adrian both owned two-seater sports cars, so the four were obliged to go out that night in the Burgaynes' Riley. Edward drove, with Linden sitting alongside him, Penny and Adrian close together in the rear seats. While the other three bandied wit and repartee, Linden was preoccupied; the encounter earlier with Hugh Burgayne was gnawing at her. It was not so much that he had contrived to paw her – and yes, she was coming to the conclusion that he had contrived it – but he had also invited her out that night behind the back of the girl to whom he was already engaged. That told her he was the sort of man no woman ought to trust, and yes, she felt sorry for Laura Birch even though she did not know the girl.

What sort of girl did he think she was to suggest such a thing? Did he imagine she would be easy? Did he think that just because she was an employee of the Blower's Green Steelworks she should fall at his feet and be thankful for the opportunity to be groped? Did he really think his superiority gave him the right to manhandle her just because she was a lowly employee from the typing pool? Of course, Hugh could make things uncomfortable for her if he chose to. If he wanted to be really vindictive he could also make things awkward for her father. She hoped things would never come to such a pass, but she would have to be careful; such was the clout he possessed.

She pondered whether she ought to tell Penny about the incident. When they were alone together she might. Then again, she might not. Penny was Hugh's sister and blood was thicker than water. She was beginning to feel, because of the incident, that she was out of her depth with these people, that she really ought to refuse any further invitations. But it would be such a pity . . .

The car pulled up in the vast car park of a newish hotel

called the Foley Arms, but better known locally as the Stewponey. An old pub had stood on the site before, but it had been recently redeveloped, was manorially vast, and even boasted a lido on to which the world, his wife, and his entire family all descended at sunny summer weekends and holidays.

'Listen, I can hear a band playing,' Adrian remarked as they each clambered out of the car. 'Let's see what's going on.'

When they were asked to pay to enter they realized it was a dance. Over the hubbub of raised conversations and laughter, the endeavours of the band and the shuffling of feet to a quick-step, Adrian bought them drinks. They stood around the bar for a while surveying the scene, soaking up the smoky ambience. Edward, Adrian and Penny lit up cigarettes.

'I say, you're quiet, Linden,' Edward commented. 'We haven't heard a peep out of you for ages? Is there something amiss?'

She smiled apologetically and shook her head. 'No, nothing at all.'

'You have been rather deep in thought, though, haven't you? Missing that boyfriend of yours?'

She rolled her eyes. 'Not at all. It's a nice change having a Saturday night away from him.' She wanted to say that it was rather nice being there with Edward at her side, but thought better of it.

'I say, d'you fancy a dance?'

'Yes, why not? Thank you, Edward.'

Edward stubbed out his cigarette; they put down their drinks, and made their way to the dance floor, leaving Penny and Adrian to their own devices. The band were playing *Night and Day*, a Cole Porter song.

They faced each other, linked hands, he put his hand to her waist, and they launched themselves into the surging sea of dancers.

It was a pleasure to feel her body next to his, as she moved to the rhythm of the slow foxtrot. She was so youthfully slender and felt so warm and yet so delicate in his arms. The gorgeous aroma of her perfume was so clean and fresh. Freshness was a quality she had in abundance, unmistakably, and 'fresh' seemed a perfect word to describe her. She was about five feet three, he estimated, delightfully petite. The sight of her skin was beginning to torment him; it must be fabulous to the touch.

Her straight dark hair, cut in a fashionable bob that curled inwards around her neck, framed her beautiful oval face perfectly. Such a pity that she was already seeing some other chap; he could not be sure of the strength of feeling she had for him, whoever he was. She seemed dismissive of the poor blighter whenever he was mentioned, but that could be shyness.

'You dance well,' he said hopelessly inadequately, unable at that moment to conjure an original sentence.

'Thank you. So do you.' When she looked into his eyes and smiled, the curve of her lips was so seductively kissable. 'Do you go to many dances when you're in Cambridge?'

'There's this place called the Dorothy Ballroom. Sometimes I go along with friends.'

'And there are lots of girls, I suppose?'

'Usually.' He wanted to say, *but none like you* . . .

'I bet you're looking forward to getting back to Cambridge,' she suggested.

'I have no choice, of course,' he said. 'I have to continue my studies . . . But the thought of hanging around here a while longer, with the possibility of getting to know you better, does appeal.'

She lowered her lids at this surprising revelation, and her heart suddenly beat faster. 'I thought the . . . the semester? – Is that the right word?'

He nodded.

'I thought that didn't start till September or October.'

'I'm going back early to further my flying. Did I tell you I'm in the University Air Squadron?'

'You did, but what can you do there that you can't do at home?'

'Well, we have lessons flying military training aircraft. And I just love flying.'

'I do hope you'll be careful. Talking to Hugh, he seemed a bit concerned for your safety.'

'Oh, Hugh . . .' He laughed dismissively. 'Well, what would he know? Which reminds me: how did your photo session go this afternoon?'

'Hard to say, really. I won't know until I see the pictures. They might not have come out very well.'

'He'll very likely have them done over the weekend. I'll try and get a peep at them before I go back to Cambridge.'

'Oh, I wouldn't bother. They're probably dreadful.'

'A girl as pretty as you? Oh, I doubt it.'

The band finished their tune and Edward unhanded her as they looked towards the stage for an inkling of what was coming next. It was 'I'm in the Mood for Love'.

'Another?' he asked.

'If you like.'

They held each other again, drifting along to the music.

'Tell me about yourself,' Edward said. 'I know so little.'

'There's really not much to tell. I live in Dudley, and I come from very ordinary parents. My father works at your father's steelworks, and my mother is just a housewife. I don't have any brothers or sisters – but please don't ask me why because I don't know. I've been fortunate enough to have had a decent education – for which I'm grateful – thanks to the sacrifices my father made.'

'You play tennis well at any rate.'

She looked into his eyes and laughed as they whirled around. 'So you say. All part of the education, I suppose.'

'Do you play any musical instruments?'

'The piano. We have an old pianola in our front room.'

'Your front room?' He laughed a little.

'Please don't mock. Our front room is my mother's pride and joy, and only ever used on Sunday afternoons if the weather's fine and we don't have to light a fire . . . or when we are expecting visitors.'

He laughed again. 'I wasn't mocking, Linden, honestly. I respect enormously the sanctity of your front room.'

'Yes, you are mocking,' she said, frowning, pouting deliciously and feigning umbrage. 'You said the "sanctity" of it. That's taking the mickey.'

'Maybe "sanctity" is the wrong word,' he conceded. 'Maybe "sanctuary" might be more fitting.'

'Yes,' she agreed, happy to do so. ' "Sanctuary" is better – as in "shrine". I admit it's my mother's shrine to respectability and convention. In our street, if you don't have a spotless front room to entertain the vicar, you're doomed. It's the same as pegging the washing out on a Monday. Dazzling white is essential. One day I came home and the whites my mother was pegging out on our line were grey. I was mortified, and I wanted to give her a piece of my mind there and then, because our washing looked a disgrace. But because she was talking to our next door neighbour I kept my mouth shut. It was just as well I did – it turned out that the same grey washing belonged to the neighbour and my mother was only pegging it out for her because *her* line was full.'

'That's a form of snobbishness.'

'Is it?'

'I think I'd like to meet your mother.'

'She really isn't anything special. Oh, I love her and all that, with all my heart, but she doesn't stand out in a crowd. She's quite ordinary. That's what I mean.'

'I detect some . . . I'm struggling for the right word here, so if it comes out all wrong to your ears please don't take offence, because none is intended . . . But I detect some embarrassment . . . some humiliation . . . in you, because of who you see yourself as, or because of where you come from.'

She sighed uneasily. 'I am aware of my background, Edward – especially compared to yours. Please don't imagine for a minute that I'm ashamed of it, though – I'm not—'

'Linden, you have absolutely nothing at all to be ashamed of. And if you for a second imagined that I might harbour some disdain I'd be mortally offended. I don't hold with outmoded concepts of class distinction.'

She flashed her eyes at him delectably. 'I'm happy to hear it. And I know Penny feels the same – not because she's said as much, but I *feel* her friendship and I sense no barriers.'

'I hope you feel there are no such barriers between you and me either.'

'Certainly I don't feel any.'

He smiled openly and she warmed to him the more. He had such a lovely open smile, and his eyes twinkled and crinkled so sexily. She wanted to give him a hug, but did not dare.

'I'd like to think we can be good friends, Linden, and that you can discuss all sorts of things with me.'

'Thank you. I think I can . . . But I'm not so sure that Hugh is of the same mind.'

'As regards what?'

'As regards the class difference between him and me.'

Edward shrugged. 'He's inclined to be a bit snobbish, a bit aloof, is Hugh, but you're not likely to have that much to do with him . . . are you?'

'At work, maybe.'

'But he's not unfriendly towards you, is he? He took some photos of you, after all.'

'No, actually he's been *very* friendly towards me,' she said ambiguously.

'Well, there you are,' Edward remarked, not grasping her meaning.

She wanted to add that she believed Hugh had tried to take advantage of his pre-eminence over her, but could not bring herself to say so. It would be grossly unfair to be the cause of any rift or mistrust between brothers.

The band stopped and threatened a jitterbug for the next dance, so Edward suggested they rejoin Penny and Adrian. By this time, they had found a table at the back of the room and were sitting very close together.

'You're back soon,' commented Adrian.

'Well, I'm no great jitterbugger,' Edward replied. He picked up his drink and lit another cigarette.

'But drop the "jitter" bit and you are inclined to be something of a bugger – or you aspire to be.'

It was late when they'd returned to Kinlet Hall, and everybody had gone to bed. Penny, loath to trouble Jenkins, made coffee which they supped around the table in the breakfast room. Edward and Adrian lit up cigarettes, and they talked disconnectedly about the evening and where they'd been.

'It's been ages since I've had so much fun,' Linden remarked.

'Me too,' Penny agreed. 'We must all get together again next time Edward comes back from Cambridge.'

'It'll be the middle of winter,' Edward said. 'It'll be overcoats and scarves and gloves.'

Linden rolled her eyes typically. 'Oh, please don't remind us. I hate winter and having to scrape the frost off the inside of my bedroom window when I get up.'

'Do you really?' Edward asked.

'If it's that cold, yes.'

'Don't you have a fire in your bedroom?'

'There's a fireplace, but my mother reckons lighting a fire in a bedroom is far too extravagant.'

'You poor thing,' Penny said. 'Not so cosy after all, eh?'

'Not so cosy.'

Penny yawned, and stretched her arms out.

'Are we keeping you up?' asked Adrian.

'Yes, rather. I think I'm going to turn in. Are you coming up yet, Linden?'

'I ought to.' She rose from the table and looked at Edward longingly, trying to glean his intentions.

'Adrian and I will have a drink first, eh, Adrian?'

'Capital idea, old man. Got any brandy?'

'I'll go and find some.'

'I might see you in the morning, Edward,' Linden said.

'Oh, I doubt that,' Penny claimed. 'It'll be a miracle if he's up before you leave.'

'I'll say goodbye now, then, Edward. And to you, Adrian.'

'Goodbye, Linden,' Adrian replied. 'It's been great fun tonight. Goodnight, Penny.'

Linden was a couple of steps behind Penny as they left the breakfast room, when Edward called her.

'I say, Linden . . .'

She turned to face him and he walked up to her, put his hand to her waist.

'I just wanted to say goodnight,' he whispered intently, and kissed her on the lips.

It lasted only a second but, in that magical moment, Linden felt the blood surge through her veins. Edward looked her directly in the eye, challengingly, then kissed her again, lingering this time.

'I hope I'll see you again when I return from Cambridge,' he said, his voice low.

'I hope so too,' she replied, conscious that hers would break up if she said more.

'Till then . . .' He took her hand and squeezed it tenderly.

Eight

Hugh's darkroom was a part of Kinlet Hall's cellaring that he'd petitioned off. In that small area he'd had running water installed as well as electricity, a geyser, two large sinks and two work benches, one for wet work, one for dry. On the wet bench lay three enamelled trays containing developer, vinegar in water for removing and neutralizing the developer, and hypo for stabilizing the prints. On the dry bench stood a photographic enlarger with a masking frame on its baseboard, a timer for timing the exposure of the negative to the light-sensitive print paper, and an electric print glazer. The whole was suffused in a dim orange glow from two safelights.

Hugh pulled a half-plate enlargement from the sink where several were being washed in running water, and inspected it by the meagre illumination. A pair of bright, smiling eyes looked back at him in the gloom. His eyes lingered, devouring the image of feminine loveliness. He finally put it down, removed the excess water, then placed it face down on the hot glazer, which would give the photo an attractive gloss. Then he pulled out another print and inspected that too, and his desire heightened. *What a gorgeous pair of legs . . .*

As Hugh was ascending the steps from his darkroom carrying a large envelope containing the set of finished photographs, Edward was on his way to find him. They met in a corridor at the rear of the house.

'Ah, Hugh . . . I was hoping I'd catch you. Have you developed and printed the photos of Linden yet? I was hoping to beg one to take with me to Cambridge.'

Hugh waved the envelope in front of him. 'They're here. I've just finished them. Take a look if you want.' While Hugh withdrew them from the envelope, Edward watched with eager anticipation. 'Here . . .'

Edward took them and scrutinized the first one, then looked

back towards the light coming in through the fanlight over the door. 'Let's take them into the light. It's a bit dim here . . .' He moved towards the door and opened it to let in more light, followed by Hugh. 'Gosh, she takes a smashing photo,' he beamed. 'Don't you think so, Hugh?'

Hugh gave a cursory nod, as if it were of no importance.

'Oh, I say, look at this one . . . sporting a lovely bit of thigh . . . Would you mind if I took this one, Hugh?' He looked at his brother expectantly. 'I expect you have another copy?'

'I can always make one. Take it.'

'Thanks, old bean.'

'I understand you were out with Linden last night, Edward?'

'Yes, we had a great time. She's a jolly good sport, you know. Of course, she's Penny's friend first and foremost, but because Penny and Adrian seem to be getting it together, I was obliged more or less to accompany Linden. Mind you, it was no imposition. She is rather a nice girl.'

'Lord knows what Penny thinks she's doing, befriending people from the works, and inviting them here,' Hugh said ominously.

'Oh? What makes you say that?'

'Well, I mean . . . familiarity . . . It doesn't do to get too familiar with employees. She'll very likely blab it around the place. It undermines the family's authority.'

'So why did you ask her to sit for you?'

'She asked me. I told her I was keen on photography and she asked if I'd take some of her. She said she'd never had a decent photo taken of herself.'

'I understood it was the other way round.' Edward shrugged, really not sure who was right.

'Anyway, you seem quite taken with her, Edward. My advice to you is, mind what you're doing with a girl like that.'

'What do you mean exactly by "a girl like that"?'

'Well, look at her . . .' He tapped the photo with the back of his fingers. 'I didn't ask her to pose like that, flaunting her legs. She flashed a sight of her knickers a couple of times, too – deliberately, of course. As I said, she's only a shorthand typist at the works – an employee,' he added, with sham disdain. 'Her father works on one of the rolling mills. She's hardly aristocracy.'

Edward looked at his brother with astonishment. 'I really

don't see what that's got to do with anything. As a matter of fact, I've already discussed her background and upbringing with her and, frankly, who cares whether she's the daughter of a rolling-mill hand or a duke? It's not her fault she's who she is . . . But I actually find her refreshingly different. I rather enjoy her company, you know. She's quite cultured for the daughter of a humble rolling-mill hand, and an unbelievably smashing girl.'

'Edward, just don't get too involved. It's odds-on favourite that she's out to entrap one of us. It just wouldn't do. She might be all right to practise on, and doubtless you'd have fun practising, but Mother and Father expect you to do better. A lot better.'

'Oh, Hugh . . .' Edward laughed in an effort to disguise his exasperation. 'I rather think you're jumping the gun there. I'm hardly likely to elope with her. In a day or two I shall be off to Cambridge and the possibility of seeing her, or even hearing from her until I come back, really is rather remote – more's the pity. Actually, I could become very distracted by Linden Woods, but while I'm at university I don't think it would be such a brilliant idea.'

'Well that's reassuring, at least.'

'Well don't be too reassured, Hugh. It's not to say I wouldn't like to.'

'So I trust nothing untoward went on last night.'

'Nothing untoward?' Edward gasped with indignation. 'Unless you consider dancing, then eating fish and chips out of newspaper in Wall Heath untoward.'

'Fish and chips?' Hugh scoffed with a leer. 'Good god . . . Well, I expect Linden felt very much at home tucking into fish and chips,' he added sarcastically. 'Especially from a newspaper.'

Edward was incensed at his brother's attitude. 'Look, Hugh . . . Thank you very much for the photo. At least now I won't forget what she looks like. But your comments about the girl are rather churlish. I'm actually quite surprised – especially as she thinks you are quite friendly towards her.'

It was on the Tuesday at the office that Hugh Burgayne requested Miss Woods to do some secretarial work for him. She left her desk with a mixture of trepidation and anticipation. His brushing her thighs was still fresh in her mind, and she was anxious as to what his attitude might be. Carrying her notepad and pencil she tapped on the door to his office.

'Ah, Miss Woods. Please take a seat . . .' So, he was formal today; because they were at work: master and minion.

She sat down primly and just as formally, looking at him with secretarial expectation. But his eyes avoided her. Instead of looking at her he sorted through a small sheaf of papers on his tidy desk, while she looked around the room patiently. The walls were oak-panelled, like each of the offices where the more prestigious people worked. Framed photographs ornamented the walls, of white-hot molten metal being poured into ingots, of men operating a rolling mill, as well as an aerial photo of the entire works. A clock with Roman numerals faced a barometer on opposing walls. A wooden filing cabinet stood beneath the said clock, a table was covered with a neat pile of blue engineering drawings, and on Hugh's desk sat two identical black telephones, and a photograph in a frame which, although she could not see it, Linden presumed was of Laura Birch, the absent fiancée.

'Very well, Miss Woods, when you're ready. I have half a dozen letters and memos I need done urgently. It will be a good thing when my secretary returns from holiday. Then we can return to normality and you won't have to trip along to this office to do my work.'

'I really don't mind, Mr Burgayne,' she responded pleasantly. 'It's all the same to me whose work I'm asked to do. It's all good experience.'

'You enjoy this work?' he asked curtly, as if such an attitude were foreign.

'Yes, I love it.'

He glanced at her indifferently then began his dictation. One letter was a reply to the Ministry of Defence and was about increasing the production of steel for building warships. Another was an enquiry about the best material for the production of air-raid shelters. The documents only served to reinforce Linden's opinion that the world was going mad, that all the speculation of war she heard on the wireless and read about in the newspapers, was not all hot air.

And Hugh Burgayne was being very business-like, she thought. So much so, that you wouldn't have known she'd been at his home over the weekend, treated almost as one of the family. You wouldn't have known that he'd taken photos of her, just the two of them together, and that he'd contrived to feel her leg.

Linden finished taking dictation then returned to her desk to type it up. When she returned to his office with the work completed she stood before him like a schoolgirl in front of the headmaster's desk, awaiting judgment on an exam paper.

'Would you like me to wait while you check and sign the work?' she asked.

'Yes, wait, please.'

He read through each letter and memo, and signed them before handing them back to her.

'No mistakes?' she queried brightly.

'None that I've spotted, Miss Woods.' He looked up and managed a smile. His manner was thawing. 'Oh . . . incidentally . . . I've got your photographs . . .' He opened a drawer in his desk and withdrew an envelope, which he offered her.

'Oh, thank you, Mr Burgayne. May I look at them now, while I'm here?'

He nodded. 'You might as well sit down.'

'Thank you.' She sat down, opened the envelope and slid out the photos, glancing only cursorily at them. 'Oh, gosh, I'm showing a bit of leg there,' she commented, and looked at him with a speculative expression of wide-eyed innocence.

'Nothing too untoward.' He smiled, and his voice was smooth. 'I should say it's rather attractive, actually. I daresay that young man of yours will like it anyway.'

'I'm not even sure I'll show him. It'll only invite too many daft questions . . . And I had such a lovely time with Penny and Edward . . .'

'Which you'll want to keep quiet about,' he suggested. 'About the photos, Miss Woods . . . It would be best if you didn't show them to anybody here – your work colleagues, I mean.'

'Oh, of course not.'

'People might jump to the wrong conclusions. Leastwise people might wonder why you were at Kinlet Hall in the first place . . . It could lead to speculation about favouritism, which some people might resent.'

'I do understand,' she affirmed. 'It's not something I intend to shout from the rooftops. I value my friendship with Penny, but it's my business – nobody else's.'

He smiled again, making a steeple with his fingers and resting his chin on it as he leaned back in his leather chair. 'And your friendship with Edward?'

'I value that too,' she replied frankly. 'Although I haven't known him long, I must say he seems to have accepted me completely, and for that I'm grateful. I like him a lot.'

'Well, not too much, I trust . . . Edward needs no distractions while he's studying at university. I'm sure you understand what I'm saying.'

'I think I do . . .' Linden was taken aback and annoyed, but she had to keep her cool, remain diplomatic and polite. 'But if you don't mind me saying so, Mr Burgayne, I don't think you have much to worry about on that score.'

She felt deflated and humiliated at what Hugh was suggesting. He was warning her off. But why? Whatever went on between her and Edward had nothing to do with him.

'Anyway, I understand you had a good time on Saturday evening after the garden party.'

'Yes, we did, thank you,' she answered, endeavouring to conceal her irritation.

'Oh . . . and, Miss Woods . . . When I invited you for a meal . . .'

'Yes?'

'You mustn't read anything into it.'

'Of course not.' *Didn't he mean anything either when he deliberately felt my leg and made it look like a casual incident?*

'With Laura away, I was at a loose end. It occurred to me that you might be too. I was merely trying to be chivalrous. Nothing more. I wasn't aware you had already arranged—'

'Really, Mr Burgayne, you don't have to explain.' She rose from the chair, conscious that her indignation was by now peeping through her normal composure; it was time to return to the safety of the typing pool. 'Anyway, thank you very much for the photos. Please let me know how much I owe you.'

He waved his hand in a dismissive gesture. 'You don't owe me anything. I would ask, though, that you give me permission to use one as an entry in my photographic society's annual exhibition. I think they're all good enough.'

She shrugged. 'Of course.'

'And I'd relish the opportunity to take some more soon . . .'

That interview with Hugh Burgayne prompted Linden to take another look at her relationship with Penny. If Hugh resented the presence of a lowly employee at Kinlet Hall, maybe she should make her excuses if further invitations were forthcoming. She had no wish to jeopardise either her own job, or that of her father, by upsetting one of the directors. In a way, she understood Hugh's point of view, but she was also acutely aware that it conflicted directly with the ideas of both Penny and Edward. And it was Penny and Edward who were her friends, not Hugh. It struck her that it would be best discussed openly and frankly with Penny.

But the situation also impelled her to a greater closeness with Ron. She had kept him at arm's length, poor chap, preferring the company of the younger Burgaynes, allowing him nowhere near them. Having spent time with Edward, dancing with him, flying with him, talking alone with him, she had perceived his interest in her, which in turn had aroused her own interest in him. But she was fooling herself if she thought that anything would or could come of it. Even if it were to bud, it would not be allowed to blossom.

So Ron enjoyed warmer responses from Linden. When they went to the cinema she allowed him to lead her to the back row. She allowed his arm around her in the darkness, allowed herself to indulge in some serious and prolonged kissing, especially in the slower parts of the films. He was a decent, reliable chap after all. Her mother and father approved of him because they regarded him as steady and hard-working, from a respectable family who were not well-off, but who were – well, *respectable*. Yes, she decided, she could do a lot worse than eventually marry Ron. If only she *fancied* him more . . .

She tried to imagine them married. She tried to picture herself lying in bed with him, doing what all young and newly married couples did – at least till the novelty wore off, as she was assured by some that it did. Somehow, the prospect did not excite her. Rather she viewed it as unsavoury. That is to say, the notion of doing it with Ron was unsavoury – not the business of sex itself. In fact, the business of sex had occupied her thoughts often and held a great deal of promise. She had allowed and tolerated Ron's ardent kissing, found pleasure in allowing him to get worked up into quite a lather sometimes, even allowed him to fondle her breasts – and it had all been startlingly enjoyable; but going all the way with him? No, definitely not. Going all the way with somebody else, though? Edward Burgayne, for instance? Well, that might be a different kettle of fish.

She'd only ever received two brief kisses from him: his goodbye to her before he left for Cambridge. Yet it was enough to stimulate her imagination, even if its promise was doomed for eternity.

Ron, meanwhile, was beginning to believe she had overcome her infatuation with the Burgaynes when he had relished four consecutive Saturday nights out with Linden. He was unaware, however, that she had pleaded unavailability to Penny on a couple of occasions, preferring not to incur the further awkwardness that her presence at Kinlet Hall might provoke in Hugh.

But amidst all Linden's doubts, Charles Burgayne was only ever the epitome of politeness and pleasantness. Occasionally he had used her secretarial proficiency when his own secretary had been otherwise occupied. Charles not only acknowledged openly that she was a friend of his daughter, but seemed to respect the fact too. He addressed her by her Christian name, preferring not to stand on the distancing formalities of calling her 'Miss Woods'. Everything he asked her to do for him she did with pleasure and with an efficiency that did not go unnoticed. In short, he felt that her whole attitude was just right.

Time moved on but the world remained afflicted by growing international dementia. In Germany the biggest ever Nazi rally was held at Nuremberg, with Hitler claiming that his nation needed more territory and that they would be demanding colonies in the east. The Japanese invaded China and the Italians had overrun Abyssinia.

Despite this global chaos ordinary folk went about their daily lives, eating, drinking, sleeping, working and playing, hoping that none of this madness would touch them and theirs. The serious business of living had to continue. There were wages to be earned, children to be raised and schooled, families fed, old folk to be looked after. It was to everybody's benefit to better themselves. But the unsettling shenanigans of the Nazis would not go away, and the future looked more and more uncertain.

One Monday in October, Penny Burgayne, wearing a smart two-piece suit in indigo, which complemented her flaxen, sun-bleached hair, accompanied her father to the steelworks. She made a beeline for Linden, calling her to an unoccupied office. The two girls greeted each other warmly.

'Haven't seen you for ages,' Penny gushed. 'I swear you've been avoiding me.'

'Nothing of the sort,' Linden replied. 'I've been really busy. Things Ron had organized mostly.'

'How is Ron?'

'He's well. And how are things progressing with Adrian?'

'I'm being dreadfully aloof at the moment. So much so that I'm fairly proud of myself. He's seen the promised land, now it's up to him to make a move. And I reckon the best way to egg him on is to ignore him. So I've made myself unavail-able. Meanwhile, it's time you and I had fun elsewhere. Pastures new and all that.'

'Pastures new?'

'Male-wise. How do you fancy coming over and staying the weekend? There's a party on at the house of one of my friends. A twenty-first. It should be a riot. There'll be loads of blokes.'

'I don't know, Penny . . .'

'Why, what's up? Has Ron finally got to you?'

Linden smiled sadly and shook her head, inadvertently avoiding Penny's eyes. But Penny was quick to notice her friend's reticence.

'What's wrong, Linden? Why the introversion?'

Linden hesitated to say.

'Well?' Penny urged.

'Promise you won't be upset.'

'Of course I won't be upset. Just tell me what's on your mind?'

'I've been warned off . . . sort of.'

Penny looked at her in amazement. 'Warned off? Warned off what? Who? Where?'

'I really wasn't going to say anything.'

'You *must*, Linden. What's going on?'

'It's Hugh – your brother.'

'Tell me.'

'It's a long story . . . For a start, he warned me off getting too attached to Edward. He made it clear that Edward didn't need me as a distraction while studying. I actually think he was being a bit of a hypocrite to—' She stopped in mid-sentence, thinking what best to tell Penny, what best to leave out.

'Go on,' Penny urged gently, realizing this was a sensitive issue for her friend.

'Did you see the photos Hugh took of me?'

'Yes. I thought they were very good.'

'Well, as he was taking them, he asked me to sit on a table . . . When I did, he came to me, raised the hem of my skirt, without so much as a by-your-leave, and ran his fingers up my thighs. Not very far, but he did – he felt my legs – and if you remember we were wearing no stockings. It happened so quick, and I didn't know whether it was accidental or intended. But the more I thought about it afterwards, the more I realized it was intentional. Afterwards, he asked if I'd like to go to dinner with him to some restaurant . . .'

Penny rolled her eyes in exasperation. 'What a bloody cad! I can only apologize, Linden. He fancies you, evidently, but that's no excuse for behaving like a cad.' She pondered a moment. 'And if he fancies you, perhaps he's jealous that there might be something stirring between you and Edward.'

'But he's got Laura. He should be satisfied with that.'

'Laura's no oil painting.'

'Even so . . . Anyway, just to confuse matters even more, Hugh made it plain as well that an employee of the company oughtn't to be too friendly with members of your family. I suppose he meant that if you get too familiar with employees you lose your authority over them, and I can see what he means . . .'

'And that's why you've refused all my invitations,' Penny divined.

Linden nodded glumly.

'The cheek of the man,' Penny exclaimed. 'I choose my own friends, Linden, not who Hugh or anybody else thinks is suitable. I will not have him interfering in my life and upsetting my friends. Who the hell does he think he is?'

Linden shrugged in response.

'Well, let me make this plain, Linden: Hugh certainly does not speak for the rest of us. We all adore you. My father thinks you are wonderful, and my mother was asking about you only on Saturday.'

'I'm glad to hear it,' Linden said inadequately, and sighed with relief that it was out in the open. 'So what should I do? Should I visit Kinlet Hall again and incur his wrath, or should I keep my distance?'

'You most certainly will not keep your distance. You are invited this weekend as my guest, and we'll go to that party. Hugh can bloody-well fizz up and burst.'

'How is Edward, by the way?' Linden enquired. 'I take it you've heard from him.'

'Oh, he's fine. He telephoned yesterday. He sends his best wishes, actually.'

'To me, you mean?'

'Yes, to you, Linden.'

Linden's face lit up.

Nine

Linden had no idea whether Penny had taken issue with Hugh over their friendship, but that weekend she was made to feel comfortably at home with the rest of the Burgaynes. When she did run into Hugh he was perfectly polite, although he affected to be a little detached. Yet for all his aloofness, whether contrived or real, Linden felt his eyes on her all the same, as if he were mentally undressing her.

As the weeks passed, Linden found herself thinking about Edward Burgayne increasingly, wondering what he was doing, who he was spending his time with. She desperately hoped he had not met another girl on those Saturday-night jaunts to the Dorothy Ballroom in Cambridge, for if he had, she – Linden – would be the last to know. While her longing for Edward increased, her interest in poor, long-suffering Ron waned in direct proportion. Her spirits were raised, however, when just prior to Christmas she received an invitation to Kinlet Hall that Penny, privately aware of her friend's yearnings, intimated she should not miss under any circumstances.

'You must come to the Boxing Day Hunt,' Penny said as she and Linden, who was at work, spoke over the telephone.

'But I've never ridden a horse in my life,' Linden pleaded.

'Oh, you won't need to. You'll be a spectator.'

'But you'll ride, won't you, Penny?'

'Oh, nothing will stop me riding. I adore the hunt.'

'So who shall I watch it with? I expect Edward will ride as well, won't he?'

'I expect he will. And so too will Hugh, so you'll not be stuck with *him*. But my father and mother won't ride. So you'll be a spectator with them.'

Ron, however, did not see it Linden's way. She had great difficulty explaining why she would not be able to visit his parents and have dinner with them on Boxing Day, as had been the custom during the time she had known him.

'So what shall I tell my mum and dad?' he asked, peeved. 'That you'd rather be with your posh friends?'

'It's not that I'd *rather*,' she replied, trying to be diplomatic, 'but I'd actually like to see a hunt, and this one just happens to fall on Boxing Day. You surely can't begrudge me wanting to see it?'

'I can and I do. I'm getting a bit fed up with these regular excursions to them Burgaynes. I'm never invited, am I? I suppose you never put in a word for me to go with you? It's almost as if you're ashamed of me.'

'Course I'm not ashamed of you, Ron. What a daft thing to say.'

'Then it strikes me there's something going on. I reckon you've got your eye on that son of theirs – him with the aeroplane – or he's got his eye on you. I suppose he's the real reason you want to go. I suppose he *will* be home for Christmas?'

'How should I know?' she answered, feigning indifference. 'Why should he let me know what his plans are?'

'All the same, I expect he *will* be home.'

'Whether or no, he's no nearer me, nor is he the reason I want to go.'

'Huh! Says you.'

'I told you, Ron, I want to see a hunt.'

Linden would normally never wear trousers, but that misty Boxing Day morning she headed for the Cat Inn at Enville, prepared for the cold, wearing a pair she had bought especially for the occasion. To complement them, she wore a scarf, hat, gloves and a thick overcoat, and was perfectly coordinated. Charles Burgayne drove her and the other non-participating members of the family to the meet in his Bentley. Dorothy sat beside him while Linden sat in the back seat alongside Laura Birch, Hugh's fiancée. She had not had any opportunity to speak with Laura beyond their initial introduction.

'It's a fine day for it,' Charles exclaimed as they sped between hedgerows bereft of leaves.

'You've not been to a meet before?' Dorothy enquired.

'Never,' Linden replied. 'Nor did I ever think I would.'

'It's a fine spectacle,' Charles affirmed. 'And a long-standing tradition here on Boxing Day.'

They arrived at the Cat Inn which, by dint of a special dispensation from the vast Enville Estate of which it was part, had been allowed to open specially for the occasion. It was set on a narrow bend in the main road from Stourbridge to Bridgnorth, and the spectacle was to start from there; the wide open space at the side served perfectly as a gathering point for the riders, their horses and the hounds. To the rear were cottages belonging to the estate, forming an idyllic terrace that lined the drive to Enville Hall and its thousands of acres of rolling fields, over which the mist was beginning to lift.

Already the place was teeming with scarlet and black coats, grooms and sightseers holding warming drinks. Horses, sensing the excitement of the chase, stamped and scraped at the gravel snorting with anticipation, and were duly checked and made to hold still while their riders made jokes and laughed, and talked animatedly about crops and cattle and sheep as they quaffed their favourite warming tipple. Linden watched it all with awe.

She heard somebody cough behind her and knew at once it was Charles Burgayne, whom momentarily she had not missed. He had slipped unnoticed into the pub, and returned carrying a tray on which stood innumerable tumblers containing an amber liquid.

'Whisky,' he said to Linden with a wink. 'To warm you.'

'Thank you,' Linden said with a grateful smile, and took the glass. She sipped it tentatively, and it trickled, bitter and sweet down her throat as it consigned its pleasant burning sensation.

'Hugh should be here soon with the other three,' Laura commented from beneath a tightly stretched and unflattering woollen hat that seemed to emphasize her ample nose. 'They were riding here over the fields together.'

As she spoke, Linden saw Edward, Penny, Hugh and Adrian appear together in the drive that led to the hall, their horses trotting in a group. 'There they are, look.'

She was disappointed that she had not had a chance to speak to Edward when she arrived at Kinlet Hall earlier, but she felt her heart skip a beat at the sight of him now, unsettlingly handsome in his pinks, sitting high astride a beautiful chestnut stallion.

'Merry Christmas, Linden,' Edward hailed from atop his mount. 'It's lovely to see you again.'

'You too.' She felt her smiling face go hot and flushed despite the cold as she raised her glass to him. 'So how's Cambridge?'

'Cold,' he replied with an appealing grin. 'But no colder than it is here.'

He reached down to accept the glass which his father was offering him, and nodded his thanks.

Meanwhile, the whipper-in was trying to assemble the hounds and flicked his whip at those that broke ranks in their excitement.

'You should get a good view of the proceedings from the Alveley road over the hill beyond the church,' Edward shouted to her above the cacophony of eager animals and people.

She smiled up at him. 'Maybe your father will drive us up there,' she called back.

'Oh, you'll have a job getting him away from the pub,' Penny remarked. 'But certainly you should get a better view there.'

'For a while at any rate,' Adrian added.

'Then maybe Laura will go with me,' Linden suggested.

'Of course I will,' Laura agreed.

'And do be careful, you lot,' Dorothy Burgayne warned. 'No heroics on those horses, do you hear? I want you all back in one piece for lunch.' She turned to Linden and said privately, 'I do worry about them when they're on a hunt.'

'I'm sure they'll be very sensible,' Linden replied.

'Well, you know, Linden, Edward *is* normally quite sensible, it's a fact; but Penny can be a dreadful daredevil. She's far more reckless than the boys.'

'Don't you just love this?' Penny yelled, relishing the atmosphere, unaware of her mother's concern.

Within seconds they heard a hard, resonant cry. Ears pricked and hoofs grated amid a haze of steamy breath, and the field surged forward en masse.

'We're off!' Edward proclaimed. 'See you all later.'

'And please be careful,' Linden called, realizing as soon as she'd uttered it that she earnestly meant it.

Edward raised his hand in acknowledgement and waved as he turned his horse round and broke into a trot. To the massed crackle of hoofs chafing the gravel, and hounds yelping as if

suddenly sprung from traps, he followed the rest of the field
heading towards the chase.

'Shall we make our way towards the church now?' Laura
suggested.

'I'll drive you there, else we'll miss it,' said Dorothy. 'We'll
leave Charles here and come back for him later. It'll do his
chest no good to be outside in this cold air. He's much better
off in the pub where it's warm.'

From the lane beyond the church that led to Alveley the
three women watched, along with other spectators eager to
monitor proceedings, and Linden saw how majestically still
the fields and distant woods were in their winter bleakness.
Trees stood bare, but tinselled in rime which was promising
to thaw as the winter sun rose blandly over the hills. In the
distant they could hear the sound of hoofs thrumming over
the hard, frosty ground. Then the hunt came into view
pounding through the shallow valley below them, and Laura
pointed.

'The hounds have checked, look. They must've lost the
scent. See how they are sniffing about.'

'Have you seen the fox yet, Laura?' Linden enquired.

'No, but the hounds have certainly had a sniff.'

Then one hound bayed as he picked up the lost scent, and
the pack surged on behind him. The horn blasted, and the
mass of red and black gushed forward again, rising and falling
in waves over the hedges.

'Can you pick out any of them?'

'Not from here, Linden,' Dorothy assured her. 'Everybody
looks the same from this distance, especially with my eyesight.
We should have brought the binocs.'

They watched, glued, until the hunt was out of sight, then
returned to the Cat.

'We'll snatch another warmer with Father before we go home,'
Dorothy said. 'If we stay here it could be ages before we catch
sight of them again. They'll probably end up in Alveley anyway,
or even by the river at Hampton Lode.'

It had taken many months of feminine wiles, but eventually
Penny Burgayne, twenty years old, had got the man she wanted,
and Adrian seemed content with his catch and with being
caught. Linden was delighted, for they were happy together.

Both were spirited and indomitable, but it seemed to her that they respected that quality in each other, and neither would seek to hold dominion over the other. She had a feeling they might eventually make it to the altar.

That Boxing Day evening, after the excitement of the hunt and the informal lunch and the more civilized dinner which followed that, the four braved the cold and went out together. Christmas festivities were still rampant in the pubs, for it had been a holiday for most, but tomorrow work would be beckoning. The four tarried in a series of hostelries, each new one closer to Dudley than the last, as they fulfilled their plan to deliver Linden home eventually.

Naturally, they had talked about the hunt, recounted it almost field by field, and Linden was not sorry to learn that the poor harassed and harried fox had managed to evade his pursuers. It was a fair outcome, she thought, but it was an opinion she kept to herself.

After closing time, Edward drove towards Dudley and Hill Street in the Riley, with Linden beside him in the front passenger seat, telling him the way to go, while Penny and Adrian canoodled in the rear, whispering nonsense to each other and giggling over it between ardent kisses.

'When do you go back to Cambridge?'

'Oh, later this week. But I shan't be back for Easter, unfortunately. Flying school. I hope I shall see you in the summer, though, Linden.'

'Yes, I hope so too,' she replied, smiling with secret pleasure in the darkness that he should say so, but sorry it was so far in the future.

'I have a photograph of you, you know. One of those that Hugh took.'

'You haven't!' Any disbelief in her tone was smothered by her delight at the surprising revelation.

He laughed at her reaction. 'Yes, I have, and you look extremely glamorous on it. You're my pin-up, you know. Gracing the wall of my room for all my friends to see. You don't mind, do you?'

'Mind? No, of course I don't mind. I'm flattered . . . Oh, go right there.' She pointed out the road junction.

'It's a smashing photo. And this way, I can't forget what you look like . . . If we could meet at some time in the summer hols I'd like that very much. We could go to a cinema maybe. Would you like to?'

'I'd love to, Edward. Thank you. That would be really nice . . . Oh, turn right here at the end, by the pub.'

'Well, it's a long time to wait.' He steered the car around the corner and they began ascending a steep hill – Hill Street. 'But we'll let Penny be the go-between, if that's all right.'

'Do I have to be?' Penny enquired, breaking off a luscious kiss.

'Yes, you do,' Edward replied good-naturedly. 'Now just get on with your knitting.'

Linden chuckled at their banter. 'Here we are, Edward. This is where I live, just on the right.'

He looked out of the window at the terraced house and saw that the front room window was illuminated.

'Would you all like to come in and say hello to my mum and dad?'

'Has he got any brandy?' Adrian enquired, full of bravado.

'Brandy? My father? He might have a bottle of beer or two.'

'I think we're late enough already, Adrian,' Penny suggested. 'It's half past eleven, and those good people have to be up in the morning.'

'No, you're welcome to come in,' Linden insisted. 'There's still a light on, look. They haven't gone to bed yet.'

'It's very kind of you, but we have a half-hour drive back as well.'

'Sorry, I was forgetting.'

'See you next summer then,' Edward said, looking at her intently, seeking eye contact in Hill Street's poorly lit dimness.

'Yes, next summer.'

He leaned towards her and it was obvious he was going to kiss her, so she met him halfway and offered her lips. He put his arms around her and hugged her as their lips met. She closed her eyes, and relished the sensation of his lips on hers, aware of her heart beating fast and furious. It was such a scrumptious kiss, she wouldn't have minded if it were to last all night.

But a harsh tap on the window on her side of the car caused them to break off prematurely. Her heart turned a somersault at the startling interruption. She peered into the darkness trying to discern who it was, afraid it *could* only be one person.

'God! It's Ron.'

'Oh, bugger,' groaned Edward.

Ron was beckoning her to get out of the car, and seemed inordinately agitated.

'I'd better go.'

'Shall you be all right? Shall I have a word with him?'

'No, Edward. Best not to. I'll be OK. Look, I'd better go.'

'Be careful, Linden,' Penny urged. 'I'll ring you at work tomorrow.'

Linden opened the door and clambered out of the car as she bade them goodnight. She faced Ron, who was hovering with proprietorial agitation.

The car drew away.

'I'll kill the brute if he so much as lays a hand on her,' Edward said grimly, pulling up fifty yards further up the road. He turned round to see what was happening through the rear window of the car.

'He's not that sort of bloke,' Penny remarked. 'She's talked to me about him, and he doesn't sound the violent type.'

'Jealousy can turn a man upside-down,' Edward replied grimly. 'And he's jealous all right. There's no knowing . . .'

'It's nothing to do with you anyway, Edward,' Penny said. 'It's Linden's business.'

The eyes of all three of them in the car were fastened on Linden and her predicament and ready to intervene should she need it. The couple, illuminated by the light of a gas street lamp, were arguing agitatedly in the middle of the road, but then seemed to calm down. The three watched Linden move calmly away from Ron towards the house, then saw him catch up with her and put his arm around her. Then she waved to them, obviously a signal that everything was all right.

Edward sighed dispiritedly. 'He's taken her into the entry. I suppose he's smooth-talked her round. Maybe she's already pressed against the wall giving him some of those divine kisses I just sampled . . . Blast! Ah, well . . . I suppose that's the end of that little dream. What will be will be . . .'

He released the brake and the car crept forward.

But Edward was labouring under a misreading of what had actually occurred . . .

'So that's your game,' Ron rasped. 'Just as I thought. You're having it off with your posh mate's posh brother.'

'It's not what it looked like, Ron,' she answered defensively. 'He's just a friend. He was just saying goodbye.'

'He was halfway down your throat.'

'That's a bit of an exaggeration. He's only a friend. It was a peck on the lips. Anyway, he's going back to Cambridge in a day or two till the summer. It's just his way of saying goodbye. It doesn't mean anything.'

'It meant something to him. I ain't daft, you know.'

They were still standing in the middle of the road and Linden moved away in a huff.

'You don't own me,' she protested. 'If you don't like it, you know what to do.'

'Typical,' Ron replied, putting his arm around her.

She shrugged him off, aware that the car was still lingering, faces watching, just discernible at the back window. Sensing that Ron was calming down, uncertain whether he believed her or not, she waved to signal that all was under control and, as she walked into the entry with him the vehicle moved slowly away over the crown of the hill.

'Yes, I know what to do,' Ron hissed defiantly. 'I ain't prepared to put up with it, I know that much. If you'd rather be out with that lot, then that's up to you, and I ain't gonna lose anymore sleep over it. There's plenty more fish in the sea, you know. But I tell you, you'll come to a sticky end with the likes of them . . .' He nodded in the direction of the disappearing car. 'Them pair in the back should be locked up for indecency. His hand was right up her leg . . .'

'Oh, you could see that much in the darkness? Anyway, lucky her,' Linden goaded rebelliously. 'I didn't realize you were such a prude.'

'Huh! If that's the sort of coaching you get . . . You're turning into a right tart, Linden Woods. A right tart, and no two ways.'

'Is that what you think of me?' Linden asked, indignant. 'A tart? You, better than anybody on this planet, know I'm not a tart.' Tears welled up in her eyes and glistened.

She looked heartbreakingly beautiful in the gloaming, and

so vulnerable that Ron wanted to take her in his arms there and then. But he'd overstepped the mark, insulted her, and he would get no response – not tonight at any rate.

'I think you'd better go, Ron,' she said huffily, and pulled a handkerchief out of her coat pocket. She dabbed at the tears as she turned away from him and strutted up the entry.

'Linden . . .!' he pleaded.

She stopped and turned to face him, a forlorn shadow in the darkness. 'I am *not* a tart, Ron. Goodbye.'

Instead of telephoning, Penny made it her business to go to the works next day just to see Linden. She wanted to ascertain for herself that her friend had survived her ordeal with Ron. So when she arrived at the Blower's Green Steelworks she at once sent for Linden.

'Well, you look all right,' Penny said. 'Are you all right?'

'Course I am,' Linden answered, grateful for Penny's concern.

'Then in the dinner break we'll go out, you and me, and you can tell me all that went on.'

Linden smiled. 'OK.'

Penny duly drove her into Dudley, where they ordered sandwiches and a pot of tea at the Midland Café overlooking the market with its red and white striped awnings. It was cold and dull, rain had set in, and the street glistened as it reflected the glow of the naphtha lamps from the market stalls.

'So you made it up with Ron?' Penny commented, keen to know as much as possible about what had transpired. She had saved her questions till they were settled in the warmth and comfort of the café.

'I most certainly did not. What gave you that idea?'

'You must have seen us stop a little way up your street.'

'Course I did.'

'To keep an eye on you. Edward was beside himself that you might need some help.'

'Bless him.'

'But when we saw Ron put his arm around you as you walked into the entry, we assumed you'd patched things up straight away.'

A waitress delivered their tea and sandwiches. The girls thanked her and Linden took the lid off the teapot to give the tea a stir.

'It wasn't like that at all, Penny. Ron was jealous. I'd never seen him jealous before, but he'd seen Edward give me that goodbye kiss. He called me a tart. Actually, it upset me no end that he should think me a tart, because he knows better than anybody that I'm not. So I went into a huff and left him.'

'But fancy him going to your house when you'd arranged to come to ours.'

'I *know*,' she said, revealing her indignation. 'I think he was there to spy on me. He knew I'd have to come home sometime because of work next day. So he came and sat with my mum and dad, waiting for me. As soon as he heard your car outside he shot out, my mum said, and was down our entry in a flash.'

'Just to catch you.'

'Just to catch me.' Linden shrugged. 'To see who had brought me back home.'

'So have you arranged to see him again?'

'Do I look daft? I don't want to see him again, but I daresay he'll be round our house quick enough when he's thought things over and calmed down . . . knowing *him*.'

'But if you don't want him, Linden, don't you think this is a golden opportunity to be rid of him?'

'I do,' Linden replied. 'And I intend to be. It strikes me I'm best off without men at the moment.'

'Edward was very quiet all the way home. You do realize he's taken with you, don't you?'

Linden smiled with pleasure at hearing it confirmed, but behind her smile was sadness borne of the conviction that nothing could possibly come of it. 'Yes . . . I think I know . . .' She took a bite of her sandwich and looked intently at Penny. 'I rather like him too, you know, Penny,' she remarked forlornly. 'Maybe more than is good for me. But with him away at university so much we'd neither of us be content courting from a distance.' She gave a little laugh as if to dismiss any notions of such an arrangement. 'I know I wouldn't. So I think the idea of promising undying devotion would be a bit impulsive, to say the least. Besides, we could both do without the distraction. If he lived permanently at home, it might be different . . . Anyway, he'll very likely meet some bright, exquisitely beautiful and educated girl in Cambridge, and be swept right off his feet.'

'Maybe he will, Linden, maybe he won't. But how different you and I are,' Penny exclaimed. 'If it was me, I'd be jumping in with both feet after the man I wanted. That's the way I am, though – impulsive. Too impulsive, perhaps.'

'You've not been impulsive with Adrian, though.'

'Crikey, I've had Adrian in my sights far too long to imagine he's an impulse.'

'I must say, though, I think you're ideally suited.'

'I think so too . . .' Penny looked intensely thoughtful as she divested her slender fingers of crumbs. After a moment or two she said, 'Can I ask you something, Linden? I consider you my best friend these days, and there's something I'm frightfully curious about.'

'Yes. Ask away.'

'It's frightfully personal, Linden.'

Linden sighed with exaggerated drama. 'For you, Penny, my life is an open book. You should know that by now. What d'you want to know? Just ask away.'

Penny leaned towards her and, so as not to be overheard, said in a low voice, 'Have you and Ron ever done it together? Had sex, I mean. You know, gone all the way? Penetration, and all that?'

'Lord, no.' Linden giggled infectiously at the notion. 'I couldn't. Not with *him*. I've never fancied him enough.'

'So you're still a virgin?'

'For better or worse. But I *am* only eighteen . . .' She rolled her eyes as if it were appalling to have remained a virgin at her age. 'I quite envy girls who aren't, you know. So what about you, Penny? Are you still? Now you've asked me it's only fair that I ask you.'

'Me? No . . .' She shook her head and took another bite. 'Adrian *was* the first, mind. I know I got a bit of a reputation as something of a fast cat in certain quarters, but I lost my virginity to Adrian, and not before. Well, I love him fearfully after all, you know, Linden, and he loves me . . . And it just all seemed so damned natural . . . It's brought us much closer.'

'Oh, but that's ever so romantic, Penny. I really envy you . . .' She sighed dreamily. 'Did it hurt, though? First time, I mean? I'd love to know what to expect when my turn comes.'

'Oh, it stings a bit at first.' Penny chuckled as she recalled it. 'They say it does.'

'But it's surprising how romantic and practical the back seat of a car can be. There was a spot or two of blood in my knickers afterwards, though,' Penny added for good measure, 'but not enough to put me off. It's the first time I ever washed my own knickers, you know.' She put her hand to her mouth to smother her laughter. 'Well, it wouldn't do to have the maid speculating. Some things are sacred after all.'

Linden giggled again. It felt good to be so close to another girl – a friend with whom she could share such intimate secrets. Meanwhile, some of the other patrons in the café looked on and smiled, no doubt wondering what it was that amused two pretty girls so much.

Ten

Nineteen thirty-eight stormed in, bringing more anxiety and uncertainty to the world. Everybody was issued with a gas mask lest gas warfare was waged on Britain, and children were given gas-mask drill at school, made compulsory by a new law. Germany annexed Austria and, as the Nazi troops marched into Vienna, the Austrians were overzealous to the point of obsequiousness in their eagerness to welcome them. The Japanese bombed Canton and the number of innocent victims subsequently killed ran into five figures; nobody knew exactly how many there were.

Linden applied herself conscientiously to her work. Her shorthand and typing speeds were increasing satisfactorily, and every task, every letter and memorandum that she handled brought more confidence. Occasionally she was obliged to do work for Hugh Burgayne and she began to feel more at ease in his company. She never enquired of him how Edward was, for to do so would reignite the flame of disapproval. But she talked to him about other things, including his photography, and he seemed to become much more amenable. She even agreed to sit for more photographs.

Hugh drove her one pre-arranged dinnertime in spring to the ruins of the old Priory in Dudley. He wanted photos of her to enter in his camera club's annual exhibition. The wind was gusting but the sun was shining, and he got her to pose in the grey limestone arches that remained standing, and on the crumbling limestone walls, with the newly fledged trees and the old castle keep, high on its hill behind her, as a backdrop. This time though, she avoided letting him near her. She did not risk allowing him close enough to touch the hem of her light summer dress and so afford him the opportunity to feel her leg again, but he did suggest that she should hoist the skirt herself for what he called 'a few glamorous poses'. Much of the time she had no need however; the capricious wind seemed more than willing to take on the onus, one minute pressing it sensually around her body and outlining her lovely figure, the next blowing her skirt high, to reveal her shapely legs and more. Linden made the necessary motions to modestly hold down her wayward skirt, but was inevitably too late; Hugh was quick to press the camera's shutter at exactly the most revealing moments. She excused herself and him; it was harmless enough done this way. Of course, the whole exercise was contrived to titillate him, poor pathetic soul, and Linden was content to go along with it. These days, apart from this one immature quirk, Hugh was behaving reasonably well.

Yet it was strange that he never showed her any of the photos he took on this particular occasion.

In August, the Burgaynes hosted another garden party, to which Linden was invited. She was aware that Edward had returned home earlier, but was disappointed that she had not heard directly from him. After his having said he wished to meet up with her during the summer she now resigned herself to the discouraging likelihood of his having met and fallen in love with a very lucky girl at Cambridge.

As she walked and talked in the grounds of Kinlet Hall with Penny, the weather was cooler than it had been the previous year and grey clouds rolled across the blue sky, causing prolonged overcast periods. Linden did not mention Edward, but neither did Penny.

Then, a familiar voice called her name somewhere behind her, and her heart lurched.

'Edward,' Linden sighed, looking becomingly surprised, and hoping the shock would explain her blushing.

'It's good to see you again, Linden. Come and have a chat . . . if Penny can spare you.'

Penny, with a knowing look, declared that she'd be happy to.

Thankfully, Edward seemed eager to drag her away as he led her to the marquee. He hauled two fold-up chairs to a table and they sat down opposite each other. Linden was privately encouraged as they smiled like sincere friends genuinely pleased to see each other, however occasional the meeting.

'How've you been?' he enquired.

'Well, thank you. And busy at work. I've been doing quite

a bit for your father lately . . . and Hugh. Are you well? How's university?'

'I begin my final year when I return. Lots of studying, lots of exams to contend with.' He sighed ruefully.

'And lots of flying?'

He smiled at that. 'Oh, yes, lots of flying.'

'And you still want to join the RAF?'

'Of course.'

'Aren't you worried, though, Edward, that there's going to be a war? That you'll be expected to fight?'

He shrugged as if it were of no consequence. 'It's what the RAF is for. Why? Are you worried about me?' His smile was devastating.

'Why? Shouldn't I worry about you?'

His eyes devoured her. 'I'm awfully flattered if you do. I worry about you too, you know.'

'Me? Honestly?'

He lit a cigarette and puffed a cloud of smoke into the apex of the marquee. 'I worry about you and that chap Ron.'

'Gosh, you needn't worry about him. He's history.'

'So I gathered from Penny, but it's good to have it confirmed. All the same, I bet he can't leave you alone.'

'He still calls round to see my mum and dad.'

'To see you, you mean.'

It was Linden's turn to shrug. 'That might be his intention, for all I know.'

'Of course it is. You must see that?'

'But there's nothing there for him anyway. He knows that much. Maybe he's just having trouble breaking the habit.'

He drew on his cigarette again, his eyes still feasting on her. She looked so achingly desirable in her simple yellow cotton dress that accentuated her slender waist and pert young bosom. The dress was sleeveless and her arms looked slender and smooth and beautifully contoured. He longed to hold her. 'I hope you're still free of him when I finish university.'

She blushed at what his words implied. 'I see no reason why I shouldn't be,' she replied softly.

'I want you to know, Linden, that I'm terribly fond of you.' His voice sounded choked with pent-up emotion. 'And Penny suggested a while ago that you . . . well, that you might be fond of me, too . . .' He drew on his cigarette and flicked ash nervously into the ashtray on the table, his eyes never leaving hers.

Linden smiled, aware of his nervousness, and decorously averted her eyes.

'I understand your . . . your reticence in not wanting to take it any further while I'm at university,' he went on. 'That's something else Penny mentioned.'

'Well . . . I do think it's sensible, don't you?' she said quietly, regretting her words as soon as they were spoken. 'I mean, you won't need the distraction . . . that's all.'

'Well, I have tremendous respect for your common sense, although it grieves me sorely . . . But look . . .' He drew on his cigarette nervously. 'When I've finished university . . . do you think you might still be here for me?'

She felt her heart suddenly pounding hard within the bodice of her yellow cotton dress. 'D'you think it's wise to be making such pledges, Edward?' she said, her tremendously respected common sense eclipsing her emotions. 'I'm sure there must be lots of worthy girls in Cambridge.'

'So there are, but none like you.'

'So you say. All the same . . .'

'All the same, it's what I would dearly like.'

That night she and Edward went out with Penny and Adrian. Determined to enjoy the occasion, they had great fun. Things that they wanted to say to each other had already been said and were not referred to again. Everything was understood between them. At this stage it would not do to become intense about one another, but both sensed the promise of the future . . .

It would have bolstered Linden's faith if Edward had asked her out for another evening before he returned to Cambridge. She would have loved to spend more time in his company, but he made no such suggestion; neither did she. Both comprehended that to spend a further evening together, holding hands, kissing ardently and promising undying devotion as they said goodbye, would only have escalated the affair prematurely. It would have been romantic if he'd suggested they write while he was away, but that would only have heightened their mutual longing and intensified their absence. To wait was a notion implicit between them, for they knew it made sense. If they each met somebody else in the meantime, so be it.

No binding promise had been made, none would therefore be broken.

In any case, the future was too uncertain for promises to be made and to expect their fulfilment, and they both realized it. Linden read the newspapers avidly and listened to the wireless, and was filled with apprehension. She was appalled and afraid for the Jews in Vienna given two weeks' notice by their employers to quit their jobs, just because they were Jewish. Clearly, some colossal, unstoppable evil was afoot.

Summer shifted surreptitiously into autumn, and Linden learned that Mussolini had expelled all Jews arriving in Italy after 1918, while others were rounded up and charged with plotting against his government. There was trouble in Czechoslovakia too; in carefully orchestrated rallies and riots the Sudeten Germans were calling for union with Germany, but the Czech government's response was to impose martial law, and appeal for calm amongst countrymen hostile to Germany. Hitler called a conference between Germany, Britain, France and Italy, to discuss the crisis. On 30 September, Mr Chamberlain, the British Prime Minister, flew home from that conference and promised, as he waved a copy of the signed Anglo-German accord, that there would be 'peace in our time'. Linden viewed it with deep suspicion, and wished she were Prime Minister; it was so obviously a sell-out.

So she was not surprised to read that on 1 October the Nazis had marched into Czechoslovakia and occupied the Sudetenland, and that other parts of the country were being annexed by Poland. Hungary too was laying claim, and duly annexed southern areas of Slovakia and Ruthenia. In December the German Navy announced plans to double the size of her fleet of U-boats.

But life went on. The Blower's Green Steelworks continued to produce and roll steel and, on Boxing Day, another hunt departed from the Cat Inn at Enville, to which Linden was once more invited. Once again she told Edward of her fears.

By March of 1939 it was clear that Poland itself was under threat from Nazi Germany, but Britain and France pledged to defend the country under any circumstances. In April the government announced conscription. For Linden, this was the clearest indication yet that war was just around the corner.

But, affording some light-heartedness into those anxious

days, the month of May brought Linden's twentieth birthday
– and something else . . .

Miss Hardy from the Personnel Department sent for Linden.
  'D'you think it will be to give me a rise for my birthday?'
she asked Vera.
  'You're kidding,' Vera replied tartly. 'They don't give rises
here just for birthdays.'
  So Linden trotted to the Personnel Department.
  'Do sit down, Miss Woods.'
  Linden did as she was bid.
  'How long have you been here now, Miss Woods?'
  'It'll be two years in August, Miss Hardy.'
  'And you appear to have settled down very well to the
work.'
  'I think I have,' Linden replied. 'I enjoy it.'
  'You are very highly thought of in certain quarters, you
know, and I have been asked to "sound you out", so to speak.'
  'Oh?' Linden's face was a delightful icon of bewilderment.
  'You may or may not be aware that Mr Charles Burgayne's
secretary Miss Evans is due to retire at the end of June . . .'
  Linden was suddenly aware of her heart beating faster at
the prospect of where this might be leading. 'Yes,' she replied.
  'Mr Burgayne himself has put your name forward as a
possible successor, and I have been asked to get your reaction.'
  Linden beamed excitedly. 'Become Mr Burgayne's secretary? Gosh!' She laughed delightedly. ' I . . . I . . . I'm
speechless.'
  'Consider it an honour, Miss Woods. I have never before
known that a woman of your tender years be considered for
such an elevated position. But your work has been carefully
monitored all the time you've been here, and Mr Burgayne
obviously believes you are worthy of the post and capable of
making a success of it. There would of course, be a significant
increase in your salary to reflect the additional responsibilities
and extra work you will be expected to undertake.'
  'What extra work, Miss Hardy?'
  'Well, Miss Evans has been more than just a secretary –
more a personal assistant and, as such, she often works with
Mr Charles and other members of the Burgayne family, sometimes even at their home on things of a more personal nature.'

'I see,' Linden said thoughtfully. 'It sounds very interesting.'

'You would, of course, get to know other members of the family, ready for the hand-over at the end of June.'

Linden was almost tempted to confess that she knew them all already, but decided it best to keep it to herself; she wanted no insinuations of favouritism.

'And what would be my new salary, Miss Hardy?'

'Thirty-nine shillings and sixpence per week.'

'Gosh!' *Think of the new clothes and shoes I could buy, trips to a hairdresser . . .*

After the dinner break Linden received another summons, this time to the office of Charles Burgayne. She tapped on his door deferentially and she heard him respond with a 'Come in,' and his customary cough.

'Ah, Linden . . .'

'Good afternoon, Mr Burgayne.'

'Please take a seat . . .' He shuffled some papers on his desk and leaned back in his chair proprietorially. 'I imagine you know why you're here, young lady?'

'Yes, I think I do, Mr Burgayne, and I have to thank you—'

'I'll let you into a little secret, Linden: ever since the very first time you did some work for me – and you'd only been here five minutes – I was impressed with your work, with your demeanour, in fact, your whole attitude, and I had you earmarked then for my future secretary, come the retirement of Edith Evans. I'm confident we shall continue working satisfactorily together.'

'Oh, I am, too, Mr Burgayne.'

'You already have the advantage of knowing me and my family, as well as the understanding, I would imagine, that we all think very highly of you. The fact that you get on well with them all, and that you are not a stranger of whom we should be wary at Kinlet Hall, was yet another factor in making you my choice. So congratulations, Linden . . .' He stood up, reached across the table for her hand and they shook, Linden beaming with joy.

'Now tell me: what have they offered you in the way of salary?'

'Thirty-nine and six a week,' she replied.

Charles winked. 'I'll see if we can't better that by at least another five bob, what?'

Her eyes widened with astonishment and joy. 'I really don't know what to say . . .'

When Linden arrived home that day, Gladys was emerging from the cellar heaving a bucket of coal. Her hands were as black as the coal she was lifting, and she placed a few lumps on the fire that was burning in the immaculate, black-leaded grate.

'What's for tea, Mum?'

'I got a bit of cod from the fishmonger's. It'll be nice with some parsley sauce.'

'Shall I carry the bucket out for you?'

'No, you'll get yourself all black and spoil your frock. I'll do it.'

'Well, if I spoil my frock I can always buy a new one.'

'Miss Moneybags, eh? Have you had some money for your birthday or summat?'

Linden grinned. 'In a way, yes.'

Gladys took the coal bucket out and Linden followed her through the veranda to the brew house. 'I thought you was looking pleased with yourself, our Linden. What's happened then?'

'You'll never believe it.'

'You'll have to tell me first.'

'I've been promoted, our Mum. I'm going to be Mr Burgayne's new secretary when Miss Evans retires at the end of June.'

'My God!' Gladys looked at her daughter in delighted astonishment. 'I always knew you'd do well, our Linden, but I never thought you'd come to be the gaffer's secretary. Wait till your dad knows.'

'And I get a whopping great rise. I can scarcely believe it.'

'Ooh, then I think we'll have a bit of a celebration tonight, eh, our Linden? I'll pop down to the outdoor after and fetch us a bottle of sherry.'

'I'll pay,' said Linden.

They heard footsteps in the entry and turned to watch Joe Woods come through the veranda door. He was beaming as he greeted them.

'Blimey, here's another grinning like a Cheshire cat,' Gladys ribbed. 'And what sort of a day have you had, dear husband?' she asked, in a mock-cultured tone.

'You'll never believe it,' Joe responded. 'They've made me up to foreman. Me – Joe Woods. I can scarcely believe it.'

'Looks like a double celebration, our Linden, eh?'

'Does that mean two bottles of sherry, then?'

'Why what's happened?' Joe asked.

Linden told him.

'Bloody hell. Looks like our ship's really come in at last.'

Eleven

The telephone on her desk rang, interrupting her work. Linden, installed in her own office as the recently appointed personal private secretary to Mr Charles Burgayne, answered it.

'Telephone call for you, Miss Woods,' the firm's telephonist announced.

She waited, hearing a few clicks.

'Linden?'

'Speaking.'

'Edward Burgayne here.'

'Edward!' she replied, suddenly trembling at the sound of his voice and instantly sitting up straight. 'Gosh, what a lovely surprise. It's lovely to hear from you. Are you home?'

'Got home last night actually. Late. Awful train journey. Hey, I'm told congrats are in order – they promoted you, I hear.' He sounded so cheery and friendly despite the crackles over the line that contrived to make his voice sound hard and distant.

'I know. Great, isn't it?'

'How's it going?'

'So far so good. Now I get to know some of the Burgayne family secrets.'

'You'll get to know more than me, no doubt.'

'Who knows!' she laughed. 'So how did your exams go?'

'Pretty well, I think.'

'Are you finished university now?'

'Yes, thank God. That's it now. *Finito*. Which is why I called ... I'd like to see you, Linden. In fact, I'm dying to. These last few weeks have dragged awfully. Tell me you haven't changed since last I saw you.'

Her heart skipped a beat. 'I don't think I've changed. Oh, except maybe for the hairstyle. That's all.'

'So you're even more beautiful now?'

She uttered a self-effacing laugh. 'That's always been a matter of opinion.'

'No, it's a matter of fact. So . . . *Can* we meet?'

'I'd love to. When?'

'Tonight?'

'Tonight?'

'D'you have something else arranged?'

She sensed the apprehension in his tone because of her unwitting hesitation. 'No, nothing, Edward. Tonight's perfect. Where? What time?'

'Can you be ready by eight?'

'OK.'

'I love the way you say "OK", just like they do in those Yankee films.' Now she heard the relief in his voice. 'So I'll pick you up at eight. We have a lot to talk about.'

'Yes, I know.'

She was ready and waiting when she heard the sound of Edward's motor car reverberating through the entry, followed by the beep of its horn. With her heart in her mouth she skipped down the entry to the street, smiled broadly as she saw him. He was in his MG two-seater, the canvas roof was down, and his eyes followed her as she skipped round to the passenger seat to sit daintily beside him. He leaned over and planted a kiss on her cheek.

'It's so good to see you, Linden. And you *are* even more beautiful than I remember.'

She grinned appreciatively. 'You say the nicest things, Edward Burgayne.' As he sped away the wind blew her hair awry and she laughed. 'I've spent ages doing my hair and as soon as I get in your car it's all over the place.'

He turned to look at her and beamed admiringly. 'I really don't know what you're worried about. You look absolutely ravishing, especially with your hair blowing everywhere. Well, you said you had it in a different style. It's longer. It suits you. Makes you look more chic.'

'But it's not meant to blow all over my face.' She laughed at herself. It was as if they had never been apart. At once she felt sublimely at ease with him. 'Where are you taking me?'

'Kinver Edge. It's a lovely evening, don't you think? The sun's still shining gloriously, and we need to talk. And what more beautiful place to sit and watch the sun go down? We could go for a drink somewhere afterwards, if you like. Talking can be thirsty work.'

They arrived in the peaceful village of Kinver, drove through the quiet main street, and turned left up a narrow lane, which became even narrower, steep and twisting. Eventually he stopped at a quiet spot on top of a hill. The view was magnificent, and they clambered out. He helped her over a rustic stile and they walked through a coppice hand in hand, content to be alone together.

'Let's sit on the grass here and enjoy the view,' he suggested.

She sat down beside him, smoothed the creases in her skirt with her hands, and looked at him expectantly.

'I've thought about you such a great deal, Linden,' he said, his voice low. 'I've thought about this moment a great deal too, trying to picture in my mind's eye what it might be like. I had a little speech all worked out . . . but it's all gone . . .' He laughed diffidently. 'You know, I can't remember a word of it.'

'Did you think you needed a speech?'

'No, I don't,' he said, still laughing. 'I realize that now.' His expression changed, and he looked serious. 'I just need to know whether you feel what I feel. Now I'm free of university, and I guess I'm just a little impatient for things to happen. I seem to have waited so long for you . . .' He took her hand and engaged her soft hazel eyes that were looking back at him so intently. 'You admitted you were quite fond of me before . . . Has anything changed?'

'Nothing's changed, Edward,' she breathed. Their eyes held and she looked so divinely intense. 'Nothing's changed from that day of the garden party. I've waited for you, and waited . . . and waited . . . just like we said . . .'

She paused, as if disinclined to bare her soul more just yet, and looked up into the sky momentarily; a buzzard was drifting on the breeze as he hunted for his supper.

'And?' he urged gently, sensing her reserve

'Well . . . I felt sure my feelings for you would fade, but they haven't. Not even a little bit. I thought I might be tempted elsewhere, but I haven't been – nor have I been short of offers.'

He squeezed her hand, and leaned forward to kiss her. 'I'm so glad, Linden. I only ever dreamed of hearing you say such things. I only ever wanted *you*, you know.'

'I only ever wanted *you*, Edward and I've been counting the days . . . Anyway, I hoped you'd ring me at work at some time to let me know you were home. But I could never be sure you would. Sometimes these things are said with all good intentions, but in the heat of the moment, and are forgotten just as quickly. And Penny's been far too engrossed with Adrian to worry about me.'

'So I gather.'

'So it's been a long and lonely wait.'

'But you waited.'

'Because I thought you were worth waiting for . . . And because I believed you were waiting for me just the same.'

'I was,' he whispered. 'Will you kiss me?'

They kissed – rewarding, prolonged, lingering kisses that drew out once more all the mutual longing that had been pent up through three long seasons and more. She melted at his touch and it was a vivid foretaste of how easy it would be to lose control of herself with this man whom she desired utterly.

'Making up for lost time?' she asked teasingly when they broke off. She was resting in his arms and they were lying in the grass.

'I've dreamed about your kisses, Linden,' he whispered. 'Every night before I went to sleep I kissed you in the photograph I have of you and tried hard to remember your real kisses. If I tried hard enough, I really could imagine it all pretty well.'

'Well, we're together now . . .' She smiled as she fingered the shallow dimple in his chin, still barely able to believe she was here now, by his side in the accommodating long grass of Kinver Edge. So much had happened to her in the last few weeks – so much good, so much to be thankful for. 'But I think we should keep quiet about it for a while, don't you?' she suggested. 'I should hate your parents to think I'm getting too big for my boots, getting my claws into their younger son as soon as he's back from university.'

'Do you think so?' he queried.

'I've only just taken this job as your father's secretary. I think it would pay us to be discreet. I don't want to appear to be overstepping the mark. You do see, don't you, Edward? Although your father obviously thinks I'm suitable as his private secretary, it doesn't mean he thinks I'm a suitable daughter-in-law. I'm just a working-class girl, remember – one generation away from a chambermaid, because that's what my mother was before she married my dad.'

'I hadn't really considered that aspect, Linden. But you know how I feel about such silly prejudices. Though not everybody does, I realize.' He sighed disappointedly. 'Maybe you're right.'

'Well, it's a certain fact that Hugh won't approve.'

'Hugh . . . Gosh, yes. Ages ago he tried to warn me off you. I thought he was rather taking too much for granted at the time.'

'So it might not be all plain sailing, Edward.'

'Penny will be all right, though. You're her best friend.'

'Yes, Penny will be all right.'

'Well, I'm prepared to outface the others if you are, if and when the time comes. I'll defy any outdated preconceptions some members of my family might have. I promise you that, my love. I take it *your* folks will be all right?'

'Oh, my mother will adore you, and my dad will hold you in fawning respect just because of who you are. Yes, my folks will be all right. I can just imagine my mother at her sewing circle gossiping and saying, "Oh, our Linden's done well for herself".' She chuckled at the thought. 'You must meet them soon, Edward. In the meantime, let's just enjoy what we have . . . Kiss me again . . .'

As Linden sat daydreaming at work, her thoughts were disturbed by the ringing of the telephone on her desk.

'Miss Burgayne for you, Miss Woods,' the telephonist announced.

The customary clicks and crackles ensued.

'Linden. You dark horse. Edward's been telling me everything. You never said, but I'm not a bit surprised, you know.'

'But you don't mind, do you, Penny?'

'Mind? About you and Edward?'

'Yes.'

'Gosh, no. Why should I mind? I'm delighted. I think you are an ideal match.'

'Thank you, Penny. I just hope the rest of your family think so.'

'Well, keep it under your hat for now. Listen, we want to make up a four for tennis before dinner. Edward says he hasn't arranged to see you tonight, so can you come? We'll be eating quite late, Mother says.'

'I could, but your father's not here to take me. He's out this afternoon . . . And I'd really rather not ask Hugh. If he thinks Edward and I . . .'

'Understandable. So book a taxi and charge it to the firm. Legitimate expenses, I understand.'

'I'll have to fetch my tennis things from home.'

'So use the taxi,' Penny instructed. 'Edward will take you home afterwards. I suppose he'll want his kiss and cuddle.'

Linden laughed. 'I'll want mine, too. Shall I be staying for dinner, Penny?' She was almost afraid to ask.

'Naturally.'

'Then I'll need something decent to change into as well.'

'Book the taxi for four o' clock, Linden, so you can leave work early. Try and get here by five. If Father's away he'll be none the wiser.'

At Kinlet Hall Edward greeted her with measured politeness as he would any other house guest, but only to avoid arousing any suspicions. Out of sight of prying eyes he put his arm around her, hugged and kissed her affectionately.

They played tennis till about half past six, then returned to the house, showered, and changed before going down to dinner. Showering was for Linden an exotic change from the tin bath on the hearth, or a thorough wash down at the stone sink in the brew house.

'Drinks outside,' Dorothy Burgayne announced to Penny and Linden as they reached the bottom stair together. 'It's such a beautiful evening.'

A table and seven folding wooden chairs had been set randomly on the lawn, which was dappled with wavering shafts of sunlight that pierced the foliage of the high trees. Charles had returned from his business trip meanwhile, and the menfolk joined them.

This is very civilized, Linden thought, sipping sherry.

Taking Penny's lead, she sat down and crossed her legs, dangling a sandal from her foot while both Edward and Hugh focused on the well-turned ankle and sensuous curve of her calf.

Talk was about the international crisis, while Dorothy tried vainly to steer clear of it, with talk of plans for the next garden party in August.

'If we're not already at war by then,' Hugh commented.

'Oh, nobody wants a war,' Linden said, glancing at Edward and thinking how traumatically it would affect their new relationship.

'Of course,' Charles agreed, 'but if and when it comes we must be prepared to fight.'

'I'll not fight, Father,' exclaimed Hugh. 'I'm a pacifist at heart. I shall register as a conscientious objector.'

'You mightn't need to,' his father replied sharply, obviously unimpressed by his older son's declared conviction. 'As a director of a steelworks you might find yourself in a reserved occupation anyway.' He coughed violently and went red in the face before he continued, watched anxiously by everybody. 'Damn this cough . . . But I must say, Hugh, I dislike and mistrust this creed of not being willing to fight on grounds of pacifism. We could all adopt that attitude, but then where would we be? It smacks of cowardice, my boy, especially when your younger brother is so obviously prepared to give his all, even training for the RAF.'

'Edward's willingness to fight is Edward's business, Father. It doesn't mean I have to be the same. Nor should you try to make me feel ashamed. I see nothing honourable or commendable in one human being slaughtering another in the name of patriotism.'

'And if we all felt the same Hitler would invade us and marvel at the woeful lack of resistance, when, after all, his obnoxious Nazi fascism is actually based on a fervent belief in belligerent patriotism.'

'I really do wish we could change the subject,' Dorothy interjected, trying once more to divert them and avoid a family argument. 'It's all too depressing. Let's talk about holidays instead. Do you intend to go to the seaside this summer, Linden?'

Linden glanced again at Edward. 'No, not this year. I'll just stay at home and maybe go out for daytrips, providing the weather holds.'

'And do you intend to go to France with the Birches this summer, Hugh?'

'I think not, Mother, even if they decide to go, and odds are they won't, the way things are shaping up on the Continent.'

'Look, I think dinner's ready,' Dorothy said, espying Jenkins. 'Shall we go in?'

*　　*　　*

Linden was thankful when dinner broke up. Throughout it she had sensed Hugh's eyes on her and she had felt self-conscious.

Because the evening remained fine, Dorothy suggested they all take a stroll through the garden. It would do Charles's chest good too to get in the fresh, warm air. They could take coffee later. Nobody was inclined to refuse, and Penny attached herself to Adrian, also a dinner guest, taking his arm devotedly as they strolled in a fragmented group.

Loath to be seen as being too attached to Edward, Linden found herself behind the others being partnered by Hugh. They said nothing for the first minute or two, only smiled tentatively at each other, listening instead to Dorothy and Charles as they stopped to admire this or that rose.

Hugh lingered at a clutch of red-hot pokers, purporting to admire their vivid colours, but clearly intending to detain Linden. He said, 'Have you ever seen the fish pool?'

'Can't say that I have.'

'Come with me. I'll show you.'

She looked for Edward, whose company she needed right then, but he was strolling way ahead, in conversation with Penny and Adrian and oblivious to her plight. She wanted to call him, but how could she utter a cry for help without drawing attention to their relationship?

Hugh led her through a gap in an ancient grey-stone wall where she imagined a gate must have existed long ago. On the other side of it, was a large ornamental pool surrounded by a well-tended lawn, and flower beds thick with blooms. Strange that she had never seen this part of the garden before.

To her great surprise and disappointment Hugh's hand reached for hers. She was shocked, but made no attempt to take it back and reproach him for it, not really sure what she should do.

'I need to speak to you, Linden.'

'Oh?'

'You see, I have a confession to make . . .' He stopped and looked at her, still holding her hand. 'I find I have feelings for you that simply won't go away.'

Oh, God . . . Of all the stupid idiots . . . Linden averted her eyes, looking somewhat guiltily at the grass beneath her feet, biting her top lip in her angst.

'I understand this might come as rather a shock to you, Linden, but I can't go on and not let you know how I feel. I hope you might give it some thought and favour me with a positive response.' He regarded her steadily.

She heaved a deep sigh of anxiety. 'I don't see how I can,' she answered, picking her words carefully. 'You're engaged to Laura after all.'

'I'm not in love with Laura. So there seems little point in continuing the relationship. It only remains to make the break.'

She let go his hand and turned away from him. She had to stop this foolishness somehow. *God, if he knew about Edward and me . . .*

'But I couldn't let myself be the cause of any unhappiness for Laura, Hugh.'

'Is Laura the only obstacle?'

'Actually, no . . .' She frowned, in two minds whether to confess there and then about Edward. But to name him presented too many difficulties yet, and she struggled to find a plausible excuse. 'The thing is, Hugh . . . Something as serious as you're suggesting needs the assent of both parties. It would be a bit one-sided, you see . . .'

'You mean because you don't feel the same for me?'

'Exactly . . . Oh, I'm very flattered – don't misunderstand me. But I don't think I – in fact I'm sure I couldn't . . .'

'Return the affection?' he prompted.

'Exactly.' She frowned again as she looked candidly into his eyes.

'But I overheard Penny say you're no longer involved with that chap you used to see.'

'That's true. But there's somebody else now anyway . . . and I'm very fond of him . . . Actually, I find this rather embarrassing, Hugh . . .'

'I'm sorry.'

'I'm sure your feelings will change.'

'Oh, don't worry, Linden, I'll try to keep them under control . . . though I can't promise.'

For the first time she noticed the fish in the pool; large and golden and lethargically graceful as they slipped silent and untroubled between lily pads and reeds.

'I think we should get back to the others,' she suggested.

'In a moment.'

'I'm a bit taken aback,' she said, feeling herself becoming bolder, more able to handle this situation. And now was perhaps a good time to tell him what she really thought. 'Especially after you'd given me cause to think I wasn't good enough even to visit Kinlet Hall, being only a servant of the company and coming from a working-class family.' There was nothing like the feeling of throwing something distasteful back in the face of the person who'd conceived it.

'Good God, if I gave you that impression, Linden, I can only apologize. It certainly is not the case.'

'Well, you did give me that distinct impression; yet now you confess undying love for me.' Her voice was low, but her temperature was rising. Now was not the time to mince her words. She had the protection of his father now, as his private secretary, as well as the potent friendship of Penny and Edward.

'Maybe you misunderstood something.'

'Maybe I did, Hugh, maybe I didn't. But I think it would be unworkable anyway. In the office tomorrow you'll be Mr Burgayne, and I'll be Miss Woods.'

'And ne'er the twain shall meet. Is that what you think?'

'Master and servant. I think that sums it up.'

She heard a voice call, 'Oh, there you are.' It was Edward.

She turned, smiled with relief and headed towards him, never so glad to see somebody in her life before. 'Hugh was just showing me the goldfish pond.'

'Lovely, isn't it? Have you seen Big George? He's a real whopper. You can't miss him.'

'I'm not sure.'

'Never mind. Some other time . . . Hugh, I'm going to steal Linden from you. We're off to the pub with Penny and Adrian. Fancy coming along?'

'No, no,' Hugh responded, deflated. 'I think I'll have an early night anyway.'

Hugh watched Edward and Linden walk away, and noticed how very much at ease this utterly desirable girl seemed with his younger brother. He was envious of how they smiled at each other and laughed with such obvious mutual affection, and found it difficult to subdue his jealousy. Was Edward the latest beau in her life, the man she'd referred to?

Twelve

The mood at the Burgaynes' 1939 garden party, held on 26 August, was noticeably more sombre than usual. The usual guests, as well as some new faces, trooped about in their summer finery with smiles on their faces. But conversations were generally confined to the imminence of war.

Linden and Edward had a deep desire to be alone that afternoon.

'Why don't you take me to the fishpond to see if Big George is around,' she suggested.

Casual visitors were generally kept away from the fish-pond, which was regarded as somewhere to be kept private. Being there now reminded her of that unfortunate encounter. She had said nothing of the incident to Edward, not wishing to cause dissention between the two brothers, but in the quiet serenity of the place she thought with hindsight how ingenuous she must have been with Hugh. Well, she had let him know how she felt, as politely as she knew how, and he had been decidedly cooler towards her since. Yet for all his newly contrived reserve, she still felt his eyes upon her from time to time, looking her up and down.

'We haven't had two months together yet, and already I'm going to lose you,' Linden complained, as they sat on the low wall surrounding the pool, their arms about each other. 'I'm so scared of what might happen.'

'I'm scared too,' Edward whispered. 'Not of fighting the Germans particularly, but of being away from you.'

'It's the not-knowing, the uncertainty of it all. God, I shall miss you, not knowing how long it'll be before I see you again.'

He hugged her tighter. He had no other comfort for her.

'You'll be kept busy at the works at any rate, my love. With any luck you'll be too busy to dwell on thoughts of me.'

'You are joking, aren't you? I'm thinking of you all day long as it is, and you haven't gone away yet. I won't know where you are, what you're doing . . . What makes it worse is you'll be flying a plane. You'll be a prime target.'

'I might be a prime target, but I've got the biggest and best incentive in the world to get through it unscathed . . . you.'

She turned her face to him and he kissed her – a deliciously long kiss. When they broke off, she sighed, 'Oh, I do love you, Edward.'

As Linden opened the door to her office on the first day of September, her telephone rang. It was Edward.

'My sweetheart,' he greeted her. He sounded down.

'Hello, love.'

'Just thought I'd better let you know – I got my call-up papers this morning.'

Her heart sank, but it was suddenly beating wildly at the prospect of losing him. 'Oh, no,' she sighed.

'I have to travel to Cambridge tomorrow to join the RAF Volunteer Reserve. They even sent me a travel warrant.'

'So soon?' she groaned. 'War hasn't even been declared yet . . . has it?'

'Not yet, my love, but it's a formality. Give it a couple more days at most. I just heard on the wireless that German troops invaded Poland at quarter to six this morning.'

'So it's begun,' she breathed. 'Oh, Edward, what are we going to do?'

'Well, if you're willing, I'm going to call for you tonight, and I'm going to lose myself in your arms while I still have the chance. Does that sound agreeable to you?'

'Most agreeable, but it won't last long enough. That's the trouble.'

'I'll pick you up about half past seven.'

'I'll be ready.'

'How've your mother and father taken the news?' Linden asked as she sat beside him in the MG.

'Badly,' he replied sombrely. 'You could see father's colour drain away as I told him. Somehow, I think he blames himself – for encouraging me to fly, I mean – not least for buying me the Gypsy Moth for my twenty-first.'

'He should be proud of you,' she said, sensing that the mood between them needed brightening. 'I'm proud of you anyway.'

'I think he *is* proud of me. He's just apprehensive.'

'Has Hugh said anything else about registering as a conshi?'

'He's said nothing to me at any rate.'

'He ought to be ashamed,' she said bluntly.

'I doubt whether he is. It's based on what he believes.'

'He only ever thinks of himself, Edward. I don't think I ever met a more self-centred person.'

'You really don't like him, do you?'

'Not very much.'

'Why? What's he ever done to you?'

'Oh, nothing . . .'

They remained unspeaking for a while as they drove through country lanes towards Enville Common, the only place they knew where they could be really, truly alone. It was a vast expanse of common land clad in abundant fern and dotted with silver birches but, importantly, devoid of people: an ideal spot for spooning under the stars if you had the means to get there.

'Are you all right?' Edward asked after too long a silence.

She smiled her reassurance. 'Yes, course I'm all right.'

Edward drove the car over some rough ground as they left the lane, towards a spot they'd visited once before. Some way in, surrounded by trees, he stopped the car and switched off the engine.

'I need a kiss.'

She turned her face towards him, leaned into him, and they kissed.

The unsettling events that day had heightened the emotions of both, and prompted heady thoughts of highly charged romance that night, the last night for heaven knew how long – possibly for ever.

'Tell me you love me, Linden,' he whispered. 'I need to hear you say it.'

'You know I love you, Edward. With all my heart and soul I love you.'

He hugged her, nuzzling her hair. 'And I love you. More than I ever thought possible. Hell, I'm going to miss you.'

She began to feel a warm stirring within her and snuggled up to him. Again he kissed her softly on the lips. Eagerly she responded, and her tension eased with every second of that embrace. Then he broke off to reach for the blanket stashed behind his seat. It was a signal, never before spoken, never before alluded to, but she understood its meaning. Wordlessly, he clambered out of the car in the greyness of dusk, and spread the blanket on a patch of grass, hidden by the dense ferns.

She was shutting the car door when he scooped her up into his arms and laid her gently on the bed he had made, as if it were fit for a bride. She offered no resistance; there was no resistance left in her; there was no point in resistance – this was not Ron: this was Edward whom she adored, and they were deeply in love. As he lay beside her, she turned her face to him and smiled conspiratorially. She closed her eyes and felt his lips caressing her smooth eyelids with the lightness of a butterfly's wings. He found her mouth and she tasted him again with tantalizing pleasure, running her fingers through his hair in an ecstasy of bliss at her absolute love for him.

In the twilight her love shone unmistakably through her clear, earnest eyes, and he kissed her again. Her lips felt so good. It would be forever impossible to have a surfeit of her kisses. He could happily kiss her till eternity.

After a while they broke off their kiss and his lips first brushed her throat and her neck, as light as the touch of a feather, then lingered at her ear. As she felt his warm breath she experienced sensations up and down her spine that she could not control. She could feel him pressing against her, urgently, and her heart beat faster at the pleasure of it all. They kissed more, savouring each other's lips. His knee slid evocatively between her thighs and the feel of him pressing against her heightened her own desire.

It was time.

There was no more time to waste.

There might never be another time.

He was going to war; he might never come back.

As if reading her mind, and without further hesitation, Edward unfastened the buttons at the front of her dress, albeit ineptly.

'Wait, love,' she whispered, intent on helping. 'Let me take it off.'

She sat up and took off her dress, then her brassiere. He looked in awe at the tantalizing curves of her breasts, then the sensuous indentation of her navel as she undid and pushed down her underskirt. Soon, she was standing before him naked except for her white knickers, her slender body pale but exquisitely beautiful in the insipid, failing light. She lay down beside him with all the grace and agility of a young feline. Her skin was chilled by the evening breeze soughing across the common, but she paid it no heed. He rolled on to her, kissing her on the mouth once more, one hand cupping a firm and incredibly smooth, virgin breast.

'In my thoughts,' he whispered, 'when I was trying to get to sleep at university, I used to kiss your breasts . . . Of course, such thoughts kept me wide awake.'

She hugged him, smiling to herself. His hands, so smooth, so caring, were gently fondling her, and it was such magical pleasure. As she felt his mouth on hers again she was suddenly aware just how desperately she needed this fast-flowing tide of passion.

His mouth skimmed her breasts delectably, his tongue teasing her nipples till she thought they would burst. He hooked his fingers behind the elastic of her knickers and she raised her bottom to ease their removal. As he slid them down her slender, shapely legs his lips ran tormentingly over the gentle curve of her belly, lingering where her delta of soft dark hair began . . . then between her legs. She lay sprawled, naked under the emerging stars of a clear evening sky, clenching the curls of his head between her fingers.

'Oh, Edward,' she sighed, paralysed and astounded with pleasure.

There could be no turning back now.

Too soon, she thought, he sat up to remove his jacket and his shirt. He pulled off his boots, then his trousers and his underpants. She watched him, as naked then as she was. Lust, simple and shameless – and entirely new to her – was increasing inexorably within her as he knelt beside her.

'Oh, sweetheart . . .' He looked down at her longingly in the fast fading light, and ran his fingers lightly up between her thighs till they settled at the mystical triangle that had been the focus of so many erotic fantasies. She was so warm there, so soft and so deliciously wet, and she parted her legs a little to make herself more accessible.

She was intoxicated when he caressed her there. Never

could she have imagined anything like this even in her wildest, most sensual dreams. Never could she have envisaged either such willing, enthusiastic submission.

'Oh, sweetheart,' he breathed again, as if she had no other name. He bent down to her, kissed her lips and gently lay on her. As she felt the pressure of his warm naked body, his chest smooth against her compressed breasts, she sniffed his skin, breathing in her own ardent desire that seemed unquenchable.

'Oh, Edward,' she sighed with longing. He entered her and she recoiled slightly. 'Oh, Edward,' she whispered again, trembling a little but trying to control it.

He drew back at once. 'Did I hurt you?'

'Please don't stop. It's hardly anything.'

He kissed her closed eyelids, her soft, round cheeks and her neck. He was so gentle, so afraid of hurting her, but each sharp pain that accompanied each tender, tentative push was a delight, and she raised her legs to accommodate him the more as he probed deeper, deeper into her. The twinges of pain were numbed in direct proportion to the pleasure, which increased with each mollifying, careful stroke, and they soon found themselves intertwined in a steady rhythm that was becoming more pronounced the longer they were joined. Her breathing came in short gasps as she rubbed herself more firmly against him which, she quickly discovered, intensified the pleasure, until all comprehension, all sense of who or where she was, was immaterial.

In those precious, unforgettable moments she was conscious only of Edward and this strange, ethereal sensation rising in the pit of her stomach which she was subconsciously willing to a greater intensity. Her world was him. His quickening breath combined ineffably with hers, his heart hammered against her own, becoming one. She hugged him ardently, clinging first to his shoulders, then his waist, then his firm, round buttocks in a fervour of passion as he thrust with increasing passion into her. He groaned . . . and sighed . . . and eventually ceased to move . . . Tears ran down her cheek as she cleaved to him, tears of relief that she finally had a reason to give herself entirely, because she was utterly, enchantingly, desperately in love.

Tomorrow he would go away and the waiting to be with him again would be intolerable. He would come home on leave and they would make love like this again; but afterwards there would be only more anxious waiting. This was the way it had to be from now on. This was the future. It was also the present and, for now, she wanted time to stand still, to exist only in this moment. She wanted this wonderful feeling of peace, which emanated from the very centre of her body and seemed to spread to her toes and her fingers, to last till eternity.

He felt her tears wet against his cheek. 'Sweetheart, you're crying.'

She clung to him. 'Tears of happiness . . . Tears of sadness as well . . . because too soon we shall be apart.'

'I know,' he said, with intense feeling.

He rolled off her and she felt moist with perspiration where he had lain on her, a little tender where he had been, but content. Oh, utterly content.

They lay silent.

All she wanted was to sleep in his arms, to awaken with him at dawn and smile into his soft eyes . . . and perhaps make love again. Within her was a growing awareness of the enormity, the significance of what they had done, a growing awareness of the forbidden heights of ecstasy they had scaled. There was no sense of shame, no guilt, no regret. Certainly no regret. It was done and there was no going back.

Thirteen

4 September 1939
My own darling Linden,
I do so wish you had been able to see me off at the station on Saturday. It was all well and good my father and Penny taking me, despatching me with their peculiar brand of bonhomie, when the one person I really wanted there was you, and you couldn't be. I am so looking forward to the day when we can be candid and open about our love, and I feel certain it will not be too long. This war, if anything like the last, will change attitudes along with everything else. What this war will drive home, if nothing else, is that we are all God's children, no matter what artificial, man-devised stations in life we have occupied.

Well, when I arrived at Cambridge a whole host of chaps like me were assembling at the station and we were marched en masse to where we were being billeted. We have since learned that before we are allowed anywhere near an aeroplane we are to go through a period of parade-ground drill, marching up and down till we can keep in perfect step. I can think of nothing more pointless or soul-destroying. Lord knows how long it will go on, but now I'm here I'm itching to fly. At least marching allows me one luxury though – thinking about you relatively uninterrupted.

In truth, I cannot get you off my mind, my love, nor our wonderful evening last Friday. I relive it constantly, hardly able to believe that something so terrifyingly beautiful happened to me. I long to be with you again. It was really quite the nicest goodbye imaginable! When I go to my bunk at night I allow myself to wallow in thoughts of what might be if the future is kind to us. Of course, it's all pie in the sky at present, because nobody can reasonably make plans, but I have a dream, a vivid dream of the future with you, my darling, and I intend to hold on to it. It will see me through all this madness.

Please write to me soon, my own darling, at the address above for now. When the square-bashing is over we'll be posted elsewhere.

I love you, and will always love you,
Edward.

Tuesday 5 Sept
My dearest darling Edward,
I was so relieved to get your letter. I am thinking about you constantly. I hope and pray this war will all be over by the time your training is finished so that you will be able to come home to me unscathed.

I spoke to Penny yesterday to ask if they'd heard from you, but she reckoned I was sure to be the first. It's just that I thought you might have telephoned them to say you'd arrived OK. Anyway, Adrian has decided he's going to join up and was due to go to a recruitment centre yesterday. Penny believes the army is his preference.

Already a blackout has been imposed, and you daren't even smoke a cigarette outdoors lest the glow be seen by the Luftwaffe who might be overhead. Everywhere is bible black, and my dad said he could hardly find his way up the back yard to our privy last night, to which my mother's beautifully logical reply was that he'd best go before it gets dark in future. You have to laugh. They send their love, by the way.

You will notice that I have written this letter by hand, not on my typewriter. I always think a type-written letter is impersonal and I'm sure you would much rather get a hand-written one. I'm writing it in my dinner break, still at my desk.

I am ending this letter with a kiss. A real one, an imprint in lipstick of my lips at the foot of the page, so you can kiss me by proxy, knowing my lips have been there too. It's the nearest we shall get to the proper thing till you come home on leave.

Please write back at once, my darling. I need you and love you always.
    Your very own Linden.

'Linden, I've decided to spend more time working from home,' Charles Burgayne said one day as she was poring over some files in his office. 'I'm rather aware that this chest of mine is not best served in the atmosphere that prevails around the works. I can benefit from the fresher, rural air of Kinlet Hall three or four extra days a week.'

'I think that's very sensible, Mr Burgayne.'

'Either Hugh or yourself can bring me any correspondence, production reports, sales figures, et cetera, that need my attention. So, if you don't mind, you'll find it necessary to spend more time there working with me at Kinlet Hall. Besides, there'll be a lot going on as regards the family now we're at war, and my wife will appreciate having somebody who can help her with her own correspondence and help her organizing things. How do you feel about that?'

She turned to him and smiled. It was considerate of him to ask whether she minded, but that was typical of the man. 'I really don't mind, Mr Burgayne. Whatever is best for you. I agree with you about the atmosphere around here though.'

'Splendid. Arrange with the taxi firm to collect you from home those mornings I want you at Kinlet Hall, and to deliver you back in the evenings. I'll have one of the unused bedrooms converted right away into an office for you, and we'll try and get a telephone extension installed as quick as the GPO can manage it. Order yourself a new typewriter and have it delivered there too – there's no point lugging the other one around with you – and arrange for a supply of stationery.'

Linden enjoyed working at the Hall. Cups of tea were on tap, she was fed well and enjoyed the welcome intrusions of Penny and Dorothy for chats from time to time. The work was not entirely Blower's Green Steelworks business, although steelmaking was thriving owing to the war effort, so the amount of work she had to get through grew accordingly, and it all kept her busy. Charles was a hard taskmaster, but he was extraordinarily fair and considerate, and always impeccably polite and pleasant. She was perfectly happy doing what she was doing.

Penny decided that her own time could be usefully employed

by joining the Women's Royal Voluntary Service ready for when things began to 'hot up'. Dorothy deemed it necessary to do her bit for the war effort too and, between them all, they agreed to make Kinlet Hall available as a sanatorium for the recuperation of injured servicemen, and Linden became involved in its organisation. The ancient house was duly inspected and judged suitable by the Red Cross, and several rooms were prepared. Part of the house thus began to resemble a hospital. To Penny's consternation, Adrian had joined the Staffordshires and begun his training.

One day in the middle of October when Linden was working at Kinlet Hall the telephone rang. She waited for a member of the family to answer it, since it would most likely be a private call, but it seemed to ring for ages. So, she answered it using the newly installed extension in her office.

'Kinlet Hall.'

'Hello. Who is that?' the voice at the other end enquired uncertainly.

She recognized it straight away, and her heart leaped.

'Edward! It's me. Linden.'

'Sweetheart! Great Scott! I never expected to be speaking to you. How are you?'

'I'm well, but missing you terribly.'

'I'm missing you too, sweetheart. God, I'd give anything to be there with you right now. Working for the old man at the house today, are you?'

'Yes. There's lots we can do from here. How's the square-bashing?'

'Oh, ludicrously tedious. Did you get my letter today?'

'I did. You sounded really fed up.'

'I am fed up. Horribly. It seems such a waste of time marching up and down a parade ground when I could be doing something really useful, like patrolling the skies.'

'I'm sure it won't be long now,' she remarked in consolation, even though she would have preferred, for her own peace of mind, that he remain marching on the parade ground.

'We won't be allowed in combat anyway for some time, so you needn't worry,' he said reading her thoughts. 'We have to train in aerobatics, navigation, night flying and gunnery – all sorts of stuff – before we're let loose on an unsuspecting enemy.'

'By which time the war might be over.'

'That I doubt,' he replied darkly. 'The Germans will take some beating, believe me. From what we've heard here, it seems there will be little trench warfare in this war. You only have to look at the speed and efficiency with which they rolled into Poland. "*Blitzkrieg*", they're calling it – lightning war. Before their army moved in the Luftwaffe knocked out the railways and shot the Polish air force out of the sky. You have to hand it to them.'

'You're scaring me, Edward.'

'Oh, please don't worry, my love. We'll be a different kettle of fish, I can assure you. They won't find us such a walk-over.'

The operator interrupted them to let him know he needed to put more money in the slot if he wanted to continue the conversation, and he replied politely that he only had a shilling. He fed it into the public telephone's coin mechanism, and she could hear its clatter.

'Who did you want to speak to, darling?' she asked, remembering he had not expected to speak to her.

'Oh, anybody. Mother, Father, Penny. But you'll do nicely,' he said warmly. 'Will you tell them I rang and that I'm all right?'

'Course I will. Shall you ring up again?'

'If I get the chance, of course. But there's no guarantee I'll be able to speak to you, is there, my love?'

She knew what he meant. 'Unfortunately not, but I'm sure your mother is going to be all right about things. We get on pretty well, you know.'

'Great. I'm pleased. Anyway, I'll write again tomorrow and let you know the latest in parade-ground politics. The money's running out, sweetheart. Look after yourself.'

The phone line went dead and, feeling both sad and uplifted, Linden rested the handset back in its cradle just as Dorothy Burgayne opened the door.

'Oh, Mrs Burgayne . . . that was Edward on the line. You just missed him.'

'Edward? Is he all right?'

'He sounds fine. He's just bored with all the drill they have to do, but he's in good health, I think.'

'You had a good long chat with him?'

'Not really,' Linden answered truthfully. 'He was speaking

from a public call box and his money ran out. But it was lovely to speak to him all the same.'

'I wish I could have spoken to him, Linden.' Linden felt her colour rise. 'You should have called me. I was only in the hallway.'

Then why didn't you answer the phone? 'Next time I'll be sure to, Mrs Burgayne.'

> *12 November 1939*
> *My very own little darling,*
> *Just a quick note to say I arrived at the RAF College Cranwell about lunch time, and I want to let you know my new address. Please write to me here from now on.*
> *It looks as though we'll be here about four months, but at least we'll actually be flying. I might even be lucky and be allowed a spot of leave soon. Even 48 hours would be brilliant, so fingers crossed.*
> *Will write again tomorrow.*
> *My love always,*
> *Edward.*

Edward was indeed granted leave some few weeks later, and on Christmas Eve Penny was about to collect him from Wolverhampton.

'I say, Linden, I bet you'd like to come with me.' Penny suggested, knowing how much it would mean to her friend. 'Do you have a huge amount of work to do for the old man?'

'Not much at all now, but I can't just go without saying something.'

'Leave it to me.'

Penny left Linden and returned, beaming, a few minutes later.

'You're coming.'

Linden grinned happily. 'How on earth did you manage that?'

'Oh, I merely told Dad I wasn't sure where the station was,' she answered dismissively. 'I told him you knew, so was it all right if you went with me? He said yes, of course. Simple.'

'You're an angel, Penny. Gosh, I'm so looking forward to seeing Edward again. But I'm so nervous.'

Christmas Eve was cold and damp and the two girls were wrapped in their overcoats, hats, scarves and mittens as they climbed into the Riley. Linden was trembling – more from anticipation at the prospect of seeing Edward again after nearly four months away than the chilly weather.

'It's a pity Adrian can't be home for Christmas too,' Penny commented miserably as she drove through grey country lanes. 'God, I miss him.'

'I know,' Linden replied, aware of exactly how her friend was feeling. 'Have you heard from him today?'

'Yes, I got his usual letter this morning. He says there's not much happening in his part of France. I must say, Linden, it's a funny old sort of war when the only fighting is being done by the navy at sea and the Finns on their border with Russia.'

'We should be grateful,' Linden said. 'At least it's keeping our boys safe.'

'But how long will it last? We all thought we would have been bombed out of existence by now, but there's been nothing.'

'Let's count our blessings.'

As soon as she saw him step down from the train in his RAF uniform her legs began to feel wobbly and her heart pounded. Edward was an icon of military fitness – leaner, fitter, taller, broader as he looked about him with a confidence that had not been apparent before. He was no longer the dewy-eyed, curly-topped university student she had fallen in love with, but a more masculine, more rugged-looking man and oh, so much more desirable. The locomotive that had hauled him home hissed and roared as she eagerly weaved her way towards him through the mass of folk spilling on to the platform. As soon as he saw her he dropped his suitcase and held out his arms. She ran into them and pressed her head into his chest, tears of joy and relief misting her eyes.

'Oh, Edward. Thank God you're home again.'

'If only for a little while.' He took her chin gently, lifted her face and kissed her on the lips. 'My, you don't know how good that feels, Linden.'

'Oh, yes I do,' she said with feeling. As she beamed up at him she saw the bright gleam in his eyes, a look of greater worldliness and authority. He put his arm around her waist, picked up his bag, and ushered her towards the exit.

'I take it you came with Penny?'

'Yes, she drove here. There she is.' Penny was waving wildly, happily. 'You're much leaner, Edward,' Linden said as they approached Penny. 'I think I fancy you even more.'

He laughed. 'And look at you.' He gave a succession of hugs around her waist, assessing her trimness. 'You can't say that you've gained weight either, while I've been away.'

'It's the food shortages,' she said, smiling contentedly, for she was aware that her figure was sleeker now – a sleekness she was content with. 'Nobody will get fat in this war the way the Germans keep sinking our merchant ships.'

Later that afternoon, Linden presented herself at Charles Burgayne's study and tapped gently on the open door. He turned to look.

'Ah, Linden.'

'If there's nothing else this afternoon, Mr Burgayne, I'll be going home now.'

'That's fine, my dear,' he answered kindly. 'Is the taxi here for you?'

'Edward very kindly offered to drive me home, so I cancelled the taxi.'

He smiled. 'Very well. I see you have the post.'

'Yes. I'll drop it in a post box on my way home.'

'And don't forget to take all your Christmas boxes either.'

She smiled appreciatively. 'Thank you all very much. Everybody's been so kind.'

'Merry Christmas, Linden.'

'Merry Christmas, Mr Burgayne.'

When she had gone, Charles went to the breakfast room where he knew Dorothy would be, and requested a cup of tea of Margaret Jenkins, the maid. He sat down opposite Dorothy.

'I have a sneaking suspicion that there's romance blossoming in our midst,' he said quietly.

Dorothy looked up from the list of queries she had made regarding the convalescent rooms, still unoccupied. 'Oh?'

'Edward and Linden. She's cancelled her taxi in favour of Edward driving her home.'

'Now that you mention it, Charles . . . He rang a few weeks

ago and she answered his call. Nobody else had a chance to
talk to him, and she blushed like a rose when I said something. Do you think we should discourage it?'

Charles waved his hand dismissively. 'Hell, no. There's a
war on, and you can hardly blame the lad – she's such a pretty
thing. Let them have their fun. Frankly, I admire his taste. If
I were in his shoes I daresay I'd be doing the same. I take it
he hasn't said anything to you, Dorothy?'

'Nothing.'

'Then it'll probably amount to nothing.'

'Let's hope he doesn't do anything rash. You know the old
saying about absence making the heart grow fonder.'

'Well, as I see it, we can hardly discourage it if we don't
know for certain that there's something going on.'

'We can discourage his driving to Dudley and back willy-
nilly, with petrol rationed the way it is,' Dorothy said.
'Especially in this blackout as well. It's just too dangerous.'

Edward stopped the car at a post box at Linden's request, and
they took advantage of the break in the journey to indulge in
a kiss or two at the side of the road, heightening their already
intense hunger for each other.

'Where can we go where it's quiet?' Edward asked.

Linden racked her brains trying to think of a suitable loca-
tion. 'I know: Oakham. There's bound to be somewhere by
the golf course.'

There were no lights to guide them, no car's lamps to see
by. The blackout was total, save for the sporadic lighting up
of the sky, as the various steelworks around randomly tipped
their white-hot slag. The resultant flares reflected vividly off
the low clouds. But, driving slowly, meeting very little traffic,
they found their way. Edward turned into a narrow, bumpy
lane that came to an abrupt end in the yard of a deserted,
worked-out quarry some way off the road. He stopped the car
and switched off the engine.

'I've missed you, Linden. God, I've been longing for you.'
He took her in his arms. 'I haven't been able to get you off
my mind. I simply can't forget that night we had before I left
for Cambridge . . .'

'I'm glad,' she breathed, her heart thumping. 'I keep thinking
about it as well. It was so beautiful.'

He felt her shiver in his arms. 'You're cold, my love.'

She nodded against his chest. 'But I'm warm inside now I'm with you.'

'Kiss me.'

She tilted her head, offering her lips, and they kissed . . . a long, lingering kiss that inflamed their mutual desire.

'Let's get in the back, for God's sake,' he suggested.

In the darkness she smiled to herself, remembering Penny's comment months ago that the back seat of the Riley could be a wonderfully romantic place. Biddably, Linden clambered between the two front seats into the rear. Edward followed.

Outside an owl hooted, the only witness to this secret escapade in the darkness. In the concealing safety of the blackout, they fell into another embrace, more passionate. He unfastened the buttons of her overcoat and unwrapped the scarf that was around her neck. He undid the row of buttons on her winter cardigan, then the tiny buttons of her blouse. As he unfastened her brassiere she felt the chill of that cold December evening on the smooth skin of her bared breasts, and shivered. But the cold would not deter her. She was with the man she loved and the warmth of desire was lighting her up as his hand softly kneaded one firm but exquisitely pliable breast. She found herself sliding down against the backrest until she was lying horizontally along the full width of the seat, and her skirt had ridden up in consequence, baring her legs. He thrust his knee between them and she felt him hard against her. With nervous, shaking hands, she undid the buttons of his trousers, thrust her hand inside, carefully withdrew him and held him, tenderly stroking.

Without shame or inhibition, she allowed him to pull the hem of her skirt up to her waist and run his hands hungrily over her thighs, lingering at the bare satin-smooth skin above the tops of her stockings. He felt between her legs, slid his fingers inside the leg of her knickers, and she was as aware as he was of her own wetness as he tantalizingly caressed her. When she raised her backside he slid her knickers down her legs and she dislodged them from her feet with a small deft kick. She eased herself beneath him and shivered with pleasure at the sensation of his lean, manly body on top of her. Both were panting like hounds on a hunt when she slid her hands into the waist of his trousers and eased them over his backside. Her hands gripped his buttocks, pulling him to her, and she sighed with little sobs of pleasure as she guided him in . . .

It had been so long and the sensation was so exquisitely sweet. She had been so lonely without him, despite being surrounded by her own family and his. As they settled into an easy rhythm that belied their inexperience, tears of joy welled up in her eyes at the relief and absolute bliss of being so physically and spiritually close to him again.

Afterwards, they lay in silence, stunned at the utter beauty and power of their love, and at the sheer pleasure they were able to give each other. Their hands still roamed affectionately over each other's cooling skin, for they were still gaining familiarity with each other's bodies.

But the cold was creeping in and it was time to go. Her folks would wonder where she was.

'That was as fine a Christmas present as I ever had,' she quipped as she fumbled in the darkness for her knickers.

'For me as well.'

'Well, I've bought you something else, as a matter of fact. I left it under the Christmas tree. I hope you won't mind the inscription. It *is* rather personal.'

'Inscription, eh? So what have you bought me?'

'I'm not telling . . . Oh, here they are . . .' She had found her knickers and she slid them up her legs and under her skirt. 'Anyway, shall I see you tomorrow? I know you won't be able to come for your Christmas dinner – that wouldn't be fair on your family – but can you come for tea? Mum and Dad would love you to.'

He pulled her to him as she was fastening the buttons of her blouse. 'About six?'

'Oh, earlier, if you can. Say five.'

He kissed her. 'Five, it is . . . I love you, little Linden Woods.'

At that moment it struck her that she only had him for two more days before his return to Cranwell, and she shivered at the impending loss. *Life before Edward has been nothing*, she thought. *Life without him now would be unbearable . . . And if I'm pregnant after this I won't mind at all.*

The inside of the car was all steamed up and, as Linden deftly scrambled through to the front passenger seat, Edward grabbed a chamois leather from the parcel shelf and wiped the windows.

'We've certainly generated some moisture,' he quipped, and she tapped him playfully on the arm.

Fourteen

The Christmas tree that stood tall and broad in the hallway at Kinlet Hall had been grown on the estate, and Linden had helped to decorate it with Penny and Dorothy a few days earlier. That Christmas Day it glittered and glowed as the family handed their gifts to each other in turn from beneath it, creating mounds of torn wrapping paper on the floor.

'Here's another from Linden,' Dorothy remarked, picking up one of the remaining gifts, a small cube. She turned it over and read the label. 'For you, Penny.'

Penny took the cube and opened it carefully. 'Perfume, bless her.' Her blue eyes brightened along with her smile of appreciation as she took the top off the pretty bottle and sniffed the contents. 'Oh, it's beautiful. It must've cost her a fortune. Smell it, Mummy . . .'

'Mmm . . .' Dorothy gave a nod of approval before she stooped down to pick up another. 'And another from Linden . . . for Edward . . .'

Edward took the small package hesitantly, but made no attempt to open it, merely waiting for the next gift that came to hand to be doled out.

'Aren't you going to see what it is?'

'If you insist,' he answered reluctantly, and all eyes were on him as he unravelled the tasteful wrapping paper. After a second or two he withdrew a silver object. 'A cigarette lighter,' he beamed, and immediately placed it back in its box to avoid reading the inscription Linden had told him about in front of them.

'I asked her to come and see the hunt on Boxing Day,' Penny said, aware of Edward's discomfiture. 'But she said she wasn't sure. She said she didn't think it was fair that we should have to travel to fetch her with petrol rationing the way it is.'

'I'll fetch her,' offered Edward. 'There's petrol enough in my car. If you think about it she could stay Boxing Night as well, then she'd be here ready for work the following morning. That would save fuel as well.'

'But might not her parents have something to say about us depriving them of their only daughter over the Christmas holiday?' Hugh suggested. 'Let's face it, she spends an awful lot of time here already working for Father. Why should she want to come here during her Christmas holiday?'

'Because she enjoys our company?'

'If you don't mind my saying so, Edward, dear,' Dorothy interjected, 'you seem quite keen to enjoy Linden's company yourself.'

'I'm very fond of Linden, Mother.'

'And I suspect she's fond of you too,' Hugh said grudgingly. 'I always thought she was Penny's friend, first and foremost, as well as being Father's private secretary.'

'Yes, well I consider her my friend as well these days,' Edward retorted. 'You might as well all know that we've been writing to each other, ever since I joined the RAF.'

'Ah.' Dorothy glanced at Charles for his reaction before she turned back to Edward. 'Are you sure that's a good idea?'

'I don't see why not, frankly.'

'There's always the danger that it might develop into something more,' Hugh said.

'Danger?' Edward queried. 'You make it sound horribly undesirable.'

'It rather depends on the girl, I suspect, and her suitability.'

'Oh, I think Linden is eminently suitable – and if there's any likelihood of romance I certainly won't shy away from it.' Edward turned to his father. 'What's your opinion of Linden, Dad. She *is* your private secretary.'

'She's my private secretary because she works hard, is jolly reliable and very capable. I also happen to think she's a rather sweet girl, and quite delightful to behold. I can understand perfectly Edward's interest. So, if she and Edward see fit to write to one another while he's away, I certainly won't begrudge them their pleasure.'

'Thank you, Dad,' Edward said.

Hugh turned away and went to his room.

*   *   *

Gladys and Joe Woods were neither surprised nor resentful of the suggestion that their only daughter should be whisked away to the country home of Charles Burgayne for the remainder of the Christmas holiday. They had taken to Edward as if he was the son they'd never had. They were delighted for her, in their typically unselfish way. Linden had done well for herself, and her proud parents wondered whether there might be marriage at the end of it, the war and survival permitting. What more could they possibly ask for? The sacrifices they had made, in order to pay for her education and raise her above the mediocrities of the life they were used to, were paying off handsomely. Just think if the Burgaynes and the Woods should become related by marriage . . .

So Linden left them with a fond kiss, while Edward carried her small cardboard suitcase, bearing her clothes and toiletries, down the entry to his car.

At Kinlet Hall the Christmas festivities the family enjoyed were on a level completely new to her. Penny and Hugh played piano duets together with such gusto and technical expertise that Linden felt compelled to applaud enthusiastically. Dorothy Burgayne also excelled on the grand piano with renditions of Chopin, only to be followed by Hugh who changed the mood completely with modern pieces by George Gershwin. Then Penny sang, accompanied by Hugh, a song that she said was for Adrian; it was 'I Get a Kick Out of You', and Linden thought it seemed rather poignant in the context of his absence. After that, she was surprised when Hugh beckoned his fiancée Laura to his side at the piano and suggested she sing her favourite song. She obediently sang 'They Can't Take That Away from Me' with a stunningly mellow, jazzy voice, and delivered the song with surprising panache.

The girl has hidden talents, Linden thought. *She can't be stupid, so why can't she make more of herself and her talents? Furthermore, why can't she see through Hugh?*

Eventually the mood became more sombre as the entertainment gave way to talk of the war. Depressed by such talk, Dorothy Burgayne decided she'd had enough and decided to retire to bed. Charles followed not long after. Hugh poured himself another drink and offered Laura a top-up, since she too was drinking port.

'No, I'm off to my room, Hugh. It's been a hectic day and

I'm awfully tired,' she said. 'See you in the morning. Are you coming up, Linden?'

'Maybe it's time we all turned in,' Edward suggested. 'We'll want a clear head for the hunt tomorrow.'

'But you're not riding, are you?' Linden said.

'Gosh, no. I'm safer in a plane than on horseback, the way I ride,' he answered with a self-effacing laugh. 'And anyway, it wouldn't do at all to get myself maimed being thrown from a horse after the government has spent a fortune training me to fly fighter planes.'

She smiled. 'I'll see you in the morning then. Goodnight, all.'

Led by Laura, they went to their respective rooms, leaving Penny, and Hugh downstairs finishing off their drinks.

Linden shut the bedroom door behind her and went across to the window lit by the glow of the fire burning in the grate. She parted the curtains and peered out. The silhouettes of trees were just visible against the lighter night sky. *Who would believe we were at war?* she thought to herself. *It's so peaceful.* She let the curtain fall, and walked back across the room to the light switch and flicked it on, hoping no light was escaping into the night to be seen by marauding German aeroplanes. She opened her suitcase, hung up the clothes she had brought with her and found her nightgown. As she undressed, carefully hanging her dress and folding her underwear and stockings, she wondered whether Edward would risk coming to her room. Her heart pounded at the prospect. Maybe she ought not to put her hair in curlers that night, just in case . . .

Later, Hugh Burgayne left his bedroom and closed the door shut as quietly as he could. Laura's room was along the landing in the west wing of the house, and his intention was to pay her a nocturnal visit. It was a practice he'd employed for some time on those occasions when she stayed the night, and hitherto had proved perfectly safe and satisfying, for nobody was ever any the wiser. But then he remembered that Linden's room was in the same direction and he was seized by a befuddled impulse, fuelled by too much alcohol, to visit her instead. After all, she was a sight prettier than Laura, and so much more desirable. She might even welcome him into her bed; she'd been more socially amenable of late, and Edward's perpetual absence could hardly be satisfying for her.

To any onlooker, the exaggerated stealth of his movements to avoid creaking floorboards suggested that not only was he about forbidden commerce, but that the port he had drunk was taking its toll. He reached Linden's door in the darkness, the only light from the starry night sky entering through an oriel window. It was chilly and he shivered as he curled his fingers around the cold brass doorknob. She might have grown attached to his brave, heroic brother; they were writing regularly – or so he had declared – but she was certainly not yet secured, or even claimed. With Edward away for so long maybe now was the right time to turn her head. Maybe he ought to groom her, for the lengthy periods that Edward would be away; she was sure to feel the need from time to time. And how he ached to feel her warm, naked body wriggling in ecstasy in response to him.

But he hesitated. Was this quite wise, this creeping about the house to the bedroom of the girl who was also his father's secretary? What if he were caught? What if instead of welcoming him she screamed in horror and awoke the whole household? What a downright cad he would look, what a complete bounder. His sometimes warm, sometimes cool affair with Laura would be finally decided. His mother would be ashamed of him, as would his father. Linden would spread it around the works that he was a thoroughly lecherous beast. He would be a laughing stock, unable to uphold his authority as a director of the Blower's Green Steelworks.

Maybe it was the cold that was bringing him to his senses. In any case, he loosed the door knob.

Then, to his horror, he heard the creak of a floorboard and was sure the sound did not emanate from beneath his own feet. Instinctively, he darted away in the opposite direction to that from which the sound had come. His heart started pounding at his own rashness and the closeness of his escape. He hid behind a corner, waited, and watched. The almost non-existent light was just enough for him to see the ghostly, pyjamaed figure of Edward, creeping almost as stealthily as he had done . . . to Linden's room.

Things seem to have progressed beyond mere letter-writing, he thought, thankful that he had not done what he had so foolhardily set out to do.

* * *

In the new year two million British men between the ages of 19 and 27 were called up for military service. Among them was Hugh Burgayne, who suffered the indignity of having to visit Dudley Labour Exchange to justify his claim that he was in a reserved occupation as an executive director of a steel-works employing nigh on a thousand men in the borough, and involved in government contracts. If this plea was turned down, only then would he resort to declaring himself a conscientious objector, since he was aware of how much his father disapproved of that stance in the face of Edward's bravery. After due investigations, Hugh eventually learned that his plea had been accepted and registered. He could remain at work, doing a vital job.

That out of the way, he decided it was time to appraise his relationship with Laura Birch, and coldly ended the affair.

Linden's natural apprehension about the reliability of her monthly visitor was lifted, and she happily shared the news with Edward. She understood how the heat and urgency of their passion had removed from their minds all regard for the possible consequences. Next time, providing there was a next time, they really must take more care.

In early March Linden received a letter from Edward. She read with eagerness of his love and longing for her, but one paragraph contained news she had been secretly dreading. It read:

> *After months of perfecting slow rolls, stall turns, bunts, spins, dives and all manner of clever aerobatics, after hours in the air practising map-reading, low flying, night flying and high-altitude flying, I have finally got my 'wings'. Pretty soon now I shall be transferred elsewhere for practice in the chivalrous art of gunnery. I'm told we shall be sitting on the tails of other aircraft trying to blast away a little red cone trailing behind it. Sounds like fun.*

In April the slow, 'phoney' war, as it was being called, where nothing seemed to happen, was over when the Germans invaded Denmark and Norway, and British and French troops joined the battle, albeit somewhat ineffectually.

May brought with it Linden's twenty-first birthday. The

Burgaynes held a small party for her at Kinlet Hall and Edward, by prior arrangement, rang up and reversed the charges so he needn't worry about having sufficient coins. Penny related the latest news of Adrian before she handed Linden the receiver.

Linden smiled gratefully at her friend and a knowing look passed between them as she put the receiver to her ear.

'Hello, Edward . . .'

'Sweetheart, many happy returns of the day, and congratulations of course.'

'Thank you.'

'I just wish I could be there to share it with you.'

'I do too.'

'Did you realize you are old enough now to marry me without me having to ask permission from your father?'

'Yes, I know.' She warmed inside, her smile broadening to a contented grin.

'Well, at least you don't sound displeased at the prospect.'

'I'm not. Not at all.'

'Just sounding you out, sweetheart. Who knows what the future might bring?'

'Yes. Who knows,' she repeated guardedly.

'What's the matter, angel? Are you tongue-tied?'

'It's not that,' she said quietly into the mouthpiece, turning away from the rest of the family.

'Oh, I see. How stupid of me. You're surrounded by large, flapping, Burgayne ears, aren't you? So when I tell you how much I love you, you can't say the same to me.'

'Not without some . . . you know . . .'

'Embarrassment?'

She laughed. 'Exactly . . .'

'How's rationing affecting you?'

'We'll none of us get fat, that's certain. Anyway, what's the latest with you?'

'We finish our gunnery training in a few days, then I'm being posted.'

'Where to?'

'No idea yet.'

'Are you likely to get some leave soon?' It was an uncontroversial question, of general interest.

'That I couldn't say, either. Do you miss me terribly?'

'You know I do,' she answered quietly.

'Oh, darling, I miss you too. This dratted war . . .'

'I know.'

'But write tomorrow, eh? As soon as I know my new address I'll send it to you.'

'OK.'

'I do love the way you say that.'

'So you say.'

'Does anybody else want to say hello while I'm on the line? You'd better ask.'

'Hold on . . . Does anybody else want to talk to Edward? . . . Yes, your father does.'

'Bye, then, darling. Write soon. I love you.'

'Bye.' With a self-effacing, half-guilty smile she handed over the receiver to Charles.

A few days later, on 10 May, Holland and Belgium fell to Germany's *'Blitzkrieg'*. It was obvious that France was next, and Britain would certainly follow. On the same day, Winston Churchill assumed the role of Prime Minister of an all-party coalition government after Neville Chamberlain, utterly discredited, was forced to resign against a background of military and political catastrophes. By 21 May, German troops had reached the River Aisne in France and were only sixty miles from Paris. Their advance was so rapid that by the twenty-seventh they had taken Boulogne, cutting off British and French troops. The only escape was via Dunkirk, and British soldiers were bombed and machine-gunned as they waded out towards ships and small boats that had been despatched in their thousands to retrieve them.

The battle for Britain was on.

Fifteen

On 6 June a visitor called unexpectedly at Kinlet Hall, a day when Linden was working there. Jenkins let in a highly agitated and emotional woman who asked to see Penny. Amelia Farrance was in her late forties but usually looked as if she was in her thirties. But not today. Today, she looked older than her years and careworn. As soon as Penny saw her she knew the news would be traumatic.

'Oh, Mrs Farrance,' she cried, a horrified look on her otherwise pretty face. 'Oh, dear God, no . . . It's Adrian, isn't it?' She rushed to the older woman and threw her arms about her, both for support and to give consolation. Tears were suddenly flowing uncontrollably.

'I just had a telegram to say he's been wounded in action, Penny,' Mrs Farrance said quietly, endeavouring to remain calm. 'But we don't know to what extent. It happened at Dunkirk while he was trying to board a boat.'

'Where is he?'

'In a hospital in Brighton. As I opened the telegram I feared the worst. Thankfully, he's only wounded. I hope and pray it's not too serious.'

'I'm going to see him, Mrs Farrance.'

'Oh, Penny, I hoped you might, and I'm so glad. I wish I could come with you, but I really couldn't bear to see him suffering, maybe even fighting for his life. It would crucify me.'

'Depending on how bad he is, maybe I could even arrange to get him here as a convalescent.' Penny's face lit up at the prospect.

'Maybe. Who knows?'

'Thank you so much for coming to let me know, Mrs Farrance. I really do appreciate it.'

'I had to come,' the older woman replied. 'It hardly seemed appropriate to let you know by phone.'

'Gosh, no. Do come into the breakfast room and I'll get Jenkins to make you a cup of tea. My mother's at a Red Cross meeting this morning, but I want to get the all-clear from Daddy for a trip to Brighton. Come on through . . . please . . .'

Penny led Amelia Farrance into the breakfast room, sat her down and ordered a pot of tea. 'If you'll excuse me a moment, Mrs Farrance.'

Penny raced to the room that had been converted into Linden's office.

'Are you all right?' Linden enquired, looking up from her work. 'You look as if you've seen a ghost.'

'Oh, Linden. Adrian has been wounded. He's hospitalized in Brighton. I'm going to see him. Would you mind very much going with me?'

'Of course I will, Penny, if it's all right with your father.'

When Penny awoke, she looked about her, bewildered. She was in a strange place . . . a hospital ward . . . It took a second to assimilate where she was and what had happened. She was on a chair, but she had been leaning forward, and her head was resting on a bed.

Adrian's bed.

So the nightmare was real . . .

Linden was there too, still asleep, sitting up in a chair on the other side of the bed, also drained after the long train journey. Outside in the corridor Penny heard footsteps, and the door swung open.

'Good morning, nurse . . .'

Nurse Radcliffe stopped when she reached the bed. 'Miss Burgayne,' she answered gently, overflowing with sympathy. 'You're awake. How does he seem?'

'I dropped off to sleep, Nurse Radcliffe,' Penny answered apologetically

'You've been here all night with the poor lad, haven't you? Why don't you go for some breakfast, or a mug of tea or something?'

'What time is it?'

'Just after seven.'

The nurse inspected Adrian, whose upper body was swathed in bandages through which blood had oozed, and was probably still oozing. She took his pulse. He had not regained consciousness and the doctors had told Penny that after losing part of his right shoulder and his arm his chances of survival were slender. It was on learning this that Penny had decided she must stay with him until the end, appalled as she was at the extent of his wounds and at witnessing his dear life ebbing away.

'Have you got time to stay with Adrian for a few minutes?' Penny enquired. 'I badly need to have a wash and clean my teeth.'

'I shall be on the ward all the time, Miss Burgayne, so I shall be able to keep my eye on him,' the nurse replied kindly. 'Why don't you wake your friend and the two of you go together?'

'Thanks awfully.'

Penny roused Linden, who awoke equally disorientated. The groans of other soldiers and seamen, also suffering atrocious wounds, quickly reminded her of her whereabouts.

'How is he?' Linden whispered, rubbing her eyes.

'No change, apparently.' Penny sighed heavily. 'Come on, we're going to freshen up and find a mug of hot tea. Some breakfast too, if you can stomach it. Nurse Radcliffe will keep an eye on Adrian.'

Linden got up from the chair and rubbed her neck where it ached from its unusual and uncomfortable angle of repose. She stood up, smoothed out the creases in her skirt and picked up her handbag. She looked again at poor Adrian, and was horrified. If this should be Edward . . .

'I'm so sorry to inflict all this on you, Linden. You really are a true friend. It must be beastly hard on you, too – I know you must be thinking about Edward. I know you must be dreadfully worried.'

'I try not to think about him ever getting hurt, Penny. Otherwise it drives me mad. Come on then, and we'll spruce ourselves up.'

Penny telephoned Amelia Farrance. Briefly she told her about Adrian's condition, preparing her as gently as she could for what was inevitable. Then they went to the boarding house Linden had sought on their arrival in Brighton, not knowing how long their stay might be.

They washed and changed, each drank tea and ate a piece of buttered toast, before hurrying back to the hospital.

'I've been to see him a few times, Miss Burgayne,' Nurse Radcliffe reported on their return, 'but there's no sign of him coming round.'

'Think I should try to wake him?' Penny asked.

'Why don't you just try talking to him?'

Penny nodded and smiled sadly. She sat beside the bed and leaned across to Adrian. 'Adrian,' she whispered. 'Adrian, can you hear me? . . . There's so much I want to tell you, if only I thought you could hear me . . .' She took his hand, which was lying on top of the counterpane and stroked it lovingly. 'Do you remember the very first time Edward introduced us, Adrian? I fell for you straight away, you know, but you'd always got that silly Juliet around you, hadn't you? Yet I knew that some day we'd be together . . . that I'd marry you. Well, hear this, my love – I'm going to marry you when you get out of here . . . So please get well . . . Please . . . I don't mind how long I have to wait. I'll wait for ever if need be, only please, please get better. And when you're feeling better I'll get you sent to Kinlet Hall to convalesce, and I can look after you myself . . .'

Linden heard it all and was touched. Tears ran down her cheeks.

'Last night, you know, Linden, he came round for a second or two.' She sniffed and wiped her tears on her handkerchief. 'He looked at me and smiled. I'm sure he knew me. At least, that's what I shall keep telling myself. He hasn't come round since, though. But he seems a bit feverish now . . .' She sighed again, resignedly. 'Feel his forehead, Linden. Tell me what you think.'

'Oh, I'm no doctor, Penny,' Linden answered quietly. Nevertheless, she felt Adrian's forehead. 'Yes, he does feel hot. Maybe we should open a window.'

'I need a cold damp cloth to put on his forehead to help cool him down.'

Just then, a doctor appeared. He ordered the screens to be put around Adrian's bed and asked Penny and Linden to leave them for a few minutes.

Outside in the cool air of morning, Penny laid her head on Linden's shoulder and wept bitterly, while Linden consoled her in her arms. Linden understood what her friend was going through, the mixture of emotions that were tormenting her;

and she pitied her. The tighter Linden held her and the greater the manifestation of her sympathy, the more Penny cried. But she was not the only woman crying in Britain over the loss of a son, husband or lover, wrought by the evacuation of Dunkirk.

'Come on, Penny,' Linden said kindly. 'Let's go and sit on one of those benches over there. Have a good cry and talk to me. I'm sure it helps, just talking.'

'Oh, Linden, I want to die . . .' Penny snivelled into her handkerchief, trying in vain to stem her weeping. 'I love him so much,' she cried.

Her crying came in plaintive wails during which Linden said nothing, merely holding her, allowing her friend to weep to her heart's content. Linden figured it was something Penny must do to get Adrian Farrance out of her system, though it might take months and even years, for she had set her heart on this man as her lifelong partner.

When they returned to the ward, the same doctor saw Penny and asked her to step into the office.

'You are not the wife of Captain Farrance, are you?'

'No, Doctor, he doesn't have a wife, but I am his fiancée,' she answered. 'Captain Farrance's mother was unable to come owing to family commitments, and she asked me to come instead.'

The doctor nodded his understanding. 'So I may speak frankly and in confidence?'

'Of course.'

'Captain Farrance is in a desperate condition, I'm afraid. I am firmly of the opinion that gangrene has taken a hold – hardly surprising in view of the length of time between his getting wounded and receiving any medical treatment. I'm dreadfully sorry to have to say this . . . but I think you should prepare yourself and his family for the inevitable. I really am most terribly sorry, Miss Burgayne.'

'How long has he got, Doctor?'

'Hours . . . at most.'

'Oh . . . bugger!'

Captain Adrian Farrance passed away at ten minutes to one that same afternoon, and Penny Burgayne wept over his lifeless, blood-stained body.

Some days later at his funeral, wracked with grief, Penny

decided that she needed to do something for other men
wounded and maimed in this war.

'Linden, I've got to make myself useful in this damned
war,' she announced. 'I'm going to train to become a nurse.
Convalescents are already being sent to Kinlet Hall, and
my help would be welcome there, as well as being useful
experience.'

'I think that's a brilliant idea, Penny,' Linden concurred.

Events moved on. The Germans took Paris, and Hitler himself
was present when the French signed their surrender, gloating
over their humiliation.

So Britain was left to fight on alone. The Luftwaffe attacked
shipping in the English Channel, and decided that Britain's
air superiority must be destroyed before the kingdom could
be invaded. Thus began the systematic bombing of airfields.

Linden received a letter from Edward dated 15 August 1940,
part of which read:

My own darling Linden,

*I am writing this letter late into the night. I was going
to leave it until morning, but I can't sleep because I am
so hyped up after the day's events, that I feel I must
write to you about them and get them out of my system,
or I'll never sleep.*

*The day started insignificantly enough, but just after
midday all hell broke loose and we heard the scream of
a Spitfire squadron as it took off. My squadron was
scrambled soon after and we took to the air under no
illusions as to the significance of what this all meant,
because two squadrons of fighters are not sent up unless
something drastic is afoot.*

*You can imagine how extremely apprehensive I was.
Strangely enough, though, my fear was very soon
replaced by sheer excitement, with the result that I have
never in my life been as alert as I was then. Having your
wits about you on occasions like this is what saves your
life. Once over the sea we maintained a height of about
12,000 feet and were about twelve miles out when we
first spotted a closely-packed formation moving across
the sky towards us in a swarm. Of course they were too*

far away to identify, but as we closed in it was obvious it was bombers escorted by fighters. I wanted it to be all over and done with, as if some time-slip could take place and pitch me out at some point in the future beyond the inevitable action. Yet another part of me was eagerly anticipating the encounter, for this is exactly what I have been trained to do.

Anyway, the instruction came through my headphones that I, along with the rest of my section, was assigned to deal with the fighters. So we split up and six of us headed towards them; and I must tell you we were grossly outnumbered, about four to one. No matter; one of my team, Harry Drummond it turned out, scored a hit first time and I saw a Messerschmitt 109E blow up into a ball of flame, showering scraps of metal through the clouds below. My first thought was 'There but for the grace of God go I.' At that, the rest of the German fighters forsook the bombers they were escorting, leaving them at the mercy of our two other sections. Suddenly, a Messerschmitt passed right in front of my very nose and I followed him, firing tracers after him. And guess what – I got him. He didn't burst into flames but down he went. I must explain that in the split seconds all this was going on, moral principles didn't matter and the thought crossed my mind that this could feasibly have been the very pilot who had hit Adrian with machine gun fire while he was trying to scramble on to a ship. If so, justice had been done, and I was not in the least sorry, only anxious to inflict more damage.

That's what I felt then, but looking back now from the peace and comfort of my bed, I do hope that the pilot, whoever he was, made it safely to the relative tranquillity of the sea below and was picked up. You see, he is somebody's son, fiancé or husband and if he was killed, that somebody will be grieving over him, in much the same way that Penny is still grieving over Adrian. Not only that; it could so easily have been me.

Of course, when we landed we were all so excited. In all, our squadron and the Spitfire Squadron combined, had twenty confirmed downs and a dozen unconfirmed, with dozens more damaged. We escaped with no losses.

*If nothing else, the escapade confirmed our superiority
in the air, both in expertise and machinery . . .*

The Luftwaffe continued the aerial bombardment of Britain
and Edward was invariably involved. Then came the news that
Biggin Hill airfield had been heavily bombed, and was un-
serviceable except as a base for one squadron only. Edward
was thus posted to Exeter where his squadron was needed to
protect the important naval bases at Portland and Plymouth,
as well as to intercept bombers on their way from occupied
France to sorties over Wales and the north-west of England.

Flying Officer Edward Burgayne, recently promoted, settled
himself in his bunk before tea with a fountain pen and writing
pad, and began writing his letter to his beloved sweetheart.
No sooner had he finished the first paragraph than they were
scrambled again. It was half past five in the afternoon. Edward
checked on all his men, some of whom were showering, some
asleep, but within five minutes the squadron of eight Hurricanes
was airborne.

'Control reports thirty-plus bandits approaching west of
Penzance, currently headed northwest over the Celtic Sea from
Brittany,' Edward heard in his earphones. 'Probably on a
bombing mission to Liverpool or Manchester.'

The voice was calm, measured and reassuring, and Edward's
keen eyes searched the empty sky. Visibility was good. The
air was frosty, the sky was cloudless with the moon and stars
clearly visible. The squadron flew north-west across the Severn
estuary in tight formation at about fourteen thousand feet,
scanning the void around them for sight of the invading formation. The enemy were reported to be over the Celtic Sea, that
area of the eastern Atlantic bounded by the southern portion
of Ireland, Wales and Cornwall. The extreme western coast
of Pembrokeshire was just about visible in the darkness. A
few minutes after, a voice screamed into Edwards headphones.

'Bandits at ten o' clock. Bandits at ten o' clock. About two
miles.'

With practised precision, the eight Hurricanes turned as one
towards the enemy aircraft.

'Approach from the side,' yelled the squadron leader. 'I
repeat, approach from the side.'

The rest of the squadron understood. This tactic would give

the eight Hurricanes a better chance of damaging the German bombers with prolonged bursts of machine-gun fire strafed along their fuselages.

Suddenly, the curtain of night was torn apart by tracers, then by the brilliant flash of a German Dornier DO215 bomber that had taken a direct hit on a fuel tank. It exploded spectacularly. The sight obviously deterred the other bomber pilots, for they peeled off to the south-west towards the south of Ireland, jettisoning their bombs into the sea. Within seconds, however, the Hurricanes were caught up in a frantic dogfight with a dozen or so accompanying Messerschmitts.

Edward dived and turned round again in a tight circle. He decided to follow the fleeing bombers and inflict as much damage on them as possible. This he did alone for some fifteen minutes, crippling several Dorniers, but unable to discern exactly how many, if any, he had 'killed'. But then the cooling tank in his Hurricane exploded as he took a hit from return fire, and with a frightening judder, his cockpit began to fill with smoke and fumes.

Edward cursed. He yelled into his radio to his colleagues, but there was no response, only crackles. His first thought was to bail out. Mentally, coolly, he rehearsed the procedure. He could hardly see for the smoke filling the inside of the cockpit, but he decided to stay aboard his aeroplane and try to bring it down safely. There was nothing below him but the ice-cold sea, and the prospect of spending even a minute bobbing up and down in it did not appeal. It did not appeal at all. Better to try and nurse the aircraft back, so he turned around, leaving the remaining Dorniers in peace.

It was then that he realized his compass had also been damaged, and was permanently stuck indicating south-west. His only option was to lose height and speed and try to open the cockpit to clear it of smoke and so aid visibility. His breathing was not so much of a concern, since routinely pilots wore oxygen masks. He descended to two and a half thousand feet and was limping along at something less than a hundred miles an hour. The fumes were making his eyes water despite the goggles. He managed to open the cockpit canopy and the savage, deafening onrush of air sucked the fumes out. At last he could see out.

But where was he?

He decided it didn't matter unduly where he was; his priority was to land, just so long as it was on British soil. He determined the North Star through the open cockpit and believed that if he took his bearings from that he should find himself over Wales. There, he would try to find somewhere suitable to land . . . but in total darkness it would be difficult, more especially on unfamiliar ground – always provided the engine of his Hurricane would hold up, or that he would not run out of fuel . . .

But the Hurricane's Merlin engine was seriously overheating and spluttering alarmingly. It seemed impossible to eke sufficient power out of it to enable him to fly much further. Perhaps he would have to ditch it into the sea after all. He wished then that he had paid more attention to inflating the Mae West he carried, in which he would have to drift until he was picked up.

Then, below him, he saw the dim outline of the coast as white waves lashed almost luminously in the moonlight against the shore. Relief swept over him. Wales. All that remained was to look for a landing spot – a field, a clearing of some sort, or even a stretch of road.

He saw the lights of what had to be a farmhouse, and by the moonlight he could just about discern fields. *A good thing in this instance that not everybody observes the blackout*, he thought. He let down his undercarriage. The Hurricane spluttered and backfired as he descended. A hedgerow whizzed past beneath him and his altimeter told him he was about a hundred feet above sea level. But how far above sea level was this ground he was only just clearing? Down, down, gently down . . . He felt the bump as the wheels touched the ground, then the instant, sickening impact as the undercarriage struck something solid and immovable. The Hurricane embedded itself nose down into the hard, unforgiving ground, and Edward lost all consciousness under the impact.

Sixteen

'Tell me, Linden,' Charles Burgayne said as he lowered his spectacles and peered over the top of them with soulful eyes, 'have you received any letters from Edward in the last few days?'

At once Linden felt sick. Edward's lack of letters had been a concern. She normally received one every day, but neither that fact, nor the sudden absence of them was something she wished to mention to his family just yet.

'I haven't had a letter for three days,' she replied. 'Some days I know he doesn't even get time to write. On the other hand, some days I get two letters. Why? Are you very worried, Mr Burgayne?'

'It was his mother's birthday yesterday, as you know, but she didn't receive a birthday card from him. Unusual. He's normally so particular. Nothing in this morning's post either. Needless to say, she's fretting like billy-o.'

'Yes, it is a worry, isn't it?' she agreed, trying to keep the angst out of her voice. 'But I'm sure he's all right. He said to me once – if this is any comfort, Mr Burgayne – that because telegrams travel pretty quick, no news is good news.'

He smiled with gratitude at this simple logic. 'He's quite right of course. But I know he's been heavily involved in protecting the Naval bases at Portland and Plymouth and beyond. I'm also aware we've lost a few pilots in the prosecution of it.'

'I know,' she said softly.

He sighed deeply, which induced a coughing spasm. 'Ah, well, Linden. Back to business. Where were we?'

Linden looked down at her notepad. 'Shall I read back what you've said so far?'

Within a mere hour of that fretful conversation, when

Linden was typing the letters in her office at Kinlet Hall, she was aware of a commotion in the hall. Jenkins had answered the front-door bell and was yelling for Mr Burgayne in a distraught cry. Alarmed, Linden left her desk and descended the broad, winding staircase, looking down on a frantic scene. Her heart went to her mouth as she ran down the steps.

'There's a telegram just come, sir,' Jenkins warbled anxiously as Charles approached looking sick with worry. She handed over the missive as if it were on fire and she didn't want to be burned by it.

'My God,' Charles breathed as Dorothy and Penny also arrived in the hall together. He looked up and saw Linden rushing down the stairs, and she in turn saw how pale he had suddenly become.

'Do open it, Charles,' Dorothy snapped with unwitting impatience.

Charles fumbled with it, his hands shaking. Unable to complete the task, he handed it to Linden.

'Read it to us, please, Linden.'

Also trembling with apprehension, she tore open the telegram and took a deep breath. 'Oh, dear God, it's from the Air Ministry . . .' She glanced at Charles; his face was an icon of suffering.

'This damned war,' he groaned. 'Go on, Linden.'

'It says, "Regret to inform you that your son Flying Officer Edward Robert Burgayne is reported missing following air combat operations on Jan. 14 1941."'

Linden slumped into the chair behind her. Her head was suddenly swimming, her thoughts a whirl of confusion, angst, doubt and hope. Above all, hope, however vain. Was this the largesse that fate doled out for falling in love with an airman during time of war – never knowing from one minute to the next whether he was alive or dead? If so, it was not fair. It was not fair at all. She had found her perfect mate in Edward, they were deeply, deeply in love, but already, too soon – much too soon – she had lost him. They'd had no chance of any life together – a life that had promised to be brimful of joy, blessed with children, and ultimately grandchildren. But, evidently it was no to be. That promise of settled contentment had been cut down in its prime, savaged, mutilated, as Edward had most likely been savaged and mutilated, also in his prime, fighting for his country and his country's principles.

An arm went around her. It was Penny.

'All is not lost yet, Linden,' she said kindly, quietly. 'It only says he's missing. It doesn't say he's dead. He may yet show up.'

'But what if he's hurt, like Adrian was, and nobody finds him?' Linden blubbered. 'I can't bear to think of it.'

'Nor can I,' Penny replied. 'Not again.'

The following day, after a sleepless night during which Linden wept most of the time, she was back in her office at the steelworks, defying the war and the ineffable distress that it inflicted. Work was the antidote to grief, and she intended to immerse herself.

The telephone on her desk rang, diverting her from thoughts of pain and disaster, and she answered it with her usual politeness.

'Linden, it's Penny.'

Linden sighed with trepidation. It was good to hear Penny's gentle, cultured voice. Penny understood perfectly what she was going through and would offer sympathy and support.

'Hello, Penny.'

'Are you feeling absolutely dreadful?'

'Oh, Penny, you, above all people, know what it's like. I'm so miserable, I want to die.'

'Well don't pop off just yet. We've just had some superbly brilliant news.'

Linden's puffy eyes widened at this unexpected lifeline. 'Oh, God. You mean he's OK?'

'It would seem so. We received a telegram five minutes ago from the Irish Military Police, so I rang you at once to put you out of your misery. He's safe and well – in Eire—'

'Oh, thank God.' Linden closed her eyes and more tears squeezed out; but these were tears of relief. 'But what on earth is he doing in Ireland?'

'God only knows. Anyway, Linden, you can rest easy now, knowing he's all right.'

'How soon before they release him?'

'We don't know that yet.'

'Gosh, Penny, I'm so relieved. He's alive and well after all.'

'And I daresay they'll allow him to write to his nearest and dearest soon. So keep an eye out for the postman, Linden.'

'Lord, I can't believe it. I don't know if my nerves can stand all this. Worrying myself stupid most of the time, then in the depths of despair because I think he might have been killed. Next thing, I'm up in the air again knowing he's all right.' She uttered a little laugh of joy.

'Will you let Daddy know, and Hugh?'

'Oh, course I will. I'll go and tell them straight away. Then I'm going to treat myself to a cup of tea. I need one, I can tell you.'

'Then I'll leave you to it for now.'

'Bye, Penny. And thank you so much for letting me know so soon.'

'I couldn't bear to think of you suffering any longer than necessary. I'll let you know if we hear anything else.'

'Thanks.' Linden put the handset in its cradle and left her office with a happy smile. At the door of Charles Burgayne, she knocked and eagerly awaited the response to enter. Still she would not have dreamed of entering his office without being bidden.

At once he saw the change in her demeanour; the lovely smile had returned, and his heart leaped.

'What is it, Linden?' he asked expectantly.

'It's Edward.' She put her hands to her face in a gesture that indicated the mixed emotions of relief and incredulity, and tears trembled on her long lashes. 'He's shown up, alive and well. He's in southern Ireland. Can you believe it? Penny just rang me.'

Charles stood up and grinned. 'Thank God . . . Oh, thank God,' he cried. 'What wonderful news.'

'I know, I know. I'm so thrilled.'

'Sit down a moment, Linden . . .'

She duly sat down on the chair in front of his huge desk, and wiped her tears.

'It's so obvious by your reaction to all this how deeply you feel for my son.'

'Oh, I can't deny it, Mr Burgayne.' She looked into her lap, avoiding his eyes.

'And I would assume he feels as deeply about you.'

She nodded, looked up at him again, her eyes wide and candid and moist again with tears. 'Yes, he does. Every bit as deeply.'

'And of course you miss him.'

'More than anybody will ever know.'

'Tell me, honestly, Linden. How long have you both felt that way?'

She felt herself blushing at what might be regarded as an intrusion into her personal affairs, but she continued smiling and looking into the eyes of her employer, who was after all the father of her sweetheart. 'Since the summer of 1939. About eighteen months.'

'You don't hide your feelings easily, Linden. And neither does Edward. His mother and I both suspected romance was blossoming.'

'But you don't mind, do you, Mr Burgayne?'

'Mind? Good God, no. Frankly, I'm delighted. If you are patient enough to tolerate what will seem like an endless wait, I wish you every happiness.'

Linden grinned contentedly; this was another monumental step forward. 'Thank you so much, Mr Burgayne. You have no idea how much that means to me. You see, Edward didn't want it to be known we were in love in case you all disapproved of me.'

'Why would we disapprove of you, Linden?'

She shrugged. 'Because I'm a nobody. Because I'm from an ordinary working-class family. Because I'm just an employee of the Blower's Green Steelworks.'

'But there's nothing wrong with any of those things.'

'I'm so glad you think so. But some people might think differently.'

'Then to hell with them, Linden, that's what I say. I have no such petty prejudices. We're not in the nineteenth century now, you know. Times have changed. You are a necessary, admired and welcome member of the Burgayne household. Always remember that.'

'I'll never forget it, sir.'

'Oh, and, *miss*,' he said returning the address with mock formality, 'less of the "sir". In future, when we're not in front of employees, do call me Charles.'

*   *   *

Shortly after, another telegram arrived from the air ministry confirming that Edward had been found and was being held in an internment camp. Linden began to worry again when she received no immediate letter from Edward. Perhaps they didn't allow prisoners to write to their families, she thought, and her concerns then were that he was being mistreated. But just a few days later on her return home from work, her mother smiled as she waved a letter teasingly.

'Postmarked Eire,' Gladys announced, as proudly as if she herself had been Edward's mother.

Linden grinned, doffed her overcoat, and took it eagerly. 'Thank God.' She ran upstairs to her bedroom with it and, as she threw herself on to her bed, she tore open the envelope, opened up the sheets of paper folded inside, and began to read.

Linden, my one true love,

I can only stress how sorry I am that I have not been able to get a letter posted to you earlier. They tell me here that my family have been notified of my incarceration, and I know Penny would have informed you. I won't bore you with details of how I lost my way – that can wait until another day – but I simply had to let you know that I am all right, and actually being treated rather well.

I crashed my Hurricane in a field while landing in the dark, and the impact knocked me unconscious. Miraculously, the only injury I received was a bruised shoulder. I actually thought I was landing in Pembrokeshire, but I was miles out because my compass had stuck.

Anyway, it was not until I came to and heard a gabble of voices all speaking with an Irish accent, telling each other excitedly to get me out, that I began to realize where I was. A group of people were inspecting me with flash lamps as I hung by the webbing in the open cockpit of my upturned plane. Then, when they could see I was still alive and awake they decided to act. The farmer, whose land I had crashed on, together with his family and the entire neighbourhood I think, were extremely hospitable. They took me into their house and fed me royally before they sent for the police, who then decided I was a military concern and handed me over to the Military Police. I was then taken away and locked in a cell, yet still treated kindly by my captors, and not without some sympathy.

I am now in permanent residence at a place called K-Lines, an internment camp at the Curragh of Kildare, very close to an IRA internment camp, a race course and a golf course. Already, there are several RAF pilots and crews here who have made the same blunder as I have and mistakenly or unavoidably landed on Irish soil. There are some German airmen too, who have been here almost since the start of the war. No doubt we shall be a happy band once we get to know each other better.

I have been informed during my interview with the camp commandant, Colonel McNally, that we are allowed certain privileges not countenanced in a POW camp, namely, we are allowed out during the day on parole, and may actually play golf! Astonishing, but true. Restrictions have been lifted here recently and we are even allowed to go to any of the three cinemas and pubs locally, and wearing civilian clothing at that. The purpose of civvies, I am informed, is so as not to stand out among the locals, some of whom dislike the British and are sympathetic to the aims of the IRA. Some, on the other hand, hate the Germans and support the British. Of course, we are kept under surveillance, but they tell us it is for our own protection. Apparently, we have to buy the civilian clothing ourselves – they don't give it us – but my salary will be paid as usual, and I should be able to get hold of something very soon.

I know and understand how relieved you will be that while I am interned here I am unable to fly. On the other hand, I feel such a fool for getting myself into this mess, and am longing to get back into a Hurricane and do my bit.

The weather here has been dreadful, by the way, with deep snow and drifting. Just before I arrived there was an escape attempt, but I think the weather impeded the chances of the chaps getting too far, and they were all

*rounded up after a day or two. Still, you are obliged to
try. It's expected that you will.*

*I have no doubt that my letters to you will be censored
before they are allowed to leave here, so maybe we
shouldn't bore the poor chap who has to read these
missives with endless admissions of love and devotion.
They go without saying. Suffice to say, my darling, that
I love and need you dreadfully, and I ache to be with
you again. But how long that will be really depends on
how long this war is going to last. I see no end in sight
yet, but if Germany invades England I urge you to try
and leave the country for your own safety and go to
Canada.*

*Meanwhile, be patient, my darling, as I have to be
patient.*

My love always,
Edward.

Penny's training to become a nurse was at the Royal Hospital
in Wolverhampton, but when at home she and Linden would
help out with the convalescents at Kinlet Hall. It was there
that a young army lieutenant named Harry Wilding came to
Penny's attention. Harry had served in France, as Adrian had
done, and had also been wounded as he'd tried to flee Dunkirk.
One day she asked him whether he happened to know Adrian,
but he shook his head. Sorry, he said, he did not, but the likelihood was remote with so many thousands of men involved.
He was, however, ready and willing to talk about his experiences, while he, in turn, listened intently while Penny told
him about Adrian.

Harry seemed a decent and likeable chap, cheerful and good-
looking, and Penny was drawn to him. He was from Bury St
Edmunds in Suffolk, an only son of a reasonably well-to-do
family . . . and unattached . . . and she began to spend more
time with him, watching him recover from his wounds, ready
to lead a normal life in future. This was exactly what Penny
needed. Another man to think about helped her overcome the
pain of losing Adrian.

But, inevitably, the time came when Harry was considered
well enough to leave Kinlet Hall, and the day prior to his
departure Penny walked with him in the grounds, hand in

hand. It was a bright March day, typically blustery, and the daffodils, in full bloom, were abundant.

'One question I've avoided asking you, Harry,' Penny said as she lead him through the hole in the old limestone wall towards the fish pond.

'What's that, pet?' He looked at her admiringly.

'Will you have to rejoin your unit?'

He shrugged. 'That, I don't know. I reckon I'll have to be assessed first. If they think I'm fit enough, then yes, I guess I shall have to go back and do a bit more.'

She sighed, looking despondent, and he guessed what was troubling her.

'Look,' he said kindly, 'I'll do my best to keep out of the way of any German bullets, but the trouble is, you don't generally see 'em coming.'

'I told myself, Harry, that I would never get too attached to a soldier or a sailor or an airman again, yet here I am, head over bloody heels once more. If you do have to go back please don't get yourself killed. I don't think I could stand it.'

'Chances are, if I am recalled,' he said, 'they'll give me a sit-down job in some stores or something. I might not even have to go abroad again. How would that suit you?'

'That would suit me perfectly, Harry,' she replied, beaming. 'Especially if we could be together from time to time.'

'Then give me a kiss and let's set a seal on it. In the meantime, you won't forget to write to me, will you?'

'Of course not, silly.'

They stopped walking to hold each other and concentrate on a decent kiss. It was good to feel a man's lips lingering on hers again, and he kissed so terribly nicely. The promise of greater closeness was tantalizing, for Penny missed the tenderness of intimacy as well as the passion.

'And don't you get falling for some other service chap who comes here convalescing,' he said as they broke off their embrace. 'You kiss so nice, I couldn't stand the thought of somebody else having the benefit.' He grinned appealingly. 'D'you hear?'

She smiled back, a light of mischief shining from her blue eyes, as in the old Penny. 'If I do, you'll be the first to know.'

'Ah, you mean the last, of course. That's the way it normally works.'

'If I'd already found somebody else by the time you knew, then it wouldn't matter one way or the other,' she teased. 'But I promise I won't,' she added.

Seventeen

'Can I ask a huge favour, Charles?'
'No harm in asking, Linden. What is it?'
Linden had just entered Charles's office at the works and was standing holding the edge of the door, her head tilted towards it appealingly. She had allowed her dark hair to grow of late and she wore it swept up and pinned in a roll, a style that enhanced the youthful set of her neck.

'I'd like a few days holiday if you can spare me . . . I had in mind the week after Easter . . .'

'Oh? Well, I daresay we can arrange for somebody else to fill in for you. But why now? The weather's likely to be inclement for a month or two.'

She shut the door behind her and approached his desk. 'I have a special reason, Charles . . . I want to go to Ireland. I want to see Edward.'

'Ireland? Will you be allowed to see him?'

'I don't see why not. He says the rules are very relaxed. Besides, you could use your contact in Dublin . . .'

He smiled at her enterprise, full of admiration at her natural grasp of how useful it was to have contacts, however acquired. Since Edward's internment, the British Representative in Dublin had written to Charles, telling him of the visit he'd made to K-Lines in order to meet Edward, and to reassure him that his son was indeed in good health and being well looked-after. They had subsequently kept up a correspondence, letters which Linden had typed.

'Sir John Maffey. Yes, I suppose I could ask him to try and ensure you a safe and easy passage.'

'Would you, Charles? Please?'

'Of course I will.'

'You see, Edward is allowed out of camp whenever he wants.'

'So I understand.'

'I'm sure he'd be able to meet me. Apparently, they even encourage the internees to take Irish girlfriends to keep them happy and not homesick.'

Charles smiled. 'Some internment! But where would you stay?'

'No idea. An inn or hotel, I expect. There must be some.'

'So when do you want to leave for Ireland?'

'Say the Tuesday after Easter Monday.'

'Get your pencil and pad, Linden. Let's get a letter off to Sir John Maffey in Dublin and ask him to pull a few strings.'

Linden grinned contentedly. 'Thank you so much, Charles.'

On Tuesday 15 April, armed with a travel permit and a copy of a letter from the British Representative in Dublin, Linden stood on the deck of a ferry bound for Belfast, braving the wind and the rain as it lashed her face. She was thrilled, and not a little nervous, at the prospect of actually being with Edward soon, of being able to touch him, able to hear his voice, feel his lips on hers again after so long. Gulls wheeled above, their persistent shrieks a perfect contrast to the roar of the restless, surging sea. Other passengers eyed her curiously – a young woman travelling alone across the Irish Sea – for this journey was not without its dangers, not least from the mines that were regularly dropped by the Luftwaffe around the approaches to Belfast. Nor did she look Irish; she looked English to the core. But she was prepared to risk all, and willingly, for the chance of being with the man she loved, however brief their encounters might turn out to be.

As she leaned against the wooden rail, relishing the buffeting of the wind, the rain, and the pleasant smell of the sea, they came within clear sight of land. Soon the ship was ploughing a wide stretch of water known as Belfast Lough, lined with docks, shipping, towering cranes and gantries, although some had clearly suffered damage from recent bombing. In the distance stood church towers and steeples, and forests of tall chimneys volleying smoke into the steel-grey sky. She strained her eyes against the rain for a better glimpse, and saw the green hills of Ulster beyond.

The ferry docked and Linden stepped on to the quay. She enquired how far it was to Great Victoria Street Station. On

the way the clouds parted and the low sun burst through clear
and strong, leaving everything tinged with grey-orange. At
length she arrived at the station and bought a return ticket for
Dublin. The next train was not due till half past ten that night
owing to wartime rescheduling. So she decided to buy a newspaper, the *Belfast Telegraph*. Trains hissed and clanked as they
pulled in and out of the station, dropping and collecting passengers. Feeling hungry, she made herself comfortable in the
station cafeteria where she bought a ham sandwich and tea.
She looked at the clock: it was ten minutes to eight. While
she waited she read the newspaper from cover to cover.

At length, the blue liveried locomotive of the Great Northern
Railway Ireland pulled in, hauling it's line of carriages. No
sooner had Linden stepped inside one and placed her suitcase
in the luggage rack than she heard the sound of air raid sirens.
She'd read in her newspaper the criticisms and invective of
how Belfast had been so unprepared for the bombing raid
around the docks and the shipbuilding yards just a week earlier.
Another reason why this journey was so fraught with danger.
How fortunate that she'd already left the docks, for the
Luftwaffe was evidently back for another strike.

The train, which was full, pulled out of the station slowly,
its blue locomotive huffing and rasping under the strain. Linden
glanced at the other passengers, all of whom looked apprehensive. Just as apprehensively, she lowered the window in
the door of the compartment and looked up. After the earlier
rain, the sky was clear but for some drifting cumulous clouds.
A three-quarter moon reflected off them and lit up the landscape. It was then that she heard the unmistakable low drone
of aircraft, many of them, even above the sound of the gasping
locomotive.

'Did you hear the sirens this morning?' somebody asked
sitting close to her.

She turned to see if the person was talking to her. Evidently
he was; a man in his fifties wearing a trilby and mackintosh.

'This morning? No,' she replied. 'I didn't arrive in Belfast
till this evening.'

'English, hah?'

She nodded and turned back to the window.

'You should be used to the sirens then. But we're not.

Leastwise, we weren't. We thought the Germans had forgotten about us, but we should've known better. We've got the Harland and Wolff shipbuilders, and Short's aircraft factory here.'

'I know,' she said sympathetically, but didn't know what else to say. Nor did she feel like encouraging conversation with a stranger right then.

The train travelled on, away from the confines of the city, and Linden continued to gaze out of the window. She didn't mind the wind buffeting her. The insistent drone of aircraft overhead continued. Belfast was in for it tonight, and no mistake. Lucky for her she had left, but oh, those poor people who couldn't . . .

Then, behind them the sky lit up. Linden stood and thrust her head out of the window to watch in horror. The first wave of German aircraft were dropping flares which came tumbling down out of the darkness to bathe the whole city in a blindingly brilliant silver glare, creating artificial daylight that slowly turned to orange before it died.

But before the light faded droves of aircraft followed, raining incendiaries, high explosive bombs and lethal parachute mines on to Belfast. Even from the train, travelling away from the city, you could hear the incessant barrage of explosions and anti-aircraft gunfire in one long, rumbling, grim cacophony of terrifying sound. Even the ground beneath them seemed to be transmitting its resulting tremors through the floor of the moving railway carriage. There would be hundreds of casualties.

As the train snaked on, meandering southeast beyond Portadown, you could see the incandescent sky to the northeast aglow with the fires and explosions that were ripping through Belfast. It was a sight that nobody who had witnessed it would forget.

It was well after midnight when the train arrived at Dublin's Amiens Street Station. Linden left the station, uncertain what to do next. Because it was late she decided it would be best to try to find somewhere to stay the night. It then dawned on her how bright the streets were – of course, there was no blackout here. Across the street she saw what looked like a hotel and headed for it. The sign above said 'North Star Hotel'. At least she might be able to get a good night's sleep there before continuing her journey.

Next morning, refreshed, she returned to the station and caught the next train to Newbridge. She was getting closer to Edward and could soon be in his arms, and these thoughts began slowly to nudge aside the nightmare of last night.

Once in Newbridge, she took a taxi to the Curragh, and her heart began pounding when the taxi stopped at the gates of a compound that was enclosed by high barbed-wire fencing, with a sentry box at each corner.

This had to be the K-Lines internment camp.

And this was where Edward was.

She paid the driver and thanked him, then braced herself for this extraordinary visit, not knowing what sort of reception she was likely to get at the building facing her, which looked the best place to start. It was a guard house.

'I'm a visitor from England to see Flying Officer Edward Burgayne.'

'Yer cum ter see Burgayne?' the guard replied with a friendly grin. 'Well, I'm sartain sure he'll be glad to see somebody as pretty as yourself, miss, dat he will. Yer see dat hut over dere . . .' He pointed. 'Ask for him in dere. Boi der way, dat's a luvly hat you be wearing.'

Linden smiled graciously. 'Thank you.'

She made her way to the next hut and repeated her request.

'What's your name, miss?'

'Linden Woods.'

'Linden Woods,' he repeated, as if savouring the words on his tongue. 'For the sweet love o' Mary, dat's a pretty name, so 'tis. I tort so when I saw it writ down.'

'You've seen it written down?'

'Ah, to be sure, we been told to expect yer, miss – in a memorandum.'

Sir John Maffey had been helpful then, according to that snippet of information.

The guard looked up at her and smiled politely. 'Would you like to go inside Mr Burgayne's hut, or will I send Mr Burgayne out to yers?'

A choice. Goodness. What to choose . . .

'Maybe if you could send him out to me, please . . .' He might be surrounded by other internees inside, which might inhibit him.

The guard left his post, and she waited.

It seemed like an age, having come this far, but it was actually no more than three minutes before she spotted Edward through the rows of intimidating barbed-wire fences, being escorted by the guard and another officer. He was smiling and, as far as she could tell from where she stood, he looked well, and was dressed in civilian clothes. Her heart was pounding like mad at the prospect of being so close to him again after all this time. Slowly – it seemed an age – he approached. When he saw her standing waiting he grinned, waved excitedly, and quickened his pace. Eventually he reached her, and they embraced, while the two Irish servicemen tactfully retired to their hut.

'Look at you,' Edward said, almost breathlessly. 'You look wonderful.' He held her at arm's length and simply admired her.

'Oh, Edward.' She gave him another hug. 'I can't believe I'm actually here.' She felt self-conscious under his gaze, but tears of joy were making her eyes tingle, and she gave them a wipe with the back of her glove. 'Gosh, just look at me. I'm such a sentimental old fool, aren't I?' she added self-effacingly.

'It's absolutely wonderful to see you. I'm so grateful you made the trip, you can't imagine.'

'I just had to come. Ever since you wrote and told me you were allowed out I've been hatching my plan. It seemed such a waste not to come.'

'I was petrified for you when I heard about the bombing in Belfast.'

'I know,' she said. 'Thankfully, we just missed it. As the train pulled out of the station you could hear the drone of the planes coming over. There seemed to be hundreds. We saw it all unfold from the train. It really was terrifying. The poor people of Belfast . . .'

'We heard about it first thing. Thousands of houses flattened, apparently, hundreds dead. Of course, they don't know the full extent yet. But it's one reason I want to get back in my Hurricane – to pay the bastards back.'

'Anyway,' she said with a smile, wiping the watery remnants of tears, 'I haven't come here to discuss the war. You look well. But they're treating you well, you say.'

'We're treated more like guests than prisoners.'

'So it's not so bad?'

'Actually, it's rather boring. But not now you're here,' he said warmly. 'How long can you stay?'

'Till Saturday. Then I'll have to start back. Goodness knows what problems there'll be when I get back to Belfast.'

'Well, let's worry about that nearer the time. For now let me show you the Curragh. Have you found somewhere to stay?'

'No, I've only just arrived.'

'Then we'd better get you fixed up. We'll go out.'

'We're leaving the camp?'

'Of course.'

'What a funny old prison,' she remarked.

He laughed. 'Well, all I do is sign a parole slip, and Fanny's your aunt. One of those chaps who came out with me is the parole officer.' He turned around and called to one of the men in the guard house. 'Captain Fitzpatrick . . .! May I have a parole slip, please?'

As Edward walked towards him, the parole officer grinned and took a slip from a drawer in the desk before him. 'To return by what time?' he asked, looking Linden up and down. 'Shall we say o-two hundred hours?' he suggested with a knowing look.

'That sounds perfect. My wife would like somewhere to stay for a few nights, Captain. Can you recommend anywhere in the Curragh?'

'Wife, did yer say? To be sure I didn't know you were married, Flying Officer,' the guard said incredulously.

Edward winked at him in response.

'Try Osberstown House, Flying Officer,' Captain Fitzpatrick said. 'Yer must've been to the hunt dances there.'

'Of course. Along the river Liffey, near Naas. Thank you, Captain.'

'Now, if you'll just sign your parole slip . . .'

'Of course.' Edward duly signed it. 'We'll need a taxi, Captain.'

'For the sweet love o' Mary!' Captain Fitzpatrick exclaimed satirically, 'D'yer tink dis is a holiday camp?' He smiled, willingly picked up the telephone and dialled a number.

Within five minutes a taxi appeared at the main gate.

When they had departed, Captain Fitzpatrick picked up the telephone again and rang Osberstown House to let them know that an English internee from K-Lines, Flying Officer Edward Burgayne, was on his way with his young wife, and asked them to ensure she was given the best room available.

On the way to Osberstown House Linden said quietly, 'Given all this freedom, why don't you just walk away, catch a train and escape? You could be in Belfast before they even missed you. It's not as if you are wearing your RAF uniform. It would be the simplest thing.'

'But it's really not that simple, darling,' Edward answered, taking her hand as they sat close to each other in the rear of the taxi. 'You saw me sign that parole slip. Well, it's a conditional release from the camp, a privilege granted by the Irish authorities. As officers of the RAF we are obliged to honour its terms and return by the time noted on that slip. Failing to do so brings dishonour not only to ourselves, but to the RAF and our country.'

'But there's a war on, Edward,' Linden protested logically. 'And the RAF needs you – not to mention me.'

'And, believe it or not, if I escaped while on parole, the authorities in Northern Ireland would only send me back here. I could even be court-martialled for breaching the terms of my parole.'

'So your word is your bond.'

'Spot on, sweetheart. Absolutely. However . . .' He smiled and she saw again that disarming twinkle in his eyes that she loved so much. 'On the other hand,' he went on, 'we are also obliged by the RAF to do all in our power to escape and return to our squadrons, but only while we are interned and not on parole. In fact, when we are not on parole the Irish expect us to try and escape. Hence all the barbed wire.'

'What a cock-eyed world this war has created,' she sighed. 'So you couldn't even return home with me? And I thought I would so easily persuade you . . .'

'I only wish I could, my love. It would be my dream. But it just ain't possible.'

As they drove through Newbridge Edward asked the taxi driver to stop, and he got out of the car.

'I won't be a minute,' he said.

Five minutes later he returned, a broad, self-satisfied grin on his face.

'You look pleased with yourself,' Linden remarked.

'Oh, I am,' he answered smugly. 'You'll see why presently.'

Presently they arrived at Osberstown House, a large, sym-metrical Georgian country house with distinctly classical Greek design features, including a pillared portico. Linden paid the taxi driver and watched him drive off.

'Here, take your gloves off,' Edward said with the familiar gleam in his eye as he put her suitcase on the ground.

Linden looked at him puzzled.

'Now give me your hand . . . No, your left hand.'

She did as he asked; he slipped a ring on her finger, and she looked at him with all her love in her eyes.

'I'm afraid it's only a curtain ring,' he said apologetically. 'It's what I stopped to get in Newbridge. But so long as they see what looks like a wedding ring they'll be happy. The folk who own this place are Catholics . . .' He winked an eye at her, and she nodded as she realized his ploy.

The young man on the desk at Osberstown House glanced at Linden with approval and at Edward with envy, but he smiled and bade them welcome as he handed him the key to a double room upstairs. Once inside it, Edward again put down Linden's suitcase. At the window he parted the curtains and looked out on to the rolling countryside of Eire and the River Liffey meandering through it.

'Come here,' he said softly.

She stood before him looking alluringly coy, and he took off her hat, then her coat which he tossed on to a chair in a swish of material. They fell into a passionate embrace, lips hungry for each other. It was so wonderful to feel her in his arms again after so long, to be alone with her and nobody else in the world to trouble them. They were together again at last, and it barely seemed possible. It would not have been possible, but for Linden's vision and her unwavering deter-mination to make it happen. She could have been killed in the attempt, too, had her train not left Belfast only minutes before the blitz.

'Let's get undressed,' he whispered.

They did so quickly, and dived naked between the sheets.

'Gosh, it's cold,' she remarked. 'Maybe we should've asked for a hot water bottle.'

He grinned contentedly. 'Absolutely no need, Sweetheart. I'll very quickly warm you up. It's a promise.'

As the cold of the sheets enveloped her she snuggled up to him, and he luxuriated in the warmth and the silkiness of her skin against him. He held her tight; their lips met again and they kissed passionately, instantly entwined in earnest mutual desire. There was scarcely time for foreplay, scarcely any need. He rolled on to her, pressing himself urgently against her as he sought entry. She gripped his buttocks and, with a little gasp of pleasure, felt him slide gloriously inside her with such blissful sweetness.

'Oh, Edward,' she sighed, relishing the luscious sensations that were flowing through her. 'I've wanted you so much . . . so much . . . If only you knew . . .'

So this is how it is for a husband come home from the wars after long years, Edward thought as he wallowed in the love she eagerly bestowed on him. The feel of her slender but curvaceous body beneath him, her eager response as he moved inside her was delightfully familiar, yet because it had been so long since last they'd made love, somehow it all seemed so new, so fresh and unexplored. It was a sheer, invigorating joy.

Afterwards they lay silent in each other's arms for some time, perspiring contentedly. Outside the sun was shining and its reflections off the River Liffey were dancing on the ceiling of the bedroom. Edward absently watched this frolicking display for some time, while Linden lay with her eyes closed, a look of serenity on her beautiful face.

Thank God he had Linden. As well as being an enthusiastic lover, she was obviously exceedingly brave and resourceful to have made this trip. It was a measure of the strength of her love – strength she would need when he announced his intentions, which were noble enough, to his family.

'Linden, are you awake?'

'Yes, I'm awake, my love,' she answered softly. 'I was just thinking how lovely it would be to wake up next to you every morning.'

'On that very topic, I want to ask you something'

'Ask away,' she sighed, and turned to face him.

'Will you marry me when all this is over?'

'Will I marry you?' She raised her head resting it in her hand, her wrist propped up on her elbow, her hair dishevelled from their passion. 'Oh, a thousand times, yes, Edward. Of course I'll marry you.'

'We'd be happy, wouldn't we, you and me?'

'Happier together than we are apart, that's for certain.' She fingered the patch of sparse hairs that were sprouting on his chest.

'I just worry about how my folks will take the news.'

'Edward, you don't have to worry about that.' She leaned forward and kissed him on the lips, her breasts brushing his chest tantalizingly. 'We have your father's blessing.'

'We do? How come?'

'Because I told him how it is between you and me. He was delighted. He wished us well.'

'You never said in any of your letters.'

'I would've. But now I've told you to your face. A much better way. Don't you think?'

'I know what I do think, Linden, my gorgeous little poppet . . . I want to make love to you again.'

'I think I want you to, Edward . . .'

Eighteen

The Friday night before she left for home, there was a dance in the ballroom at the Osberstown. It was obvious to Linden that many of Edward's chums here had already made friends with local girls, some of them well-heeled socialites and members of the Kildare Hunt, because they danced and laughed with obvious familiarity. However, some girls were accompanied by their mothers, who kept an ever watchful eye.

Through the haze of cigarette smoke and wafts of scintillating perfume, Edward introduced Linden to other internees, Douglas Newport and Herbert Ricketts, crew members of a Blenheim bomber, who had been forced to bale out over County Donegal: Aubrey Covington, tall and good-looking with an equally handsome moustache; and Paul Mayhew from Norfolk, a Hurricane pilot who had got lost over Ireland in circumstances similar to Edward's.

'How long have you been at K-Lines, Paul,' Linden enquired, making conversation.

'Since early October last year,' Paul replied. 'Though I did make one unsuccessful attempt to escape in January – just before Edward arrived, I think. But the weather was foul – against us more than any other factor. However, I've not at all given up the idea, I can assure you . . .' He took a quick drink from his glass. 'I too have a rather charming fiancée back home who I'm dying to see.'

'And you, Aubrey?' Linden asked. 'You obviously haven't escaped yet.'

'But not for want of trying,' he answered. 'I try regularly, but I must say, it is rather comfortable here. I'd just as soon be in the officers' bar as risk being shot at.'

'You have a bar, as well as all this freedom?' she asked incredulously.

'Well-stocked at that,' Aubrey replied. 'I must say I've rather developed a taste for Guinness.'

They were standing near the ballroom's bar which was tended by a tall blonde girl whom they called Josephine.

'How do you get along with the German internees?' Linden asked Douglas Newport, over the sound of some quickstep the band was playing.

'We don't have much to do with them,' Newport answered, hugging his beer glass to his chest. 'For obvious reasons. They come in here sometimes, but they tend not to mix with us. In any case, it wouldn't do to get too chummy.'

The group chatted about this and that for some time; then Edward, itching to get close to Linden, leaned towards her and said, 'They're playing a waltz, sweetheart. Dance with me.'

She put her glass down on the bar and held her hand out to him with a smile, and they stepped on to the chalked parquet floor together.

'So what do you think of my fellow airmen?' he asked as they set off in a whirl around the slippery floor.

'They all seem terribly nice,' she answered, hearing herself and at once aware that she was beginning to sound like them. 'But I do feel sorry for them. They're all itching to get away from here.'

'Me included,' he admitted. 'All the time there's talk of escape. They're always discussing ruses – where to dig tunnels and all that. But Paul – you know, the Hurricane pilot from Norfolk – he's the leader of our escape committee, if you can call it that. I believe he's got contacts.'

'Shall you try and escape, Edward?'

'They'll have a job to hold me back.'

'But do be careful, darling. I'd rather you were here and still in one piece than at home and in several bits.'

He laughed.

'Actually, I've got something to tell you, Linden,' he said, pressing himself against her and with a dreamy look in his eyes.

'What?'

'I've manage to get special parole. I don't have to report back till tomorrow night.'

'Oh, Edward!' Her eyes were wide with elation, and looked heartbreakingly beautiful in the subdued light of the Osberstown's

ballroom. 'Is that what was in the bag you brought with you –
overnight things?'

'Toothbrush, comb, shaving tackle. If you can stand to see
me in the same clothes tomorrow . . .'

'Oh, but, Edward, that's brilliant.' Suddenly there appeared
a hint of devilment in her eyes as she looked up at him. 'Shall
we slip off early?'

He laughed happily at her saucy suggestion, delighted at
her utter lack of prudishness, her lack of inhibition. She was
one in a million. 'I wanted to suggest the same myself but
was a little reticent. I'm pleased as Punch you did.'

'And could you come with me as far as Dublin tomorrow?'
she asked.

'That's my avowed intention.'

'Oh, Edward.' She hugged him tight. 'I love you so much . . .'

That night was made all the more delectable, all the more
passionate, because it was wrested from the peculiarity of
their circumstances. Edward, the RAF pilot who was interned
in a benevolent sort of prison where, incongruously, he was
free to come and go as he pleased, but not allowed to return
home while aching to do exactly that; Linden, the resourceful,
romantic girl who needed to know that her man was thriving,
and who was unshrinking in her intention to make the absolute
best of their limited time together. It had been a magical week,
an unforgettable experience and she regretted nothing, save
the horrors she had seen perpetrated on Belfast. Yet, inevitably,
the time came when she and Edward had to part.

As he had promised, he travelled with her to Dublin, leaving
Osberstown House early, so that she could catch the ten o'
clock train to Belfast. They said their goodbyes on the platform at Amiens Street Station, and even more goodbyes as
he hurried alongside the train as it gathered speed, keeping
up with Linden at one of the open windows, until he ran out
of platform. Then she craned her neck to see him waving,
until eventually he disappeared from view behind a hoarding.
It was a perfect cue for tears to fall again.

Linden, when she could get her mind off Edward and think
about her journey, was apprehensive about how things would
be in Belfast. Work was already underway clearing up, folk
were smiling, and she admired their unconquerable spirit.

All that remained now was to hope that the ferry was still operating.

Charles Burgayne was eager to see her as soon as she arrived at the office on the Monday morning.

'How is he, Linden?' He sounded anxious.

'He's extremely well, Charles,' she said brightly, to immediately allay any fears.

'It's very gratifying to hear it. Very gratifying.' He coughed. 'And you enjoyed yourselves?'

'We had a brilliant time. I wouldn't have missed it for the world. It was lovely to see Edward again. He sends his love, of course.'

'His mother will be delighted to hear it.'

She told Charles at length about the very favourable conditions of Edward's internment, and the extent of his liberty – except, of course, for his extended parole and their subsequent night of passion at Osberstown House – and explained, too, the concept of the parole system that allowed it. 'But I wouldn't be at all surprised if some of them don't try and make a break for it,' she remarked. 'They're all desperate to get back to their squadrons and fight. I just hope they don't get shot in the process.'

'I have the feeling it would be better for all concerned if he were to remain there, Linden,' Charles said with a solemn frown. 'We took a hit here at the factory the other night, you know,' he said. 'Did your father tell you?'

'Yes,' she replied. 'It's lucky nobody was killed.'

'Well, one or two hurt, but not seriously, thank God. Number Two Melting Shop is out of action meanwhile.' He shrugged resignedly and coughed again. 'We're lucky we haven't been hit before. As a steelworks, we're a legitimate target.'

Spring turned slowly and surely into summer and, along the way, the Germans pushed the British out of Greece. London suffered the worst air raids of the war so far. The hitherto indomitable spirit of Londoners seemed to weaken under the ferocity of the attack. In May the German battleship *Bismarck*, reckoned to be unsinkable and the terror of Atlantic shipping, was finally destroyed after a three-day chase across the ocean from Greenland. German troops, wearing New Zealand army uniforms, invaded Crete, but were repulsed largely by New Zealand troops, as well as British and Greek forces.

Significantly, in late June, the Nazis invaded Russia.

On Monday, 30 June, Linden was at her desk at the steel-works when she received a message from the telephonist that a telegram had just arrived for her. She hurried to collect it, her heart in her mouth, sat on a chair in the reception hall and opened it gingerly. Her mind was suddenly swimming with possibilities that it contained bad news about Edward. But logic rapidly took over. It could not be. The authorities would have sent any bad news to Charles, his father, his next of kin. This must be good news, and from Edward himself. Heartened, she unfolded it and read it.

'Am in Belfast. More later. Meanwhile don't write. Please tell family. Edward.'

Excitedly, she ran to Charles's office and burst in unceremoniously, waving the telegram.

'It's from Edward,' she gasped breathlessly. 'He's in Belfast. It can only mean one thing – he's escaped.'

Charles stood up, astounded. 'Are you sure?'

'Why else would he be in Belfast? He's across the border. It stands to reason he's escaped.'

'May I see?' He held his hand out for the telegram and she passed it to him. As he read it a smile spread over his face. 'I do believe you're right, Linden. So what do we do now, I wonder?'

'We wait,' she suggested. 'He says, "More later." Maybe he'll ring.'

'Maybe I should ring the Air Ministry to see if they know anything about it.'

'I wouldn't,' she said assertively.

'You wouldn't?'

'No, because it could draw attention to it. If they start investigating, it might jeopardize his chances.'

Charles looked at her with admiration as he rubbed his chin pensively. 'You're a canny girl, Linden, and I think you may be right. But waiting . . .' He coughed. 'Not knowing . . .' He coughed again.

'I know.'

'Still, I agree, we should make no ripples, just in case.'

She nodded. 'Just in case.'

*   *   *

The waiting seemed interminable. Days passed with no word and no clue as to what had happened to Edward. Linden was beginning to imagine all sorts of horrendous possibilities: that he'd been recaptured and sent back to K-Lines; that the RAF had sent him back; that he'd been shot; that he'd been run over by a bus; that it had all been some sort of cruel joke.

Then, magically, on the following Sunday evening, after nearly a week of anxiety, she answered a knock on the veranda door, and through the glass she saw him standing there, a perfect grin on his manly face. She rushed to open it, and flung her arms around his neck.

'Oh, Edward . . . Edward . . .' Tears of joy tingled in her eyes.

'My angel . . .'

'So you did escape, after all.'

'Nine of us got out. Six of us made it.'

'How? How did you do it.'

'Later. Kiss me, Linden. God, I've missed you.'

They kissed, ardently and long.

'Come in and see mum and dad,' Linden said to Edward as they broke off their embrace. She took his hand and turned, leading him inside.

'Look who just happened to be in the neighbourhood,' she said joyously to Gladys and Joe, who were sitting listening to the wireless and had not heard the knock on the door.

'Well, I'll be buggered!' Joe exclaimed, getting up from his chair and offering his hand. 'It's young Edward. Thank God you'm all right, my son – our Linden's been worrying herself daft over thee . . . Turn the wireless off, Glad.'

Glad did as she was bid.

'It's good to see you again, Mr Woods. It's great to be back.' He turned to Gladys. 'Mrs Woods . . . Lovely to see you again.' He bent down and kissed her filially on the cheek.

'So you escaped that concentration camp,' Gladys exclaimed. 'Good for you. I never did trust them Irish. You only have to look at that swine de Valera to see what a crooked so-and-so he is.'

Edward grinned happily. 'Well, it was hardly a concentration camp,' he said. 'More like a holiday camp, to tell you the truth. But I'm glad to be out of it. I'm glad to be back in England.'

'I'll put the kettle on, eh? I bet you could do with a cup of tea. I know I could.' But she hesitated, standing by the door to hear more of Edward's exploit.

'When did you get back?' Linden asked.

'About three this afternoon. I was taken to London for a couple of days before I was allowed home. Dad collected me from the station.'

'Sit yourself down, son,' Joe invited, 'and tell us how it all happened.'

'It was all too easy really,' Edward responded as he pulled a chair from under the table and sat on it. 'We'd planned it all very carefully, of course. The top and bottom of it was that we'd been to the races, and some of us had had a jolly good day—'

'The races?' Joe queried, incredulous.

'Yes, Dad,' Linden butted in, rolling her eyes. 'I forgot to tell you there's a race course next to the camp, and they're allowed to go.'

'Well, on our return, we all pretended to be the worse for drink, a condition not at all unusual among us, I have to confess. Later, while we played cards, we pretended to drink more, with lots of empty bottles around us to enhance the effect. So when the guards came to check on us later they were lulled into a false sense of our security, so to speak. At bedtime some of our lads asked to go to the parole hut with the excuse that they wanted to send a telegram, and of course the guard complied. While they were taking their time composing it, two other chaps – with perfect timing – returned from parole, signed in, and together we overcame the guards. We didn't knock them about, of course, they were thoroughly decent chaps. All that remained was to get through the outer perimeter fence. Well, our appointed leader, Paul Mayhew – you remember you talked with him, Linden – had managed to get hold of a pair of wire cutters from somewhere – I told you he had connections. In seconds we were through, and out on to the golf course.'

'Golf course?' Joe said, incredulous.

'Yes, Dad, I forgot to tell you – they were allowed to play golf as well.'

'Glory be! I wouldn't mind being shut up in that camp meself.'

'And that's it, basically,' Edward continued. 'Once outside we split up, of course, and most of us managed to get to Belfast by one means or another. I've seen Paul since in London, and he hid up in a tree for about twenty hours, he reckoned, before he crossed the border.'

'Who else made it?' Linden asked.

'Ricketts, Newport . . . You met those chaps at the Osberstown dance. The others you didn't.'

'So who didn't make it?'

'Poor old Covington, for one. You know, the tall, good-looking chap with the moustache. The others I'm not sure about. We only planned for six to go, but nine went in all. Opportunists, the other three who saw their chance to go, and tried their luck. You can hardly blame them.'

'Well, what a story,' Gladys said. She was still hovering by the door ready to scurry to the brew house to fill the kettle. 'I'll make that tea . . .'

'No, wait, Mrs Woods. There's something else I have to tell you, that you'll be interested to hear.' He looked at Linden and she saw that delicious look in his eyes again. 'When Linden came to Ireland I asked her if she would marry me.' He reached out to where she was standing, close to him, and pulled her on to his lap giving her a hug around the waist. 'I have no idea whether she's mentioned it to you, but anyway, she said yes.'

'Our Linden!' Gladys exclaimed, emotionally. 'You never said. How come you never said?'

Linden shrugged. 'There didn't seem any need, Mum. Edward was interned and he might have been there for years. There seemed no point in everybody raising their hopes when it looked like being a long wait.'

'Anyway,' Edward pressed. 'With your blessing I hope, I intend to apply for a special licence while I'm home, and I hope that within a very few days we shall be man and wife.'

'This week?' shrieked Linden excitedly. 'Gosh, Edward, You really do know how to spring a surprise. Will it be a church wedding?'

'I hope so.'

'Gosh, I'll have to see if I can buy a decent wedding dress. Do your mother and father know? And Penny, and Hugh?'

'Oh, yes, I've announced my intention.'

'And?'

'And they're delighted. We shall hold the wedding supper at Kinlet Hall. All that remains is to fix the day and book the vicar.'

Nineteen

On the arm of her father, who was as proud as any man had a right to be, Linden walked into the cool dimness of the lovely sandstone church of St Mary in Enville, to meet Edward. Following her was Penny, content to be the solitary bridesmaid, her reward for the hours she had spent helping to organize this wedding. Edward stood awaiting his bride, looking pleased with himself and undeniably handsome in his steel-blue RAF uniform. He turned to greet her and gave her a broad, happy smile as she reached his side, and she felt her heart pounding hard. Linden's beautiful eyes misted with emotion, but tears did not fall.

Yet how quickly the ceremony seemed to pass, as if it was all a dream. One minute she was making her vows, the gold ring was firmly on her finger, she was lifting her veil and tilting her face to receive Edward's smiling kiss. Then, before she knew it, she was in the vestry signing the register – signing her name, Linden Woods, for the last time. She was surrounded by people, being kissed, hugged, having her hand shaken, and was aware of a perpetual smile on her face.

Then she caught the look of intense desire turned on her by Edward's best man, his brother Hugh, and felt uneasy. The same look he had given her at the fishpond: a look of ardent longing. But she saw something more in his eyes now, something darker; resentment, even jealousy, perhaps. At that moment Linden felt inordinately sorry for Hugh. He was an enigma, unfathomable, a troubled soul perhaps because of her. She had never really liked him; something about him made her flesh creep, though she'd never bothered to try to understand him. Now that she was his sister-in-law perhaps she should.

Back down the aisle again, but this time on Edward's arm. She was smiling radiantly as the organ triumphantly thundered out the Wedding March. People on both sides, smiling their admiration and best wishes, were watching her intently as she walked slowly past them with her handsome new husband. Then they were out in the porch, greeted by warm, summer sunshine, and a press photographer whose editor had heard of Edward's recent escapades and considered his escape from internment, just to return home and marry his sweetheart, was romantic and newsworthy.

More photographs by the private photographer whose services Penny had managed to secure. Linden's mother and father – happy, smiling figures – stood contentedly in the group along with Charles and Dorothy Burgayne as the photographer did his stuff. Then showers of confetti, tossing her bouquet to Penny, getting into a chauffeur-driven car and being taken back to Kinlet Hall.

'I think you look stunningly beautiful,' Edward said warmly as they sat close together in the rear seat. 'Considering what little time you've had to prepare for this, I'm astonished.'

She smiled up at him. 'I'm glad you think I look nice. I feel nice.'

Indeed, Linden seemed to have garnered even more slender beauty when she put on the white satin gown, the misty veil, the chaplet of orange blossoms, none of which had been easily come by, and which had cost a small fortune.

'So kiss me,' he said.

She kissed him.

'I do hope my mum and dad don't show themselves up,' she remarked, out of the blue. 'They're not used to the way of life you Burgaynes are used to, Edward.'

'Is it bothering you?'

'A bit.'

'They'll be just fine,' he reassured her. 'It's not as if they're bumpkins. I thought your mother looked very nice in her new outfit.'

'Oh, she does, and I'm glad you think so, but it was a real panic finding something that she liked that isn't too old-fashioned.'

'And your father,' he said. 'He looks very smart in his new suit.'

'It's not new, Edward. It's not even his. The trouble is, he's likely to broadcast it.'

Before long they were being driven up the long, sweeping

drive of Kinlet Hall. At the front door they alighted from the car, watched and applauded by Jenkins, the cook, servants hired just for the day, the convalescent servicemen who were sufficiently mobile – some of whom Linden was acquainted with – and their nurses. Linden and Edward stood, waiting to receive their guests, which amounted to immediate members of both families, and Harry Wilding, Penny's by now established beau, who was fully recovered from his wounds and conveniently on leave. They all returned, including the Beauchamps, long-standing friends of the Burgaynes. Linden knew of the Beauchamps – she knew quite a lot about them – but had never met them, so it was with some surprise that she learned they had offered to lend them their cottage retreat in Ludlow as a honeymoon hideaway.

'Edward is a lucky chap, my dear,' Harry Wilding commented to Penny when they arrived.

'No luckier than you are, Harry,' she riposted, tongue in cheek.

There were one or two moments when Linden couldn't help feeling slightly forlorn. Out of all these people only two were her own guests – her mother and father – and she felt they were uncomfortably out of their depth and was on tenterhooks herself because of it. She thought about her old flame, Ron Downing, and her half-hearted attitude towards him; she'd always known that he would never be the one she would marry. What would he think of her now, if he could see her?

Everybody was gracious, conversation was bright, the atmosphere was jovial. Charles Burgayne was unstinting in his efforts to make Gladys Woods feel welcome and at home, and Linden, content with this kind attention to her mother, was full of admiration for her new father-in-law. Her mother-in-law, too, Dorothy, was conversing with Joe as if they'd known each other years. It was all so gratifying.

The meal was served, there were speeches, but only a short one from Joe, who toasted the bride and groom, to which Edward responded in true tradition. Hugh, his eyes barely leaving Linden, gave his, rather more revealing speech as best man.

'I have to congratulate Edward on his choice of bride,' he began predictably. 'The very first time I cast eyes on Linden was the day she became an employee of Blower's Green Steelworks. I have to tell you that many pretty girls have graced those corridors of industrial power, and it was always a rule of mine, as a member of the family owning and running the company, that I would never ingratiate myself with any of them. But when Linden appeared that day, I asked myself whether, after all, it had been a rather silly and short-sighted imperative . . .' Polite laughter . . . 'Soon after that, Linden visited Kinlet Hall – to make up a four for tennis, I believe – a game she plays like a demon, by the way – and, to my absolute horror, I discovered that Edward had taken her for a flight in his Gypsy Moth, for in those days Edward was not the great pilot he has since turned out to be . . . Well, as you can see, they made a happy landing . . .' Another ripple of laughter and some applause. 'So now, on behalf of the very lovely bridesmaid, Penny, I give you a toast. I ask you to raise your glasses to Edward and Linden.'

'Edward and Linden,' they all repeated, and drank.

The time came for Linden to change out of her wedding dress and Edward to swap his uniform for civvies. Linden, her arm linked in Penny's, went up the stairs to the enormous bedroom that had been hastily prepared for her and Edward. It was to be their room, the bedroom where she would sleep every night, during and after her honeymoon, because it had been decreed that even when Edward returned to his squadron, she should continue to live there as a member of the Burgayne family. Oh, yes, she was a Burgayne now . . .

Linden kicked off her shoes. 'Would you unfasten me, Penny, please?'

Penny willingly obliged, releasing the hook and eye at the back of Linden's wedding dress, then the row of tiny buttons below it.

'Thank you,' Linden said as she slipped it off her shoulders and over her hips. 'You know, Penny,' she said, picking up the dress from the floor. 'I never expected to marry a man like Edward and live in a grand house like this.' She put the dress on a hanger and hung it from the picture rail.

'Your inferiority complex is rearing its ugly head again, Linden. Bloody-well stop it.'

'Oh, I expected to marry somebody, but I always pictured somebody more like that chap Ron Downing I used to see – you know – decent enough, but ordinary.' She slipped off her underskirts and stepped out of them. Her flesh-coloured stockings rendered her legs sleek and shapely. 'I rather saw myself in a little terraced house like ours – at best one of those new semi-detached ones, if he'd been lucky enough to get a good job – and then children perhaps. That sort of thing. But you know, Penny, I didn't fall in love with Edward at once. I liked him from the first, but he sort of grew on me.'

'I think that's the best way,' Penny remarked. 'That's how it was with Harry and me.'

'Yes, and I'm so happy for you, Penny.' She began to put on her going-away outfit, a light dress of printed silk, with a wide swinging skirt. 'Especially after the tragedy of Adrian's death. I thought you were never going to get over it, and there was nothing any of us could do to help you.'

Penny put her hand on Linden's arm in a gesture of appreciation for her concern. 'I know, Linden, that if you could have done anything you would've. You're the best friend I ever had, and you understand me well. Anyway, let's not dwell on all that. You were saying how you didn't fall in love with Edward straight away.'

'Oh . . . all I was going to say was, when we first met I could tell Edward fancied me, but I never really expected he'd fall for me the way he did, an ordinary working girl.'

'I told you, Linden, put your working-girl complex away.'

'Oh, I have, believe me. All the same, marrying Edward is the most unpredictable thing that could ever have happened to me. Astonishing, really.'

'Well,' Penny said, her pretty head tilted cannily, 'unpredictable it might have been, but hardly astonishing. Not only are you so *unconscionably* beautiful, but you're so outrageously modest with it, and so damned nice. Why shouldn't Edward fall in love with you?'

'I don't know. I'm just so happy he did.' She turned and looked at herself in the cheval mirror near the window. 'I'm ready now – how do I look?'

Penny rolled her eyes with envy. 'You positively glow, you absolute tart . . . Why can't I glow like you?'

Linden laughed happily. 'Oh, but you do, Penny. You just don't see it yourself.' Which was perfectly true. 'It's why Harry has fallen in love with you. And you'll glow all the more when you two get married.'

'Well, thanks for tossing me your bouquet anyway.'

* * *

Their destination was an old Georgian house, cleverly modernized, in Ludlow. Here, they would have absolute peace and security from intrusion, yet the convenience that a small market town offered. There was no maid, no gardener and no cook to serve them, but that was hardly likely to faze Linden, who had lived her life without such help.

When they arrived the low sun was already flaring behind a ridge of cloud. Edward drew up the MG before the brightly-painted front door and they clambered out. He took the key and opened it, then decided to carry Linden through, to her amused shrieks of protest.

'How kind of the Beauchamps to come and make it so pretty before we arrived,' Linden commented. 'They must have been here only yesterday.'

Edward lugged the suitcases upstairs to the large double bedroom, from which opened a dressing-room and a perfectly appointed bathroom. Together they opened them putting away the few clothes they had brought with them. While Edward went downstairs to heat some water she walked over to the windows, with their crisp white muslin curtains, and looked out over the green, undulating hills around Ludlow. The sky was beginning to darken towards the east. She stood there for some time, silently reliving the day, deliciously happy, for without question this had been the loveliest day of her life. After a while, she decided to change into clothes more practical, and began undressing.

Edward returned to the room as she was sitting at the dressing-table in only her underwear, brushing her abundant dark hair. It fell youthfully to her shoulders, shining, burnished, and her eyes looked so big and soft and inviting in the fading light as she saw him in the mirror and turned to greet him. He returned her welcoming smile, the warmth of desire bright in his eyes. He kicked off his shoes, doffed his jacket, his tie, his shirt, his trousers, his underpants and his socks, then scooped her up in his arms and laid her across the counterpane. She looped her arms around his neck then raised her bottom as he slipped her knickers down her legs. Running his hand over the silky smooth skin of her belly and down between the soft, dark delta to the south, he kissed her ardently. Then, he rolled gently on to her, and they made love leisurely, extravagantly, for the first time as man and wife.

Twenty

The following Thursday a telegram arrived at Kinlet Hall. It was addressed to Edward, but Dorothy opened it in his absence to ascertain its urgency. Penny decided that she should be the one to deliver it to the honeymooning couple at Ludlow, and drove there at once. Looking suitably glum when she arrived, she handed it to Edward who in turn also turned glum. He passed it to Linden, and her heart sank when she saw it was from the Air Ministry, requesting him rejoin his squadron at Exeter immediately.

'Damn!' she said. 'Why can't they leave us alone just a little bit longer?'

So the honeymoon was over, and with such cruel abruptness.

'Has Harry gone back?' Edward asked conversationally.

'He left yesterday,' Penny replied. 'Otherwise he would've come here with me. Look, while I'm here I'll help you tidy up before you leave.'

'Thanks, Penny,' Linden said, deflated after the contentedness that this taste of living with Edward had brought. 'I'll go up and strip the bed.'

'And I'll pack our bags,' Edward said sombrely.

Upstairs, back in the bedroom, Edward caught Linden and pulled her to him, put his hands to her waist as he looked dejectedly into her eyes. 'I'm so sorry I have to go, sweetheart,' he breathed.

'Duty calls,' she sighed with resignation. 'We knew this couldn't last forever. We both know it can't be helped, but it's such a pity they can't just pension you off as being out of practice and a danger to everybody once you've been interned in some foreign land.'

'After the time and money invested in training me? No such luck.'

'Shall you go back today?'

'Not a chance.' He smiled ruefully. 'I'm spending the night with you at Kinlet Hall. I'll go back tomorrow.'

She hugged him. 'Then more waiting for you to come home on leave . . . more worrying whether you're all right . . . or not . . .'

'I know, sweetheart.' He gave her another reassuring squeeze. 'It's the same for me. But I have a job to do, and I suppose the sooner I get back and do it, the sooner this damned war will be over. And when it is, we can resume our lives. We'll be able to put all this madness behind us.'

'I can't wait,' she sighed, and clung to him fearfully, as if this was going to be the last time ever.

Breakfast next morning was a quiet, sombre affair. It was to be their last breakfast together for some time and there was so much still to be said, so many more promises to be made. But both felt inhibited to say much more than 'Pass the marmalade, please, sweetheart', because of the presence of the others. Linden glanced at Edward meaningfully, and he would smile back at her with reassurance in his soft blue eyes. It was obvious that he too felt the same frustration.

Charles was to drive Edward to the station, accompanied by Linden of course. When breakfast was over Edward carried his suitcase to the Bentley, which had been readied outside on the sweeping driveway alongside Hugh's Jaguar, and put it down. Linden, meanwhile, was adding the final touches to her make-up upstairs. As Edward opened the boot of the car ready to stow his suitcase, Hugh appeared carrying a brown envelope.

'I just wanted to say goodbye, Edward, old man, and give you these . . .' He handed him the envelope.

Edward looked at his brother enquiringly. 'What is it?'

'Just some photos I took of Linden one spring day. I thought you might like to have them . . .'

'Thanks, Hugh,' Edward replied, his curiosity at once aroused.

'So, goodbye, old chap.' Hugh patted him fraternally on the shoulder, offered his hand and they shook. 'Keep out of trouble this time, and we'll see you on your next leave. In the meantime, I'll keep an eye on Linden for you.'

As Hugh slumped into his car and drove off, Edward opened

the envelope and pulled out the bundle of photographs, half-plate size, of Linden in various poses taken outdoors. He looked at the first. She was laughing contentedly, her pose relaxed, but her skirt was alluringly above her knees. He looked at the next. She was standing, legs apart, framed by the arch of some ancient ruined building and taken from a low angle. Her skirt was blowing up around her thighs showing much more than would normally have been considered decent. Irked by what he saw and the thought of Linden, his own wife posing so flauntingly, so coquettishly, for his brother, he slid it behind the others and looked at the next with increasing indignation. Linden was seated, her face tilted to the sun, her eyes closed, as if basking in the luxurious warmth of the sunshine. Her back was erect, her breasts pushed hard against the light material of her dress, and again the hem of her skirt was rippling audaciously high, revealing long tracts of her thighs.

Edward sighed with frustration, and turned his head to see if she was coming. He did not know how to handle this situation, how to approach Linden about it, for it could not possibly go unmentioned. Linden had never mentioned having these taken . . .

She appeared at the front door with Charles, and they hurried towards the car. It was time to go.

'I'll sit in the front with Father,' Edward stated offishly.

'You should sit in the back with your wife,' Charles suggested. 'You're not going to see her for God knows how long.'

'No, it's all right, Father. I'll sit in the front.'

Linden was hurt by this, especially when they had been married only days and about to be parted. On the way to the station she found herself looking silently at the back of his head as he spoke not a word to her, and only to his father when spoken to. Something was amiss. But what?

They arrived at the station, and the three alighted from the Bentley. Linden glanced apprehensively at Edward but his eyes avoided her.

'I'll wait in the car for you, Linden,' Charles said as Edward retrieved his suitcase from the boot. 'You don't want me in the way while you say your goodbyes.' He gave her a wink.

'Thank you, Charles,' she replied, forcing a smile.

Edward put down his suitcase, shook hands with his father and gave him a hug, then picked it up again and headed for the entrance to the station, paying no heed to Linden. Linden skipped behind him mystified and irked.

'Edward! Wait for me!'

He ignored her, striding out determinedly.

'Edward, wait,' she pleaded. 'What's the matter? What's wrong?'

She caught up with him as he reached the booth and waited anxiously while he bought his ticket, which he placed in the top pocket of his jacket. He pocketed his change and regarded her with a look of disdain.

'What on earth is wrong, Edward?' she asked again, and saw that now at least she had won his attention.

'I'll tell you what's wrong, Linden . . .' He reached inside his jacket and pulled out the brown envelope. 'Here . . .' He offered it her; she took it and opened it gingerly. 'Hugh gave me those photographs just as we left. He said he thought I might like to have them.' There was dark sarcasm in his tone.

Folk were milling around them, travellers arriving and departing, and Linden felt not only decidedly self-conscious but helpless too. They could hardly have a row – their first ever – in full view of the travelling public, and at the very moment they were to part.

She scanned the photos one after the other while he scrutinized her reaction. She felt herself blushing with embarrassment, and wanted the floor to open up and swallow her. Why had she never mentioned them?

'Well?'

She shrugged, not knowing how best to respond, but at least she understood why he was angry. 'They're just some photos Hugh took . . . oh, a long time ago,' she replied trying to make light of them. 'Before you and I were—'

'Are you always so willing to flaunt yourself in front of others?' he asked acidly. 'In front of my own brother?'

'Of course not, Edward.' She sighed with frustration, praying silently that she could extricate herself from this silly and unnecessary situation without too much harm to their relationship. 'Anyway, you didn't seem to mind the first time Hugh took some photos of me.'

'I had no claim on you then.'

'You had no claim on me when these were taken either,' she asserted in defence of herself.

'I wonder about you, Linden. The whole thing makes me wonder what sort of a girl I've married.' He looked away from her, remembering hearing that her old flame had called her a tart when he'd caught her with him after he'd driven her home one Boxing Day evening. The poor chap had been justified, too; she was being disloyal to him. Was all this – this inclination to be unfaithful, this fondness to show herself off – a flaw in her personality?

She saw the hurt look in his eyes. Tears welled up and trembled on her eyelids at his implication, at the realization that he was distressed and it was her fault. 'I am not a tart, Edward, if that's what you think,' she pouted.

'I know no such thing, Linden.' His eyes pierced hers with hot resentment. 'So why didn't you tell me about these photos? Because you thought I might disapprove? Because you were ashamed?'

'Ashamed?' she queried, her own anger rising. 'No, I'm *not* ashamed. I have done nothing to be ashamed of. I'm embarrassed, I admit, but only because it never occurred to me to tell you about them.'

'So . . . I repeat – why didn't you tell me?'

'Because I'd forgotten all about them. I've never seen them before. I remember Hugh taking them, of course. He wanted them for his camera club's annual exhibition, if you must know. It was long before you and I started courting seriously. I saw no harm in it.'

'Is there anything else you haven't told me?' he scoffed.

'Of course not . . . Oh, Edward . . .' She reached out to him, put her arms around him and laid her head on his chest submissively. 'What's got into you?' she appealed. 'Don't you know I love you with all my heart and soul? Don't you know I wouldn't do anything you disapproved of for the world? If these photos have offended you, I am so sorry, but they were taken innocently enough, believe me. Hugh asked me to pose for him . . . There was no ulterior motive on my part. It was just a single young girl having fun, enjoying being admired . . . If you can't understand that . . .' She gave a shrug.

'The subject matter doesn't offend me, Linden,' he conceded, sounding more reasonable now. 'A beautiful girl looking extremely appealing. I'm not that much of a prude, nor a hypocrite, that I can't appreciate the aesthetics. But I doubt your judgement in allowing Hugh to even photograph you. Are you sure they were taken before we started courting?'

He was softening, thank God, and he needed her reassurance. This was hurting him as much as it was hurting her.

'Of course I'm sure,' she said earnestly. 'Look at my hairstyle. It was quite short . . .' She pointed to it in one of the photos. 'It hasn't been like that for ages.'

He sighed profoundly then, admitting her claim, and gave her a hug. 'Very well . . . Look, we can hardly part on an argument, can we?' He smiled his apology. 'God knows when we'll see each other again. Promise me you won't sit for Hugh again – or anybody else for that matter.'

'Oh, Edward . . . Of course I won't.' It was a solemn promise. 'I love you, I'm your wife and I'm devoted to you. And I'll stay devoted to you while you're away. You know I will.'

'Then I apologize if I've upset you. I love you too, Linden. I absolutely idolize you . . . So kiss me.'

They kissed, regardless of the people milling busily around them.

They eventually broke off, and he peered resentfully at the station clock.

'My train leaves in five minutes,' he reminded her, with a wistful smile. 'Will you walk to the platform with me?'

She smiled back at him, more brightly, evidence of her tears still on her cheeks. 'Course I will. Just try and stop me.'

With arms around each other, they headed towards the train that was already standing by.

One evening some weeks later, Hugh Burgayne, having been under stress at the steelworks over some government contract, decided to seek the peace and tranquillity that the grounds of Kinlet Hall offered. He could not find the peace he needed inside, for talk at the dinner table seemed to be concentrated on the changes Linden wished to make to the large bedroom she was occupying, ready for when Edward came home on leave.

It was a balmy July evening and Hugh found himself passing through the hole in the wall towards the fishpond. He sat on the pool's edge and peered into the water's murky depths, beyond the outspread floating leaves of the water lilies. Some of the pool's slippery occupants swam into view, silent slivers of silver and gold.

Hugh was shouldering greater responsibility lately at the works, but not entirely satisfactorily. His father's health was in decline and he was remaining at home more, becoming less active in the day-to-day running of the colossal steel-making business. It was, of course, his chest; he had always suffered with his chest. Hugh, even as a small boy, could remember his father often being laid up in winter owing to bronchitis, and the weeks it sometimes took to fully recover. The problem was hardly improving with age. Consequently, Linden too found she had less work to do as a secretary – work she had decided to continue doing, despite the fact that she was married now and a member of the Burgayne family. Hugh often wondered how she felt about the things the other members of the typing pool were doubtless saying now she was a lady of the manor, and set apart from them. It could not be easy for her. She was bound to suffer some resentment from some of the girls, yet she seemed to carry it off with great aplomb.

Linden . . .

He recalled the time he'd confessed his feelings to her. He had chosen his moment badly, for he realized now – typically much too late – that she had been irked with him. He'd been spouting about registering as a conscientious objector when Edward was clearly keen to do his bit in the RAF. The comparison, he understood, must have been odious. Even his father had not admired him that evening. But assessing folk never had been Hugh's strong point. Seeing Linden every day, dining along with her every evening nowadays, and some lunch times and breakfast times, had not diminished his desire for her. Oh, she was the adoring wife of his younger brother, but that did not stop him casting covert, lustful glances her way, admiring her pretty face, her beautifully proportioned body. She was, oh, so beddable.

Yet why should he languish over one woman who never would be his, and never could be? There were plenty of women, any number of them, available right now. They might not all be single, but while patriotic husbands were away fighting in this ridiculous war, many were happy to make themselves available to any presentable man who showed an interest, and keen enough to sample what was on offer. Not that Hugh had ever tried his luck in that respect, but he'd heard it said. Live for today was the prevalent cry, for tomorrow we might be bombed out of existence. Oh, it was perfectly understandable. There was even Laura Birch to fall back on at a push, if he wished; she remained unattached and amenable. She even telephoned him at work from time to time. The truth was, Hugh was unsure of himself where women were concerned. He did not know how to talk to them, how to pass a compliment. He did not know how to make them laugh and so incite their interest.

The things he did have, though, were money, education, and his assured future in Blower's Green Steelworks.

Deciding to leave his thoughts at the fishpond, he stood up and ambled back through the hole in the wall. He looked at his watch. It was nearly half past eight.

Coming from the house for a turn in the grounds he saw Linden, smart in a crisp summer dress that emphasised her trim waist and pert breasts, with Penny wearing her trainee nurse's uniform. Accompanying them was a young RAF officer on crutches: one of the current crop of convalescents. The girls walked slowly, at the airman's reduced pace, one on each side of him. They were laughing at something he had said.

He watched their retreating figures, especially Linden's: the sway of her hips that caused her skirt to swing so appealingly, her well-turned ankles, how her calves looked so shapely from behind. Then Penny stopped, said something, and ran back to the house, while Linden carried on walking with this recovering RAF officer, still attentive and laughing, clearly enjoying his company, hanging on his every word.

Why would she want to do that when she had Edward for her husband? Was she so easily diverted? Could she be so easily diverted? He pondered the possibility for some time. There was something about women he did not understand . . .

That same night, Hugh made a startling discovery.

After Linden had gone to bed his mind was still active; sleep would thus elude him. He went to the attic with a flash lamp in search of another lens and masking frame for his photographic enlarger, so that he could make bigger and more impressive enlargements of some of his more treasured photographs. He did not use these things often, and there was not enough room to store them in his darkroom. But before he began to look he noticed a splinter of light coming up through the uneven floorboards. Over many years the joists had warped and shrunk, leaving the floor irregular and distorted. He saw movement below and got down on hands and knees to see what it was, realizing that this area of the attic was roughly above the old bedroom recently taken over by Linden and Edward, which was yet to be refurbished properly. Through a corresponding crack in the room's ceiling he saw, to his astonishment, that he was looking directly down on Linden. He scanned the attic with the flash lamp and spotted a coathanger with a wire hook. He tip-toed to where it hung and straightened the hook, then returned to the gap in the floorboards. Carefully he prodded the plaster below with the wire to open the crack a little. Linden was sitting on her bed wearing only brassiere and frilly French knickers. His heart started pounding at this fortuitous discovery. She was applying some creamy concoction to her face. He wanted to wiggle the wire around again to increase the size of the fissure even more, and so improve his angle of view. But it was a risky business and he did not want to make any sound; less still did he want any bits to fall from above and give the game away, so he decided not to push his luck. He could return tomorrow and effect the improvement when she was not there.

He remained watching for some minutes, congratulating himself on his extreme good fortune. He felt a familiar stirring within his trousers at the sight of her semi-nakedness, her trim backside and sleek legs. Then she sat in front of the mirror and brushed her hair for a while, her back towards him. After a while she got up from the dressing table and disappeared from view, reappearing after a second or two in a flimsy white nightgown. She slipped her knickers down her legs and tossed them aside, pulled the bedclothes back and slid into bed.

Then the light went out.

Dorothy Burgayne, although used to her husband's suffering, was more alarmed than usual at his recent spate of chestiness, and duly sent for the doctor.

Dr Vernon Mackenzie, a huge, robust man, arrived in due course and Dorothy greeted him cordially.

'The old trouble?'

'Yes, the old trouble,' she sighed.

'Then let me take a look at him.'

'I made him stay in bed, Vernon.'

'Well, that's always a safe bet.'

Dr Mackenzie followed her up the sweeping staircase to their bedroom. Charles looked swamped in the old four-poster, and very pale. He was propped up on a pillow reading a copy of *Picture Post.*

'Oh, good morning, Vernon.'

'Good morning, Charles. The old trouble, I understand.'

'The old trouble and a bit more besides, I suspect,' Charles croaked. 'I'm not normally this incapacitated at this time of year.'

'I told you years ago: you should move to sunnier climes. You could afford it.'

Charles coughed, a long, ratchety cough and winced at the pain. 'That might be eminently sensible, Vernon,' he wheezed, 'but entirely impracticable. I have a business to run.'

'And it'll kill you if you don't leave it be.' He put down his bag. 'Let me examine you.'

The doctor opened the bag and took out his stethoscope. He undid the top buttons of Charles's pyjamas, pressed the pad against his chest, and listened. 'Breathe deeply.'

It induced another searing spasm of coughing.

'Try again, slowly . . . Breathe in . . . Breathe out.' The doctor put away his stethoscope. 'The coughing is painful, Charles?'

'Rather.'

'And you're short of breath when you do anything physical?'

'I haven't done anything physical for years.'

'What about climbing the stairs?'

'Yes, that makes me short of breath.'

'Has it been worse lately?'

'Markedly.'

Dr Mackenzie sighed. 'You've suffered with bronchial problems for a number of years, Charles, that much we all know.'

'Ever since I had measles as a child.'

'And you aren't getting any younger.'

'Thank you for reminding me.'

'You have also spent much of your life in the foul confines of a steelworks, among all manner of obnoxious fumes.'

'An occupational hazard, Vernon.'

'But one that has aggravated the condition over the years, Charles.'

'So what is your diagnosis this time? What is your treatment to be? The same as before?'

'Avoid the steelworks at all costs, my friend.' He patted Charles's arm matily. 'Your condition has deteriorated to emphysema. There is no cure, you know, Charles. Only treatment to alleviate the symptoms. The temperature of your room must be maintained at sixty-five degrees Fahrenheit, and I'm going to prescribe the usual regular steam inhalations of Friar's Balsam, as well as a turpentine liniment chest rub.'

'The chest rub at least sounds exciting, Vernon,' Charles replied dolefully. 'Perhaps we can find some pretty nurse from the convalescent ward . . .'

'That, I fear, would only cause you more acute breathlessness,' the doctor riposted with a smile, 'and that won't do. Sorry, old chap.'

Back downstairs in the hall Dr Mackenzie said, 'I'm very concerned, Dorothy, about Charles's health. His condition has deteriorated without question, and I'm obliged to keep my eye on him. He is very prone to other more serious ailments, so he must be kept quiet and at rest. Don't allow him near dust or smoke, or outside in fog. Tell me, does he worry?'

'He worries a great deal about Edward, our younger son, an RAF pilot.'

'And well he might.' Vernon Mackenzie assumed a suitably grave expression. 'There's a hazardous occupation, if ever I saw one. Now . . . While I'm here I'll take a look at your convalescents . . .'

'I hoped you would, Vernon. I'll take you through.'

'Anytime you need me, just ring.'

'Thank you, Vernon.'

'You know, Linden, I really don't think you should flirt with Pilot Officer Farnell when you accompany him in those walks he takes for therapy. He takes it all too seriously,' Penny warned one evening.

'What harm can it do?' Linden queried. 'He needs cheering up after all those awful operations to save his leg.'

'Oh, you cheer him up – there's no question about that. The way he looks at you . . .'

'Yes, I know . . .'

'Just so long as you don't look at him in the same way.'

'Gosh, Penny. What are you suggesting?'

'It's just that when his time comes to leave he's going to be all despondent again, which could set him back somewhat. Don't forget his wife ran off with somebody else. It would be cruel if he fell in love with you to compensate.'

'Which hat are you wearing right now, Penny – your nurse's or an agony aunt's?'

'It doesn't matter. The advice is the same.'

They were sitting together in the breakfast room enjoying a pot of tea. Penny had just returned from the hospital, still wearing her uniform. The others had had dinner.

'Anyway, as far as Keith Farnell is concerned, he knows very well that I'm married, and I certainly haven't led him on. I wouldn't do that. I'm not interested in him that way; but he's a pleasant enough chap, and there's no harm in trying to cheer him up. Besides, him being RAF, he sort of makes me feel closer to Edward. I can't help having some rapport with him. I'm sure he and Edward would get on really well. Actually, I feel rather sorry for him. Shall we give him another turn around the garden after dinner? He does need to exercise that leg.'

'Why don't *you*?' Penny suggested.

'Just me?' Linden queried.

'Yes, just you. And put him straight about a few things. He's leaving soon, I understand. And while you do that I'll go and see father. How is he today, by the way?'

'About the same, I think.'

There was a pause in the conversation and they both drained their tea mugs.

'You know, Penny,' Linden said with a sigh as she put her mug down, 'I feel at such a loose end at the moment.'

'Oh? In what way?'

'Well . . . If Edward were home I know it would be different. But he's not, is he? Nor is he likely to be for the foreseeable future.'

'So what's your point, Linden?'

'My point is, that I am still employed as your father's secretary, and because he is so ill and not allowed to work, I have nothing to do either. Oh, I try and make myself busy with the convalescents, but there's not a lot I'm qualified to do, or even allowed to do except talk to them, help them with therapeutic exercises, and fetch and carry for the nurses.'

'There must be loads you can do outside,' Penny said.

'I'm sure there must be. I think I should mention it to Hugh. I'm sure there's work aplenty I could do if I went back to the office. They still pay me wages, but I feel I'm having the money under false pretences.'

'Rest assured, the Blower's Green Steelworks can afford you, Linden. But, yes, maybe Hugh would appreciate an assistant. I know he's overworked at present and, after all, you do know the ropes. If not, there's still the convalescents. You could drive, too. There are lots of errands you could run. Why don't you learn to drive?'

'Yes, I should, shouldn't I?' Linden replied, enthusiastic at the novel idea. 'I've never given it a thought. If I could drive I could be useful in lots of ways. Can we spare the petrol for me to learn?'

'I don't think petrol is an issue at the steelworks, Linden.'

Keith Farnell was at a table reading a newspaper when Linden passed by, and he hailed her eagerly.

'Pilot Officer Farnell,' she greeted him, formally but amiably. 'How are you today?'

'All the better for seeing you.' He was sporting a broad grin of pleasure at the sight of her. 'Have you come to take me for my evening constitutional?'

'I can, if your crutches are up to it,' she answered dryly.

'For you I'd hop on my good leg to China and back. It looks like a beautiful evening.'

'Oh, it is.'

'No Nurse Penny this evening?' he asked.

'She's with her father.'

'Ah. So I get you all to myself for once.'

He took hold of his crutches which he'd placed handily against the wall, and eased himself off the chair. He made his way to the door and she opened it for him, to let him out into the warm summer air.

'How is your leg today?' Linden enquired as they began walking over the grass, towards the slanting shadows of a clutch of elms.

'Oh, the healing continues. So much so, that I'm being let out of here.'

'So I understand. We shall miss you.'

'I'd like to think that *you* will, Linden.'

'Course I shall,' she said affably. 'I shall remember you with great fondness.'

'Great fondness?' he repeated with some disdain. 'How patronizing that sounds.'

'I'm sorry,' she said. 'It wasn't meant to be.'

'You see, Linden, *fondness* is hardly a word that expresses what I have come to feel for you.'

'If that's the case,' she answered, suddenly feeling flushed, 'I hope I haven't given you reason to think it might be reciprocated. I'm a married woman, Keith, as you know, and I'm very much in love with my husband.'

'Yes, despite how much it grieves me, I understand all that. But you must allow me to say what is in my heart. I've enjoyed your company a few times while I've been convalescing here, and you are an inspiration to me, you know. I wouldn't have improved at the rate I have if it wasn't for you, for the prospect of hearing your voice, of seeing that heavenly face, of being with you on these therapeutic walks I'm obliged to take . . .' He smiled appealingly. 'Of seeing the light in your beautiful eyes.'

'I'm flattered,' she said, unable to think of anything else to say.

'Anyway, your husband is an RAF man, isn't he?'

'You know he is.'

'I'd like to meet him sometime.'

'Perhaps you will . . . Sometime. Who knows . . .?'

'It's just that . . . Well, Linden, if anything untoward were to befall him . . . I'd like to stake my claim . . .'

Linden shuddered. 'I really don't know what to say to that, except that I certainly hope and pray nothing untoward does befall him, as you put it.'

'But you must understand that life in the RAF is mighty precarious. You only have to look at me.'

'Oh, I understand it only too well, believe me.'

'So we are both realists.'

'It pays to be,' she admitted.

'But I am also a romantic. Incurably so.'

She sighed as she looked up at him, hobbling along with the help of his crutches. 'It's not wise to be romantic where I'm concerned, Keith. I can offer you nothing in return. I'm happy to be your friend, but that's all I can be.'

'Can I write to you?'

'Would you want me to show your letters to my husband?'

He shook his head and smiled. 'Of course not.'

'So you would ask me to be disloyal?'

'Absolutely.'

'Why can't you just accept my situation and be done with it?'

They stopped walking and Keith Farnell turned to face her. 'Because I love you, Linden. Can't you see?'

She touched his arm, allowing her hand to rest on it as she looked up into his eyes, sympathetic to his emotions. 'I like you very much, Keith,' she said earnestly, 'but it can never be more than that. You have to understand.'

'Then you can show my letters to your brave husband on his return, and have a jolly good laugh about this other silly airman who suffers from the unrequited love of his beautiful wife.'

'It's just a passing fancy,' she answered dismissively as they continued walking. 'You must have known lots of girls.'

'A few, yes, of course. But I knew from the moment I set eyes on you that there could never be anybody else for me. This is not some juvenile infatuation.'

'It's infatuation all the same.' She touched his arm again and smiled considerately. 'I think we should be going back.' She was determined to put a stop to this as kindly as she knew how.

'Now I've offended you.'

'No, you haven't offended me, Keith. But there's no point in harping on about it.'

Both were unaware that this earnestly emotive scene, being enacted within sight of the house, had been seen but not over-heard by Hugh Burgayne, who was carrying a small Leica 35mm camera.

Twenty-One

Next morning Linden was up early. She had a clear double-edged plan. The first part was to go with Hugh to the office and immerse herself in work. That in turn would ensure she was not around when Pilot Officer Keith Farnell left the house for his return home and ultimately to his squadron.

As Hugh and Linden journeyed to the steelworks in his Jaguar SS, conversation was at first sparse, except for a comment from him about the relentless German advance through Russia, and how it had lessened the possibility of Britain being invaded.

'I was thinking, Hugh . . . Something Penny suggested . . . I'd like to learn to drive a car. I could be more useful to everybody if I could drive. Also, I could visit my mum and dad a bit more regularly. I just need somebody with the time to teach me.'

'I could teach you,' he offered, seizing the opportunity.

'But you're too busy. You're far too busy.'

'I think I'm the best judge of that. I'm busy during the day – there's no question, but most evenings I could find time. Besides, I understand your friend Pilot Officer Farnell is leaving shortly, so that should give you more freedom in the evenings as well.' He looked at her askance.

'Gosh, Hugh, you make it sound as if we've been having an affair,' she answered.

'I trust you haven't been.'

She laughed; it was such a preposterous notion. 'Certainly not. I'm a happily married woman, as you well know.'

'But some women, Linden, while content enough while their husbands are around . . .'

'Well, that doesn't apply to me, Hugh,' she protested. 'I'm perfectly content to wait for Edward.'

'The fact is, Linden, my dear, I've seen you and Mr Farnell

together walking in the grounds. You looked very chummy together.'

Linden felt she was suddenly on trial for something she hadn't done. 'I don't dislike the man, Hugh,' she answered defensively. 'I actually feel very sorry for him, having lost his wife, then the injuries to his leg. But that's all you could ever have seen – the two of us walking the grounds. That's hardly tantamount to having an affair.'

'I'm sure Edward would be very displeased if he found out you'd even been walking the grounds of an evening with another man.'

'In the circumstances, Hugh, I think Edward would understand perfectly, and would even condone my helping a fellow RAF pilot to recover.'

'All the same, I'm sure you wouldn't want me to tell him about it.'

'I can't imagine why you'd want to anyway. But if you think I've got a guilty conscience, you're wrong. I've nothing to hide.'

'Then I'm glad. But it was obvious by the way he looked at you that he was smitten.'

'I can't help that. I haven't egged him on.'

'All the same, he'll doubtless be sorry to leave you behind.'

'Oh, I've no doubt he'll write. He said he would. But that doesn't mean I have to answer. On second thoughts, though, it would be discourteous not to reply.'

'Of course you wouldn't have to reply, Linden. Why encourage the idiot?'

That night, Hugh set himself up in the attic room and watched Linden undress once more. These nightly observations were becoming an obsession, but he realized they were getting him nowhere – only increasing his frustration. He realized he was also jealous of the admiration she drew from other men. He was insanely jealous of Pilot Officer Farnell, who had managed to get her attention. There had to be a resolution to this torment . . . If only he could somehow prise them apart, Edward and Linden . . .

Next day he left his office and drove to Dudley town centre. There, he bought a miniature camera to take photos of Linden through the crack in her ceiling.

* * *

Hugh was left alone at the dinner table the following evening. Dorothy was upstairs with Charles, who showed no improvement, Linden had been called to the kitchen to give cook an opinion on some culinary matter in Dorothy's absence, and Penny was at the hospital on her shift.

He picked up the bottle of wine they'd shared at dinner and emptied it into his glass just as Linden returned.

'Oh, would you like some more wine, Linden?' he asked.

'No, thanks. I've already had one glass. It'll only make me tired. Especially if you're going to teach me to drive. I wouldn't want to fall asleep at the wheel.'

'Shall we go now, before it gets dark?'

'It might be best, I think.'

He quickly downed what remained in his glass and got up. 'It'll have to be the Jaguar, I'm afraid, since Penny has the Riley.'

It was another balmy evening. The sun was low, glittering through the whispering foliage of the trees.

'I don't think we'll go on to the roads today,' Hugh said as they walked towards the car. 'I'll show you the rudiments here, and have you starting and stopping.'

He opened the driver's door and gestured for her to sit inside, and she brushed past him as she did so. 'Get yourself comfortable . . . You can adjust the seat here . . . Excuse me a moment.' He stooped down and his hand dived between her shins, brushing the skin of her bare calves. He lifted the hem of her skirt a little for access to the adjusting lever, and she was reminded of the time he did something similar while posing her for photographs. A coincidence?

'Now pull yourself forward . . . Comfortable?'

She nodded.

'Now . . . these pedals at your feet, Linden . . . Part your legs a little so you can see them . . .'

He looked at her with unmistakable innuendo brimming from his narrowed eyes.

'That's it. The pedal on the right is the throttle. When you press it you go faster. The one on the left is the clutch, and you use that when you want to change gear and stop. The one in the middle is the brake.'

'I have three pedals, but only two feet,' she remarked.

He laughed at her girlish analysis. 'You use your right foot to operate the throttle and the brake, the logic being that if you are using one pedal you won't be using the other. Before we start the car, make sure that you are in neutral . . .' He leaned over her as he reached for the gearstick to demonstrate, trying to ensure he rubbed his upper arm against her bosom.

He turned his head and smiled reassuringly at her, taking in her slender figure, the flawless, lightly tanned skin of her bare arms; how her light summer skirt tantalizingly outlined the contours of her thighs as she sat. She looked so clean and fresh and he longed to feel her firm young woman's body against his own. He yearned to sniff her hair, her creamy skin, to experience her sweet gentle breath on his face. He'd been looking forward so much to being alone with her like this, dreaming of what might come of it.

'Perhaps you'd be better showing me that from the passenger seat,' she suggested, sensing his intentions.

'Perhaps I should,' he agreed, and walked around the car.

He got in beside her. 'Left foot on the clutch,' he instructed. 'Now feel your way through the gears.' He put his hand on hers and guided her through the gears: forwards, backwards, across and forwards. 'Reverse is a bit trickier . . . Do you see?'

'Yes, I've got it.' She pulled her hand from under his. 'I always was quick to pick things up,' she said pointedly.

'Now let's start the engine,' he replied, ignoring her comment. 'It's been standing a while now, so we might have to use the choke. This is the choke . . . Now, make sure you are in neutral . . .' She duly checked. 'Now turn the key and press the starter . . . There . . . and don't forget to release it when the engine fires.'

Linden felt the vibration of the engine instantly as it roared into life.

'Foot on clutch . . . Now engage first gear. Handbrake off . . .' She struggled with the handbrake, and he did it for her. 'Now let the clutch out slowly, and gently put pressure on the throttle pedal.'

Of course, the engine stalled.

'All right,' he said patiently. 'Let's try again.'

It stalled again with an alarming judder. She tried several times, until she eventually felt the car move forwards. Flushed with success, she stayed in first gear getting used to the notion that she was in control of the car, getting used to the feel of the steering, the effect of the throttle.

'Now press down on the clutch and change into second gear . . . Very good. That's very good, Linden.'

She smiled at him, delighted at her minor achievement, and drove on, twisting and turning along the drive until they almost reached the huge wrought-iron gates at the end. She felt for the brake, applied it too enthusiastically, and forgot about the clutch. They came to an abrupt halt and the engine stalled.

'Now let's try a three-point turn.'

He explained the routine and she set about doing it. It was a great deal more difficult to keep the car from stalling when reversing, but after numerous attempts she began to get the feel for it. While she reversed the car, he turned to look behind through the rear window, and his arm went around the back of her seat.

'Now first gear,' he instructed.

Another stall, but at the next attempt they moved forward.

But Hugh's arm remained behind her. 'Very good,' he said again. 'Now, just pull up here . . .'

They were well away from the house, which was hidden from view behind the many trees that stood in the grounds on all sides. The leaves above them stirred and Linden looked up to see a squirrel bounding energetically from one branch to another. She put the car in neutral and applied the handbrake as she watched it for a few seconds through the open window.

Hugh looked at her as he tickled the back of her neck experimentally. The feel of his fingers sent a shudder down her back and she leaned forward in a protest.

'Please stop it, Hugh,' she said, irritated.

'Can I ask something of you, Linden?' He was almost choking on his desire.

'What?' she replied apprehensively.

'May I kiss you?'

She laughed, but with bewilderment. 'To what end? I don't think so, Hugh.'

He eased himself towards her and pulled her to him, and tried to force his lips on hers. She turned her face away in indignation.

'Hugh, what on earth d'you think you're doing?'

'I told you, I want to kiss you.'

'Well, I don't want to kiss you, if you don't mind.'

'All right . . . Then will you go to bed with me?'

'No, I will not.' She laughed again at his absurdity. 'If I won't kiss you, I'm hardly likely to go to bed with you.'

'Oh, but the two things aren't necessarily connected,' he suggested, not about to abandon his cause. 'You could still go to bed with me, and we wouldn't have to kiss if you didn't want to. I do understand that kissing is more personal – more intimate, perhaps – than the actual sex act.'

'Whether or no,' she replied. 'I have no desire to go to bed with you. I'm married to your brother, for goodness sake.'

'Nobody need know, Linden, least of all Edward. Think of the fun we'd have. They say stolen fruits are the sweetest.'

Linden saw the squirrel run down the trunk of the tree and sit for a few moments on the grass, its tail erect, before it darted up another tree, indifferent to the problem she was facing with Hugh.

'And what if I told Edward that his own brother had designs on me?'

'You wouldn't. You couldn't possibly.'

'I will if you don't stop this nonsense right away, Hugh.'

'But I can't. Don't you see? I fell in love with you the moment I saw you. I fell desperately in love. I've been in love with you ever since. I live and breathe you. I dream about you every night. You are never off my mind.'

'Oh, Hugh!' She was shocked and disappointed that he still felt that way. 'Hugh, you should have the grace not to say such things,' she said in admonishment. At once she wanted to curl up into a ball and put her hands over her ears so she could hear no more such words. She was a married woman, after all – married to his brother.

'But you must have known it all along, Linden. I didn't try to hide it. I didn't even try to hide it from Laura.'

'I would have thought my obvious love for Edward, not to mention my marrying him, might have cured you of all that.'

'But it hasn't. We only have to be in the same room and I have this terrible urge to take you in my arms and make ardent love to you. When you're close to me, within touching distance, like now, it's absolute murder. Doubtless you are blissfully unaware of the torment it brings, Linden. Please don't be so hard on me as to refuse me.'

'I have to refuse you, Hugh—'

In a last ditch effort to seduce her he ran his hand up her skirt, let it rest on her thigh just above the knee and relished the fleeting moment of contact with her flesh, lightly moist with the perspiration of the day's heat.

Retaining her composure, Linden suffered it to stay there while she made her point. 'What do you think you are doing, Hugh?'

'Feeling your leg, of course.'

'Please stop it,' she said haughtily.

'Why should I? You evidently like it.' He slid his hand further up her thigh, felt her knickers and the warm softness of her crotch beneath . . .

She slapped his face as hard as she could at his arrogance.

'How dare you!' she protested. She opened the car door and jumped out, then hurried back towards the house, darting between the trees, avoiding the edge of the drive. Tears trembled on her long lashes as she walked. *How dare he . . . Who does he think he is?*

That night Hugh was again on sentry duty in the attic room, accompanied by his new miniature camera, ready and waiting to secretly spy on and photograph Linden as she undressed and prepared herself for bed. It had been a hot day, and the day's warmth and sultriness lingered, typically for late July. He watched her remove her light summer dress and her underskirt, then, to his unqualified joy, her knickers and her brassiere for the sake of keeping cool. She was standing there stark naked except for the gold wedding ring that glinted on her finger. Hugh's mouth went very dry, and he stared transfixed, goggle-eyed and sweating, his heart pounding like a drum in concert with the disturbing throbbing that was all at once demanding more space inside his trousers. Her breasts were ripe and beautiful like fresh fruit, more ripe and more beautiful than Laura Birch's. Her triangle of dark hair, too, was a magnet for his eyes as he watched her spread herself on top of the counterpane with ultimate femininity and grace, before she reached over to turn out the light.

He lay there a long time afterwards, mental images of her nakedness filling his thoughts. Eventually – perhaps it was even half an hour later – he got up from the floor, his frustration absolute. She had already turned him down that evening. Perhaps his approach had been too clumsy, too unsophisticated for her tastes. It was not his fault that he did not know how to win over women. It was not his fault that he was not the glib-talking ladies' man his brother was. She should understand that and make allowances.

That slap she had given him was hardly deserved.

Indeed, she might end up being very sorry for that.

He took off his shoes and quietly, stealthily, crept down the back stairs and made his way to the landing and Linden's room. Breathing hard, a lump in his dry throat, he stood outside the door in the darkness. The rest of the household was already in bed and asleep. Why hadn't he thought of this before? It was a desperate measure, but he was desperate – desperate to have her, but also desperate to make her see she had chosen the wrong man. His only decision now was whether to wait a little longer to be sure she was asleep, or simply go in there at once.

He couldn't wait. Patience had never been one of his virtues.

Gently, he tried the doorknob and it turned. The catch released with a metallic click, and he pushed the door open. He could smell her sweetness, could hear the faint sound of her steady breathing. At once he was affected. How was it possible that one girl could have such a massive impact on a man? She was asleep already. His eyes were accustomed to the darkness, and he could just discern the pale, slender curves of her body as she lay sprawled tantalizingly on top of her bed. Her dark hair was loose, and flowing over her pillow like rivers of ink.

His eyes never leaving her, he took off his clothes silently and they fell to the floor. He approached the bed, lay down on the side where Edward would sleep, and remained still for a moment, just looking at the soft curve of her throat and the delectable mounds of her creamy breasts. How delightful it would be to nuzzle his face in their spongy smoothness. Well, very, very soon . . .

His heart was pounding like a drum, the blood coursing through his veins, and his mouth was bone-dry. After this, she would either love him irreversibly, or hate him.

Gently, he reached out to her and let his hand skim lightly over her belly. The unbelievable smoothness of her skin made him want to weep, it was so unutterably beautiful. He could feel the enticing warmth of her body radiating towards him. His hand ventured carefully to her bare thighs and luxuriated in their silkiness, less moist than earlier when he had snatched that quick, defiant grope up her skirt. Encouraged, he roamed smoothly upwards and reached the triangular mound of soft hair . . . Oh, bliss . . . She stirred, parted her thighs and sighed, and his heart pounded with anticipation as he caressed her gently in that soft, moist place.

'Oh, Edward,' she breathed softly.

Her response was immediate. Her arm came around him, her mouth was on his, and she snuggled her body to him, sighing contentedly. He cupped one firm round buttock in his hand as she pressed herself against him, then ran it gently over her thigh. His luck was in at last. This woman was far too desirable to be the property of one man. Gently, he rolled on to her, enjoying these stolen, but incredibly delicious kisses she had denied him earlier.

But for Linden, rousing from a dreamy sleep, there was something different about these kisses. They did not feel like Edward's kisses, did not taste the same. Funny the tricks dreams play on you. Besides, Edward was not at home. Or had he returned on leave in the night and slipped into bed with her?

'Edward?' she whispered.

'Yes, I'm here.'

'Gosh, you're home . . .' She sighed contentedly, smiling to herself in the darkness.

Edward was already on top of her, rather edgily, too eagerly she thought. However, her legs were apart, and she was ready and just as eager to receive him as he pressed urgently for entry. But she could feel that he was not lined up quite properly – a lack of practice, maybe – hence the difficulty. She reached down, took him in her hand to guide him inside her.

And then a horrific possibility struck her with all the force of an earthquake and she hesitated.

What if this were Hugh? She would not put it past him.

She unhanded him and deftly shoved him off. She could hardly take the risk. If it was Edward she could make a valid excuse, that would be the end of it and they would resume. If it was Hugh, she would have made the right move. These thoughts formulated, and were decided on, in a fraction of a second, a second in which she reached over and switched on her bedside lamp.

She shrieked in horror. 'Hugh! For God's sake! What d'you think you're playing at?'

For once he looked decidedly sheepish, blinking at the brightness of the light as he slid off the bed. Linden instinctively rolled the counterpane around herself for both modesty and protection.

'Are you mad?' she cried, thoroughly indignant, swathed in the soft material.

'I don't know. A little, I suppose,' he answered pathetically. 'I couldn't help myself, Linden. You know how I feel.'

'I didn't know anybody could be so underhand. You should be locked up.'

She could find no words strong enough to express what she felt. What she was beginning to feel deep inside, but had as yet not formed into a coherent idea or indeed a solution, was that she could consider neither herself nor her virtue safe in this house while Edward was away. There was a lock on the door, but never had she thought for even a moment that she ought to use it in the family home of her husband. From now on, though, she must keep the door locked.

'I'm not ashamed, Linden,' Hugh said defiantly, recovering his composure. 'I want you, and I gave you fair warning.'

'That you did, but never would I have thought you could stoop so low as to try and take me in my sleep. If you ever come near me again I swear I shall tell your father.'

'I wouldn't, if I were you,' he said ominously. 'It would be all too easy for me to tell Edward how you invited me to your room while he was away.'

'You wouldn't dare tell such lies.'

'Wouldn't I?' He smirked as he strutted across the bedroom, unabashed, and picked up his clothes. 'Consider this a truce we have for now, Linden – but for you at any rate it'll be an uneasy one. I suggest you consider your position very carefully. It might be so much simpler, and so much more satisfying just to submit to me. Think on it.'

'I'll do no such thing,' she said vehemently. 'Now will you please bugger off.'

*　　*　　*

Next morning, Hugh arose early with the intention of leaving for the office without Linden. Before he went, though, he sought Jenkins, and found her in the breakfast room laying the table for the others.

'Whatever post we receive from now on, I want you to put it away unseen by anybody, and hand it to me on my return home. I don't want my father troubled unduly.'

'All right.'

'Do you understand what I'm asking?'

'Yes. You want me to hand you the post and not give it to anybody else.'

'Correct.'

'But what if somebody else gets to the post first?'

'You know what time the post arrives, Margaret. Be sure you are there, ready and waiting for the postman.'

'What about if it's a letter from Mr Edward for the new Mrs Burgayne?'

'You know what Mr Edward's letters look like?'

'Course I do.'

'Then let "*the new Mrs Burgayne*" have them. But only letters from Edward. All others you will hold on to for me. I repeat: keep all other post and hand it to me – nobody else.'

'Very good . . . sir.'

Twenty-Two

L inden realized that her virtue was more likely to be left intact if Penny would teach her to drive and allow her to practise in the Riley. This she did throughout August, and gradually became a proficient driver. On the last Sunday in August, Linden, accompanied by Penny, took Edward's MG and, with the canvas hood lowered and the wind blowing through their hair in the summer sunshine, left Kinlet Hall to spend the day with Gladys and Joe Woods in Dudley.

Linden's absence that day presented Hugh with a perfect opportunity to do what he had been thinking of doing ever since she had so unfeelingly spurned his love and rebuffed his advances, for Hugh was nothing if not vindictive. Withholding her favours, for which he was so ravenously hungry, was nothing short of a crime in his eyes. She needed to understand that neither he nor his feelings were to be trifled with. In the end he would have her. He just needed to clear the path.

So he sat at the typewriter upstairs in Linden's Kinlet Hall office and fed two sheets of paper, separated by a sheet of carbon paper, between the rollers. He squared them up, and began to type; a letter he had more or less mentally composed already.

31 August 1941
 Kinlet Hall
Dear Edward,
 First and foremost I must give you the latest news on Father. Dr Mackenzie has been calling regularly, administering potions and poultices, but the old man as yet shows no detectable signs of improvement. If anything, he is worse. It seems his bronchial problems emanate from when he was a very young man and will never improve wholly. His spirits are also low, because he is

unable to occupy himself usefully, having been made to give up working, at least until such time as there might be some improvement in his condition. That, however, is very unlikely to happen. He has also lost his appetite, is barely eating anything, and has lost much weight in consequence.

You may rest assured, of course, that he is enjoying the best care possible, so I would not want you to worry about him unduly, or even consider applying for compassionate leave to visit at this stage.

However, there is another particular turn of events, about which I feel it is my bounden duty as your brother, and acting head of the family, to inform you. It grieves me greatly to have to write on the subject, but after due consideration of the seriousness of events and how they directly affect you, I feel I have no choice.

You may or may not know that a young airman was convalescing here at Kinlet Hall by the name of Pilot Officer Keith Farnell. It seems that he and Linden, your beloved wife, struck up quite some friendship after you had returned to active duty following your internment in Ireland and your subsequent marriage. As evidence of this I enclose some photographs that I managed to take of them together in the grounds, and I'm sure you will easily discern, merely by their poses, the obvious familiarity that exists between them. It transpires that letters have passed between them since his return home, and I have been fortunate, inasmuch as I have been able to acquire a couple that Linden received from him. They are enclosed for your edification and enlightenment. You will agree, I am certain, that there can be no doubt from the very strong emotions and desires expressed in these letters, that PO Farnell and your wife are, or have been, conducting an illicit and ardent love affair, albeit at a distance for the time being. Unfortunately, I have not been able to get hold of her replies, for obvious reasons, but I have no reason to suppose they are any less fervent. And all this while she is no doubt also writing fervent love letters to you. One cannot begin to comprehend the fickleness of women.

It pains me even more to relate that I myself have

been propositioned by your wife on more than one occasion, even invited to her bedroom. Needless to say I was astounded, not to mention affronted, that she would even consider that I could betray my loyalty to my own brother, but some people, we must regrettably acknowledge, do not share our moral values. I would not normally have mentioned these occurrences, but in the context of the foregoing I am confident you will agree that it is entirely relevant and reveals a pattern to her behaviour and laxness of morals.

I have no reason to suppose there have not been others. Indeed, I saw Linden once meet that other person she was friendly with when she first commenced her employment at Blower's Green Steelworks. It was outside the works and it was when you two had begun your then undeclared courtship. His name eludes me at the moment.

I perceived from the outset that your liaison with Linden was both foolhardy and doomed. You may recall that I tried in my own way to warn you of this, and to register my disapproval. The old saying, 'There are none so blind as those who will not see' certainly holds true in your case. One must put it down to the impetuosity of youth. I even tried to discourage her, but my words fell on deaf ears. After all, to a common working girl, you were quite some catch, and she was hardly likely to let go easily.

So I trust the foregoing will open your eyes to the diabolical flaw in the personality of Linden Woods and the things of which she is capable.

I deeply regret having to inform you of these appalling events for I know the revelation will upset you greatly, but I would be failing in my duty as a brother if I were to ignore them. Edward, you are young enough and strong enough to put all this behind you and start anew. A better life, with somebody more suitable and more responsible, on your return from active service, is what I earnestly wish for you.

Affectionately yours,
Hugh.

Hugh pulled the letter from the typewriter, read it through, signed it, and put it into the envelope he had addressed along with the incriminating letters from Keith Farnell that he'd intercepted, and the tell-tale photographs. Then he sealed it, picked up the rest of the correspondence, and drove to the nearest pillar box to post his letter, somewhat pleased with his efforts.

The pink hue of an early September dawn was turning to turquoise over the English Channel as two southbound Hurricanes scanned the skies, patrolling for German aircraft. Over the last few days and nights the Biggin Hill RAF base had been attacked again, and reduced to a shambles by 1,000 pound bombs dropped by a dozen bombers approaching at low level and undetected by radar. Many personnel lost their lives. There was no reason to suppose other airfields would not be likewise struck; hence the aerial patrols.

Pilot Officer Royston Hughes flew one of the Hurricanes, the other being piloted by Flying Officer Edward Burgayne, cruising at 16,000 feet. Edward's eyes, even through the tears which misted them, instinctively searched every section of the sky around him, above and below. A long way off, a speck in the sky, an unidentifiable aeroplane was limping for the French coast with a plume of smoke trailing – somebody else's victim, and they made no attempt to pursue it.

Then the voice of Royston Hughes rasped through the headphones. Six fighters, possibly Messerschmitt 109Fs, were approaching at a height of about 12,000 feet. Edward gave the order to descend and engage them. The danger was that if an enemy plane could get behind you and beneath you, you were at his mercy. Conversely, if you could get behind and below the enemy planes you would have the advantage.

But Edward Burgayne had lost all enthusiasm for any chase. Bigger, more important things were preoccupying him – personal things. Only the day before he had received an extremely disturbing letter from his brother Hugh. Hugh rarely wrote, and the very rarity of correspondence from Hugh served to underline its gravity; and the information it contained was grave indeed. Edward was scarcely able to believe that Linden, to whom he had given his all and whom he had believed he could trust, could betray him after all. His doubts about her and her integrity had been first raised when Hugh had presented him with that batch of photos as he was due to leave Kinlet Hall to rejoin his squadron. Now Hugh had produced even more evidence, unmistakable in the form of love letters from a man of whom he had no prior knowledge, and clear black-and-white photographs, which showed her holding affectionately on to the arm of this other airman as she stood smiling coquettishly at him with her big expressive eyes. That look, he had always believed, was reserved only for him.

It was heartbreaking to have one's illusions shattered, to be told that the woman you adored was not worth a light. In the torment of sleepless nights he had pondered over and over their moments together, searching for some clue that would give the lie to Hugh's devastating claims. Yet all he could ever recall was Linden's eager response to him, her unstinting demonstrations of love. But to turn all that on its head; was that same eager response, were those same unstinting demonstrations of love, merely the subterfuge of a woman out to sell herself to a man she considered worth having, or – even worse – the baser instincts of sexual gratification? He understood there were such women; they were often discussed bawdily in the mess rooms, referred to as nymphomaniacs, and everybody wanted to meet at least one in his life. Maybe Linden was one such nymphomaniac, if Hugh's further assertion that she had propositioned him was anything to go by.

He had been blinded by love, by desire, and ought to have seen it coming. He pondered the first time they had made love, when her eagerness, her lack of modesty belied her claims to virginity; virginity which she had affected convincingly enough at the time. Yet she had undressed in front of him without turning a hair, flaunting herself before him in only her knickers in the dense ferns of Enville Common – hardly the behaviour of the demure young thing she purported to be. How easy her seduction had been in hindsight; her forwardness had astonished yet delighted him. In truth it had been tantamount to her seducing him.

Having received Hugh's letter, Edward had decided not to write again to Linden until he had considered the matter further. It would be difficult to know what to say to her ever again after receiving this intelligence. How could he write and accuse her

of having affairs, and blame her for the impending break-up of
their marriage, without revealing that it was Hugh who had fed
him the information? But if he failed to write, what then? She
had to know how things stood between them and the reason
why. It was an impossible situation, and his mind was in a whirl
of confusion because of it. He was hardly mentally fit to be
flying his Hurricane in this state – deprived of sleep, of the
love of his wife, having to make split-second decisions that
could jeopardize the life of his fellow pilot Royston Hughes.

He flew on, preoccupied, with Royston flying alongside
just a few feet to his left. The Messerschmitts had evidently
spotted the pair of Hurricanes and were preparing to attack,
peeling off from their formation to come on broadside.

Then began a terrific dogfight. Royston Hughes manoeuv-
red himself cleverly and opened fire, disabling two of the
Messerschmitts. He screamed with triumph through Edward's
headphones as he saw them lose altitude, riddled with bullet
holes, spewing black smoke behind them.

Edward watched all this impassively, almost as if he were
a spectator and aloof from the action. Partly through sheer
mental fatigue, partly through the acute heartache he was
suffering, what he was doing now seemed triflingly immaterial. Once he had been happy, oh so happy, but would he ever
be happy again? He had loved Linden Woods with all his
heart and soul, but could he ever love any woman again?
Would he ever be able to trust a woman in future? – any
woman? What he now knew put a different perspective on
every aspect of his existence. So was there any point in living?
And here was the perfect opportunity to escape this life and
all its ineffable tribulations . . . with honour.

He saw the line of tracers from one of the Messerschmitts
that were intended for him, and had time to either dive or
climb to avoid them. But he did neither. Even he was unsure
whether he maintained his course through fatigue, apathy,
indecision, or whether it was entirely deliberate.

The first bullet ripped into the Hurricane's nose, ripping
away the fuel lines to the engine, which spluttered and died
in a jet of flames that lapped fiercely around the nose. The
next strafed the tail, blasting part of the rudder away.

Edward was still conscious, but unmoved, still impassive,
still aloof, utterly fatalistic as his Hurricane nose-dived

uncontrollably towards the sea below, failing to respond to his fellow pilot's shouts in his headphones.

After some anxious days devoid of a letter from Edward, Linden sought the advice of Hugh. They had hardly spoken since that awful night when he had invaded her bed, and the atmosphere between them was palpable.

'Jenkins tells me you have given instructions that all post be handed only to you,' she said coolly on his return from the steelworks one evening. 'Are there any letters from Edward you might have been hiding from me?' She flashed a look of sheer scorn that was unmistakable in its message.

'Indeed not, Linden,' he replied, his haughtiness matching her disdain. 'Jenkins has instructions to hand you any correspondence addressed to you personally. It is only business mail I am concerned about, merely to protect my father from the worry of dealing with it while he is so ill.'

'Thank you,' she said politely. 'But you might as well know how worried I am that I've received nothing from Edward for a few days now. I think it fair you should know. Unless, of course, he has written to his father or mother, in which case I would appreciate being made aware of it for my own peace of mind.'

'There have been no letters at all from Edward.'

'Are you sure?' Tears welled in her eyes.

'Of course I'm sure,' he declared aggressively, affecting to resent what he believed she was implying.

'I see. Then perhaps you should be worried too.'

The telegram from the Air Ministry arrived that same evening, addressed to Mrs Edward Burgayne. She took it from the telegram boy, trembling with trepidation. She had been down this path before. It had turned out well in the end, but the heart-rending anxiety, the devastation, the feeling that life suddenly seemed pointless, was unbearable. Whatever it said in this telegram, she was going to suffer those same traumatic emotions again, whether or not it would turn out well this time. But there was no escaping it. So she opened the telegram and read it, watched apprehensively by Dorothy and Penny.

It ran:

> *The Air Ministry regrets to inform you that your husband*
> *Flying Officer Edward Burgayne has been reported*
> *missing in action, believed killed, following operations*
> *over the English Channel on the morning of 3/9/41.*
> *Letter to follow.*

Linden fell into the arms of Penny and wept hysterically.
Dorothy gently prised the telegram from Linden's fingers and
crept away to break the dreadful news to Charles, leaving
Linden to grieve in Penny's tender care.

Charles was sitting in a wicker armchair in the bedroom,
wearing his dressing gown. His hair was awry and he had not
shaved that day, so that grey whiskers sprouted from his cheeks
and chin, exaggerating his pallidness. He looked up when
Dorothy entered, at once alarmed by the grave expression on
her face.

'What is it?' he wheezed. 'You look as if you've seen a ghost.'

'Here, Charles. This just arrived.' She offered him the
telegram. 'It's bad news, I'm afraid.'

'Edward?'

She nodded. 'You'd better read it.'

'No. Read it to me.'

She duly read it.

A cold shudder ran down his spine. 'My God,' he whispered, as tears started rimming his eyes. 'It's as I always
feared—' A spasm of painful coughing seized him, interrupting
him. Eventually it subsided and he continued. 'I rue the day
I gave him that damned Gypsy Moth. Why ever did I encourage
him to fly?'

'You weren't to know there would be a war, Charles,'
Dorothy consoled, struggling to maintain her self-control. 'Or
that he would be so intimately involved in it. And even if you
hadn't given it him, who's to say he wouldn't have become
an RAF pilot anyway?'

Charles shook his head and wept. 'I feel responsible,' he
croaked. 'I contrived to kill my own son. I have helped to
engineer his death.'

'We don't know that he's dead yet, Charles.' Dorothy knelt
beside him and took his hand. 'He's reported missing. He
might well show up.'

'Over the English Channel? If he crashed or was shot down over the English Channel . . . he would have drowned anyway.'

'But there is hope, Charles. We must be patient, and pray that he is still alive.'

'Some hope,' he answered despondently. 'How is Linden taking it?'

'She's utterly distraught.'

'That was a silly question, wasn't it? I'd have expected her to be nothing less.'

The promised letter arrived two harrowing days later. Jenkins, realizing what it was and its importance, sought Linden as soon as the post arrived and handed it to her. She was sitting with Penny in the breakfast room, pushing an uneaten rasher of bacon, her ration for the week, around her plate. When Jenkins appeared, she looked up.

'I think your letter has arrived, ma'am,' she remarked softly.

'Oh, Margaret. Thank you.' Linden got up to receive the letter and opened it as she sat down again. As she read its contents tears formed once more in her eyes, which were already red from continued weeping. There seemed to be no end to it.

'What does it say, Linden?' Penny asked gently. 'Do you want to read it to me?'

Linden handed it over silently and Penny digested its contents.

> *RAF Exeter.*
> *6 September 1941*
> *Dear Mrs Burgayne,*
> *By the time you receive this letter, you will have had a telegram informing you that your husband, Flying Officer Edward Burgayne has been reported missing as a result of Air Operations. It is with sincere regret that I write to you conveying as I do the feelings of my entire Squadron. On the morning of 3 September at approximately five o' clock Edward and a colleague, Pilot Officer Royston Hughes, took off from this aerodrome to patrol the skies over the English Channel for signs of approaching enemy aircraft. The enemy has been conducting low level and high level attacks on our aerodromes with a view to*

*crippling our air superiority. Unfortunately, your husband
failed to return, and his aircraft was seen losing height
and in a severely damaged condition by PO Hughes.*

*Your husband always displayed keenness and consid-
erable ability, and had many friends. We lost one of our
finest and bravest men when his aircraft failed to return,
and one for which a great future had already been mapped
out with this Squadron. His presence is greatly missed
and his loss is regretted by all.*

*Your husband's personal affects have been gathered
together and will be retained for a short period in the
hope that better news will be received. You may be aware
that in quite a large percentage of cases aircrew reported
missing are eventually reported prisoner-of-war, and I hope
that this may give you some comfort in your anxiety. It is
likely that the Red Cross will inform you before I get to
hear.*

*It is desired to explain that the message in the telegram
notifying you that your husband was believed killed, was
included with the object of avoiding his chance of escape
being prejudiced by undue publicity in case he is still
alive and at large. This is a precaution in the case of all
missing personnel.*

*Once again please accept the deep sympathy of us
all, and let us hope that we may soon have some good
news of the safety of your husband.*

*Yours Sincerely
B. Bingham
Wing Commander*

Twenty-Three

L inden hurried up the stairs to show the letter to Charles, and tapped gently on the door to his bedroom. He was grievously affected by the loss of his younger son, which had an adverse effect on his overall condition. Right then he was alone, slumped in his wicker chair in the window that looked out on to the grounds of Kinlet Hall. But his eyes were shut to the world.

'Charles?' she said gently, in case he was asleep.

He roused, slowly turning his head to face her. He looked like death, and Linden was alarmed at his apparent worsening since the day before. He was so vastly changed from the proud, confident captain of industry she had worked with and admired.

'Linden,' he croaked, and managed a smile. 'Come and sit by me.'

She did as she was bid, pulling the stool from the dressing table close to him.

'This letter just arrived, Charles. It's from Edward's Wing Commander. Full of regrets, of course. Would you like to read it?'

'My eyes are not so good, Linden . . . Please read it to me.'

She read it out, slowly and precisely.

'It's not like the last time when he turned up in Ireland, is it?' she commented with a profound sigh afterwards. 'This is altogether different.'

'Altogether more serious,' he gasped, finding breathing more difficult. 'It really doesn't offer much in the way of hope.'

'But he might turn up,' she said, in an effort to cheer him a little. 'Even if he's alive and been captured, at least that means he'll be freed when the war ends.'

'Whenever that might be,' Charles replied dolefully.

'Are you comfortable, Charles? Is there something I can get you while I'm here?'

'You're a good girl, Linden,' he said with a sad smile. 'I hope and pray that Edward turns up for you. I've never seen him so happy as when he's with you.'

'It's the same for me too, you know. I'm like a ship without a sail without him.'

'I know, my dear.' He reached for her hand, and she met him halfway, clasping his affectionately. 'It must be so very painful for you, Linden.'

'Painful for us all . . . But, Charles, I do have some good news that might cheer you. At least I hope it does.'

He looked at her enquiringly, the light in his eyes, dimmed for so long, brightening a little. 'Do tell me.'

'I'm having Edward's baby . . .'

It took a second or two to sink in, coming, as it did, as a complete surprise. 'But that's simply tremendous news, Linden. You're going to give us a grandchild. Oh, I couldn't be more pleased. Congratulations, my dear.'

'Thank you. I thought it would please you. I do hope it's a boy and that he's the image of his daddy.'

Charles's smile was one of delight. 'Oh, wait till the rest of the family know.'

'Oh, no, Charles, I don't want anybody else to know yet. This is just between the two of us. It's not absolutely certain yet, although I am pretty sure.'

'But it's just the tonic everybody needs.'

'Please, Charles. Please don't say anything yet. Let me tell them in my own time.'

He squeezed her hand. 'Very well . . . I just hope I don't talk in my sleep and blurt it out in front of Dorothy.'

She smiled caringly. 'Thank you . . . You know, you've always been very good to me, always very kind. I want to thank you for that as well.'

'Because I've always thought the world of you, Linden. And I'm proud that you are my daughter-in-law. I just hope the future bodes well for you.'

'Mmm,' she agreed. 'So do I.'

'Well, speaking frankly . . . and realistically . . . If dear Edward does not show up – and we all pray he will, of course – you should know that the Burgaynes will always look after you and your baby when it arrives. Your child will be a Burgayne, Linden. He, or she, will be treated as such. Always remember that.'

Linden was touched, and tears trembled on her long lashes. 'Thank you, Charles. Naturally, I've suspected for a week or two that I've been carrying a child, and it has been a concern as to what would happen if Edward were ever lost – even before he was lost. It's pretty hazardous being an RAF pilot.'

'Too hazardous for my taste,' Charles concurred. He sighed deeply, gasping for breath.

'Are you all right, Charles?'

'I feel quite hot and faint all of a sudden. Could you please help me into bed?'

'Of course . . .'

She stood up, and helped him to his feet, steadying him as she took the few awkward steps to his bed. He slumped down and, as he rested back on his pillows, she lifted his legs and tucked his feet into bed, then helped him lean forward and plumped up his pillows. He was sweating profusely, and his breathing was coming in sharp rasps.

'Thank you,' he gasped, polite as ever, even in his extreme discomfort.

'I'll call a nurse from the convalescents' room.'

'No, stay,' he implored. 'Dorothy should be here very shortly. Tell me what names you have thought of for your baby.'

'I haven't given it a thought yet,' she admitted. 'But if it's a boy, then I shall call him Edward. Certainly Edward.'

'A good choice, and hardly surprising. And if it's a girl?'

'Mmm . . . I need more notice.'

He smiled through his suffering, and closed his eyes, his breathing still laboured. Within a couple of minutes it was clear he was asleep, and Linden planted a kiss on his cheek before she tip-toed out of the room.

She immediately sought Dorothy, and Dorothy hurried to his room, then hurried back downstairs to the telephone. She called Dr Mackenzie.

'Charles is running a temperature, Vernon, and I am concerned,' she explained.

'I see. I'll be there shortly.'

After Dr Mackenzie examined Charles he diagnosed that he had developed pneumonia.

'Which is exactly what I was hoping to avoid,' he added.

*   *   *

Charles Burgayne passed away on Sunday 21 September 1941. Linden sat with him much of the time during his suffering, watching this once-great man, a true gentleman, fade away. In the early stages, Dr Mackenzie said it was possible he might recover, but Linden could see that even he didn't really believe recovery was likely. Besides the illness, Charles had taken the additional punishment of the loss of his son, and felt partly responsible for that loss. The trauma of grief had taken its toll and expedited his death, for he had lost the will to fight for his life.

Kinlet Hall was engulfed in sorrow. The loss of Edward was hard enough to bear, for there was still no news, but Charles too . . .

The funeral was held on Friday the twenty-seventh. As the clock struck twelve, every pew inside the ancient sandstone church of St Mary at Enville was filled. The Burgayne family were huddled in the front pew, behind them relatives, friends and business associates, as well as a numerous contingent from the steelworks, including Joe Woods, Linden's father. Just a few short weeks ago Linden had been married here.

Then everybody filed outside to the churchyard in a sombre procession and stood in random groups around the precisely cut rectangular hole in the ground. The day was grey, misty and autumnal. The wind had freshened, and the flowers placed lovingly on the graves of the long dead in the churchyard quivered in the vases that held them. The breeze brought with it some spots of rain that rustled and pattered in the tops of the trees.

Linden looked out across the valley behind the village and recalled the first time she had watched Edward, Adrian and Penny riding across with others, hooves thundering and hounds baying during the first Boxing Day hunt she'd been invited to. Little had she realized then that she would be looking across the same valley, uncannily silent on this day, mourning Edward's loss in war just a few short years later, and the death of his father also.

Dorothy Burgayne sniffed and wiped her tears, and Hugh, with a great show of filial love, put a comforting arm around her. Penny shifted silently to Linden's side, and Linden felt her friend's arm around her waist. Linden realized that Penny too needed comforting, so they gloomily held on to each other, like the devoted sisters they had become.

For Linden especially, this was a double funeral. The only thing missing today was Edward's body, but only God knew where he lay. The tears came, irrepressible, insistent. A million tears she had cried already, but clearly it was not over yet. Helplessness and grief still sickened her, as did the sense of the futility of loving somebody, when that person's life could be snuffed out so easily and so unjustly. She resented the hopeless waste that made a mockery of his bravery and his sensitivity, for he had ultimately been a sensitive man. His loss, and the loss of others like him everywhere, was the consequence of the ambitions and politics of remote and aloof people in positions of extreme power, and had been wrought by their agencies. The suffering they caused ordinary people was beyond endurance.

She resented too the premature demise through more natural causes of Charles, a man she had always admired and had grown to love as a daughter loves a father, whose actual funeral this was. These sudden, unexpected deaths disdained all the striving for betterment, negated the value of wealth and position, for neither money nor influence, however abundant, could have made Charles a well man. Nor could they bring Edward back.

Yet inside her was growing the next Burgayne – Edward's son or daughter. However much of a mockery death made of her hopes and her dreams, she must protect this life, for it was all she would ever have of Edward now.

To take her mind off things, and to try and make herself useful, Linden did her best to immerse herself in work, and she drove herself everyday to the steelworks. She occupied the same office she had occupied before and found that she missed Charles greatly. She half-expected him to call her into his office, or venture into hers and ask her to do this or that for him, but because it didn't happen her sense of his loss was accentuated.

Some of the other girls had harboured resentment of her heightened status, but were genuinely sorry that after such a tragically short time married, she was now, suddenly, a widow. They sensed her sadness and shared in it. After all, they were equally likely to suffer similarly, since their husbands or sweethearts were away fighting this dreadful war. But for all the closeness that sympathy engendered, there were still material differences

between Linden and the others. When she went home she did
not go back to a small, damp terraced house with a privy in the
back yard, where baths were relatively infrequent and taken in
a tin tub in the scullery, but to a mansion in acres of beautiful
wooded grounds, with bathrooms and servants. Why, she even
had the use of a motorcar with which to drive herself to and
from work. They seemed to forgive her for that too.

Hugh was evidently still smarting. For rebuffing his ardent
advances, he rarely spoke to Linden, so she drove herself to
work in Edward's MG. When he did deign to speak it was
curtly.

Yet Hugh still harboured this dark, secret lust for Linden,
fuelled by his still regular, secret spying on her through the
crack in the floor of the attic. By now he had built up quite a
collection of photographs, some showing her naked and some
scantily clad in her underwear, which he kept in a file marked
'LW' in a draw of a cabinet in his cellar darkroom. It was a
sin that she was going to waste, unloved and unserviced, in
that big bed in that vast, all but empty house. He strove to think
of the best way of getting her to be his friend again, and ultimately his lover. After all, his father was no longer alive and
could not be an obstacle, Edward was out of the way, Penny
was spending more and more time in nurses' accommodation
at the Royal Hospital in Wolverhampton, and his mother would
be oblivious to anything anyway because of her grief.

Besides, he controlled everything now. He had ultimate
power; over the works, over his employees, over his father's
entire estate, and over his mother. He could do just as he
pleased and nobody would dare gainsay him for fear of getting
on the wrong side of him. He was God.

To demonstrate the fact he would do away with his father's
Bentley which he had inherited. He had never liked the car
anyway; it was far too stodgy for a chap in his late twenties.
If only he could get hold of one of those American jobs – a
Cord, or a Cadillac would be much more preferable, much
better suited to the image of himself as the wealthy, dashing
young man about town he was keen to become. It could only
do his standing with women a power of good.

Then he had a brilliant idea. He thought he could see a way
to gain Linden's friendship, her admiration, and a certain route
into her knickers. He rang her office.

'Linden, it's Hugh. Would you like to step into my office a moment?'

She put down the receiver, got up, and made her way to Hugh's office with a notepad and pencil, wondering why on earth he wasn't using his own secretary. She tapped on his door, and waited for him to acknowledge her.

'Sit down, Linden,' he said pleasantly.

'What can I do for you, Hugh?'

'You can listen to me.' He smiled, an amiable smile that had the opposite effect to that which he was trying to achieve, and immediately put her on her guard. 'I wish to offer the hand of friendship, Linden. We live in the same house, you and me, and I see no sense in us living in enmity. Don't you think it would be much more comfortable, much more agreeable if we could forget our differences and get on with our lives as friends?'

'It sounds logical,' she replied, privately sceptical of his intentions.

'I understand how you have suffered, your grief over Edward. I know too how fond you were of my father. I would like to make some recompense.'

'So what are you proposing?' she asked, trying not to sound sceptical.

'First of all, I propose to give you my Jaguar car. You've done very well learning to drive so quickly. It's yours, to use as you please. It's small recompense.'

'That's very generous, Hugh . . . Forgive me if I sound cynical, though, but what do you want in return?'

He held his hands up in a gesture of candidness. 'Nothing. There are no strings attached. I merely want us to live in peace and accord.'

'So you won't want access to my bedroom?'

'That *is* being cynical, Linden,' he answered calmly. 'Anyway, you lock your bedroom door,' he added, and she wondered how he knew that if he hadn't tried to get in.

'It's very kind, and I thank you, Hugh, but I don't know if I should accept your offer. You see, Edward's MG is now mine. It falls to me as his widow, so I don't need another car. I can only drive one at a time.'

'So you are spurning my offer?'

'Not spurning, no. I see no practical reason to own another

car when the one I have is perfectly adequate. But I do appreciate your offer of a truce between us. As you say, it will
make life much more agreeable at Kinlet Hall, instead of us
trying to avoid each other.'

'So we have a truce at least?'

'You're my brother-in-law, so yes, let's have a truce,' she
agreed. 'I welcome a truce.'

Hugh had broken the ice, and laid the foundations for his
plan, but his idea of a truce was somewhat different from
Linden's. To him it meant a resumption of former endeavours, with Linden remaining friendly and even becoming
compliant. To Linden it meant a truce – peace, pure and
simple.

A week passed and Dorothy, having developed a cold, was
sent packing to bed by Hugh with a bottle of aspirin. He had
become overbearing and impatient with his mother, had come
to regard her as a burden since his father had died. Penny,
meanwhile, was still living in Wolverhampton at the hospital.
Linden was sitting on one of the settees in the drawing-room
reading the latest issue of *Picture Post* and its update on the
war, when Hugh sat himself beside her.

'Don't you get lonely nowadays, Linden?' he asked clumsily.

'How could I possibly be lonely with you at my side?' she
answered, looking up.

The sarcasm went straight over Hugh's head and he said,
'Do you mean that, Linden?'

For a man who was capable of running a steelworks, which
he did with ample aplomb, he could be decidedly dim, she
thought.

'If I thought you meant that,' he added, 'I'd kiss you.'

'There's no need to go to such drastic lengths, I assure you.'
She resumed reading *Picture Post*, feigning a nonchalance she
did not feel. He was up to his old tricks again, surely.

His arm came around her shoulder and gave her a hug. 'I'd
like to think that I could be more than just a friend, you know,
more than just your brother-in-law,' he said smoothly. 'I've
always admired you tremendously, Linden, you know that.
And with Edward not around anymore . . .'

Linden shifted smartly along the settee away from him.
'That's just about the most insensitive thing anybody could

say to me, Hugh,' she protested, pushing back tears. 'Do you think that because Edward has been posted missing—'

'And is most certainly dead,' he interjected.

She sighed. 'Do you think that because Edward has been posted missing,' she repeated patiently, 'I don't love him anymore? He's on my mind constantly. I never stop thinking about him, hoping that I'll receive some news that he's alive and well, and in some prisoner-of-war camp in Germany. Don't you know that that's all I live for now? Yet you seem unable to comprehend it. You seem incapable of understanding anybody's feelings but your own.'

'You're right on that count, I understand my own well enough. I understand that I want you and that I've wanted you from the outset; yet you are always so offish . . . and it hurts. Are you such a cold fish?'

'Not with the right person.'

'You mean like Pilot Officer Farnell?'

'No, I don't mean like Pilot Officer Farnell,' she answered indignantly.

'Have you heard from him since he left?'

'No, I haven't. Why should I?'

'You and he seemed very fond. So he had his fun and scarpered, eh, disappearing into the land of Babylon?'

'I really don't know what you mean, Hugh, but it sounds offensive. I thought we had a truce. I thought we agreed not to rub each other up the wrong way.'

'That's true, and I'm sorry. I just get so frustrated with you so near and yet so far away.'

'There's nothing I can do to help you there.'

'But there is, Linden, don't you see? Just give yourself up to me. I'll care for you, I'll look after you. I'll make you the happiest woman in the world. You can have whatever you want. Your wish is my command. I'm a wealthy man since my father died. I control his entire estate. You could have access to it all, through me. All you have to do is sleep with me.'

'Is that all?'

'Well . . . You know what people do when they sleep together?'

'You make it sound very tempting, Hugh,' she replied, trying to hide her disdain.

'I hope it might help sway you. This too . . .'

He leaned over and kissed her on the lips. For a fleeting second, she was too taken aback to resist. It was a mistake. In that same fleeting second, he translated that lack of resistance as resignation, and his hand went straight to her breast, slightly plumper now.

'Hugh!' she protested, pulling away.

'Oh, come on, Linden,' he said impatiently. 'Grow up.'

Without further ado he pushed her down so that she was lying on the settee and spread himself on top of her, still trying to kiss her, his free hand clawing at her skirt. She turned her face from him, protesting vehemently, trying to push his hand from up her skirt. But he was bigger and stronger than she was. He forced his knees between her legs, hurting her, and she yelled in complaint. His hand went around one cheek of her bottom and she could feel the elastic of her knickers tighten around her waist as he yanked on it.

'*Hugh*!' she shrieked again. She began thumping his back with clenched fists, but it made no difference. He was tugging her knickers relentlessly down her legs, and she felt them rip under the strain as she resisted. Pressing his whole weight upon her, pinning her down, he unfastened his fly and she felt him unleash his manhood. Unless she could do something drastic in the next few seconds she was going to be subjected to it. The thought made her feel nauseous and she screamed in protest. She had idly wondered as a girl how she would feel if she were to be raped, not thinking for a minute that it would ever happen; yet here she was now, held fast and hard beneath a man intent on having his way.

'You must understand, Linden,' he rasped through clenched teeth as he put all his strength into tearing away her knickers, 'that I am the master in this house, and so long as you live here you will do as I want you to do. The sooner you accept this, the happier you will be.'

The last resisting threads of torn cotton and elastic gave way and he tossed her knickers aside. Linden made one last gasping attempt to free herself, to dislodge him from between her legs. She managed to get one arm free, and she brought her hand up to his face, and tore down it, feeling the resistance of his temple and the flesh of his cheek as she dug her fingernails in deep.

He yelled with pain, loosed her, but slapped her hard across the face in retaliation.

'You minx!' he roared. 'You'll not get away with that.'

'*Hugh*!' a voice called conveying absolute disapproval 'I have never witnessed such scandalous behaviour in all my life.' It was Dorothy. She was standing watching in outraged astonishment, hands on hips. Linden had no idea how long she had been there, but her intervention at any rate was timely. 'You should be utterly ashamed of yourself . . .' She approached Linden, who was struggling to regain her composure, feeling suddenly embarrassed and practically naked minus her one important item of underwear. 'Linden, my dear . . . Are you all right?'

Linden, flushed from her struggle, ran her fingers through her hair, which was all over her face in an unruly mop. She picked up her torn knickers from the floor and threw them scornfully at Hugh as a souvenir. Shamefacedly, he restored his drooping manhood to its rightful place.

'Thank you, Dorothy,' she gasped breathlessly. 'I think I'm all right, thanks only to you. You couldn't have cut it any finer, though. I hope you could tell I was not a willing party to all that.'

'That much was obvious,' Dorothy replied with re-energized contempt for Hugh in her icy look and her voice. 'My dear, I can't think what has come over him.'

'Well one thing is for certain, Dorothy,' Linden said, smoothing the creases out of her skirt self-consciously. 'I can't stay in this house a moment longer.'

'You're leaving?'

'Tonight. Would you stay a moment longer with *this* maniac on the loose?'

'No. I confess, in your position I would not . . . after witnessing what I have just witnessed. But it is not my wish that you leave, Linden.'

'Nevertheless, I shall pack my things and go. I've never been so humiliated in all my life.' She glared at Hugh. 'This is not the first time he's tried this, Dorothy, and I really have no intention of putting up with it.'

'I really had no idea, Linden.'

Just then Jenkins appeared, alerted by Linden's screams and curious to know what the fuss was about. Dorothy saw her and shepherded her quickly away.

'There's no need for you to be concerned, Jenkins,' Dorothy

said calmly. 'Linden just had a little fright, but it's all over now.'

'I thought somebody was being murdered,' Jenkins remarked, sceptical of the inadequate explanation.

'Oh, somebody will be if he's not very careful.'

Linden rushed upstairs to her room, packed as many of her things as she could cram into a suitcase, and left in the MG.

Twenty-Four

Penny returned home next day to enjoy some free time away from the hospital. She had exams coming up and needed somewhere quiet to study, and Kinlet Hall was the ideal place. Besides, she would have some mail to catch up on. There were sure to be letters from Harry Wilding, and she looked forward to them; a bit of sentimentality was a welcome change from the gruesomeness of the hospital wards.

It was just before seven when she pulled up before the house, and it struck her how quickly the nights were drawing in. She was glad to be home before dark, for she did not enjoy driving in the blackout. The evening was cool and dark clouds loitered above the tree tops in the western sky as she made her way across the gravel drive to the front door.

Inside, she looked for the unclaimed mail, on the vast and ancient chest of drawers on which it normally waited, but there was none. Odd.

'I'm home,' she called.

The house felt strange, cold, lacking in atmosphere, and she put it down to the difference the death of her father had made.

Jenkins appeared. Her ready smile and her usual cheerfulness were lost.

'Hello, Margaret. Where is everybody?'

'Oh, Mr Hugh's in the cellar, miss, working in his dark-room, and Mrs Burgayne is in the drawing-room.'

'Thank you, Margaret.' She pointed to the old chest of drawers. 'Is there no post for me?'

'Er . . . Mr Hugh still insists he takes the post, miss.'

'Oh, really? Then I'll see what he has of mine when I've seen my mother, and chastise him for being so presumptuous.'

Penny took off her jacket and handed it to Jenkins, then headed for the drawing room. She greeted Dorothy with a

kiss and sat on the settee beside her, cross-legged, dangling
her sensible shoe from her toe by its tongue.

'How have you been, Mother?'

'Me? *I've* been quite all right considering . . .' Dorothy was
knitting socks for the war effort.

'You make it sound as if nobody else is.'

'There *has* been a problem, Penny.' She looked up from
her work with a frown. 'Quite a problem.'

'Concerning who?'

'Concerning Linden.'

'Linden? Where is Linden?'

'Unfortunately, she's left.'

'Left? You mean she's gone from here?'

'That's exactly what I mean.'

'How come, Mother? What's happened?'

'I'm afraid her presence had become quite too much for
Hugh.'

'In what way? I don't know what you mean.'

'In the worst possible way that a man can be affected by
a thoroughly pretty girl.'

'Oh . . .' Penny nodded her understanding. 'I always
suspected he fancied her on the quiet. So you've sent her away?
Mother, I can't believe you've sent her away because of that.'

'I haven't sent her away.' Dorothy resumed knitting. 'I didn't
want her to go. She left of her own free will, and frankly, I
would've done the same in her position. Hugh suddenly made
her life impossible here. He tried to rape her, you know.'

'He *what*?'

'In this very room. On this very sofa. I had gone to bed
early with a cold, then shortly afterwards I heard these terrible
screams. I intervened at what appeared to be a critical
moment—'

'Oh, spare me the details, Mother.'

'Well, Hugh hasn't forgiven me for the interruption, and I
haven't forgiven him either for being such a callous bounder.
So we co-exist in a world of silent brooding. His father would
have gone mad.'

'Father would've *killed* him.'

Dorothy sighed profoundly and put down her knitting.
'Anyway, I'm so happy to see you, Penny. At least I'll have
somebody to talk to.'

'But poor Linden,' Penny said. 'I must go and see her. I presume she's gone back to her mum and dad?'

'I presume so. She hasn't been in touch.'

'What a complete idiot Hugh is. He's grabbed hold of my post, I understand. Where does he keep it?'

'In his room, I imagine. Oh, he started having the post so his father wouldn't have the worry of dealing with business communications while he was ill.'

'But all business stuff goes to the works,' Penny argued logically. She shrugged. 'He certainly gets some strange notions. I take it there's no news of Edward?'

'None, dear.'

Penny watched tears well up in her mother's eyes at mention of Edward's name, and decided she should turn the conversation.

'How are the convalescents?'

'Thriving, as far as I am aware. We've taken in three new lads in the past week.'

'Maybe I should go and inspect them. There might be a likely candidate among them,' she said flippantly.

'Oh, don't joke about such things, Penny. Hugh insists that Linden's been having an affair with one RAF chap.'

Penny gasped with indignation. 'Whatever Hugh might think, Mother, I can assure you that Linden most certainly was not. I know her and she's not that sort of girl. She idolized Edward.'

'That's what I always like to think, but Hugh was adamant.'

'Well he's bloody-well wrong. He's way off beam. So when did he tell you this pack of lies. Before or after his skirmish with Linden?'

'After . . . during a fit of remorse. No doubt trying to justify his beastly actions against her.'

'The poor girl. I'm going to give him a piece of my mind.'

'Please, say nothing, Penny. All's quiet now. Let sleeping dogs lie.'

'Jenkins says he's in the cellar, buggering about in his darkroom. I'm going to see him.'

'Don't say anything, Penny.'

'I'm making no such promise, Mother.'

So Penny grabbed a flash lamp and made her way to the cellar, prepared for a fight. The door to the sectioned-off area used as Hugh's darkroom was shut, and when she tried it she found it was locked.

'Hugh?' she called. 'It's Penny. Can I come in?'

'You'll have to wait,' he called back tersely. 'I'm in the middle of something.'

'Well hurry, it's chilly down here.' She wrapped her arms around herself in an effort to ward off the cold, and waited.

Eventually she heard him unlock the door and open it. The main light was on, as well as his orange safety lights by which he did his photographic printing. The acrid smell of hypo assailed her.

'What d'you want?'

'Oh good evening, Hugh, how lovely to see you,' she said with exaggerated sarcasm. 'Gosh, I haven't seen you for ages and all you can say is "What d'you want?" First of all I want my mail. What right have you to stash it away?'

'You can have your mail when I go upstairs.'

'What right have you to stash away anybody's mail, come to that?' she queried, stressing the point.

'What else do you want?' he asked, avoiding giving an answer. 'I assume there's something else.'

'Yes. I just heard about the disgraceful incident with Linden. You really ought to be ashamed of yourself. Have you no sense? Have you no regard for the way the poor girl feels about Edward, grieving over him as she is? A decent, innocent girl like that.'

'Innocent?' he muttered scornfully. 'She's not so innocent.'

'Oh, I know what you think,' Penny hissed with equal disdain. 'You're stupid enough to think she was having an affair with Pilot Officer Farnell.'

'As a matter of fact, I do. I have some photographs of the two of them together that prove it.'

'Oh? Do show me.'

He went to the filing cabinet, opened the top draw guardedly, his back turned directly towards her so that she couldn't see, and flipped through various files. After some seconds he handed her two prints.

'There . . .'

They certainly depicted Linden and Keith Farnell together. She was looking into his eyes and laughing, and her arm was on his in a gesture of familiarity.

'You bloody fool,' Penny scoffed. 'These don't prove anything. Linden is a friendly girl. She always thinks the best of everybody, and she's sharing a joke with Keith. She always touches people she gets on with. She's the sort of person who does it without thinking. It's her nature. It means nothing.'

'Think what you like,' he said grumpily. 'I know what I saw.'

'Whatever you saw – or think you saw – it gives you no right to try and rape her. Who on earth do you think you are? God? – sitting in judgement? The poor, poor girl. I presume that because she can't stand the sight of you anymore she's given up her job, too?'

'There was a letter of resignation from her at the works, yes.'

'So now she's left with no means of supporting herself. That's *very* good, Hugh. That really is *terribly* clever. Do you realize what a true and abiding arsehole you are?'

Gladys and Joe Woods were entirely happy to receive Linden back into their home, and she occupied her old bedroom looking out on to Hill Street.

'When the bab comes, our Linden, we'll have the box room cleared out ready so's we can put a cot in there, eh?' Gladys was quick to suggest. 'It'll be lovely having a bab in the house. It'll help keep us young.'

Linden smiled indulgently, pleased that they were pleased. Their attitude made life so much more bearable, and she soon settled into the unpretentious roll of their dependent young daughter once again, as if it had always been that way.

She had been back in Hill Street no more than a week when a letter arrived for her. It was from Irene Attwood, one of Linden's school friends. When last they had seen each other, at the dance held at the grammar school, they had all expressed a wish to hold a reunion four years later. Well, Irene had tracked down most of them and she had hired a room at the Dudley Arms Hotel for Saturday, 8 November at 7.30 p.m. Was she engaged or even married yet? It would be lovely to see her and catch up on each other's lives since leaving school. And would she please reply as soon as possible?

So Linden replied, saying yes, she would love to go and see the others, to find out how they were getting on in this awful war.

The same day the letter arrived, so did Penny. The two girls greeted each other tearfully, with sisterly hugs, and Linden said Penny should sit and have a cup of tea with Gladys while she changed and made herself presentable, for they would go out.

The air had a definite autumnal nip as they walked down the entry to Penny's Riley and clambered into it.

'Right. Where are we going?' Penny enquired.

'Anywhere,' Linden replied. 'Just drive off and stop somewhere quiet. I didn't want to talk in front of my mum and dad.'

'I imagine they don't know everything, then?' Penny said, starting the engine. 'I heard from my mother about your awful spat with Hugh. What a complete nincompoop he is. I really gave him a piece of my mind over that. I can only apologize for his outlandish behaviour.' She put the car into gear and drove off.

'It's over and done with, Penny, and I never want to see him again. But my mum and dad know nothing of that. It would only upset them . . . Then there's something you don't know, Penny . . .'

'Oh?'

'I'm having Edward's baby.'

Penny stopped the car at once, in the middle of the road. 'That's absolutely the best news I've heard in years. You're delighted, of course?'

'Of course I'm delighted.' Linden grinned, pleased at Penny's reaction.

'So when is it due?'

'You know, I haven't worked it out accurately, but it'll be sometime towards the end of April.'

'Gosh, I'd say that's about as accurate as you can get. Let's see . . . You must've conceived on your honeymoon.'

'Of course. When else?' She laughed self-consciously. 'In Ludlow . . . Or maybe even at Kinlet Hall when we returned – the night before Edward rejoined his squadron. I like to think it was that night . . . We hardly slept . . .'

'Lucky you,' Penny offered. 'I should hope you didn't. Of course, there's no news of poor Edward. Have you given up hope?'

Linden sighed. 'Oh, Penny, I ache for him. But I do try to

be realistic. If he was still alive, somebody somewhere would have found him by now, and he'd either be held in a prisoner-of-war camp or sent back to his squadron, depending on who found him. There's no word either way, so I'm inclined to think he's lying at the bottom of the sea, probably still in his shattered Hurricane.'

'You paint a horrifying picture, Linden. But we have much in common, you and me. I lost Adrian and was convinced my world had ended. Now you've lost Edward, and no doubt you think your world has ended too. But it hasn't, Linden, believe me. You'll get over the heartache. It'll take time, but you'll get over it.'

'At least I've got a baby to look forward to, Penny,' she sighed. 'At least I shall have something of Edward to remind me of him. He'd be so proud . . .'

'So he would,' Penny concurred softly. 'So am I. Bloody hell, I'm going to be an aunty, for Christ's sake. I want to be the child's godmother, too. Will you let me?'

Linden laughed. 'Course. I would've asked you anyway . . . So what's the latest on Harry Wilding?'

'He's got a desk job with the Royal Army Ordnance Corps. No more front line fighting for him. You have to agree it's much safer.'

'Good to hear. But I don't mean his army career. I mean the romance.'

'Oh . . . Well, the fool's asked me to marry him . . . and I think I will . . .'

'Oh, Penny, that's brilliant. I'm so pleased. When?'

'We haven't decided yet. We can either wait till this damned war's over and then do it, or do it when he's next on leave.' She shrugged. 'What would you do?'

'Do you love him dearly?'

'Yes, I love him dearly.'

'Then why wait?'

'Mmm . . . There is a certain logic there, Linden . . .'

Linden was delighted to see her old school friends again. In the four years that had passed, several had married, most to servicemen who were away fighting in the war. She, Irene Attwood and Doreen Gilbert, her closest school pals, drifted off into their own private clique where they brought each other up to date with their lives as they supped. Linden told her story to appropriately timed oohs and aahs, and sincere expressions of sympathy at the recent loss of her husband, rendered all the more poignant since she admitted she was already pregnant with his child.

'So what shall you do?' Doreen asked.

'Oh, I'll try and find another job till I get too big and can't work any more,' Linden answered. 'I can't expect my dad to keep me, and the baby will be another burden for him when it arrives. The trouble is, folk don't want to employ somebody who's going to have to leave soon to have a child.'

'What about when it's born? Will you still work?'

'I won't be able to,' Linden said. 'I could hardly expect my mother to look after my child while I went out to work. Anyway, I shall want to look after it myself.'

'I think his family ought to help you out,' Irene remarked, trying to be helpful. 'I mean to say, it's not as if they're short of money if they own that big steelworks down Peartree Lane. And it will be their grandchild.'

'If Edward's father were still alive, I'm sure they would, Irene,' Linden said. 'But I don't get on with the new head of the family, Edward's older brother. He's the reason I gave up my job there and moved out of their home.'

'You fell out with him?'

'You could put it that way. I won't get a penny because of him. But neither would I want anything off *him*.'

'So what happened to that chap Ron who you used to go out with?' Doreen enquired. 'He was nice. Wouldn't you fancy seeing him again?'

Linden shrugged and smiled. 'Once I met Edward, I wasn't interested in Ron anymore,' she replied. 'Anyway, I presume he's in the army or air force now, like most other chaps, if the Germans haven't got him.'

'He's in the army,' Irene declared. 'One of the girls I work with lives near him, and she knows him. We were talking about you – that's how it came to light.'

'Whether or no,' Linden remarked. 'Why talk about him? Let's talk about you two. Tell me what you've been up to.'

Twenty-Five

Weeks and months passed and the gruesome war spread and grew. Hong Kong fell to the Japanese and the Allies failed to stem their relentless advance through Malaya. In February 1942 the Japanese had taken Singapore. The Germans were getting the better of the British in the Western Desert too. At the end of March the RAF began a terror-bombing campaign, dropping thousands of incendiary bombs on German cities. The Nazis responded in April by bombing British cities listed in their Baedeker guidebook, and Exeter, Bath, Norwich and York were all hit in consequence. But the Germans were meeting fierce resistance from the Red Army in Russia, which was making heavy demands on manpower and machinery. It seemed the Germans might have bitten off more than they could chew.

Linden was slowly coming to terms with Edward's loss. Some days were better than others. Some days she tended to dwell on thoughts of him for longer than she should, and made herself miserable in the process. The lack of any news told her he had never been found, otherwise she would have heard; Penny would be quick enough to inform her of any letter or telegram that arrived.

On 30 April, Linden was full of reflections, and feeling particularly downcast.

Her child was due but still she had no pains, no signs that the birth was imminent. She could feel it kicking healthily inside her, so she was not worried about going over her time a little. All the same, she wished she could get it over and done with so she could sleep more comfortably and move around more easily. In the afternoon, she decided to take a walk, despite her big belly, and told her mother she would be about an hour. She wanted to be alone, to walk in the soft April rains under the canopy of trees that was Oakham Road and remember Edward.

As she walked, her mind was full of him, the precious
moments they had shared. Memories flooded back ceaselessly.
She recalled the very first time she'd met him when she'd
been invited to Kinlet Hall to make up a four at tennis, and
Penny was doing her best to entice Adrian into a love affair.
Little had Linden thought then that she would eventually
become Edward's wife, much less his widow. It was the widow-
hood that was so brutal a circumstance, a circumstance that
really tore at her emotions. She'd had so little time as his
wife, so little time to enjoy marriage before he had been so
cruelly snatched away. No longer could she talk to him, no
longer could she touch him, take his hand, feel his sweet lips
on hers, be caressed by his warmth . . . Her child would never
know its father.

She recalled the exhilaration of that flight in his beloved
Moth and how privileged she had been to have experienced
it with him; because of it she could appreciate his love of
flying. She remembered the first evenings out in foursomes
with Penny and Adrian, dancing so close to Edward at the
Stewponey, talking with him, laughing, eating fish and chips
from Wall Heath late at night; the time that first cold Boxing
Day when she had been invited to see the Enville Hunt. She'd
been so lucky to have done all that – an ordinary working
girl. She recalled their first serious kiss just before he had
returned to Cambridge, when Ron had so rudely interrupted
them. Was that an omen for the future she had not recognized? Why had they held back their love, she and Edward?
Why hadn't they made the most of what time they had while
he was alive, by committing to each other before he had
finished his university studies? They could have met during
those times; she could have gone to Cambridge for weekends,
or they could have met halfway. What languid, loving nights
they would have had. But, instead, they had waited.

Her thoughts wandered to the first night they had made
love in the open air at Enville Common, hidden by ferns.
Never had she felt so happy, so close to anybody. She recalled
how he had been as nervous as she was, but how she'd tried
not to show it, and had actually led that fateful expedition
into virgin territory. Then the long, long wait before they could
be together again, and the weird but vigorously romantic time
in Ireland. She recalled the joy and pride she had felt when

he'd escaped and announced that they should be married, and the panic to get everything organized in a week. Now he was gone, and the promise of happiness was gone with him. How futile it had all been.

At least, though, she was about to have his child, and she welcomed it with all her heart. She had no thoughts, no notions of meeting another man when the passage of time had finally healed her broken heart. She could love no other man like she loved Edward. Her child would be her saviour.

The rain came heavier, drumming on the burgeoning spring foliage of the trees around her, but she walked on defiantly. If only she'd thought to bring a brolly. She turned up her collar and nestled deeper inside her coat. The rain and the wind could not hurt her. She would weather them, like she'd weathered the heartache. The rain began to seep into her coat; her hair, hatless, was becoming limp and bedraggled and the drops trickled down her face like an overabundance of tears. What would Edward think of her if he could see her now with her nine-month belly, and soaked to her very skin, looking decidedly unglamorous? She hardly looked like the pristine and personal private secretary she had once been at the height of her efficiency. But she would weather it. She would re-emerge from this all the wiser, all the more worldly, and all the more compassionately.

And then she felt it: the first pang that told her that her baby was on its way.

Elizabeth Penelope Burgayne was born on 1 May 1942, a healthy baby weighing seven pounds five ounces, with blue eyes like her father and dark hair like her mother. As the days and weeks passed it became clearer that little Elizabeth was destined to inherit her mother's looks and daintiness.

Motherhood came naturally to Linden. She idolized her child and watched her bloom into a healthy, contented baby. Elizabeth helped take her mind off Edward, as she had known she would, although she would have given anything to see Edward with his child; he would have been so appreciative, so admiring, so proud. Gladys and Joe both doted on the baby and it seemed to Linden that all she had to do was feed the fragile and precious bundle.

Linden's figure soon returned to its former slenderness and

her belly, she was pleased to see, was free of stretch marks. What excess weight she had put on during her pregnancy she soon lost, although it was challenging to get fat on the reduced diet of food rationing.

Then, one day in the heat of August, Linden and Gladys were taking a break from the day's chores, enjoying a cup of tea. Linden took advantage of the break to feed Elizabeth and the baby was at her breast, when they heard a knock on the door of the veranda. Gladys, corsets creaking and with a sigh at the interruption, got up to answer it. 'Oh, my God!' she exclaimed. 'Look who it is.'

Linden, alerted by her mother's surprised utterance, stood up to get a look also.

'Jesus Christ!' she said to herself.

Wearing his uniform, standing there waiting to be let in, was Ron Downing.

Gladys greeted him with a broad smile as if he was a long-lost son. 'Come in, my lad. How nice to see you. You home on leave?'

'Yes, I got a few days' leave, Mrs Woods,' Ron replied, a little unsure of himself and what welcome, if any, he might receive. 'I thought I'd come and say hello to you and Linden. I heard she's had a bit of a bad time.'

'It's nice of you to think of her,' Gladys said. 'She's in the house feeding the baby. Come and say hello. She'll be thrilled to see you.'

Ron was a little embarrassed to witness Linden with the child at her breast, but she knew better than to rob the baby of its feed and induce squawks and tears of protestation. So she carried on unruffled. He tried not to look, but she smiled her greeting at him from her chair with fewer inhibitions. Childbirth had taught her that where babies were concerned, bashfulness and self-consciousness were entirely out of place.

'You won't mind if I don't get up, Ron.'

'Don't worry, chick, I can see you've got your hands full.' He smiled amiably. 'How are you anyway?'

'Well enough, thank you.' She looked him up and down appraisingly. 'You as well. You look very smart in your uniform.'

'Think so?'

'I do. Don't you think so, Mum?'

'He looks very smart,' Gladys agreed.

Ron smiled appreciatively. 'So who's this little person?'

'This is Elizabeth,' Linden informed him. 'And isn't she beautiful?' She eased the child away from her nipple and turned her towards Ron, for him to see her better. 'Don't you think so?'

'She's gorgeous,' he agreed. Little Elizabeth, robbed of her dinner, opened her eyes momentarily in protest and he saw how vividly blue and clear they were. He also saw how very smooth and appealing Linden's pale, exposed breast was, but Linden did not appear to mind. She returned the child to it and Elizabeth continued suckling keenly.

'I heard you'd got married, Linden,' he said, trying to tread carefully. 'I bumped into somebody who knows Irene who you were at school with. Anyway, *she* told me. She said your husband was posted missing.'

'Yes,' Linden replied economically.

'I'm ever so sorry. It must have been horrible for you, especially as you was having a baby as well.'

'Well, you can imagine, can't you?'

'And there's nothing more been heard of him?'

Linden shook her head and glanced at the baby. 'And you, Ron?' she said, turning the emphasis away from herself. 'Are you courting, or engaged, or anything?'

'Me? No . . .' He wanted to say that there could never be anybody but Linden Woods for him, but he thought better than to let it be known there and then, even though it was the only reason he was there.

'I'm surprised,' she commented. 'A nice-looking chap like you. I'd have thought the girls would've been falling over themselves. Are you sure there's nobody?'

'Well, nobody serious . . . It seems that all those couples who are serious get wed quick. This war has led to more and more folk getting married earlier – rush jobs.'

'So how long are you on leave?'

'Three days. Not long enough o' course . . . But while I'm on leave . . . if you fancy going out one night . . .'

'Oh, that would be nice, our Linden,' Gladys intervened, hardly masking her enthusiasm. 'Why don't you? Once the baby's been fed and put to bed, I can look after her.'

Ron looked at Linden imploringly, awaiting her response.

'I think my mother's keen to get me married off again,' Linden joked.

'Oh, don't be daft, our Linden. But it wouldn't hurt to go out with Ron. You used to go out with him often enough . . .'

'For old times' sake, eh, chick?' Ron said brightly. 'You can tell me all about your husband. I'd like to hear.'

Linden smiled. The baby had finished feeding, and while Ron's eyes were averted momentarily, she discreetly wiped her breast and covered herself up, then put the baby to her shoulder to coax up any wind.

'OK, if you like,' she agreed. 'But I can't promise I'll be the best company you've ever had.'

'It'll be nice just to catch up on each other's lives after so long,' Ron said. 'We'll have plenty to tell each other, I reckon.'

Ron stayed about half an hour over a cup of tea. Secretly he wondered how he would have felt if the little child before him had been his. Under different circumstances she might have been. She really was a lovely little thing.

'Can I hold the baby a minute?' he asked.

'Are you sure?' Linden looked at him doubtfully.

'Yes,' he reassured her. 'I'd like to.'

Linden passed Elizabeth to him carefully. He held her tentatively at first, then with greater confidence when she did not struggle to escape his arms like some vigorous young puppy. He rocked the baby gently for a minute or two, looking down at her with tenderness.

'She's like you, Linden,' he said, handing her back.

'Everybody says so, but I can see her daddy in her more and more.'

Ron called for Linden the following evening. It was warm and sultry, as August generally is in England, and they walked together up Oakham Road, where Linden had walked alone the day before Elizabeth had been born.

'I was really sorry to hear about your husband,' he said sincerely. 'I think it's a terrible thing for somebody your age to be a widow. So many good lads have perished fighting in this war, and there's so many girls like you . . . in the same boat, I mean.'

'Oh, I know,' she replied. 'I know I'm not the only one. But that really doesn't help much.'

'No, I don't suppose it does.'

'So what about you, Ron? What have you been up to? It's been – what? – four years since we last saw each other?'

'About that,' he agreed. 'I joined up soon after the outbreak of war. I was sent to France and got out OK in the mad scramble of Dunkirk. I've just got back from the Western Desert. Rommel's been giving us quite a bashing out there, but now Montgomery's taken over you'll see a change.'

'How are your folks?'

'Mum and Dad are OK.'

'Give them my best wishes.'

'Oh, I will. They send theirs, by the way.'

'That's nice of them.'

They walked on in silence for what seemed like an age. Conversation did not seem to flow naturally like it used to, and Linden put it down to mutual nervousness. After all, she had rejected him in favour of Edward; it must be playing on his mind. It was playing on hers.

'I've never been interested in anybody else but you, you know, Linden,' he suddenly remarked, breaking the silence.

'There's plenty other fish in the sea, Ron.'

'Oh, you say that, but having lost the love of your life, does it feel that way to you?'

'No,' she admitted, and smiled sadly. 'I take your point.'

'Well then . . . Anyway, who knows? . . . When this war's over, you and me could do worse than get back together again.'

She laughed at that, not dismissively but self-consciously. 'You're a glutton for punishment. I'd have thought you'd had enough of me after the merry dance I led you before.'

'Never. If I thought there was a chance of it, I'd wait for you.'

'You mean you'd be prepared to take on another man's child? Your old rival's child?'

'Course. The baby would be all part of the bargain, eh?'

'Well, I can make no promises,' she said gently. 'You have to understand that Edward was the whole world to me. It's going to take a long time to get over him. Oh, Elizabeth helps – I love her to bits; but as yet I can't see that far into the future.'

'I understand, chick,' he said kindly. 'But there'll come a time when this war is over, and folk will want to start to lead normal lives again. You'll need a man to look after you, to help bring up your baby. You can't depend on your father to keep you. You'll need a bit of security in your life, and so will your child. I'm prepared to provide it if I'm spared this war. I'd just like you to bear it in mind.'

'Oh, you're a good and kind soul, Ron,' she answered. 'You're decent and reliable, the sort of man many a girl would give her all for, and I appreciate your offer. But it's too much of a sacrifice for you to make. It's too soon for me yet in any case. I'd be no good for you. I'm still raw from losing Edward. Ask me in another two years if this damned war is still on then – if you still feel the same.'

The war ground on and, during that time, Penny married her Harry Wilding. While he remained in the army she remained nominally at Kinlet Hall, but spent most of her time at the Royal Hospital in Wolverhampton. She found it difficult to live in the same house as Hugh. He had contrived to commandeer his father's entire estate, and allowed his mother a pittance only for clothing and the little luxuries of life when, throughout her married life, she had been used to having the best of everything, and in abundance. To satisfy the law he made her a director of Blower's Green Steelworks, but unpaid, and made all decisions himself; he controlled the company entirely. Dorothy was allowed no independence, and became almost a prisoner in what used to be her husband's house. Since Charles's death Hugh effectively owned the property. He suffered the convalescents only because he didn't relish a confrontation with the Red Cross and how it would look if he cast them out. Nor had Penny seen any of her father's inheritance that she felt sure was due to her. Consequently she had to live on her nurse's pay. No doubt there was recourse through the courts to what was rightfully hers, but the potential costs of litigation precluded her doing anything yet. She decided to wait till the war was over and she had settled down to a normal life with Harry before she embarked on something which was undesirable anyway and would tear apart what remained of the Burgayne family.

Elizabeth had her second birthday, and Linden her twenty-fifth, and Gladys made a cake with which to celebrate, despite the constraints of sugar rationing. Penny, by this time a fully fledged nurse, was invited to the little party, and they all made a pleasant evening of it. Aunty Penny helped put Elizabeth to bed and read her a story; she had been allowed to stay up later than usual as it was her birthday. Gladys and Joe retired to bed at half past ten, with the excuse that Joe must be fresh for work next morning, but diplomatically leaving Penny and Linden to talk, which they did over a bottle of beer.

Penny brought Linden up to date with Hugh's latest tyrannies, and news of Harry's pen-pushing in the Royal Army Ordnance Corps in France.

'It will be grand to have him on leave again, but I don't expect to see him now before the end of the war,' Penny said resignedly. 'How about Ron? What's happening with him?'

'Oh, we still write,' Linden replied. 'He's asked me to marry him and, I must say, the older I get, the more it makes sense. After all, I can't allow myself and Elizabeth to be a burden on my mum and dad forever.'

'Is that the only thing that would induce you into marriage again? – being a burden?'

'No, but it's a consideration.'

'So you might marry Ron, but not because you are in love with him?' Penny queried.

'He knows how I feel, Penny,' Linden answered defensively.

'But you're still a young woman, Linden, and in your prime. If you're anything like me you still have a healthy sexual appetite too, even though it can't be satisfied very often. Would Ron do for you in that department, if you don't actually love him?'

'If I were Ron's wife, of course he would have to do for me. I suppose sex would have to be part of the arrangement, whether or no. Lots of girls marry, Penny, but not always for love. Life isn't like that. Some women marry for security, for a roof over their heads. Anyway, Ron is not actually repulsive. In fact, he's quite handsome – he's certainly improved with age. It's just that I never used to fancy him that way. And as you get older, I imagine that side of things becomes less important.'

'Not to me it doesn't, and nor will it to you, I suspect. Not for a long time yet. You and Edward were like rabbits. You said so yourself.'

Linden grinned impishly. 'We were. We couldn't get enough of each other. It was an addiction with us. Nothing will ever come close to that again. Nothing.'

'So when Ron is about his nightly exercise upon you, you will be lying back and thinking of Edward—'

'Wishing it could be Edward.'

'So it won't be the same, Linden, because it's not Edward. You will resent it. It will become a chore.'

'I think I know this, Penny.'

'Yet you are prepared to put up with it for the sake of not being a burden on your parents?'

'I must.'

'And is this forthcoming marriage, of which I don't really approve, imminent?'

Linden shrugged, typically. 'That I don't know. It depends whether he gets some leave soon.'

'Well, I ask you to think about it very seriously.'

'I have thought about it, Penny,' Linden replied, avoiding Penny's eyes in her admonishment. 'Very seriously . . .' She looked up more challengingly. 'Do I take it then, that you wouldn't consider being my maid-of-honour?'

Penny sighed. 'You are my best friend, Linden, so I will do whatever you want. It's simply that I don't – I can't – condone your marrying Ron. Nor will it be fair on him, don't you see? There must be hundreds of chaps more worthy of you – chaps you'd fancy.'

'I also have Elizabeth to consider. Ron would be very good with her.'

'So would any number of men. I just think you're making the ghastly mistake of going along with the first man who offers himself. Don't do it, Linden. After Edward, you're vulnerable. I think you're still on the rebound, even after all this time.'

Twenty-Six

Despite Penny's protestations, Linden agreed to marry Ron Downing. She had thought it through very carefully and the benefits seemed to outweigh the impediments. Ron was a good man, he loved her, he would cherish her, and he would be a sound father to Elizabeth. He understood what Linden had gone through, and was prepared to make allowances if her responses to him were not as heartfelt as they had been with Edward. All this they had discussed very frankly in a series of letters. In time, she would grow to love him dearly, he had predicted, and she was inclined to agree that she might – if nothing else, he was deserving of her love. The days, the dreams of living her life as Edward Burgayne's devoted wife, in the secure embrace of a wealthy and influential family, had long disappeared. What a dream it had been, but reality had to be faced.

The war was all but won by this time, and Ron was due home on leave for Christmas before being posted to the Ardennes where the Germans were making a last ditch attempt to recapture Antwerp, in Belgium, so as to cut off supplies to the advancing Allied armies. Linden had made all necessary arrangements for the registry-office wedding. All that remained was for Ron to appear – he was due home on 20 December 1944 – and to obtain the special licence that would enable them to become man and wife on Friday the twenty-second, just in time for a very merry Christmas.

On the nineteenth, the day before Ron was due, Linden took Elizabeth in her pushchair to the Post Office at St John's Road on Kates Hill to collect her allowance. There was a telephone kiosk on the corner there, and she had arranged to ring Penny who would be home at Kinlet Hall that day. It was cold and damp, but people were wearing smiles on their faces at the welcome prospect of Christmas, victory and an end to the war.

'It's all set, Penny,' Linden said into the handset. 'I'm just waiting for him to get home on leave. We shall be married on Friday.'

Silence.

'Say something, Penny . . . Please wish me well.'

'Oh, Linden, of course I wish you well,' came the reply at last. 'I shall be there, don't worry.'

'Oh, I know you don't think it's for the best, but I have to make my own mind up about these things, don't I? If Edward were still alive I wouldn't be doing this anyway. But Ron's a good man. We'll be all right, Elizabeth and me.'

'Ignore me, Linden. I'm a silly romantic at heart, and I just don't see much romance in what you're doing. Now, with Edward, it *was* romantic.'

'But it is practical. So will you come to the house first on Friday?'

'Yes, I'll come to your house.'

'Come early then, because there'll be lots to do, and we shall depend on you for a lift.'

'You sound quite excited, Linden.'

'I suppose I am, really.'

'How's my niece, by the way?'

'Oh, fine, except that she got covered in writing ink this morning, the little monkey. Mum left a bottle within her reach. Of course, she managed to get hold of it and opened it. It went everywhere. I just hope we can wash it off her by Friday.'

Penny chuckled. 'Kids! What I wouldn't give for a houseful.'

'Your chance will come, Penny.'

'Yours too, for many more.'

'Eventually, who knows? . . . See you Friday.'

She put down the receiver and carried Elizabeth back to her pushchair. Yes, she was quite excited now at the prospect of marrying Ron.

Penny made her way back to the drawing room where her mother was mending – sewing a button on a blouse she'd had for years. Jenkins arrived there at the same time carrying a tray, a pot of tea and two cups and saucers, and set them down on an occasional table before Dorothy.

'Well, it's all set,' Penny announced resignedly. 'Linden's

marrying her old sweetheart when he arrives back on leave for Christmas. I don't hold with it; I think she's doing it for the wrong reasons, but she has her own ideas.'

Dorothy cut the cotton thread and put her needle back into a pincushion. 'I think I can understand how she feels,' she commented. 'A young woman with a child must be anxious that they are both cared for. It's her duty as a mother to see that her child gets the best on offer.'

Jenkins was listening, and hesitated to leave.

'I do understand that, Mummy, but she doesn't love this chap, although she does like him – more as an old friend, though, than a paramour.'

'But that's nice,' Dorothy said, tying the strand of cotton off. 'If that's the case, maybe he won't make too many demands on her.'

'I think the boot's on the other foot, Mummy. She won't make many demands on him, but I think it'll be a different kettle of fish with him. He's hungry for her, and has been for years. He'll not be able to keep his hands off her.'

'Oh, Penny, you can be quite coarse sometimes. It's so unbecoming. I'm sure it must be mixing with common nurses that does it.'

'I've always called a spade a spade, Mother.'

'Young Mrs Burgayne's getting married again?' Jenkins interjected, still hovering.

'On Friday, Margaret. Didn't you know?'

'No, I had no idea, miss. But I wouldn't have thought it the proper thing to do, under the circumstances.'

'What circumstances? As a widow, unencumbered by a husband, as she is now, she is free to marry if she so desires. I just don't think she's chosen the right man. Or, put another way, I don't think the right man has chosen her, for that's what it amounts to.'

'Does Mr Hugh know that young Mrs Burgayne is to remarry, miss?'

'One presumes he knows. Why? Does his opinion matter?'

'No, I just wondered, miss,' Jenkins said, and made a rapid exit.

The big day arrived, and after breakfast Penny rang for Jenkins to come to her room to help her get ready. She was sitting in her underwear, rolling her stockings up her legs and looking pensive when Jenkins arrived.

'I think I shall need a vest on today if I'm going to have to stand out in the cold, Margaret. What do you think?'

'Yes, I think so, miss. I would if I were you at any rate. It seems a bit chilly out.'

'There's one in my drawer over there.'

Jenkins went to the chest of drawers. She withdrew a vest and placed it on Penny's bed.

'I think young Mrs Burgayne's very wrong to get wed again, miss,' Jenkins declared, out of the blue.

'So you agree with me, then, Margaret?'

'Well, I mean, miss – what about if Mr Edward is still alive in a prisoner-of-war camp, and he comes home after the war and finds his wife has got married to somebody else?'

'That would be tragic, I agree. Not to mention making her second marriage illegal. But we all know there's little chance of it happening in this case.'

'Pardon me for saying so, miss, but Mr Edward is still alive.'

Penny looked at her with a frown of curiosity. 'What on earth makes you say that?'

Jenkins shrugged. 'There have been letters . . .'

'Letters? What kind of letters?'

'Letters, miss.' She shrugged again, guiltily, and her colour rose.

'Letters from whom, Margaret? You must tell me.'

'I dunno who from, miss . . . Mr Hugh always had them.'

'Letters from Edward?' Penny asked with incredulity.

'Letters . . . and cards.'

Penny felt herself go hot. 'So where are these letters and cards now?'

'I dunno, miss. Like I say, Mr Hugh always had them.'

'Yes . . . He did, didn't he?' Penny said, instantly prepared to give the notion more credibility than heretofore.

Letters . . .

If there had been letters about Edward, why hadn't Hugh handed them over? What would he do with such letters anyway? Well . . . he was normally a stickler for order and organization. Maybe they were still around somewhere . . .

'If he knows I've said anything, miss, he'll kill me,' Jenkins bleated.

'No he won't,' Penny said impatiently. 'Because I shan't impli-
cate you. Look, you can go now. I can manage from here on.'

'If you're sure, miss.'

'I'm sure. Go and make my mother a cup of tea or
something.'

'Very good, miss.' Jenkins left the room, closing the door
behind her.

Surely Hugh would never hide letters that revealed information about Edward, even if such letters existed. Yet he had
been vetting the post. He had even taken hold of her own
letters until she had fought him over it. Had that order never
been rescinded? Was Jenkins still faithfully handing him the
mail every day? To what purpose? But what if the person for
whom the letters were intended was not here to receive them?
What if that person was Linden? Penny's thoughts raced on,
gathering momentum by the second. Hugh had tried to rape
Linden. His true colours had come to the fore. His regard for
Linden had subsequently turned somersaults and, since she
had uncovered the monumental flaws in his character, that
high regard had since tumbled to absolute disregard. Would
he, could he have kept all letters addressed to her out of pure
spite? He was certainly capable of it. You only had to witness
how he treated his poor mother to realize how ruthless he
could be.

Then Penny remembered the incident when she'd had to
ask him for her own mail – letters from Harry. She'd had
to go to him in his darkroom and suffer the ignominy of
awaiting his convenience to retrieve them. Once inside he
had showed her photographs of Linden and Keith Farnell,
which he kept in a file . . . *in that filing cabinet.*

Penny quickly finished dressing herself. She put on her coat
and hurried to the cellar. The entrance was outside in the cold,
down some stone steps on the north side of the house. She
found the door was locked. The key had to be somewhere.
Back inside, she rushed upstairs to Hugh's room. This door
was not locked. Jenkins had been in, neatly made his bed,
tidied up and dusted. There was a dressing table, a tallboy, a
chest of drawers. The key to the cellar should be somewhere.
She rifled through them. In the fifth drawer she found a bunch
of keys. One was large and old, made of iron, big and bulky
but smoothed through years of use. This had to be it.

She took it, raced outside again and down the stone steps
to the cellar. She inserted the key. It turned in the lock. She
opened the door and hurried across to the partitioned area
which was the darkroom. That door was locked too. Penny
fumbled through the assortment of keys looking for a likely
contender. She tried a couple. One fitted the lock; it turned
without resistance, and that door opened too. She headed
directly for the filing cabinet. Hugh had opened the top drawer
to find the photos when she had been there before. She tugged
on it, but that, too, was locked. Of course, it would be. Once
more she sorted through the keys and found one that looked
about right. She inserted it into the keyhole and it slid in
unhindered. It turned. She pulled the drawer again, and it
glided open . . .

Penny was breathing hard by this time. What on earth was
she likely to find in here? What evidence of Hugh's evil vindic-
tiveness was she likely to uncover? She trembled at the
prospect. God, if he were to come in here right now he would
kill her. She flipped through the files, lined up neatly and
squarely in the deep drawer. They were all neatly labelled:
Bank, Cameras, Cars, Chemicals, Legal, Developers, Fixers,
Insurance, LW, Miscellaneous, Receipts, Records Various,
Sheet Music, . . . One stood out in that alphabetical list. No
name, just initials.

LW . . .

Linden Woods . . .

Penny withdrew the file, laid it on the dry bench and opened
it. She gasped when she saw how many photographs there
were of Linden in various states of undress, many taken when
she was stark naked. They all had one thing in common: each
was taken from a position above her, looking almost directly
down on her. And taken through a spy hole if the fuzzy outline
at the edges of most was anything to go by. How could he?

Penny continued to flip through the photos and papers. The
photos he'd already shown her of Linden with Keith Farnell
were there, and still they proved nothing. Then she came across
a carbon copy of a typewritten letter . . . How typical of Hugh
to keep a carbon copy: 'for the sake of good order' – that was
always one of his sayings. She pulled it out. It was addressed
to Edward, and dated 31 August 1941 – just a few days before
he had been reported missing. She read the letter with increasing

horror. It told Edward of Linden's 'affair' with Keith Farnell, how she had even tried to entice Hugh into her bedroom. It painted the poor innocent girl a whore, and was written in a very convincing style.

Penny was incensed. This very letter might have been the cause of Edward's death. Saddened to the point of despondency he could have made sure he got himself killed in action, tantamount to committing suicide, rather than suffer the pain and anguish of what his loving, caring brother had so eloquently described. But surely, Edward would never have believed such nonsense? Surely he would have seen straight through it? Events, however, suggested not.

She put the letter down, scarcely able to believe that Hugh could be so vicious. Then she came across another, still in its envelope. It bore the emblem of the Red Cross, and she opened it with trembling hands . . .

> *Friday 28 November 1941*
> *Dear Mrs Burgayne,*
>
> *It is with some trepidation that I write this letter. Part of our remit is to trace missing relatives via our international network and our work is invaluable in bringing comfort and succour to missing servicemen and their relatives from all countries.*
>
> *It has come to our attention that your husband was posted missing believed killed on 3 September 1941 as a result of air combat. However, reports from our network suggest that an RAF pilot was picked up in the English Channel at about 08.00 hours of that morning by a German motor torpedo boat. We are hopeful that this airman was indeed your husband. With the help and co-operation of the Air Ministry we are actively seeking confirmation from the German Authorities that Flying Officer Edward Burgayne is alive and well and is interned in a German prisoner-of-war camp.*
>
> *As soon as we have more information we shall of course be in touch.*
> *Yours faithfully,*
> *Richard H Charlton*
> *pp The British Red Cross*

Maybe this was what Jenkins had meant when she'd said there had been letters. She would have seen the Red Cross emblem on the envelope and put two and two together. Yet either her loyalty to Hugh, or her absolute fear of him, had prevented her from saying anything to anybody – until Linden's second marriage was imminent.

And look just how imminent it was! She looked at her watch anxiously.

There was another letter – also in a Red Cross envelope. She tore it open angrily, read it avidly.

> *14 January 1942*
> *Dear Mrs Burgayne,*
> *It is with very great pleasure that subsequent to my previous letter, I can inform to you that due to the invaluable help from the Air Ministry, information has been secured regarding the fate of your husband Flying Officer Edward Burgayne. He is reported to be interned currently in Dulag Luft Dulag 12, a transit camp for receiving and debriefing captured RAF personnel prior to transit to a prisoner-of-war camp. How long your husband might remain there is not known.*
> *It is important for you to know that the Red Cross operates a postal message scheme which you would be advised to use to make contact with your husband. Most Citizens' Advice Bureaux act as Red Cross Postal Message Bureaux, but those that do not will be able to give the address of your nearest despatching centre . . .*

Penny found evidence that Hugh had used the Red Cross as a means of making contact with Edward, because there was a letter-card from him bearing official German rubber-stamp marks and sent via the Red Cross. It was a response to a note from Hugh, written in Edward's own hand.

> *Hugh,*
> *Devastated to hear of father's death. Dearly want to be home. What news of Linden? Moving to POW camp soon.*

Penny's eyes filled with tears when she read it. Edward was still alive when everybody believed he was dead and had rearranged their lives accordingly. Suddenly she was aware of his raw emotions as he went through all this unnecessary suffering, not knowing what was happening, the absolute and total frustration at being unable to influence matters, particularly where Linden was concerned. *'What news of Linden?'* he had said. Oh, the poor, poor man. Penny wept long and hard for him. The poor man would have been heartbroken to have received all the venomous lies about his wife. It must surely have affected him monstrously.

She eventually wiped her tears and came across another letter-card:

> *Hugh,*
> *Now at Stalag Luft 6 near a town called Heydekrug,*
> *Polish–Lithuanian border. What news of Linden? Please*
> *let me have news soon.*

Hugh had obviously risked sending a full letter, for the next document was another carbon copy of a typewritten letter.

> *4th May 1943*
> *Flying Officer Edward Burgayne,*
> *Stalag Luft 6*
> *Heydekrug*
> *Germany*

> *Dear Edward,*
> *It is indeed good to know that you are finally settled in Stalag Luft 6, with other Allied airmen I imagine, for what must prove to be very stimulating company.*
> *As for Linden, she left Kinlet Hall shortly after Father passed away. She also resigned her job as secretary. Clearly, she was seeking pastures new. I understand that only a month ago she gave birth to a child, a daughter, which clearly could not have been yours some year and a half after your absence. I undertook some undercover investigation, and it appears that her former sweetheart might be the child's father. This merely bears out what I told you before . . .*

Penny was flabbergasted. Hugh had claimed Elizabeth's birth to be a year later than the actual birth so that Edward could hardly begin to imagine himself as the father. Such wickedness. And he'd cited Ron Downing as the father.

She had seen enough. What she had seen sickened her. But she needed this proof she'd found. So she picked up the letters and letter-cards, and one photograph of the naked Linden, and put them to one side. The rest she replaced in the file, which she in turn returned carefully to the drawer in the filing cabinet. She locked it up, took the documents she'd put to one side, turned off the light, left the darkroom and locked that too, then emerged from the cellar into the dull chill of that enlightening December day.

She looked at her watch. She had to stop this wedding. It was nearly twelve already. She should have been at Linden's house by now. The wedding was at one o'clock. Just enough time. She hurried back to her room and grabbed the keys to the Riley, said goodbye to her mother, and left.

Twenty-Seven

L inden was standing at the bottom of the entry awaiting Penny's arrival, on tenterhooks because her friend was late and depending on her to take the family to the registry office. She was wearing her best coat and a new hat, fitting for a wedding, a pair of new nylon stockings that gave her legs a sleek and shapely look, and high-heeled shoes. Fastened to the lapel of her coat was a pink silk rose. She looked every inch a war bride.

Penny drew up outside number 20 and jumped out of the car bearing the filched documents.

'Gosh, you're late, Penny,' Linden admonished mildly. 'Ron will think I've changed my mind.'

'You've got to change your mind, Linden,' Penny gasped as she hurried round the car to the pavement. 'You can't marry Ron. Not while your present husband lives.'

Linden looked at Penny almost with disparagement. She would never have believed that Penny might employ such insensitive delaying tactics.

'What on earth do you mean, Penny?'

Penny was at her side now, waving the papers. 'Linden, Edward is alive and apparently well. I discovered it only this morning.'

'If this is some kind of sick joke . . .'

'If this is any kind of joke, it's not a bit funny, I agree. But it *is* true and a reason to be joyful. Look at these papers, Linden. Edward's own dear brother Hugh – may God damn him till eternity – has hidden from all of us the fact that Edward is alive and well, and in some POW camp in Germany. He's known it for two years, and the proof is here.'

'Edward is alive?' Linden seemed to reel at the news, and Penny steadied her. 'Oh, God . . . Is he really alive, Penny?'

'Absolutely.'

Tears welled up instantly and lingered on Linden's long lashes for a second before trickling down her face. Then her expression changed, to one of resentment. 'If this is a ploy, Penny, it's the cruellest ever . . .'

'It's no ploy, nor is it a dream,' Penny said gently, putting her arms around her. 'Pinch yourself. Edward is alive and well, I tell you. I promise you.'

'Oh, Penny . . . Is it really true?'

'I keep telling you.' Penny gasped with frustration, unable to comprehend Linden's reluctance to accept what she was being told. 'Why won't you believe me when it's all you've wanted to hear for years?'

'Oh, Penny . . . It's like a dreadful mist has suddenly been lifted from my eyes, and I can see where I'm going again. D'you think I'll be able to go and see him, like I did when I went to Ireland?'

'Don't be daft. We're at war with Germany. We weren't at war with Ireland. Look . . . Please read these letters, Linden.'

So Linden read the letters from the Red Cross and was convinced that Edward was alive after all. She looked at Penny, and a smile lightened her face that only a minute ago had been clouded with confusion and doubt.

'Oh, Penny, this is brilliant news . . . But why would Hugh want to hide it from us all? I don't understand.'

'I know why, and I'll tell you because you have to know. But I'm afraid it will take the gloss off this wonderful news. You see, Hugh has evidently tried to turn Edward against you . . . by inventing ridiculous lies. Here . . . You'd better read the lot.'

'Let's go in the house. I'm frozen.'

'No, Linden. Read them here before your mother and father realize what's happening. Then we'll decide how best to tackle what has to be done next.'

'About Ron, you mean?'

'About Ron first, then about Edward.'

So Linden read. When she reached the awful, malicious lies that Hugh had formulated so calculatingly, her mouth dropped open and her moist eyes widened with horror.

'I can't believe this,' she said softly. 'I can't believe anybody would want to do this.'

'Neither can I,' Penny replied. 'I would never have thought him capable of such evil, for that's what it is. It's Hugh's way of getting back at you for refusing him.'

'But this is scandalous, Penny. He should be put away. He must be sick. He should be put in a mental home . . . And what if Edward believes all this rubbish?'

'Being realistic, it must have had some effect. It's my view that when he read that awful first letter from Hugh, he actually wanted to get shot down, heartbroken.'

'My God . . . Oh, Edward, Edward . . .' She clenched her fists in frustration and anger, and more tears came.

'There's more, Linden,' Penny warned. 'Hugh's also been spying on you. Take a look at this . . .' She handed Linden the photograph. 'It's only one of many. There must have been a crack or a hole in your bedroom ceiling. Anyway, I shall investigate that when I get back home.'

'The dirty sod!' she exclaimed with mounting disdain. 'I never liked Hugh, you know, Penny. Something I could never quite put my finger on, but there was always something about him I didn't like. Something dark, something creepy. It seems my opinion was warranted all along.'

'Yes,' Penny agreed.

'Ah well . . .' Linden gave a juddering sigh, then forced a smile through her tears. To Penny, who knew Linden well, it seemed like a smile of relief. 'The wedding's off anyway. I'd better let the bridegroom know.'

'Yes, you don't have to sacrifice yourself after all.'

'I don't, do I?'

Penny perceived an element of acknowledgment in those few words, the acknowledgment that she had accepted she would have been sacrificing herself to Ron.

Back inside the house, Gladys and Joe were dumbfounded but delighted, vastly relieved also to learn that Edward was alive and well. But Gladys felt pangs of sorrow for Ron, who for years had idolized Linden.

'As one heart's mended, another's broken,' she declared with a sigh. 'But that's life . . .' She gave Linden a hug. 'I'm happy for you, my flower. At least, when this war's over, you'll be back together.'

Linden nodded and began to sob. 'I know,' she cried. 'But

you know one of the best things that's come out of this? Elizabeth will get to know and love her real live daddy.'

There was no time to get to the house where Ron Downing had always lived with his parents and where he had been spending his leave, so Penny drove Linden directly to the registry office in Dudley. It was after one o'clock when they arrived, and Ron, resplendent in army uniform, was standing outside on the pavement looking agitated.

When he saw the car draw up he smiled and went to greet her, but when he saw that she had been crying, he was instantly full of foreboding.

'Take this,' Penny said, handing her the letter from the Red Cross confirming Edward's internment. 'You might need it as proof.'

Linden opened the door and stepped out of the car as calmly as she could.

'I thought you were never coming,' he said gently, taking her hand.

'I had to,' she replied as placidly as she knew how.

But he read her well. 'What's up, Linden?'

Penny watched from the car, but could not hear how Linden explained the situation. She saw her take Ron to one side and look earnestly into his eyes as she revealed that her dear beloved Edward was still alive after all. He stood, patiently listening, rolled his eyes disbelievingly, looked away, asked her something and looked at her again, keeping perfectly still while she gave her reply. Then he nodded in Penny's direction and they both turned to glance at her. Penny gave them a little wave of her fingers and smiled. Linden unfolded the letter from the Red Cross and handed it to him; the ultimate proof that she was not simply trying to wriggle out of their arrangement. Poor Ron read it, and began to assume the look of a man who had just been handed a death sentence. He had been so close to attaining his dream, but it was being snatched away from him at the very last minute. Penny felt inordinately sorry for him as she continued watching, for she acknowledged that he *was* a decent man.

There was no need to hear the conversation, she could see it being played out, and it was ineffably poignant: the strong, fearless soldier wiping his eyes as he began to weep for the love of a woman he could not have, the sympathy that was manifest on the exquisite face of this woman he loved as she denied him what he wanted most in the world. He nodded, finally convinced of the situation, wiped an eye again with the back of his hand, then took her hand and kissed her tenderly on the cheek. He turned away; she turned away and headed back to the car.

Linden opened the door and slumped into the seat. 'God . . . Talk about cutting it fine. He's just gone in to tell the registrar the wedding's off.'

'How do you feel?' Penny enquired.

'Drained. Completely drained.'

'Hardly surprising. It's been a funny old day. Can we go yet?'

'Yes, let's go, Penny. You know, that's the most awful thing I think I've ever had to do.'

'You do tend to get yourself into some scrapes with men,' Penny replied, tongue in cheek as she started the engine.

'But I don't mean to . . .' She settled herself more comfortably in the car, glad that the ordeal of facing Ron was over. Another chapter of her life was over, and it was time to move on. 'How long d'you think it will be before the war's over, Penny?'

'Hard to say, but not long.' She put the car into gear and they moved off. 'The Home Guard has been stood down and the Germans are being defeated on every front. Months, if not weeks, I'd say.'

'And then Edward will be released and he'll be home again. Oh, I can hardly wait.'

Penny turned her head and smiled. 'You see, it wouldn't have been right to marry Ron. You'd have been a bigamist.'

'Crikey! I hadn't thought of that. Anyway, what's going to happen about Hugh? He surely can't be allowed to get away with what he's done.'

'Frankly, Linden, I don't know what we should do. He'll have to be confronted, of course, and he'll have to write to Edward again, apologizing for his stupid lies and for keeping from you the fact that he's in a POW camp. Beyond that, I don't know.'

* * *

Penny returned to Kinlet Hall to tell her mother the awful
truth about Hugh and the good news about Edward. Together
they must decide what should be done about Hugh's appalling
behaviour.

'My God, I never realized I had spawned a monster when
I had Hugh. What could have made him turn out the way he
has. He's always had the best of everything – the best education, the best opportunities. How many other men of thirty
inherit a company as large and as successful as the Blower's
Green Steelworks?'

'Maybe that's the trouble,' Penny suggested. 'He's had too
much and therefore expected everything else to fall in his lap.
Even Linden. The problem remains, Mummy, what to do about
him. Can't we stretch him on a rack, or tar and feather him?
Preferably both?'

'Our disdain will be sufficient,' Dorothy said. 'His own
sense of shame will be punishment enough.'

'Is he capable of feeling shame?'

'If not, he is lost.'

'So when shall we tell him?'

'After dinner.'

Hugh duly returned from work. He went upstairs, washed
and changed, flipped through the day's newspaper, and went
in to dinner.

It was a morbidly silent affair, with nobody able or willing
to make conversation. Penny's scornful glances at Hugh were
like daggers. Jenkins could sense the atmosphere and was on
tenterhooks. It was obvious to her that something was afoot,
especially in view of her revelations to Penny earlier.

Then, halfway through the fish course, Dorothy crashed
down her knife and fork, dabbed her mouth with her napkin
and got up, unable to control her resentment.

'I'm sorry,' she said to Penny, 'but I cannot sit at the same
table with my own son, and it breaks my heart.' Tears flooded
her eyes, and she rushed out of the room.

'What's that all about?' Hugh remarked with measured
scorn.

'About you, actually,' Penny replied, with equal contempt.

'Me? Fancy . . .'

Penny turned to Jenkins. 'Margaret, please leave us now,
would you? I have certain things I need to say to my brother.'

Jenkins gave Penny a cutting look, glanced at Hugh apprehensively, then scurried from the room, afraid she was about to be implicated.

'I have been to see Linden today, Hugh,' Penny began. 'It was her wedding day.'

'Oh? Did it go off well?'

'Much better than any of us could have imagined, actually. She's very happy. Very happily married.'

'Did she marry that ne'er-do-well she used to see before?'

'The father of her child, you mean?'

He looked at her puzzled. 'What do you mean? Is he the father of her child?'

'Yes, she's married to the father of her child. Shouldn't she be?'

'Are you saying the chap she's married today is the father of her child?'

Penny smiled; she was confounding him. 'I'm saying the chap she married is the father of her child,' she confirmed, but twisting the words.

'You're talking in riddles, Penny.'

'No, I'm not. Edward is the father of her child and that's who she is married to.'

'But Edward is dead. Linden was going to marry this other chap –this ne'er-do-well.'

'She was . . . but since she discovered that Edward is still alive and well in a prisoner-of-war camp called Stalag Luft 6 somewhere in Germany, she could hardly marry the ne'er-do-well, as you insist on calling him, could she?'

Hugh felt himself go hot. 'I suppose not. But this is great news, Penny. How on earth did she discover Edward is still alive?'

'By letters from the Red Cross initially.'

'Oh?' He looked at her apprehensively.

'Yes. First there was one that said an airman had been picked up from the sea by a German torpedo boat, then another some little time after that confirmed it was Edward, stating he'd been traced to a reception centre for captured Allied airmen.'

'Really?' He hunched his shoulders in the manner that he did when he had a conflict on his hands, and Penny saw that he was flustered.

'Yes. Then she read a copy of a letter written by Edward's loving brother, claiming she'd been having a torrid affair with another airman called Keith Farnell in this very house. It was quite awful, and utterly malicious and, if she's got any sense, she will sue for libel. Also, the effect it had on poor Edward was to make him go out in his aeroplane with the intention of getting himself shot down.'

'You can't prove that.'

'Ah . . .' Penny smiled triumphantly. It was tantamount to an admission of guilt, however inadvertently given. But her smile quickly turned to an icy glare. 'You should be ashamed of yourself, Hugh. Do you realize the heartache you have caused the people you are supposed to love? Do you understand what unhappiness and chaos you have created with your damned pointless lies and your insane meddling? What were you thinking of? And those horrible photographs you sneaked of Linden in her bedroom. It's the behaviour of a unspeakable creep. Father would have been appalled.'

'You've been in my darkroom, going through my files.'

'And a good thing, too,' she rasped, 'else we should never have discovered your insanity. Did you really think you could get away with it? It's my belief we should have you committed. And what sort of reception will you get from Edward once he is back home? The war is nearly over and he'll be released soon. If I were him I'd happily strangle you.'

'I hadn't thought of that. I merely thought he would thank me for exposing Linden for what she is.'

'But whatever you thought she was, it wasn't enough to stop you wanting her for yourself. Is that what this is all about – petty jealousy and spite? I would've thought you too big a man to be troubled by such trivialities. Obviously I was wrong.'

Hugh Burgayne left the house the next morning and did not return. Christmas came and went, and still he did not return. Subsequent enquiries, instigated with the police after the Christmas break, revealed that Hugh had obviously visited his office at some time, had possibly slept there for one or even two nights, and that the petty cash was missing. When it was time to go to the bank to fetch the money required to pay wages, it was discovered that company cheque books were

also missing. Substantial amounts of cash had been with-
drawn, leaving the company bereft.

In her capacity as a director of Blower's Green Steelworks,
Dorothy was obliged to visit the bank and urgently negotiate
facilities to overdraw so that wages and suppliers could be
paid in order for the company to remain in business.

Hugh Burgayne had disappeared off the face of the earth,
taking his own and the company's wealth with him.

At the first opportunity after that Christmas in 1944, Linden
visited the Citizens' Advice Bureau so that she could send a
note using the Red Cross Postal Message Scheme. It had
occurred to her how strange it was that she had seen nothing
in the correspondence that Penny had retrieved from Hugh's
file, that suggested Edward had tried to contact her directly.
This set alarm bells ringing. Had he been convinced by Hugh's
meddling? If so, she had nothing to look forward to but the
divorce courts on his return.

Her note to Edward, consisting of the stipulated twenty
words only, was hardly sufficient to tell him all and let him
know how she felt. But she did her best, and it read:

*Just discovered Hugh's lies. Hugh hid fact you are
no longer missing. Love you always. You have a daughter.
Write.*

She waited anxiously for a reply, but no reply came. Weeks
passed, and the weeks turned into months. But still no word
came, and Linden was back to weeping, beside herself with
worry and frustration, because there was nothing more she
could do.

Twenty-Eight

Edward Burgayne never received the message that Linden sent via the Red Cross. In mid-July 1944 – months earlier than she actually sent it – he and three thousand other prisoners of war were shifted out of Stalag Luft 6, to avoid the advancing Russians. After a gruelling journey crammed into horse trucks, they arrived at another camp in Torun in Poland where they remained only three weeks before being moved again to Fallingbostel, twenty miles north of Hanover. Conditions there were atrocious, and it was already dangerously overcrowded.

At Christmas food began to arrive from the Red Cross, and a parcel of cigarettes arrived in January 1945. By March the supply of parcels dried up, and the Germans' rations, too, had dwindled to nothing. Come April and the Germans hurriedly left the camp, chased by Russians hell-bent on revenge, and on the sixteenth the Americans turned up. They delivered food and drink to the starving prisoners that same night, and over the next two days worked on a plan to transport everyone home.

He duly left Fallingbostel on 20 April. Along with hundreds of other British prisoners of war he was taken to Belgium. From there he was flown to Aylesbury, where he arrived on 22 April. Tea, food and cigarettes were laid on and waiting, since the RAF stations in England were already gearing up to receive returning prisoners of war. Next day he was taken to RAF Cosford, near Wolverhampton, where he would be medically examined, debriefed, and kitted out . . .

Only when he was so close to home did he try to examine his feelings and emotions objectively. For so long he had been incarcerated, cut off from the civilized world. He had been unable to influence things that were going on at home, and there had been such a debilitating lack of information. He'd received no word at all from Linden during his entire internment, when he knew well enough that the Red Cross had let her know where he was by dint of the notes from Hugh. That same dearth of correspondence served only to reinforce the comments Hugh had made about Linden in that awful letter he'd received.

That soul-destroying information had unbalanced him, prompted him to offer himself as an easy target to be shot down, for he foresaw no further joy in living. Having survived it so miraculously, he was forced to consider, in retrospect, how reckless he had been. He began to believe that Fate had played a hand, and he, a fatalist, imagined there had to be a reason. He began to believe there could be life after Linden after all, and that Fate must have chosen him to participate.

Then the doubts would return, and he would tell himself again and again that it could not be true, that Linden must still love him. Yet how could she when he had heard nothing at all from her in all his years pent up in German prisoner-of-war camps? He debated it with himself endlessly. She had obviously given up the wait, had been tempted elsewhere as Hugh had told him. For the sake of his sanity, which had been tested to the limit, for the sake of finality, of a solution, he had to let go of her. He had to let go of his hopes, his dreams, and his love for her.

Yet still he dreamed of her. He dreamed of their easy relationship, the tenderness, the glorious intimacy they had shared, and when he awoke he would suffer again the heartache and anger.

He could not live with doubts; it was not possible. He had to believe one thing or the other, and it was simply easier to let go, to try and forget her, for she was evidently unworthy of remembrance. He'd had no option but to shut Linden from his thoughts and accept that, like so many other wives and fiancées he'd heard about from fellow prisoners, she was fickle, promiscuous and it was in her nature to stray. Besides, he could do nothing about it either way from within the ghastly confines of Stalag Luft 6.

That other letter from Hugh, that other sickening missive claiming there was an illegitimate child, which he received just prior to the exodus from Stalag Luft 6, merely served to confirm her easy virtue. It had unsettled him more than anything else. The very idea that Linden might have had a child by some other chap – and out of wedlock – was utterly abhorrent. Yet he had no option but to accept it. Other men's wives were unfaithful, why not his?

It was natural to give credence to Hugh's letters, sent out of a duty inspired by brotherly love. There was no reason to disbelieve what he read in them. Yet it was an absolute living nightmare; it was pure hell, insufferable. He endured it, but prayed every day that a letter from Linden telling him that she loved him deeply and looked forward to his release at the earliest moment would release him from that hell. Yet no such letter came. Nor would it.

There was a telephone booth in the main reception centre at RAF Cosford. After a few days there Edward believed he ought to make contact with his family. He ought to let them know he was safely back in England, and find out once and for all when Linden had left Kinlet Hall. It was one rather large loose end that needed to be tidied up at the earliest possible moment so that he could resume some sort of life. But first he had to muster up the courage. He did not have the strength to endure the savage confirmation of the truth. Whilst he never lacked the courage to fly his Hurricane into a potentially fatal dog fight, he lacked the courage to face up to what had plagued him for years, but which was finally inevitable; the awful proof that Linden had betrayed him and had a child by another man.

He stood looking at the telephone for some time, preoccupied, willing himself to use it. After some minutes of indecision, he slipped two pennies into the slot, lifted the receiver and made his call.

His mother answered, and the coins dropped with a clatter.

'Mother, it's me, Edward . . .' There were some seconds of uncertainty while Dorothy, suddenly bewildered at the sound of Edward's voice, collected herself . . . 'Mother?' he said again.

'Edward? Is that really you?'

'Yes, it's really me, Mother. Don't you recognize my voice? How have you been keeping?'

'Oh, Edward, Edward, where are you?'

'I'm at RAF Cosford, believe it or not.'

'Cosford? So near? Thank God you're back so soon. Our world has fallen apart since you were reported missing and your dear father passed away. I can't begin to tell you . . . But how are you, dear?'

'Reasonably well, all things considered. Lost a fair bit of weight, though, since last time you saw me. Not enough to eat, especially lately . . . What about Linden, Mother? What happened there?'

'Linden? Linden hasn't lived here for more than three years.'

'So it is true . . .' he breathed, and sighed heavily. His world finally caved in.

'When are you coming home, dear?'

'I can't say, Mother,' he answered despondently. 'It depends when the RAF will release me.'

'Can we ring you, Edward? Do you have a phone number there where we can ring you.'

'I suppose so.'

'Then let me get a pencil and paper and write it down.'

'Then hurry, Mother. I think my money's due to run out of this infernal telephone very soon, and I have no more change.'

'I'll only be a moment . . .'

Unending silence while Dorothy sought after a pencil and paper. She sounded nowhere near as sharp as he remembered.

'Thank God you're back in England,' she said at length, returning to the telephone. 'What number do you have there?'

He read the number from the centre of the dial in front of him. 'It's a payphone,' he added.

'Can you receive visitors?'

'I imagine so,' he replied, absolutely unsure of the truth of it.

'We'll visit you. There's so much to tell—'

The line went dead. His time had run out.

He slammed the receiver back in its cradle with frustration, and glared at the instrument resentfully for a few seconds, thinking his mother might ring him back. But the telephone failed to ring. Tears welled up in his eyes and he wept.

After some time he sensed a presence beside him.

'Let me guess . . . It's a woman . . .'

Edward turned to see a fellow RAF officer, of higher rank, standing next to him – a complete stranger. He nodded morbidly. 'Something like that, sir.' He dried his eyes and returned his handkerchief to his pocket.

'Nothing new there. Fickle creatures, women. Prepared to bugger off with the milkman if he takes their fancy.'

'Thanks,' Edward replied curtly. 'That's just the sort of information I need.'

'Expect nothing, and you won't be disappointed,' the officer said, undeterred. 'That's the worst that can happen, and when it does you know you've hit rock bottom. From then on things can only get better. Are you prepared to accept the worst on that basis?'

'I thought I would be able to, sir. I'd sort of conditioned myself to accept it. I'm not so sure now, though.'

'I know. You've been to hell and back. You've seen it all – the horrors, the depths of human depravity and the suffering. You've witnessed cruelty, wickedness, filth, squalor. I could go on. Things that would horrify you in peacetime and in normal daily life, you have taken in your stride. What you're facing now is no different. You'll take it all in your stride as well. You've no option, when all's said and done.'

Edward forced a smile. 'I believe you might be right, sir.'

'I know I'm right. I'm speaking from experience.'

'Sorry to hear that, sir.'

'I was married once to a beautiful girl whom I absolutely idolized. We promised each other the world, that whatever happened in this war we would remain faithful. But you know what? While I was away fighting in the RAF for king and country, she was distracted. Some glib-talking young buck, no doubt extremely handsome and I daresay sporting a huge dick, talked himself into her underwear and she ran off with him. That's the trouble with beautiful girls, you know – you daren't rest while your back's turned, because some cad will be trying his luck. And women are susceptible – so susceptible. Anyway, I was devastated. I was also angry and wanted to get my own back, and I believed the most vengeful way was to steal somebody else's wife. It seemed fair – somebody had stolen mine after all. And the world owed me that one solitary favour to redress the balance.

'And, do you know, I met one such girl who was an absolutely ideal candidate. A terrific girl. A peach of a girl. I was on bombers, you know – a pilot officer in those days – and we got shot down. I was wounded in the leg and it was touch-and-go whether I'd actually keep the bally thing.

The first thought of the surgeons was to lop it off, but they decided to try and mend it instead with some pretty heroic surgical techniques they were trying. I had countless operations, but it was saved, and I was sent to convalesce at a place not far from here called Kinlet Hall. It was there I met this delightful young thing who was married to the son of the owner of the house, by the name of Burgayne – also an RAF chap it transpired. Well, I fell head over heels for her . . . Linden, her name was . . . and naturally, I plied my charm with a vengeance. She was wonderful to me. She helped me recover, accompanied me around the grounds on therapeutic walks that were supposed to exercise my leg. She listened patiently to my tales of woe. Never have I met a woman more sympathetic or easier to talk to. She was a real gem. She had a sister-in-law too, I remember, called Penny – also a dainty dish . . .'

'But this girl Linden,' Edward prompted, intrigued. 'Did you get anywhere with her?'

The other officer shook his head. 'She was definitely not available for those sort of shenanigans. She was recently wed, was very much in love with her husband, and was not about to stray. In fairness to her, she told me exactly that from the outset, from the very first suggestion I made that I was interested in her, that she could never be unfaithful, that it was not in her nature. Undaunted, however, I subsequently wrote to her, words of undying love that might have swayed a lesser mortal. But they didn't sway Linden Burgayne. Not one solitary inch.' He laughed, shaking his head as he relived his own foolishness. 'I never heard a word from her, from that day to this. But what a woman. What a girl to be married to. Such loyalty, such steadfastness. So you see, it just goes to prove that not all girls are tarred with the same brush.'

Edward held out his hand to his superior officer with an unforced smile. 'Flying Officer Edward Burgayne, sir. Thank you for that information. You've quite given me something to think about.'

'Burgayne? Of Kinlet Hall? Well, I'm blowed.' He took Edward's hand and they shook. 'Flight Lieutenant Keith Farnell . . .'

'Yes, I gathered that, sir . . .'

*   *   *

All the worrying, the doubts, the fears, the frustration, the desolation, the anger, the futility and heartache – especially the heartache – that had been pent up for years and growing like a canker, all seemed to drain away from him in those few seconds. There had never been any hope, and now, suddenly, there was. According to this man, Linden was a gem – loyal, steadfast and true, and that mattered more than anything. Might she still be waiting for him after all?

Yet the question of the child still remained. What she had told Keith Farnell might have been true at the time, but years had slipped by. She might, after all, have grown tired of waiting, as so many did, and sought solace and romance in somebody else's arms. But all that Keith Farnell said conflicted directly with what Hugh had written. Maybe the rest of it was not true. He put a handkerchief to his face to wipe renewed tears away and stepped outside the building into the darkness of the evening.

The sky was clear, the moon and the stars were bright. A perfect night for flying, he thought. But his flying days were over. He would resign his commission.

It was Penny who rapped on the veranda door at 20 Hill Street next morning and Linden who answered it. She could tell by the expression on Penny's face that something significant had happened.

'Penny,' she greeted her uneasily. 'Come in.'

'Come on, girl, spruce yourself up, I'm taking you and Elizabeth out.'

'But—'

'No buts. I want you looking your absolute beautiful best – both of you. I'm taking you out, I said.'

'Where are you taking us?' Linden laughed, safe in her assessment that it was not going to be awful with Penny in blustering mood.

'That's for me to know and you to find out.'

'I won't go with you if you won't tell me,' Linden teased.

'Suit yourself,' Penny replied, feigning nonchalance, 'but it's somewhere rather special, and you're the one who'll be missing out. Persuade her, please, Gladys.'

'Fancy a cup of tea while you wait, Penny?' Gladys enquired.

'That would be really nice.'

So Penny sat and talked to Gladys and had a cup of tea, giving no clue as to where she was about to take Linden and Elizabeth, while they got ready upstairs.

When the stairs door opened, Linden stepped down the last step in a simple cotton dress with a tasteful floral print, nylon stockings and high heels. Her hair was perfect and her make-up exquisite.

'I didn't mean that you had to outshine me so vividly, Linden,' Penny said in mock protest. 'My God, you look divine. Doesn't she, Gladys?'

'I wish I knew where she gets her looks from,' Gladys replied. 'It certainly ain't me – nor her dad neither.'

Then Elizabeth appeared treading gingerly down the stairs behind Linden, clinging to the handrail as she'd been taught. She was clean and spruce in a pale yellow cotton dress, white ankle socks and dainty shoes, her dark hair tied in two bunches with matching ribbons.

'And you, young lady – I can see you're going to take after your mummy. You look nice enough to eat, Elizabeth.'

'Fank you, Aunty Penny,' Elizabeth replied with becoming coyness. 'Where are you taking us? Mummy says she wants to know.'

'Mummy will know soon enough, dear. Somewhere nice, anyway – for both of you.'

They bade Gladys goodbye, filed through the entry to the street and got into Penny's car.

Penny steered the conversation in the direction of generalities: about Harry, about the war, about anything and everything, avoiding any reference to Edward. They drove through Sedgley, through the centre of Wolverhampton, and were out in the pleasant suburb of Tettenhall where the road was overhung with a grotto of trees before Linden commented that this was quite a long journey for them to take by car. Penny drove on, into open countryside, and then through the sleepy, attractive village of Albrighton. Here, aeroplanes were flying low overhead, some taking off and others landing one after the other, which betokened the close proximity of an aerodrome. Then Linden saw what was unmistakably a huge RAF base, and Penny slowed down.

'This looks like an RAF place,' Linden said. 'Is this where you're taking us?'

'When I can find the way in,' Penny replied dismissively.

'Why here?'

'You'll see.'

Anxiety stirred within her. It must have something to do
with Edward. But what? Perhaps it was the commanding
officer from his squadron who was here and wished to see
her. But why? To tell her he was dead after all and hand over
all his personal effects which so far she had not seen? No, he
would have sent a letter, his things in a parcel. Besides, Penny's
demeanour would have been different. All manner of possibilities ran through her mind, except the correct one.

Penny turned into the base and stopped at a barrier. She
got out of the car, closed the door behind her and talked with
the guard. Linden saw how he smiled, and she knew then it
was nothing too grave. The guard pointed towards one of the
buildings, Penny obviously thanked him, got back into the car
and, once the barrier was raised, drove on.

She pulled up outside a brick building, turned to Linden
and said, 'Wait here, you two,' and disappeared inside.

'I'm a visitor for Flying Officer Edward Burgayne, a recently
returned prisoner-of-war,' she announced to the RAF man at
the desk.

The man smiled. 'I'll see if I can get him found and sent
here for you.' He saw the wedding ring on her finger. 'Are
you his wife?'

'His sister.'

'Ah.'

The man picked up the telephone and started making
enquiries. He smiled at Penny, and said, 'Got him. He's on
his way.'

'Is there somewhere private I can talk to him?'

'Yes, there's a room over there.' He pointed to a closed
door and Penny thanked him.

'I'll wait here. Which way will he come?'

'Through the door behind me, I imagine. He's coming from
that direction.'

'He won't come in the way I did?'

'Doubtful.'

Penny nodded, satisfied that Edward would not see Linden
until she had prepared him.

After a wait that seemed interminable, Edward arrived, and

Penny was staggered at how thin and gaunt he was. But they rushed towards each other and hugged.

'Oh, Edward,' she sighed, 'it's so wonderful to see you back.' She let go of him and looked him up and down. 'But you're so painfully thin. Are you quite well?'

'The doctors tell me I'll almost certainly survive,' he said flippantly, as if it would be a great disappointment if he did. 'The last few months we were half starved. Our calorie intake fell to about eight hundred a day, then nothing – due to food shortages, of course. But I'll soon put weight on when I'm home. Anyway, look at you – you look wonderful.'

'I'm a married woman now – Mrs Harry Wilding, no less,' she declared proudly. 'He's an army chap. Met him at Kinlet Hall when he was a convalescent. He's in Belgium now with Eisenhower's lot, clearing up.'

'I met another convalescent from Kinlet Hall last night,' Edward declared.

'Oh? Who was that?'

'A chap called Keith Farnell. A flight lieutenant, stationed here. Did you know him?'

'Bloody hell!' Penny exclaimed. 'Fancy him being stationed here. He was terribly sweet on Linden.'

'So he said – before he knew who I was. He said some very nice things about her.'

'I need to talk to you about Keith Farnell,' Penny said. 'And Linden.'

'Oh? So did they have an affair then?'

'No, absolutely not, Edward, despite what Hugh wrote. I found copies of the despicable letters Hugh sent you. There was not a word of truth in either of them except for the part where he said she'd left Kinlet Hall. She did, but only because he made her life hell. She went back to live with her mother and father. There was never ever any question of wanton infidelity, Edward.'

'I only wish I could believe that.'

Penny recalled Linden's intention to marry Ron Downing. 'Well, you must remember, Edward, that she believed you were dead. We all did.'

He looked at Penny apprehensively. 'So there have been other men? Is that what you're about to tell me?'

'No, Edward. What you are not aware of, but what you

must understand and take into account, is that Hugh intercepted the correspondence the Red Cross sent to Linden
telling her you had been found, and were alive and well in a
prisoner-of-war camp. She had no idea.'

'But why would he do that?' Edward queried incredulously.

'Spite. But more of that later. Linden has been through hell,
as we all have – the same as you have. So you must bear in
mind that she thought you were dead. She has her own story to
tell, and I wouldn't dream of trying to tell it for her. That's all
I want to say on her behalf . . . But there is one more thing . . .'

'What?'

'Hugh . . . After proving himself to be such an out-and-out
bastard he's disappeared, and hasn't been seen or heard of for
months. Driven by shame at what he's done to this family, I
have no doubt. Strangely, though, Margaret Jenkins, our maid
of long-standing, has also disappeared. We think it's more
than coincidental. We believe she was pregnant with Hugh's
child, according to some snippets of information that cook
gave us. Hugh has also robbed the company, leaving it bereft
of capital, and we're having to borrow heavily from the bank.
We shall expect you to take the helm at Blower's Green
Steelworks and see if together we can't get through the crisis.'

'There's my career sorted out then,' he said.

'You'll learn more later. There's much more. Anyway—'

'Anyway . . . back to Linden . . . Is it true she has a child?'

'Yes, Edward.' Penny answered with a smile. 'She has a
child . . .'

He groaned, plagued by the notion, and paid no attention
when Penny said, 'Now, just wait here . . .'

Twenty-Nine

Penny hurried outside. In the Riley Elizabeth was sitting in Linden's lap, and they were playing a game. Linden looked up questioningly when she saw Penny open the driver's door and get back into the car.

'Are we leaving already?' Linden asked.

'No . . .' Penny turned to face her. 'Linden, I brought you here to see Edward—'

Linden gasped, putting her hand to her mouth in shock. 'Edward?' she queried, incredulous. 'You mean he's here? At Cosford? Not in Germany?'

'Precisely that. He's inside that building.' She nodded in the general direction.

At once Linden opened the car door. 'Then I'll go and see him straight away.'

Penny held her arm. 'Wait, Linden. Listen to me first . . .'

'Go on.' Linden sat back in the chair reluctantly heeding Penny's advice.

'He's been through hell, and it shows. He's painfully thin. He's been half-starved these last few months, but he told me the doctors say he'll be OK. Those letters Hugh sent have obviously had an effect, and he's certainly not convinced that you've been faithful. I would be careful how you tell him you were due to be married to Ron. In fact, if I were you I wouldn't mention it at all yet. Not until he's settled and confident again of your love. He might think the worst. Elizabeth is also a worry, because he never knew you were pregnant and he has no notion that he is the child's father. You can thank Hugh for that, of course.'

'You didn't tell him he has a daughter, then?'

'No. Because I believe you must have that pleasure. *You* have to convince him of your love and your loyalty. With that in mind, I think you should go and see him first without Elizabeth.'

'But she's the ace up my sleeve.'

'Not yet, she isn't, Linden. You have to convince him first.'

'Do you think he still wants me?' she asked, the awful possibility that he didn't entering her head for the first time.

'Oh, of that I have no doubt, but just remember he has had doubts about you. You will need all your patience and understanding to help him overcome those doubts.'

Linden sighed. 'May I go and see him now?' she asked, almost impatiently.

'Yes, do. Go . . .'

Linden stepped out of the car, and felt herself trembling. What could she expect? Was Edward so weak, physically and mentally, that Penny had seen fit to brief her first, to forewarn her? It was one aspect of his situation she had not considered.

She entered the building and the door swung shut behind her. At the far end of the room in which she found herself, a man in RAF uniform was sitting at a desk. He looked up when he saw her, and she followed his eyes as he nodded towards a door to her left behind which sat Edward, waiting in that private little interview room. She pointed towards the door and raised her eyebrows questioningly, and the man nodded again with a benevolent smile, as if he knew.

Tentatively, quietly, she pushed it open. *He* was sitting at a table, his head in his hands, and he did not see or hear her enter. He looked desperately thin, as Penny had warned her, and his hair had lost its youthful sheen. His fingers were lean, his nails cracked and in poor condition, his knuckles bony and his skin looked sallow and flaky.

God . . . Her heart went out to him.

'Edward,' she whispered.

Wearily, he looked up. His eyes were sunken and dark-rimmed, but as he saw her they brightened with instant pleasure.

'Linden!' At once he stood up to greet her. 'My God . . .'

She held her arms out to him and at once they grasped each other tightly. Her eyes were shut tight in the ecstasy of simply holding him again, but tears still managed to squeeze out and they rolled down her cheek; he *felt* so thin. Her poor Edward was so frail compared to how he had been the last time she'd seen him.

'Oh, Edward . . .' She was unable to say more yet, for

pent-up emotion seemed to constrict her vocal chords, seemed to prevent her mouth from forming words. Eventually, she managed, in a snuffle, to utter, 'If anybody had told me when I got out of bed this morning, that I would be holding you in my arms by eleven o' clock, I would have called them a liar.'

As she shook with weeping, pressed against him, he lifted her chin and looked into her wet eyes, clear and round and earnest.

'I can't believe it's you,' he said in a croak, and a great sob of a sigh juddered through his gaunt body. 'My God, I've yearned for this moment, but despaired of it ever coming to pass. Oh, Linden . . . Linden . . . Linden . . .'

He hugged her so tightly, and it was as if he could not get enough of the sound of her name, or the joy of the sensation of saying it.

'Are you still mine?' he said softly into her ear, tears rolling down his sallow cheeks. 'It's been so long, Linden . . . Are you still mine?'

'Of course I'm still yours,' she said tenderly, and planted a kiss on his cracked, dry lips. 'If you still want me.' She looked at him beseechingly.

'More than anything, more than *anything.*'

'Gosh, I've missed you so much, Edward. I've needed you so much, I can't begin to tell you . . . Life without you has been awful . . . so lonely . . . If it hadn't been for our—' She stopped herself saying it and gazed fervently into his eyes. 'I have the most wonderful surprise for you, Edward.'

'A surprise? D'you think I need more surprises?'

'This one is a special – an extra-special – surprise.'

'Then surprise me.'

'You have a daughter.'

There. It was out. She felt him tauten at the mention of a child, understood why, understood why Penny had taken the trouble to prime her, and realized she had to proceed very carefully, as Penny had predicted.

'She'll be three on Tuesday,' Linden went on, prudently giving him a straight fact to consider, 'and she's called Elizabeth Penelope. Elizabeth after Princess Elizabeth, Penelope after Penny. She can't wait to meet you.'

He let go of her, and she stood before him as if silently accused of some heinous crime. Suddenly she felt vulnerable, because she was aware that in his mind, poisoned by Hugh, her integrity – her honesty – was on trial.

'Edward,' she said assertively. Never had she shrunk from being forthright and now was not the time to begin. 'I can understand your doubts about being Elizabeth's father, but I can assure you, you are. She was born on the first of May 1942, just nine months after our honeymoon. Do you remember our honeymoon in Ludlow, Edward? Do you remember the hours we spent, before you were recalled to your squadron, making love till we were sore? It's hardly any surprise that I should've conceived then, is it? It would have been more surprising if I hadn't . . . I can show you her birth certificate.'

He sighed with relief, at once convinced and his frown changed to a broad, open smile.

'Oh, Linden,' he sighed. 'How could I ever have doubted you?' He took her in his arms again, and held her tight.

'I suppose it's natural to have doubts when you're away from somebody for so long,' she said matter-of-factly. 'And I understand it wasn't helped any by Hugh's stupidity either—'

'If ever I lay my hands on him . . .' Edward said, finding it unnecessary to finish his sentence.

'It's over and done with, Edward. Forget him. Everything is going to come right for us. We have each other again. We've always had each other; even when I thought you were dead, at least I was still yours. Always.'

'You were never tempted?'

'I was never short of offers,' she admitted, smiling. 'But I've never been interested in anybody else that way.'

'Hugh said you were seeing again that chap Ron, who you used to see years ago.'

She hadn't reckoned on explaining those circumstances yet, and Penny had advised her to avoid the issue for the time being. But it had been introduced, and she decided it was as well to get it into the open and done with, once and for all. So she told Edward the story of how she and Ron had agreed to marry.

'And did you love Ron, by this time?'

'No. I've never felt *love* for him – not *that* sort of love. Oh, I liked him, Edward. He was a nice, decent chap. He was very supportive, and he would have been a good father to Elizabeth. But was I in love with him? No.'

'Did you ever sleep with him?'

'Never. The chance never cropped up anyway. He was always away in the army.'

'Would you have done?'

'Of course, if I'd married him, but not until. But if I'd married him, it would have been bigamy anyway, and the marriage would not have been legal.'

'And he was prepared to take on another man's child?'

'Yes.'

Edward sighed. 'I'm glad you've told me all this, Linden. Maybe we expect too much of people, maybe I expected too much of you. But we are only flesh and blood, after all, afflicted by all the weaknesses, the inclinations and instincts of mere flesh and blood. I could hardly have blamed you if you had married Ron, illegally or not. The fact that you didn't has saved us a lot of bother and a lot of heartache. I imagine he didn't take kindly to being let down?'

'He was very disappointed . . . but very understanding under the circumstances.'

'Oh, Linden . . .'

'What?'

'Shall we sit down? I feel rather tired and aching standing up.'

'Of course.' She should have realized he was not as strong as he used to be after his ordeals; he needed building up.

So they sat opposite each other at the table in that bare, chilly, unromantic room.

'Do you remember Pilot Officer Keith Farnell?' he asked.

'Yes . . .' She felt her heart-rate quicken.

'He's here . . . at Cosford. I bumped into him last night, quite coincidentally. We got talking . . .'

'You did?'

'He told me he'd been a convalescent at Kinlet Hall . . . He said some very nice things about you, quite unprompted. He implied the exact opposite of what Hugh had written.'

'Thank God for that,' she responded. 'How did he seem? His leg was badly hurt.'

'He was limping a bit. But other than that he seemed fine. Would you like to see him while you're here?'

'Not particularly,' she said. 'I'm here to see you, not him.'

He took her hands in his and looked into her eyes.

'Let me just gaze at you for a few moments,' he said, and smiled warmly. 'You're as beautiful as ever . . . I really don't deserve you, doubting you the way I have. And look at me. I'm just a scrawny ex-prisoner-of-war whose mind has been so screwed up that everything has got twisted out of all proportion. Anyway, I imagine you'll be pleased to learn that I've already decided I'm going to resign my commission. I'll do my damnedest to be a good husband for you, Linden, but I fear you might have to be patient with me sometimes.'

'I'm just so happy you're home, Edward,' she replied sincerely. 'And I'll look after you properly. I'll make you well again. I promise.'

'And I'm going to be busy running the steelworks, Penny tells me.'

'Only when you're fit and well.' She stroked the rough skin of his hand lovingly. 'Then I'll help you if you want me to,' she said enthusiastically. 'I know a bit about what goes on at the steelworks. I didn't work with your father all that time and not pick up a few tips, you know.'

He laughed. 'I think we'll be all right after all, you and me, Linden,' he said, feeling infinitely happier and brighter.

'Of course we shall. Now . . . Would you like to meet your daughter?'

'Is she here?'

'She's outside with her Aunty Penny. You didn't imagine I'd leave her out of this, did you?'

'God, I hope she's going to like me.'

'She's going to love you. Come on . . . Do you feel up to walking to her?'

'You won't keep me away now.'

As they stepped outside into the warm spring sunshine together, hand in hand, they saw Penny playing with Elizabeth on a patch of mown grass.

'Is that her?' Edward enquired, his eyes alive now with the sincere, gentle look about them that she had always loved.

'That's her, the little tinker.'

It was a monumental moment. A lump came to his throat and his eyes welled up with tears again. 'She's beautiful, Linden,' he sighed inadequately. 'Look at her lovely thick dark hair. She's just like you.'

'But she has your eyes, Edward, and no mistake.'

Linden called her and when Elizabeth looked up from her game with Penny, she beckoned her. Penny urged her forward, and the little girl came running over and Edward sat on his haunches to be at her level, waiting, a broad expectant grin on his face. She ran directly to him and he caught her in his arms, picked her up and hugged her. He was indescribably moved that this child, his child, who had never seen him before and only knew him by what her mother and others had told her, could be so understanding of the situation she was suddenly thrust into, and so instantaneously generous with her affection. He fell in love with her at once, and made a private vow that he would be the best father any child could have. He would try his utmost to make up for the years lost.

'Are you weally my daddy?' she asked, with the sort of wide-eyed innocence that would have demolished the hardest heart, but primed by Aunty Penny beforehand.

'Oh, yes, I'm your daddy all right,' Edward replied. 'And it's your birthday soon.'

The child nodded earnestly, looking directly into his eyes. 'I'll be fwee the first of May,' she declared.

'Oh, on May Day,' Daddy said, as if it were a great surprise. 'We'll see if we can rig up a maypole especially for you, and we can all dance around it. Would you like that?'

Elizabeth nodded eagerly.

Linden looked on moist-eyed but content – oh, utterly content.

'And you've been looking after Mummy for me while I've been away?'

The child nodded again, and grinned.

'Good girl. Now Daddy's back to look after both of you, and I shan't be going away again.' Edward turned to Linden. 'It's a travesty I've been away so long. I'm absolutely devastated that I've missed three years of her life – three years of her growing up. And she really is beautiful, Linden – the image of you.'

'She's a little madam,' Linden asserted with infinite tenderness in her eyes. 'I can see she'll be able to twist you round her little finger.'

'Oh, there's no doubt about it,' he happily admitted. 'But I want her to. With all my heart.'

'Anyway, she'll benefit from her father's presence.'

'Which she'll get – in abundance.' He gave the child another hug, reached out and took Linden's hand, and the three of them held each other savouring these moments, which in the years to come would remain vivid, poignant, but extraordinarily happy memories.

Edward Burgayne resigned his commission on 13 May, the day that Winston Churchill announced that the war with Germany was officially over. In the meantime, he had been allowed home to celebrate Elizabeth's third birthday and Linden's twenty-sixth a week later. She moved back to Kinlet Hall and was happy to regard it as her home once again. And with a child in the house the atmosphere was at once restored.

But, even more than that, a new and challenging adventure, another chapter in their lives, had begun . . .